NEVER BEFORE ~~HAS~~ ... KT-213-022
IN AMERICA BEEN GIVEN SO TOTAL AN
EXAMINATION. OVER 1000 GAY MEN
ANSWER QUESTIONS LIKE THE FOLLOW-
ING:

- Was your first homosexual experience good or bad?

- Do you have sex in baths? In restrooms? In other public places?

- Do you prefer having sex with lovers? Strangers? Older men? Younger ones?

- Do you pay or get paid for sex?

- Have you ever gotten into trouble with the police?

- Do you have sex with women—and do you like it?

- Would you rather be gay or straight?

This is just a small sampling of the vast variety of questions asked in *The Spada Report*. The answers may well surprise and even shock both gays and straights with their unashamed honesty and extraordinary diversity. Never before have so many different gays been so personally open about every aspect of their sexuality and themselves.

THE SPADA REPORT

The Newest Survey of Gay Sexuality Today

SIGNET Books of Related Interest

☐ **THE HOMOSEXUAL MATRIX by C. A. Tripp, Ph.D.** Ten years in the making, this monumental study has been hailed as a major achievement—a book that opens broad new perspectives on homosexuality. "Broadens our minds and explodes our misconceptions sky-high."—The New York Times (#E7172—$2.50)

☐ **LOVING SOMEONE GAY by Don Clark, Ph.D.** This perceptive guide by a gay therapist opens the door to communication and understanding by cutting through the mystery and myth surrounding gay people and gay identity. "To be read for guidance by gays and for heightened awareness by straights."—Publishers Weekly (#E8593—$2.25)

☐ **COMING OUT by Wallace Hamilton.** A sensitive, moving novel of a divorced man's entry into the gay world. (#E7425—$1.75)

☐ **THE NAKED CIVIL SERVANT by Quentin Crisp.** An unusually riveting, exuberant autobiography of a man who, in 1931, "came out" in the streets of London as a self-confessed and self-evident homosexual. "Brilliant, witty, acute . . . I loved it!"—The New York Times (#E8292—$2.25)†

☐ **THE HAZARDS OF BEING MALE: Surviving the Myth of Masculine Privilege by Herb Goldberg, Ph.D.** The breakthrough book that does for men what women's lib is doing for women. . . . "A must"—Houston Chronicle (#J8627—$1.95)

† Not available in Canada

To order these titles, please

pse coupon on the last

page of this book.

THE SPADA REPORT

The Newest Survey of Gay Male Sexuality

By James Spada

A SIGNET BOOK
NEW AMERICAN LIBRARY
TIMES MIRROR

Copyright © 1979 by James Spada

 SIGNET TRADEMARK REG. U.S. PAT. OFF. AND FOREIGN COUNTRIES
REGISTERED TRADEMARK—MARCA REGISTRADA
HECHO EN CHICAGO, U.S.A.

SIGNET, SIGNET CLASSICS, MENTOR, PLUME AND MERIDIAN BOOKS
are published by The New American Library, Inc.,
1301 Avenue of the Americas, New York, New York 10019

FIRST PRINTING, MAY, 1979

1 2 3 4 5 6 7 8 9

PRINTED IN THE UNITED STATES OF AMERICA

FOR DAN

*There is an easiness about him, the kind you feel
when surrounded by people you know will always
love you.*

Acknowledgments

The work on this book consumed many man-hours and it wouldn't have been possible to do without the help of generous people who contributed their time because of their belief in this project. Dan Conlon, Chris Nickens, John Ruggles, and Steve Amos worked with me very closely, and Bob Kiggins, Steve Ginn, Kevin Scullin, Ray Hannon, and Bob Scott contributed what time they could, and for that I am grateful.

I would also like to thank Southern Californians for Whitman Radclyffe, which published the questionnaire in their newsletter; the Gay Rights Chapter of the ACLU and its then president Dick Caudillo, who were the first to allow me to distribute the questionnaire; Jane Rotrosen, who believed in this project from the beginning and was of inestimable help in preparing the questionnaire; Jim Kepner, for allowing me access to his extensive gay library; Tony Sullivan and Richard Adams, Michael Kearns, Terry Mayo and Enid Blaustein of KTNT, Barbara Petty and Steve Mitchell, Jill Evans, Morris Kight, Tom Coleman, John Alan Cohan, Peter Thomas Judge, John Embry, Sam Murdoch, Michael Denneny, Troy Perry, Alan Rinzler, Preston Reese, and my editor, Agnes Birnbaum, for their advice, information, and encouragement; and all the publications which contributed their valuable editorial space to reproduce the questionnaire.

Last, but certainly not least, I salute the men who took the time, energy, and emotion to complete a difficult and draining questionnaire. Without you, this book would not have been possible.

Contents

INTRODUCTION 1

HOW THE QUESTIONNAIRE WAS DESIGNED, ANALYZED, AND DISTRIBUTED 10

WHO ANSWERED 12

WHY DID MEN RESPOND TO THE QUESTION- NAIRE? 18

PART ONE: COMING OUT 21

When did you first realize you were sexually attracted to members of your own sex? 23

At what age did you have your first homosexual experience? 30

Have you told your family that you're gay? 43

Do you ever pretend to be straight? 53

PART TWO: GAY MALE SEXUALITY 61

How often do you have sex? How important is sex in your life? 63

Do you enjoy one-night stands? 68

Are one-night stands purely sexual outlets, or do you consider each partner a potential relationship? 71

Do you enjoy affection during sex? 76

Do you enjoy giving fellatio? 80

Do you enjoy having your partner ejaculate in your mouth? 85

Do you enjoy receiving fellatio? 87

Do you enjoy 69 (mutual fellatio)? 90

Do you enjoy anal intercourse? *92*

During anal intercourse, are you usually top or bottom man? *97*

Do your emotions differ when you're on top from when you're on the bottom? *101*

What is it like for you to be anally penetrated by a penis? *104*

When you are anally penetrated, does your orgasm feel different? *108*

Can you reach orgasm without direct stimulation of your penis? *111*

Do you ever go to the baths? *112*

Do you ever have sex in restrooms or other public places? *117*

Do you ever engage in any unusual sexual activities? *126*

Do you use drugs, sex toys, or pornography during sex? *135*

Do you ever get aroused by uniforms, leather, garments, odors, and the like? *140*

Have you ever paid or been paid for sex? *143*

Is the size of a man's penis (including your own) important to you? *150*

How would you define masculinity? *157*

Do you consider yourself masculine? *160*

PART THREE: RELATIONSHIPS 165

How would you characterize your emotional involvements with men? *167*

Do you have a lover? *176*

What is it about your lover that made you fall in love with him? *185*

Do you and/or your lover have sex with others? *189*

Would you like a lover? *197*

Would you want to live with your lover? *202*

Do you prefer men younger, older, or the same age as yourself? *203*

PART FOUR: WOMEN 213

Do you have sex with women? *215*

Are you now (or have you ever been) married to a woman? *221*

What is it about men that you find more sexually attractive than women? *227*

What can an emotional relationship with a man offer you that one with a woman cannot?   *229*

What are your feelings about lesbianism?   *234*

Do you ever dress in women's clothing?   *238*

Would you rather be a woman?   *242*

PART FIVE: PROBLEMS   247

Have you ever been arrested for a sexual activity?   *249*

Have you ever had any of your rights denied you because you are gay?   *254*

Have you ever had any form of V.D. or other sexually transmitted disease?   *259*

Have you ever been in the military? Did you have any gay experiences there?   *263*

PART SIX: ON BEING GAY   271

Do you think there are any reasons that you're gay?   *273*

Do you ever feel guilty about being gay?   *282*

Do you think it is easy or difficult to be gay today?   *286*

What do you like most about being gay? What do you dislike most?   *293*

Would you rather be straight?   *297*

What do you think are the most important changes that have to be made, by gays or straight society or both, to improve gay life?   *299*

Do you consider yourself happy?   *310*

AFTERWORD   317

Statistical Breakdown of Replies   *323*

INTRODUCTION

The past decade has been one of tremendous change and challenge for the more than 20 million gay men and women in America. Since the advent of "gay liberation" in 1969, important social changes have been accomplished: laws against discrimination have been passed; the various media have presented a more positive image; the psychiatric community has reversed its position that homosexuality is a mental disorder; many people have come to view the gay lifestyle as an acceptable alternative.

But with the anti-gay backlash of 1977 and 1978, which brought a number of political setbacks by popular vote and legislative action, gay people were faced with a harsh reality: the advances were more form than substance. The basic fears and misconceptions about homosexuals and the gay lifestyle, which most gays believed were disappearing, were still with many members of the populace. In many ways, gays found themselves back at square one, having to explain and justify themselves and their feelings in an attempt to break down what they consider unfair and inaccurate stereotypes.

Part of the problem in the chasm between how gay people view themselves and how they are viewed by many others is that the average gay person has almost never been asked about himself. The most famous theories and analyses of homosexuality, upon which many stereotypes are based, have been the result of psychiatrists' study of their patients—homosexuals emotionally disturbed enough to seek professional help. Although these people can hardly be considered representative of the entire gay population, the conclusions drawn from this limited group were universally applied to all homosexuals once the studies were completed.

In this survey, we have allowed gay men across the country to speak for themselves. The 1,038 men who responded to this questionnaire live in all fifty states, have a wide variety of occupations and religious beliefs, and range in age from sixteen to seventy-seven. We believe that from such a far-reaching sampling of average gay men, much more reliable conclusions about gay men in general can be drawn than from the kinds of surveys done until now.

In drawing what conclusions we do, however, we do not

3

imply that they apply to all homosexual men. On the contrary, while pointing out trends and statistics, we have been careful to quote all points of view mentioned with any frequency, both as an acknowledgment that other viewpoints exist and as an attempt to understand all attitudes, activities, and lifestyles. Indeed, one of the most startling factors about the responses to this questionnaire is the enormous diversity of viewpoints. With many of these men, homosexuality may be the only thing they have in common. A sampling of some of the comments made will more than prove the point:

ON ANITA BRYANT:

"Anita Bryant, in my estimation, is a very sick woman who needs all the help that God and man can give her, because she has never learned the one commandment that Jesus held to be the most important in all His ministry: 'One final commandment I give you and that is that ye love one another!' Anita Bryant doesn't see that, and neither do all the other queer-haters like her in the world."

"Anita Bryant really truly believed she was right and what did she get for it? Not understanding, not a willingness on our part to educate her and her kind. No, she got drags at state legislatures to reinforce the fears she had the guts to express, she got pies in her face—an act of children. Well, until we grow up and live in the real world, we'll never get what we want and need. The majority of people would give us 'rights' if we showed our good side. Educate them to know us as people with values, morals, and responsibility. Don't slap them in the face and call them bigots. Some are but most are just confused—give them our patience and understanding. They'll eventually give us what we desire most."

ON THE POSSIBLE REASONS FOR BEING HOMOSEXUAL?

"I feel that part of the reason is a very hostile father. He told me when I was sixteen that he hated me from the day I was born—but he didn't really have to say it since I knew it from the time I was old enough to be aware of him."

"Growing up, I was very close to my father. He was in many ways my best friend and we spent many hours together whenever he was not at work. We have always been very open about displaying our affection for one another (e.g.

walking down the beach together hand in hand as a teenager, hugging and kissing one another). I never felt anything sexual toward him, but I'm sure it came easier for me to recognize and show affection for another man."

ON ONE-NIGHT STANDS:

"One-night stands are too quick and too impersonal. I prefer a long, slow, heavy sex act with someone who I really care about deeply. I like to just 'be there' both before and after. I like to get into touching and feeling. I want to feel I made love to a man instead of just having sex with him."

"I like discovering a man for the first time, exploring his mind and his body. I can enjoy sex physically and emotionally without having the idea of 'maybe this time' on my mind to get in the way of relaxing. Even if we never see each other again we have still given each other something of ourselves. I'd rather love a man for one night than not at all."

ON THE BARS:

"On those occasions when I have ventured into a bar or disco I see some highly slappable faces. Gay people really need to wake up and become more communicable between themselves. I'm sick and tired of seeing those driven faggots who make their entire lives revolve around the discos and the bars. They pose like statues hoping they are gorgeous and end up going home alone. Maybe I've made many mistakes in my life, but that's never been one of them."

"The bars are *good*—for meeting people, for the positive reinforcement that *that many* people are gay, too. Back to 'I'm OK—You're OK.' "

"So many gay people I know put down the bar scene and say, 'That's gay life and I don't want any part of it.' Well, that's not gay life. Have any of these people ever been in a straight bar? There's just as much insincerity, just as much cruising, just as much of a 'meatrack' atmosphere. That's *bar* life, not gay life. The problem is that bars are one of the few places gays can get together, so more are forced to go there than straights are forced to go to their bars. But I think more and more opportunities for gays to meet outside that bar scene are opening up. I hope so."

"I think gay bars are a lot better than straight bars. Gay bars are so much better and friendlier and more relaxed."

ON THE BATHS:

"I've been to the baths about fifteen times. Each time it's been very different. The first time I felt awkward and tacky—what a meatrack! But I stayed seven hours, came four times, and was the center of an orgy with three different guys sucking me off in a row. I felt like the sex object of all time. I can't stress the importance of this to a guy who always thought he was ugly and undesirable. The next time I met a guy the minute I walked in, stayed with him for the next five hours, took him home with me and saw him again after that (we still keep in touch—he now lives in a different city than I). I've had some wonderful sex in the baths—with beautiful, hunky guys I probably wouldn't have been able to be intimate with any other place (maybe they have lovers or are married). The most physically satisfying sex I've ever had was at the baths, and I now have five friends who I first met at the baths. I like them."

"There are always bodies in rooms waiting to be fucked. Time and again, they don't even turn over and one never sees their faces. I prefer someone who will hug and kiss awhile first and let me enjoy the beauties of their bodies."

"The whole concept of baths disgusts me. I can't even imagine sex without a great deal of feeling attached to it. How can it have any meaning when you have sex with a stranger or dozens of strangers? It seems to me that that's taking a thing of great spiritual beauty and making it as base as possible. I'll leave the baths to the animals."

ON COMING OUT TO YOUR FAMILY:

"My family knew long before I cared to acknowledge the fact to them. In fact, my mom was the one who first talked to me about it and said that they had accepted it and now it was up to me to accept it. Of course, it was not easy for them to accept, and for a long time I harbored a great fear that they would reject me. But today, I get along absolutely terrifically with my parents. There are never any embarrassing questions about 'When are you getting married?' It was very important to me to have this honesty with my parents because I love and care for them a great deal."

"My family did what they thought God wanted—to rid the world of their queer son. They tried to kill me on Christmas

Eve, while I was asleep. I broke all contacts with family and relatives in 1971. The last time I saw my mother and father was a few hours in July 1970. Shortly thereafter my father left my mother. She attempted to sue *me* for $50,000 and $250 a month for support."

ON FELLATIO:

"I enjoy having my mouth on an object that is a 'private part' and just with a cock in general. I think this stems from being sheltered, in childhood, from seeing the other boys and men nude—no nudity at home, no locker rooms in school, no exposure to nude men—it's become an obsession to see other penises. I almost believe that if I was forbidden to see another part of the body for so long I would be compelled to make love to it."

"I enjoy the physical feel of a cock in my mouth. It's enjoyable to feel a soft cock in my mouth and then have it swell longer and fuller to fill my mouth—the smooth warm soft outer skin over a full erection."

"I do not enjoy giving fellatio. Guess I still have hang-ups about it connected to my upbringing. Besides, my jaws get tired!"

ON THE GAY RIGHTS MOVEMENT:

"I feel that too much of the gay rights movement has been (unconsciously) directed by exhibitionist tendencies in certain radical leaders. I wish the movement represented a more responsible element. For instance, the gays who held hands and kissed at the hearings on gay rights in New York City without doubt ruined any chance the ordinance had at the time of passing in this city. I hope when the next chance comes the National Gay Task Force will see that more mainstream gays represent the minority, not just anybody who's willing to exhibit or flaunt himself."

"Thank God for the radical gays. If it wasn't for them, we wouldn't have accomplished anything. Militancy is always the way things get changed—look at the blacks. If we stay in our closets and meekly apologize we'll get nowhere. We have to shout—'Hey, I'm OK—it's you who's fucked up in your sexual hang-ups!' And we have to demand those rights which we deserve as human beings. We can accept no less!"

On Religion:

"I truly feel that religious beliefs (especially those held to a great extent in the United States) are extremely harmful, since they seem to bring out a need in those who 'believe' to control everybody else's lives. People have to stop placing themselves in the role of 'judge.'"

"I used to think I couldn't be gay and Christian. Now I know better. I joined the Metropolitan Community Church about a month ago. I am deeply grateful for the Rev. Troy Perry's ministry. I am a deeply religious man still in the process of shedding a number of hang-ups. I go to church to worship God, not to cruise, not to pick up tricks. I have been deeply blessed by MCC. Since my parents and many of my friends are now dead, I find my family at MCC. I am always proud to stand up for Jesus Christ and bear my testimony; this really turns my sophisticated friends off, but I don't care. I will not deny God and my Lord and Savior Jesus Christ."

On Having a Lover:

"I would like to have a lover because for a long time I've lived in a very safe emotional environment that I have constructed for myself simply became I am terrified of being hurt. For that reason, I've found my life to be emotionally stagnant. I don't experience emotional pain, but I don't experience the ecstasy, either. Nothing happens. I've reached a plateau and have been there for many years. Consequently I haven't grown much as a person all that time."

"Although there are certain people I would jump at the chance to have a serious relationship with, I do not at present want a lover. I need to develop a positive sense of self first. I do not want a lover so that I will have someone to depend on, lean on. I must stand by myself first, and when that is accomplished, wanting or needing a lover is a moot point."

On Penis Size:

"I am a real 'size queen.' The bigger the better, as far as I'm concerned. I think it is more of a visual stimulation than anything else, but a big dick is very exciting to me. The fact that I am well hung, I think, has played a big part in my sexual popularity in the past, and it is an important factor in the relationship with my lover."

"An average penis is usually best, because it entails the fewest hang-ups. Men with small cocks often have slight inferiority complexes which they compensate for by being overly aggressive or completely reticent. Guys with whoppers are either embarrassed (because they know from experience that there's little they can do with it except show it off) or obnoxiously over-proud and macho. It's not what you've got, it's how you use it that counts."

As this brief sampling of what is to follow clearly shows, gay men are one group of individuals who will be very difficult to pigeonhole. The men who responded to this questionnaire obviously did so with frankness and honesty. Their contributions will go a long way toward a better understanding of the complexity of gay men—and thus of all human sexuality. We offer the results of this survey in the hope of breaking down the barriers which separate so many of us. And for that alone, we owe these men an enormous debt of gratitude.

How the Questionnaire
was Designed, Anyalyzed,
and Distributed

When I first began distributing this questionnaire, I was repeatedly told that such a lengthy and complicated survey would not receive an adequate amount of replies, and those it did receive would be almost impossible to analyze. I was advised that a simple yes-or-no or multiple-choice questionnaire would receive a much higher percentage of responses and be much easier to tally.

Although both suggestions were possibly correct, I found little potential value in a strictly statistical survey. Even with a smaller response, I felt a verbal survey would be much more enlightening and meaningful, and represent a welcome departure from the kind of scientific surveying of homosexuals done up to this point.

The number of replies received was indeed heartening—many men obviously responded to my exhortation to "make your voice heard" and "stop being a statistic." Most men took great pains with the questionnaire, quite a few returning dozens of single-spaced typewritten pages of reply.

This did, of course, make analysis and categorization much more difficult and time-consuming than it would have been otherwise, but it was also much more rewarding and moving. The process was as follows:

Each survey received was given its sequential number and read for the purpose of statistical analysis. It was then read again, and each answer sufficiently explanatory to be considered for inclusion in the verbal part of this book was coded with the survey's number and transferred to a folder for that question. Responses not earmarked for possible inclusion in the book were transferred to a master folder.

The responses were then reread, and some included in the book, first on the basis of representativeness, then on how thought-provoking, interesting, or unusual the response was.

The results of the survey are based on answers to the fifty-five-question questionnaire which was distributed throughout the United States between November 1976 and July 1978. Ten thousand copies of the survey were given out at meetings and symposia, displayed in bookstores, distributed in gay bars and theaters, and sent out through the mail to those requesting copies. Notices of the availability of the questionnaire were published in *The Advocate*, the *L.A. Free Press*, *The Alternate*, the *Bay Area Reporter*, *In Touch*, *Blueboy*, *Los Angeles* magazine, and other gay and nongay publications.

The largest distribution of the survey was through magazine reproduction of the questions. The widest possible geographic, educational, social, and age distribution was sought by reproducing the questionnaire in a variety of publications—*Data Boy*, a bar giveaway serving the West Coast; *The Advocate*, the leading gay newspaper; *Christopher Street*, a gay literary magazine; *Playguy*, a sexually oriented picture magazine; and *Man's Way*, a general-interest gay magazine. With the exception of *Data Boy*, all are nationally distributed.

1,038 responses were received.

Who Answered

Respondents covered a wide range of area, age, occupation, and education. Breakdowns of these follow.

Geographical Distribution

Replies were received from all fifty states and six foreign countries. Each area was represented as follows:

NORTHEAST (New York, Pennsylvania, New Jersey, Connecticut, Massachusetts, Rhode Island, Vermont, New Hampshire, Maine, Delaware, Virginia, West Virginia, Maryland): 268 (25.8%)
SOUTHEAST (Florida, Georgia, South Carolina, North Carolina, Washington, D.C., Puerto Rico): 74 (7.2%)
NORTH CENTRAL (North Dakota, South Dakota, Ohio, Indiana, Nebraska, Minnesota, Iowa, Illinois, Wisconsin, Michigan): 162 (15.6%)
SOUTH (Kansas, Oklahoma, Texas, Arkansas, Missouri, Louisiana, Mississippi, Tennessee, Kentucky, Alabama): 97 (9.3%)
NORTHWEST (Washington, Alaska, Oregon, Idaho, Montana, Wyoming): 40 (3.9%)
SOUTHWEST (California, Nevada, Utah, Colorado, Arizona, New Mexico, Hawaii): 363 (35.0%)
FOREIGN COUNTRIES (Canada, Japan, Indonesia, England, Mexico, Italy): 31 (3.0%)
ORIGIN UNKNOWN: 3 (0.03%)

RELIGIOUS
DISTRIBUTION

Roman Catholic: 289
Protestant: 181
None: 100
Baptist: 67
Episcopalian: 65
Methodist: 65
Jewish: 44
Presbyterian: 37
Lutheran: 35
Agnostic: 20
All others: 70
No answer: 65

EDUCATIONAL
LEVELS

Some college: 303
College degree: 263
High school graduate: 158
In college: 101
Postgraduate work: 53
Master's Degree: 46
Ph.D.: 40
High school dropout: 17
Grammar school: 8
In high school: 6
Others: 4
No answer: 39

AGES OF
RESPONDENTS

16–18: 12
19–24: 224
25–30: 313
31–40: 215
41–49: 151
50–65: 81
66–74: 23
75–77: 3
No answer: 16

RACES

Caucasian: 858
Black: 71
Chicano: 29
Oriental: 10
Puerto Rican: 5
"Mixed": 4
No answer: 61

OCCUPATIONS (Terms
are those used by re-
spondents.)

Student: 118
No Answer: 85
Teacher: 63
None: 35
Retired: 30
College professor: 27
Writer: 24
Unemployed: 22
Computer programmer: 21
Lawyer: 18
M.D.: 18
Office worker: 15
Waiter: 15
Actor: 14
Male nurse: 13
Clergyman: 12
"In management": 12
Musician: 12
Hardhat: 9
Government employee: 9
Artist: 8
Librarian: 8
Engineer: 8
"Professional": 8
Store clerk: 8
Social worker: 7
Interior decorator: 7
Editor: 7
Hairdresser: 6
Bank administrator: 6

Typesetter: 5
Medical assistant: 5
Laborer: 5
G.I.: 5
Administrative assistant: 5
Bank teller: 4
Civil servant: 4
Chef: 4
Editor's assistant: 4
Bartender: 4
Truck driver: 4
Counselor: 4
Merchant seaman: 4
Police officer: 4
Airline steward: 4
Fashion designer: 4
Military officer: 3
Library clerk: 3
Telephone operator: 3
Painter: 3
Restaurant manager: 3
Shipping clerk: 3
Busboy: 3
Florist: 3
Administrator: 3
Clerical worker: 3
Newspaper reporter: 3
Author: 3

The following occupations
  were mentioned twice:

Graphic artist
Draftsman
Gardener
Landscape architect
Bookkeeper
"Work at Gay Community
  Services Center"
Blue-collar worker
Businessman
Art dealer
"In fashion industry"
Surgical assistant

Actor/playwright
Retail merchant
Journalist
Freelance designer
Radio announcer
Airlines agent
Entertainer
Mortician
Writer/editor
Publisher
Insurance executive
Mail clerk
Scientist
Shop owner
Hospital worker
Photographer
White-collar worker
Auditor
Dancer
Typist
Self-employed
Educational consultant
Cook
Office manager
Barber
Researcher
Real estate broker
Claims adjuster
Electrician
Marriage counselor
Receptionist
Bus driver
"In publicity and promo-
  tion"
Hospital administrator
Assistant office manager
"National Park Service"
Trucking industry consul-
  tant
Motion-picture production
  supervisor
Unit tester, electrical fac-
  tory

Manager, telephone company
County laborer
Interpreter
"Work at chemical dependency center"
"In nursing"
Physical-therapy assistant
Credit representative
Management consultant
Custodial worker
Supply clerk
"In theater"
Company director
"In government"
"In the medical field"

The following occupations were mentioned once:

X-ray technician
Weightlifter
Theater manager
Chemical technician
Assistant manager, furniture store
Bar owner
"In production"
Clinical psychologist
Manufacturing director of operations
Auto assembler
Secretary
Antique dealer
Jewelry designer
Theater critic
Manager for actors
Gay bookstore owner
Credit-card manager
Church secretary
Curator
Computer engineer
Director of nursing
Sanitary inspector

Compliance coordinator
Maintenance supervisor
Dispatcher
"Work in credit"
Farmer
Fuel tax clerk
Store sales manager
Marketing executive
Disneyland operator
Assistant magazine research director
Mail carrier
Printer
Psychotherapist
Health-care administrator
Senior stenographer
Data-control supervisor
Silversmith
Network executive
Negotiator
"Para-legal"
Costume, set designer
Talent agent
Insurance underwriter
"In health insurance"
Illustrator
Grocery clerk
Ichthyologist
"In display"
Mag card operator
Insurance executive
Customer service representative
Meteorologist
Motel desk clerk
Lineman
Emergency-room administration clerk
Technical controller
Industrial painter
TV producer
Steamship agency operations assistant
"Disabled"

Dental technician
Court administrator
Fireman
Factory worker
Dance teacher
Grievance officer
House parent
"Work for airline caterer"
Traffic manager
Disc jockey
Child psychologist
Silk screener
Parts manager
Electronics sales manager
Janitor
Organ builder
Musical director
Apartment manager
University administrator
Veterinarian
Postal clerk
Cost analyst
Artist in TV
Choreographer
Psychiatric technician
Church organist
Hotel executive
Hearing-aid distributor
Singer
Civic volunteer
Credit manager
Supervisor
Trust officer for bank
Gay bookstore manager
Rancher
Coordinator of operations
Restaurant owner
Manufacturer's rep
Makeup artist
Food service manager
Political consultant
Yeoman seaman USN
Theatrical employee
Motel manager

Missionary
Musical conductor
Press agent
"In advertising"
Gemologist
Marketing researcher
Change agent
Computer control clerk
Food technologist
Sheet-metal worker
Gift-shop owner
Bookstore manager
Dog breeder and groomer
College fund raiser
"In music and PR"
College curriculum director
Photojournalist
"In electrical appliance business"
Tariff compiler
"In telecommunications"
Manager of truck terminal
Stockbroker
Art director in movies
Technical writer
Sociologist
"In motion-picture industry"
"General manager"
Audio engineer
Statistical assistant to bank comptroller
Advertising coordinator
Engineer
Employment director
Eye doctor
Warehouseman
"Occupations vary"
Carpet layer
"Investor"
Obstetrical assistant
Aide to librarian
Masseur
Juvenile probation officer

Housekeeper
"Own haircutting place"
Film production assistant
Technical library director
Liquor salesman
Educational administrator
Copywriter

Motorcycle mechanic
"Work for airline"
Travel agent
"Renaissance man"
"Work with retarded"
Telephone surveyor

Why Did Men Respond
to the Questionnaire?

Why did so many men invest so much time in answering the questionnaire from which this book has been compiled? A number of them expressed their feelings about this in response to the final question, "Is there anything you'd like to add?":

"I appreciate this opportunity to express my feelings about the above questions, hoping that when the book is published, if even *one* person reads it, who has been bigoted or has not understood homosexuals, perhaps my answers will help that person to understand and be more tolerant, and accepting of our lifestyles."

"I think you have devised a questionnaire that exposes the workings of the gay mind very well. I would like to congratulate you and also thank you for undertaking the task of gathering and making publicly available all of this information."

"I wish to commend you on this survey. It is a step to educating the public that we are not criminals or mean ogres who prey on little children. Reading the results of a survey like this when I was having my coming-out crisis could have made a big difference in the time required to adjust."

"I appreciated this opportunity to respond to your questionnaire. It gave me an opportunity to think about aspects of my personality and my sexuality that I had not considered before. My attitude toward my gayness and its relevance in my life has changed under this closer examination. I mean no one, not even myself, has ever asked me these questions before. I sincerely wish you good luck in your work."

"I should like to add a note of deep gratitude to Circumstance at finding this survey. The thanks to the Life Style Survey staff for such a complete questionnaire are boundless. I consider it my good fortune to have found this material at just the time when I came out of myself. The task has been difficult at times, but the questionnaire has been beneficial to me and my wife as we have shared it all. We are better able to love, respect, be patient with, understand each other and increasingly be more ourselves. Publish away! So that the sexual mythology many of us have learned in childhood will feel the pangs of its long-awaited death."

"I think there should be more surveys like this one so gay persons can express themselves. For too long, straights had these surveys to themselves and our feelings and thoughts didn't count."

"I used to work for a social research institute and can appreciate how smart you were to leave the questions open-ended in order to reveal the 'human dimension' of your respondents. It often was very difficult to 'code' the responses of, for instance, a poor mother in the ghetto who could barely afford to support her children and who was being asked how many cars she had bought in the last year—you were only supposed to code the car and ignore the rest. Oh boy."

"Even during psychotherapy I never got to look at, examine, and sort out all the various items as proposed by this survey."

"This was much more difficult to write than I ever thought it would be. I answered because your need for information sounded like an appeal. I rarely read magazines of this type, but in this case a friend passed it on to me for the sake of your article. Since I would not have bought the magazine, I answered to give you info from someone who would not ordinarily have seen it."

"Never before have I been able to feel that I'm doing something to help people better understand each other. Thanks for asking."

"My God, I can't believe I have put this much on paper. When I started out I thought I would invest the time for probably two pages worth of answers that I could bang out on a typewriter in an hour at most. I have now worked on this for weeks, sneaking (literally) out an hour or two when I can at work. I am literally stunned by all these pages. Time and again, I would finish a question after hundreds of words and then I suddenly would feel like I was awakening from a trance. I felt as though I was talking on some very emotional topics to a close friend who never talked back but just listened. As I reread some of the material I had written, I was astonished to see what I had said, much of it verbalized for the first time in my life, not only to someone else, but to myself. I don't know what you put in your questionnaire (at first

I just ignored it as a waste of time), but you hit a lot of 'buttons' for me."

"This, to my mind, is the kind of activity the gay community needs. If the results can make only one young gay more comfortable in himself, more alive to his special being, then I would say the effort you are making is well worthwhile."

"I feel that in taking the time and effort to do this survey, I have, in some way, helped my fellow gay brothers and sisters and most of all myself. I've expressed my views, opinions, and feelings as best I could and it has made me feel fabulous. I only hope the course of my gay lifestyle will go for the best in my future endeavors. It's surveys and questionnaires like these that aid and help gays break down walls and find out there are lots of men just like them that are feeling and searching for that love and warmth that we all need and deserve. I'm glad to be a part of it."

PART ONE:
COMING OUT

When did you first realize you were sexually attracted to members of your own sex? How did you feel about that?

The answers to these questions present one of the clearest facts to emerge from this survey: most gay men have their first homosexual feelings at the same time that they have any sexual awakening at all—and it is a realization they make entirely on their own. Thirty-five percent of the respondents report their first homosexual attraction *before the age of ten,* and another 41% place it between the ages of ten and fourteen. Most of the men do not remember any heterosexual feelings at all, and those who do often report that they were accompanied by homosexual feelings as well. Further, many of the men who acknowledged their homosexuality at a later age write that they now realize certain feelings they experienced in childhood were indeed homosexual, but that they repressed them.

Homosexual feelings were as natural to these men as heterosexual feelings are to straight men, and they developed as naturally. Most report that they felt quite good about their inclinations until they realized that they were not acceptable to the majority. Despite this realization, and despite sometimes desperate attempts to change, these feelings were impossible to suppress. Such attempts often led to tremendous heartache and alienation.

Most of the respondents felt their first homosexual inclinations at a very early age:

"I first realized I was sexually attracted to men when I was four years old. Our television set was broken, so a very attractive repairman came to the house to fix it. I sat with my dad and watched the repairman. When he left I turned to my father and said, 'He was cute.' My father laughed and said, 'What?' I explained that I thought the TV man was very nice-looking. My father was amused, but made it very clear that boys don't say things like that about other boys."

"There was evidence as early as four to six years of age

23

when I was fascinated by public dressing rooms at the beach. But it really became evident when I was about ten. My friends all commented about Mouseketeer Annette's body. I found her attractive (and still do) but I did not feel those mysterious feelings of lust that they felt. *Those* feelings I had for teen idol Fabian."

"I always was gay and didn't know until about eleven that I was any different in that respect from everyone else. I wasn't particularly embarrassed about it, nor ashamed. But I learned quickly to lie about it in order to survive. The kids in school were not particularly humane toward those they branded fairies, queers, fruits, pansies, sissies, and cocksuckers."

"I can remember constantly watching nude men, being fascinated with their bodies, their genitals, their muscles, their asses, their hair—in the locker room of the country club our family belonged to. I can remember this feeling when my father was still alive, so I was three or four years old, as he died shortly after my fifth birthday. This, I suppose, wipes out the theory of lack of a father making a faggot son, as I knew I wanted men when I had a father."

"Since the fifth grade, I remember picturing guys at school naked. I remember, at age twelve, reading in a psychology book on sex and kids at home a question about worrying about kids being queer. The author answered that it was normal to age thirteen. I remember thinking, Whew! I still have a while."

"I've known forever. I thought it was a natural phase to becoming heterosexual. But, of course, that—praise the Lord!—never happened."

"I realized I was attracted to men when I was five. I told my parents of the strange sense of wonder and happiness and fullness I noted when I saw guys in beach trunks. I didn't know what it meant."

"When I was a kid, I saw a telephone lineman standing on the side of the road. Me and my parents were driving by. He was blond, had a bronze tan, and a well-defined, muscular body. He wasn't wearing a shirt and his jeans were hanging down below his pubic hairs—no underwear. He was wearing boots and a hard hat. He was beautiful. You can tell Anita he didn't recruit me. He didn't even see me. He was gorgeous and I was attracted to him and I knew it. I felt a little puzzled at first for being that attracted to a man. I never let anything bother me much, so I thought I might be gay, but I'd know better when I got older if I was or not. I left it at that, but I never forgot him."

"I was about seven when I first remember being drawn to men, not sexually so much as that I remember having a strange feeling that I never had before—an almost magnetic attraction. I was awed by it, pleased by it—until I began to realize that what I felt was the terrible thing that people were talking about. Then I felt sick."

"When I was thirteen, I wondered, Why am I not so preoccupied with girls as all the other boys are? I figured that it, like pubic hair, just took time. I sought out attractive boys as friends, but didn't know why."

"In some unexplainable manner I knew when I was about seven, but I did not actualize it till I was eleven. I remember when I was seven going with my uncle to feed the cattle at his ranch. My uncle, who had always been a typical 'ranchero,' stopped his pickup at the main gate and before opening it, he opened his fly, pulled out his penis, and proceeded to pee. I was completely captivated by the sight of his penis and its beauty. Since he was completely unaware that I was watching, he did not bother to hide it. I clearly remember feeling a very strong urge to touch it and to hold it in my hand. I still remember that incident as if it happened yesterday."

"When I was in first or second grade, my brother's class (fourth grade) gave a play and this boy came out on stage in cut-off jeans and his legs were so beautiful, I felt my stomach do a mysterious swan dive. The experience is as clear today as if it happened this morning. I was turned on by him. It took years before I attached any fear to that experience of being turned on by other boys. I just simply was turned on."

"I've always been attracted sexually to men. Those Errol Flynn pirate flicks were tops in my childhood fantasies. I guess I first realized it was not the 'norm' when I was eleven and my mother gave me *Ann Landers Talks to Teenagers About Sex*. It was then I found out what a homosexual is and how unhappy their lives are. I decided to have a 'tragic' adolescence with my 'deep dark secret—the love that dare not speak its name.' So I went around for several years being tragic. It seems funny now, but I was very serious then."

"When I was very young I realized I was very attracted to men. Across the street lived four brothers. I noticed myself staring one summer evening across the dinner table at

Lawrence's bare chest. It was well developed and covered with hair. I was fascinated by it. At the time I was four or five years old. Another brother, George, turned out to be my first love. I tried to see him and be with him as much as possible. It was customary for all the members of his family to hug and kiss me after church every Sunday. One Sunday, George refused to kiss me or allow me to kiss him. I ran out of the living room in tears and locked myself in the bathroom. His older sister Eva persuaded me to let her in. I was crying up a storm and told her, 'George hates me. He always loved me before. Why does he hate me now? I didn't do anything wrong.' Eva tried to tell me that George didn't hate me but I knew he did. She brought George over to me and he said he didn't hate me. I said, 'Then if you don't hate me give me a hug and kiss like you used to.' He replied, 'I can't kiss because men don't kiss. I can't kiss you anymore from now on.' 'But I'm not a man. I'm only four.' 'I'm not kissing you.'

"That was my first significant experience with rejection by a male. For me it was very shattering. I thought my attraction to males was very beautiful. Even though I was told such things were bad, evil, and sick, and accepted such warnings in the back of my mind somewhere, I had a feeling that such things were right for me. I couldn't understand why something so wonderful could be so evil."

"I first realized I was sexually attracted to men when I was in the first grade. There was this guy named Daniel who I thought was the most beautiful thing I'd ever seen. I once had a wet dream in which all I did was kiss him on the mouth.

"I have been sexually attracted to men as early as four years old. I must have felt very good about wanting a man because they're still my only sexual attraction. By the age of seven I was having sex with about fourteen different guys from around my block."

"Since early grade school I have been fascinated by the male body. Once when I was very young, I played 'show and tell' with a neighborhood girl. When I saw what she had, or didn't have, I was never even curious about seeing another girl."

"I knew by age eight or ten that the pictures of Tarzan in the comics were very exciting and stimulating, that the boys changing clothes in the locker room were terribly exciting. But all during those years I would never have considered the possibility of a sex relationship as even possible, and I guess I always believed that I would someday be able to function with some woman."

Most of the men, especially those whose first awareness of their homosexual feelings was in adolescence, experienced guilt, self-hatred and alienation when they became aware of society's disapproval of homosexuality. Many wanted desperately to change:

"I was attracted to men at least from the age of twelve. I felt extremely guilty about it. I cried often and copiously. I was sad as hell. I felt that I was the only person in the world with that 'affliction,' that I was abnormal, subhuman, evil, messed up, not worth taking another breath of the world's air. Rather than express my proclivities, I hid them."

"When I was in junior high school, I felt terrible as I realized I was queer, and I was a classic closet case. I vowed that no one would ever find out the awful truth about me, and I used to try to get turned on to the female body by looking at *Playboy* magazines and jacking off, but it didn't work at all. I'd always manage to find some picture with a guy in it, and *that* would really turn me on."

"In high school I felt different and ugly and alone because I was attracted to guys. It was hell. I hated high school. It made me withdraw and become a loner."

"I first realized I was sexually attracted to men when I was in first or second grade. I felt OK about it; it was natural to me. Later, as I became aware of the hostility toward homosexuality, I began to feel guilty."

"I've known all my life that I was gay but I tried very hard to hide it. As a result, I began to hate myself and even more so to hate openly gay people that I met. I became very hostile toward them."

"I first noticed my attraction to men around age fourteen. I freaked out, read a lot of books on the subject, hoped it was just a phase, cried a lot, worried a lot, my grades dropped."

"By adolescence, when I fell hard for an eighteen-year-old guy with whom I worked in a play (unrequited love—he was straight), I had absorbed enough of the anti-gay venom spewed out by churches and peer groups that I felt ashamed that I was in love. I told my mother about it in tears—she tried to explain it away as hero worship. I knew better. I could cry now for all the guys who are going through what I went through then. It's got to stop. Fuck you, Anita Bryant!"

"It horrified me. I rationalized. Read books. Convinced myself it was just a stage I was going through. I did a lot of praying, became a ladies' man, athlete extra to prove to myself I wasn't, because I didn't want to be. In other words, I tried to will myself to be heterosexual. It didn't work."

"At first the realization that I was 'queer' was terrifying. I suppose that is one reason I tried so hard to make out with all the girls I could—to undo this image I had of myself and certainly to keep most people from knowing I liked (preferred) to suck dicks. I married at eighteen to 'prove' once and for all that I was not 'queer.' What a phony I was! It was after four years of marriage and being in the service, then another year in civilian life and a divorce that I started to get really honest with myself."

"I resisted my gay feelings until I was twenty-three, and I poisoned the relationships I had after that with further resistance, until I was twenty-five. All of this was for nothing—a sacrifice of my happiness to straight society which would not let me know that gays were not limp-wristed half-women who dyed their hair pink and walked poodles. The total absence of one single role model for gays made me believe that what I felt was not what other homosexuals (those perverts) felt and that I couldn't be queer because of that. That is how I was 'saved' and 'protected' from gay role models. Instead of being a happy, well-adjusted gay, I was a miserable, lonely, self-hating gay. Nothing else was even possible. Save which children?"

"I at first refused to believe it and believed that I would outgrow it. My refusal period ran several years in which I would regress into believing that if I dated lots of girls and went out and did things socially and sexually with girls I'd make it. I could never make the sexual part and that threw my system into sorry disrepair. I began to feel completely out in left field, the complete oddball with nothing really good to believe in about myself. There was no one to turn to. While all this was going on I had discovered the adult bookstore, and with that the 'gay' section of magazines. I used to buy those books, run home sometimes shaking, and get it off looking at those pictures. Then I'd become furious at my own weaknesses. It wasn't uncommon to begin crying as I took a scissors and cut up each page of the magazine into confetti.

Several hundred dollars' worth of magazines over a two-year period met their fate this way."

"I think I knew I was attracted to men when I was very young, before school age. I certainly knew by ten or twelve and hoped I'd die young so I wouldn't have to face up to it."

A few men were lucky enough to avoid early guilt feelings, or to have positive reinforcement:

"I have always been attracted to men. I first realized it when I first realized there was such a thing as sex. I felt nothing special about that; it seemed perfectly ordinary. Later still, when I learned of other people's disapproval, it was the other people I thought of as weird, not myself. I maintain that thinking to this date. It is the bigots who are fucked up in their heads, not me."

"I felt some discomfort. Yet, it did not take long for me to accept the fact of my gayness. I had no great trauma and once I saw the probability of my orientation, I did not go through any period of denial. I accept myself as I am in total; being gay is part of that total."

"I was about eighteen when I realized that I was homosexual and had no great feelings about it except that I did not want to be forced into any other pattern."

"I accepted being gay when I was in the thirteen-fifteen stage. I was having a reasonable amount of sex. I enjoyed it and even if some of the guys called me names, they were also the ones in the back yard after dark. (I still see some of them and have sex.)"

"At ten, I felt perfectly natural about it. Even when I was told it was 'sinful,' I really did not feel that it was so because it was so *natural* to me! I can't explain it. It was at that point that I began to reject religious beliefs that could make anything ugly and wicked out of anything that was such a joyful delight, such *ecstasy*."

"My family and regional background is arch-conservative, and when I finally realized what my sexual orientation represented to my peers it was a major trauma. I immediately went to a psychiatrist expecting to be cured and made normal. Instead the doctor told me I was normal and spent two years explaining why. I was very fortunate in going to a very bright, very compassionate doctor."

"I had heard references to queers, faggots, fairies, etc. but I never identified them with what I did. Once, in seventh grade, a boy complained to our shop teacher that another boy had grabbed his ass and the teacher flew into a rage. He shook the culprit, yelling, 'What the hell is wrong with you? Do you know what they do to guys like you? Do you want to be put away for being queer?' Most of the boys laughed at the scene; I couldn't understand what the fuss was about. My father had always taught me that we are children of God and equal before His eyes. Thus I have always been convinced that my sexuality is a precious gift which I should be thankful for and which I should develop and use to my greatest advantage."

At what age did you have your first homosexual experience? With whom? What happened? What did you think about it? If you do not consider it meaningful, when was the first such encounter you had with another man?

Twenty-one percent of the men had their first experience before age nine, and most men had their first such encounter between ten and fourteen, with friends or relatives of approximately the same age. Many of the men, however, do not consider these encounters particularly meaningful—they feel that they were more the usual childhood curiosity about sex in general than a definite manifestation of their homosexuality. An often-made observation is that, although many men continued sexual relations with their friends through adolescence, most of those friends went on to exclusive heterosexuality, marriage, and fatherhood.

In the case of a respondent's first youthful experience taking place with an adult, it is usually stressed by the respondent that it was *he* who made the first advance, he who initiated and desired the encounter, and that no coercion or seduction by the adult took place. Several dozen did describe their first experience as a seduction, but just three reported the use of force.

It is evident from these responses that, in the case of both heterosexual and homosexual young men, there is a strong sexual drive and curiosity in children which is healthier for them to express than deny. Many respondents stated that sexuality in general—and not just their homosexuality—was the most difficult problem to deal with while growing up. For many, there was so much guilt instilled in them about sexual feelings *per se* that attempting to deal with their homosexuality was almost impossible.

In most of the responses that follow, a clear pattern emerges: an individual's first sexual experience is recalled by him as a beautiful awakening, a reaching out, a culmination of sexual desires. It is most often characterized as an unpleasant experience only when outside forces (parents, society) condemn it.

Most of the respondents (62%) had their first experience before age 14 with a peer:

"When I was nine years old, a classmate showed me how to 'get a good feeling.' We did it together all through the fourth grade. I enjoyed it. I didn't feel guilty. As a Catholic, I was taught it was a sin to do it with a girl or by myself. They never said anything about other boys."

"I had my first gay sexual experience at the age of six. I was with the boy next door. He was also six years old. We were walking home from the store when suddenly we walked over to a patch of grass in front of a home and got down on our knees and pulled out our penises and started rubbing them together. I remember we asked each other why are our penises so hard and veiny. That was definitely one of the purest experiences I have ever had. There was no guilt feeling or shame at all."

"When I was about ten years old, kids in the neighborhood lured me out into the bushes or an old shed somewhere to have sex. They were teenagers. This did not happen very many times because I was very inhibited. I loved it. There was no brutality in it at all. They are all married and have kids now—so I am grateful to straight people for some things. It is brutality that scared me when I was a kid—never these sexual episodes."

"I had what I later learned to call my first 'homosexual' experience when I was thirteen. There was no sex involved then. A best friend and I used to go on long winter band trips and put our arms around each other and go to sleep underneath the blankets. It seemed so natural, I never thought of it as illicit or bad; but subconsciously realized that 'the others' would not understand. Looking back, I feel he was 'out of the closet' (he was seventeen) but didn't know how to bring me out, or was afraid to. One of my great goals is to find him again and talk to him about those times—all was left unspoken then—we hadn't learned the words to express what we felt."

"When I was six years old, I played 'I show you, you show me' with a five-year-old friend. We got caught and my mother forced me to go next door and apologize. It made me ashamed."

"At twelve with a boy in my seventh-grade class. We just touched and masturbated mostly. The 'affair' went on for almost two years. I guess it was meaningful just because it went on for so long. I still know him: he's married and has one child, and is a closet gay."

"At eleven. It was with a classmate who had come over to my house to play with me. We played with each other's penis and then we felt each other's asshole. He was not circumcised and I was fascinated by his foreskin, which I insisted on moving back and forth. Eventually he ejaculated and scared the daylights out of both of us. We were so naive, we didn't even know what semen was! We debated whether to tell our parents about this incident because we felt my friend had damaged himself internally and that was the reason for the white gooey stuff spurting from his penis. Thank God we never did tell our parents! After our initial fear subsided, we continued to masturbate each other for some time and eventually I too ejaculated. It felt so good! I could now understand why my friend reacted the way he did every time he came."

"The first consequential experience was at fourteen. It grew out of an intimate friendship; my best friend and I were extremely close and it just sort of evolved naturally. We kissed, petted, and had fellatio—reciprocal. There was really no guilt involved—it was too easy and it just seemed so right. But we were terrified of being misunderstood and broken up by parents. Our fears were realized later."

"I had fun with boys ever since I can remember till sixth grade when my mother caught me down by the RR tracks with my best friend. She did everything one can do wrong. Told his parents, caused a ruckus all the way home, and threatened to tell my father, who was suffering from a heart condition. Naturally she told him and he almost had a second heart attack. It got around the neighborhood and I was harassed until I went away to college. I didn't do anything about sex until then."

"When I was two or three, I dreamed I was sucking a man's penis. I remember it vividly to this day. Although it did not involve any physical contact, I still consider it my first homosexual experience. I enjoyed it."

"I think I was about twelve when I seduced a neighbor boy about fourteen. He penetrated me anally and I loved it. We did this on numerous occasions over a few years. I penetrated him later in the relationship. All my experiences were anal until I was nineteen. One night I became so entranced by my friend's penis that I just had to take it in my mouth. I fellated him to orgasm and swallowed his sperm—on my first time. I remember a sense of pride at my accomplishment and thinking how easy it was to do something which was supposedly so distasteful."

"My first time was with a friend, we were about eleven or twelve. We were discussing feelings and dreams and he revealed he'd masturbated. I needed confirmation that we were talking about the same experience—I truly was amazed anyone else had the experience I thought I'd discovered. We masturbated behind the local Community House, in the cool night autumn air with stars above. It was unbelievably mysterious. Neither of us had but a drop of sperm. I remember he touched the drop and took his finger away, creating a thread of silk in the moonlight. It was an innocent, motiveless discovery without a trace of evil or negativity, shame or guilt anywhere in our universe."

"You may not believe this, but I haven't had a sexual experience with anyone, male or female. Wait a minute—I remember now when I was about six or seven I used to play doctor with a neighbor boy the same age. Most of the time we just looked at each other's assholes, but once I got the idea to put my friend's cock in my mouth. I have no idea how I got that idea—I thought I was the first human to ever think of such a thing. So I put his cock in my mouth for about one second and that was it. He wouldn't reciprocate. My mom almost caught us, so out of fear we quit playing doctor. That is the total sum of my sexual experiences with other people. Isn't it a shame?"

"At twelve, before I was able to ejaculate, a few other kids and I got around to playing with each other several times a week. Later we progressed as far as mutual blow jobs but I always acted very straight. It was difficult to not moan and groan in ecstasy when going down on my best friend, but somehow I managed to maintain the appearance of doing it only because he was doing it to me. I was fifteen when I first ran into other queers (besides myself) and I still acted very straight, just letting them use their mouths below my waist. I left home and my friends at seventeen. It was about another year when I encountered another gay boy at my age and made love for the first time as opposed to having sex."

Many men were adolescents before their first experience with a peer:

"I was about fourteen. I thought it was great fun and so did he. One thing led to another and over the next couple of years we got together about once a week and eventually we were trying fellatio. He's married now with a family and I'm not. Go figure. I thought he and I were the only two people in the world who had ever done such a thing."

"I was about fifteen when my school buddy masturbated me one night. I liked it and we fell in love even at that age. We are still good friends even though we do not see each other more often than once every eight to ten years; the feeling is still there. We were inseparable for about four years until the military service separated us. Then we just corresponded. He still says he loves me even though he's happily married."

"My first gay sex was when I was seventeen years old. The head lifeguard at the beach I was working at. We went to a party one night and he took me into a bedroom, locked the door, turned off the light, and got undressed. It was very beautiful. He was as tender as I was nervous. He kissed me a lot and comforted me. He was a handsome man. Yes, I did see fireworks. I can truly say it was the best experience of my life!"

"I had my first homosexual experience at seventeen. I met a young man, also in the art school at the university. We were in his dorm room, lights out. Ella singing, and we wound up masturbating each other. I don't think either of us achieved orgasm before we were interrupted by his roommate fumbling with his key at the door. We flew apart and acted a bit like Lucy and Ethel caught (barely) in the act. Luckily, the (hetero) roommate bought it. However, this pretense, in conjunction with first-time fears, only added to the negative aspects of the sex play. It was at this point in my life that I was able to finally realize that the label 'homosexual' and all the negatives I had learned about it in my very heterosexual world applied to me. It was impossible for me to reconcile my own homophobic prejudices with the idea that I was, for once and all, finally, up-front, no self-delusions left, gay. And I proceeded to attempt suicide by downing a bottle of aspirin. Needless to say, I just got sick. No one knew. I didn't share that with anyone for years. In fact, I felt so incredibly isolated at all points of major crisis in my sexual development. I am just now getting over the resentments, the anger toward my family and anyone adhering to those archaic notions concerning sex and homosexuality. I still feel bad about having to go through all that with no help, not even recognition. I was a victim. And I realize how many innocent victims there have been. It's an agonizing thought."

"The first meaningful experience was when I fell in love when I was seventeen. He was older (twenty-three), gorgeous and dumb. He soon dumped me for someone else. It broke my heart. I swore that I would never let that happen to me again. It did frequently thereafter. It wasn't until I was twenty-eight that I finally got myself together and realized that there has to be more to a person than just looks."

"I was fifteen or sixteen. It was a 'beach encounter.' A guy saw me sunbathing in the nude on a deserted beach and asked me if I wanted a blow job. I had heard about it and knew gays hung out at this beach and I was curious, so I said OK. We went over between two dunes and I got the best blow job ever. I thought it was great. I had something to compare it with—I had had sex with a girl twice before. The blow job was better."

In some cases, young men had either their first experience or their first meaningful experience with an adult:

"I had my first homosexual experience at the age of ten with my gym teacher. We were swimming in the sea and I wrestled him in the water for a couple of minutes until I had the most delicious orgasm in my life. He never noticed."

"I was about twelve. This experience was with my scout master and consisted of him performing fellatio on me while he masturbated himself. As far as what I thought about it, I liked it. It felt good and I think it made us closer as friends and someone I could turn to when I had problems."

"I may have been eleven or twelve. However, I did want it before then. I took the opportunity when it presented itself. My sister was having a party and our cousin's boyfriend was a sailor. When he went to the bathroom I followed. He knew what I wanted and so I fellated him. All I thought of was that he was a man and I was able to fill a need he had. After that Ray and his friends took me along wherever they went. Yes, it was meaningful. I gave them what they wanted and they gave me what I wanted."

"I had my homosexual experiences with other boys in junior and senior high school. My first meaningful experience was with a bus driver in Los Angeles when I was eighteen. I rode that bus every night for two weeks to the end of the line and back because the driver fascinated me with his masculine looks. Then one night he asked me why I just rode from my stop to the end and back again, and I told him I liked to watch him drive. To my surprise he said if I stayed on for one more trip he'd drive me home in his car. That affair lasted several months and to this day I remember how he taught me all the ways of sex and love."

"My first experience was at sixteen with a teacher in my high school. He knew that I was gay and that my two best friends were unwilling to go to bed with me. I think that they had talked to him about me and my propositions so he decided that he would ease the pain. It was beneficial to have an older man take an interest in me and help me deal with myself at that tender age."

"Believe it or not I was seven and at my dad's country club in the head and was so taken by the men's penises that I walked over to one man and started performing fellatio on him. At first he got rather nervous but let me go all the way. It was not distasteful to me at all. I wanted more but was afraid I would get caught so I stopped. However, from that day on any chance I got to service a male I did."

"I was sixteen years old when I met a man at the bakery where I was working. He was about twenty-six, tall, blond, and handsome. We would meet after work and sit in his car and talk of everything and anything. I really didn't know if he was gay but he was intelligent and very enjoyable. He never touched me sexually and sex was rarely mentioned. I had no idea what my motives were for meeting him. A few weeks later we went to his house, nearby, and he'd play records and serve tea and we'd talk and talk and talk. This went on for six months and never once did sex break in on the relationship. But he was about to take me home one day and I couldn't stand the frustration building up in me. I grabbed him and kissed him violently (Hollywood style). He said nothing and I later apologized but he said it was what I felt and I just expressed it. A couple of weeks later we went to bed. He was at all times gentle, patient, and caring and he gave me head and we felt each other and that was it. Soon after he disappeared but left a letter with a friend who relayed it to me. It said he couldn't cope with my youth. It was a bittersweet way to come out and I've always been grateful for his tenderness."

"My dream came along when I was seventeen. He courted me in an elegant way, taking me to concerts and restaurants, and then seduced me, with a full moon shining on the sofa, with a great deal of lyricism and tenderness. This was my first orgasm with another person and this is what made me seek love and affection rather than mere sex in my later life."

The lengths to which a young man will go to have his first homosexual experience were recounted by one man:

"At twenty, I finally realized I was homosexual and I wanted to have sex with somebody. I knew I had to do something about it. The opportunity came up one day when I went to see *Something for Everyone*, a film which involved Michael York in all sorts of sexual activities. The audience was liberally sprinkled with gay guys (I was with a straight friend). Soon, a guy sat next to me—no big deal, it was crowded. I wasn't even aware of him, at first. Then he started running his hand over my foot, and into my shoe. Well, I had never had my foot fondled by another guy before, besides which I was with a straight friend, who thought I was straight as well, so what could I do? I was so petrified, I was afraid to even look at the guy. Finally, my friend looked over and noticed what was going on. I must have given him a totally helpless look, because *he* chased the guy away for me.

"All the way home I felt miserable. Here was my opportunity, and I blew it. As a joke, I said, 'Now I understand those ads in the *Village Voice* that read, "Will the guy who fondled my foot at the Elgin last night please call . . ."' But it wasn't a joke to me. That's exactly what I wanted to do. The idea obsessed me. So I did it.

"The next week was a nightmare. The phone rang at any hour of the day or night. (God, was I stupid and naive. I really thought that only that guy would call, and that he'd call at the time specified in the ad.) Fortunately, my family bought the story that the ad was a misprint, which a very nice girl at the *Voice* agreed to tell them. (This sounds so dumb, but it really seemed like a good idea at the time.)

"During the day, home alone, I was answering the calls, hoping to find my fondler. But after about three calls I realized this wasn't going to happen. Half of the guys who called thought they'd be getting a girl. But I finally got one guy who sounded sane and nice. I knew after a few sentences that he wasn't the guy at the theater, but he seemed normal enough, and this was the best chance I figured I'd get from this fiasco, so I agreed to come over to his place. He was very kind to me and patient with me, and he taught me everything I know."

Some men had their first experience with a relative, either in the same age group or older:

"I can scarcely remember my first experience, since my older brothers were sucking me and fucking me between my smooth legs and buns at a very early age. They really loved me and were careful not to hurt me in any way. At age ten I was being manipulated in a very meaningful way, fellated and fellating; but I was not penetrated until I insisted on it at age fourteen. It hurt a good deal, but I wanted it so badly that I was willing to endure the pain, which was only temporary. Living on a remote farm and being well protected by my big brothers, I had little contact with men outside my immediate family, until my high school days. I was soon as promiscuous as the other school kids. All my brothers, by the way, are now married."

"Since my brother introduced me to sex I didn't get that sleazy feeling about it. I knew we couldn't let our parents know for we thought they would really get mad at us for doing something we shouldn't be doing. I felt a shade guilty because I knew sex was supposed to be between guys and gals, not between guys only. But for the next six months that my brother and I had oral sex, I enjoyed it even though we had to sneak about in the middle of the night to each other's bed."

"When I was five, six, seven years old I used to sleep with my father (he was divorced from my mother) and, at times, when he'd had a few drinks, he'd have a hard-on, and would encourage me to play with it, and sometimes he would suck my cock. At the time, I didn't think much about it; I remember thinking, or realizing, that this was some sort of need he had, and that he didn't have a wife. I enjoyed it, but as I grew older, I began to question it. I confided in one of my older sisters, and she said very firmly that the next time he tried anything I should tell him to stop. I did, and he did. Then I got more and more uptight about being gay, and apart from some very furtive encounters with boys a little older than I, had very little sexual experience, apart from masturbation, until I left the monastery when I was twenty-four."

"My uncle gave me cookies to do him when I was five. He was sixteen. Later he gave me a ring for Christmas. It was more than I got from my parents. I really loved him."

"I had my first experience at ten or eleven. I fellated my younger brother. He was too young (seven or eight) to know what was going on, much less to orgasm. I don't think he even got an erection. I felt guilty about it and did for many years—until, in fact, I told him that I was gay and asked if he remembered what had happened. He said yes and that he was bisexual himself and that he didn't 'blame' me for any 'harm' I might have caused him. Indeed, he felt the experience was actually good for him."

Seventeen percent of the men did not have their first homosexual experience until they were adults:

"In college I became very good friends with Robert. I knew I was sexually attracted to him but I tried very hard not to show it and I vowed never to allow any kind of sex between us. I thought it would ruin our friendship. One night we spent the night together, which we had done many times before. This one night, however, Robert really put the make on me. I fought it like hell but finally had to give in to my sexual desires. After I orgasmed I could have killed myself. I just knew Robert would regret the act. I immediately told him I was sorry but I just couldn't help what had happened. My whole life changed with his next words. He said, 'Sorry? Don't be, please. You're the sweetest person on earth. I love you! Doesn't it seem the natural thing to do?' Those were the first words of love ever spoken between us. We had been in love for a long time but hadn't ever acknowledged it."

"When I was twenty-seven I went to a steam bath with a straight friend for a steam bath. We had no idea they were gay, and we chose a locker rather than a room because of price. Nobody approached us and we left still not knowing they were gay. I went back and this time got a room. I sensed it weird as people wandered about but I fell asleep and woke to the touch of a man's hand on my crotch. I was engaged at the time and since that encounter have never had sex with a woman. *I loved it!* I felt guilty but I loved it. I went back four times that week."

"My first contact was at age forty-eight when I learned about oral and anal sex and I remember thinking that I had at last found myself. There was a great sense of relief when I at last realized that there were many out there just like myself."

"My first experience was with a friend at college. Soon after we met he told me he was gay and we talked about it, mainly at my suggestion. One night he gave me the *National Lampoon* 'Are You a Homosexual?' quiz. I passed with the rating 'Flaming Queen' and David said, 'Let's do something about it,' and he kissed me. I didn't fight it at all! This was what I had been wanting for the last seventeen years!"

"At twenty-two with a fifteen-year-old hustler in the front seat of my car in a railroad yard one night. I told him it was my first experience and he was responsive. I went home afterward in a state of euphoria at the knowledge that I had just done what I'd dreamed of doing for over a decade. The sex wasn't all that great but the fact that I was with another male and could openly touch and kiss and hold him without fear or guilt was a very liberating feeling."

"I was nineteen and a priest who was a friend of the family gave me a blow job. He asked me to reciprocate but I didn't know what to do. I felt very awkward or clumsy. I didn't think anything of the experience, it all seemed very natural the way it happened. But when I found out he had done this with all of my brothers I was irritated."

"The first meaningful relationship was when I was twenty-one. I picked up a girl at a singles bar in Los Angeles. It turned out that it was a man in drag. We engaged in mutual oral sex. We had regular sexual encounters, each of us performing anal intercourse. This was the first time I enjoyed sex with another man. He moved in with me, and we were lovers for a short time, then roommates for about a year. He eventually had a sex-change operation and became a lesbian. It sounds bizarre, even to me."

"A grad student picked me up in the college theater, took me to my off-campus room, and had his way with me. It was the first time I French-kissed, tasted come, came in someone else's mouth, and got fucked—quite a night. I think I must have been extremely lucky because, even from the beginning, I never felt the guilt that so many guys have gone through. I knew I was a good person, that what I had done had hurt no one and caused no one any unhappiness (on the contrary!). So I concluded that if it was wrong by society's mores, then the mores were wrong—that simple."

"My first real meaningful experience was at about twenty-one when I was living with a man of fifty-three. I fell madly, deeply in love with his sixteen-year-old great-nephew. He, a friend, and a younger brother skipped school one day, while Uncle Mark was at work, and came over to the house. We played strip poker, and they looked at some gay/straight magazines Uncle Mark had. After they left, Robert came back alone. He was very passive, but I knew what he wanted. I led him into the bedroom, where he pretended to fall asleep, while I took him orally, kissing his sweet young body with every ounce of love I had within me. He never satisfied my sexual needs, but I was never more satisfied with another man than I was with Robert."

"Believe it or not, my first contact with another man was a bare two years ago (at fifty) in a gay theater. The experience was almost accidental in initiation. The outcome was hardly cataclysmic, but I liked it enough to seek out other experiences of the kind."

"My first meaningful experience took place when I was eighteen. We came just by hugging each other."

Although most of the men had a positive first experience, some found their first encounter unpleasant:

"My first bold attempt to break into the homosexual experience (whatever that means) was about a year ago, with a total stranger. I answered an ad, went to his house, got drunk, went to bed because he was too drunk to drive me home, had sex, and was bored because I didn't even know him or want to know him. We didn't have much in common. He was older, too effeminate, too weird. So the next day he drove me home and I never saw him again. He tried to reach me twice but I never returned his calls. I have never had the meaningful relationship that I desire."

"Just short of my fifteenth birthday, a nineteen-year-old picked me up in a movie in my home town and took me behind the church, pulled my pants down and blew me. Scared the shit out of me and worried me into a state of pimples until I found my self looking for him one night. I consider it meaningful because not one ounce of love was involved, just the act. He wasn't even attractive. The act became almost more important than the feelings being expressed, if any."

"At about fourteen I was seduced by this fat old bastard and it was a lousy experience. I'm surprised I didn't develop straight tendencies at that point."

"At fifteen. An older man, just a friend. There was mutual masturbation, then he immediately jumped up to wash the sheets. I thought I had done something really dirty. That feeling stayed with me many years. The first meaningful relationship was about six years ago with a man who finally showed me that semen is not dirty!"

"At Hebrew summer camp I groped this person who turned out to be a famous Massachusetts rabbi. I was thirteen or so. My adolescence was generally so completely fucked up that I can scarcely think of my first positive meaningful experience. I had a very fucked up outlook on my personal sexuality until I was twenty or twenty-one, thinking for some time that 'maybe if I go out of my way to have a disagreeable homosexual experience I'll see what's right for me since after all, it is sick, isn't it.' "

"My first experience was at twenty-two with my deceased lover. Well, that's a very long story. But I can say we both were drunk out of our minds—at least I was. At first after he told me what happened I refused to talk with him for almost seven months."

"I had my first experience at nineteen. With a man (older) who picked me up in Washington Square Park. I was terrified for the longest time when cruising him because I was afraid he might turn out to be a cop. But he finally came up and spoke. He said he'd hesitated for so long because he couldn't tell if I was gay or not. He took me to his apartment a few blocks away and we did most of the things I had been dreaming about for years. I was enthusiastic but completely inexperienced. And the upshot of it all was when it was all over, I was extremely disappointed. All that anticipation built up great expectations. When it was over, I felt dirty and ashamed. I think I even cried on the bus back home."

Have you told your family that you're gay?

For most gay men, the decision whether or not to inform their family of their homosexual preferences is one of the most difficult they will ever face. Even those men who feel totally comfortable with their gayness harbor great fears about their loved ones' reactions:

"I've come out to everybody—my boss, my friends. I live openly with my lover and don't feel a shred of guilt. But I'm terrified to tell my parents. I have no idea how they'll react. We have never discussed anything sexual, much less homosexuality. They're wonderful people, and intellectually I think they'll say 'So what?' But I've seen the most awful reactions from the least likely people sometimes. I love both my parents dearly and I couldn't bear it if they disapproved of me."

There is pressure on gay men currently to reveal themselves. "Coming out" to friends and relatives is seen by many gay people as an effective way to break down stereotypes and foster a better understanding of homosexuality. A Mervin Field poll in California revealed that among those people polled who said they did not know anyone gay, the majority opposed gay rights. The opposite was true among those who stated they did know someone gay.*

It is clear that by making themselves known, gay people will advance the cause of gay rights. But what can a gay person expect after informing his family?

In this survey, slightly more men have told their family than have not. Of those who have, almost twice as many report good reactions as bad:

"You wouldn't believe the trauma I put myself through trying to work up the courage to tell my parents. I wanted to so badly, because I felt like I was deceiving them. But I was scared shitless that they'd never speak to me again. I actually got physically ill from the stress. Then I finally did it and I almost fell out of my seat when my mother said, 'Dear, it's no surprise. We figured as much. We just wondered how long it was going to take you to make it official. We love you, and if you're happy, then we're happy for you.' I practically

* Los Angeles *Times*, August 12, 1977.

cried. But, do you want to laugh? I was almost disappointed, because I had geared up so long for this dramatic confrontation!"

"I told my mother on Mother's Day. She said it was the best Mother's Day present she ever had. This was because I could never talk to her before that because of my secret. We are very good friends now."

"I told my mother when I was fourteen. She merely sat me down and asked me if it was truly what I wanted. I said yes. She tried to advise me as to all the outside world's feelings on the matter, gave me a five-hour lecture on the do's and don'ts of being a good person and a couple of hints on how to act and what to expect, and that was that."

"I told my mother, father and brother all at the same time when I came out four years ago. My father tried to understand and began reading materials I recommended. He came around, after an initial reaction of quiet acceptance, to the point that he is as well versed in the subject as I am and knows that although he fathered me, he did nothing to determine my sexuality beyond genetic contributions. My parents are 100% supportive of me, meet my friends all the time, even let my last roommate and myself sleep over during one of the holiday periods. As for my brother, he was in the service at the time and I wrote and told him. He wrote back saying that that was the way I was and he saw nothing wrong with it. He is my best friend, and I'm very lucky to have such an understanding family."

"My father, with whom I was very close, was wise and perceptive when I first discussed with him the warmth and joy which I felt in my friendship with a younger fraternity pledge-brother. I remember to this day his saying to me: 'Why don't you just call it love, and relax and enjoy it.' That more than anything else is what made it easy for me to accept the feelings I had toward this guy on whom I had a crush."

"For the most part, my parents' reaction was rational and logical. Nothing in my family life has changed because of my gayness. I'm quite proud of my parents for this."

"They've reacted well. I was amazed. I think every gay person should tell his or her family. Your family are the only people who will love you if you are anything. You should let them know what they are loving. If they don't accept, they don't really love you."

"I told them after college. They asked me if I was happy, I

said yes and they said they were happy also for me. They asked to meet my lover, who they now consider their son-in-law. My parents paid for a wedding reception after we got married at a gay church."

"I told my family when I was young. They were happy because I wouldn't have any illegitimate children."

"I told my parents in May of 1977. A letter was the reaction, saying how they still loved me and it was my life and I could lead it the way I wanted. I really feel it is an absolute must for every gay to tell their parents. We have no right to complain about how we are treated if we continue to oppress and repress ourselves. I now consider it 'anti-gay' not to tell your parents."

"My father was gay. He died two years ago and we came out to each other a couple of months before that. (Not to imply we had sex.) We were thus able to love each other fully for the first time, with no barriers between us. My brother and his wife know and accept, and love me perhaps more because of my honesty."

Many men report that while their family's initial reaction was negative, the situation has improved:

"My mother's reaction was a good cry, then her telling me not to tell my grandmother and father. Unfortunately, I complied with her wishes. My mother was very ignorant of homosexuality and we went through a six-month education process. Then she openly accepted me and my lifestyle. She has accepted my lover as her son and treats him equally with me. He's in her will."

"My mom reacted in the usual motherly fashion: she cried, was outraged, wanted to kill me, wanted me out, and just couldn't understand why I was this way. It hurt me the way she reacted at first, but then I began to understand her. I preached to her about my whole existence, how I am what I am and that above all I'm happy. It took her about a week and a half to get over it, but she has. She's a super lady. She never made me feel that she thought of gays as sissified men. She just couldn't imagine two men into each other's heads, etc."

"My parents were upset and set up an appointment with a psychiatrist suggested by the family M.D. The psychiatrist to my surprise told them gay is good, not changeable, not caused by anything they did or hormones or any other physical abnormality, and because of societal conditions would cause us all some pain. Therefore he suggested they work for change. He had been to a workshop for psychiatrists sponsored by the local gay organization. My parents accept me and my lover and invite both of us over for dinner now and then."

"At first there was total unacceptance on the part of my parents. Then they decided it was just a phase. Later they finally resigned themselves into acceptance. Now it is better than ever—the reason being I had a friend over recently and he met my father. As it turned out his father had worked under my father and they were friends. I think this made him realize other people had gay sons, too."

"When I finished telling them and talking over the sobs and tears, I was taken to the airport with the final goodbye. Since that time they have come to accept the situation, though they still do not understand the permanence, nor the fact that it is not a decision that I made. They do not accept or talk about my lover, and, I think, they see him as a real threat to my ever 'going straight.' It will take some more time but they will, one day, understand. I won't take no for an answer!"

"I sent a letter home to Montana to let my sister know. She let the rest of the family know quietly by reading my letter. The letter was very soft-sell and traced a path of love, affection, and reality from as far back as I remembered. After the initial wondering where to place the 'blame' and 'breast beating', stronger thoughts prevailed to reveal I was still their son and as long as I was happy everything was OK. Many years later I am a family 'celebrity' so to speak."

Some men have encountered a mixed reaction:

"My sister broke the news to my mother because she knew that my mother was coming to visit me and she might wonder why it was that I slept in the same bed as my 'roommate.' My mother told my sister that she knew I was gay when I was still a teenager. I only wish my mother had told me. My father found out I was gay because he opened and read a letter I'd written to my younger brother to tell him I was gay. My father was very upset. He tore up the letter (my brother never saw it) and wrote to me to tell me it was all right and to go and get some male hormone shots. I wrote back and told him that if he ever again opened a letter from me not addressed to him I'd have him arrested, that the last thing I needed was male hormone shots, that I had more than enough hair on my chest and to 'stay the fuck out of my sexual life.' We get along quite well now, although there was a period of time when he was quite distant. He was such a bigot that I figured it was the best thing that could happen to him. My brothers and sisters know that I'm gay and it's quite OK with them. My youngest brother is also gay and my sister is bisexual."

"My mom told me that most everyone has homosexual experiences and that I wasn't necessarily gay if I had gay experiences. She told me that I would probably outgrow it. She really didn't want to know that I'm gay. I'm sure she wishes I wasn't, but I know she loves me and I will always love her. When I told my dad, the first thing he said was, 'The first thing you must realize is that it's no big deal.' He told me that I shouldn't be upset because lots of people are gay and that I'm not alone. He was great."

"My mother read a letter I had written (yes, she steamed it open!) and found out. Her reaction was histrionics for a week. I finally said to her, 'Mother, Bette Davis has already won the Academy Award this year; you haven't got a chance.' My father's reaction was one of reason and caring; he was fearful only for my welfare and happiness."

"Earlier this month I wrote my eighteen-year-old son a letter for his birthday. The letter was by no means sensational. As he is entering the navy I wanted to tell him of my homosexuality and the importance of knowing oneself thoroughly. It was received most graciously—being his father, it was easy for me to note pride as well. A few days later I wrote my sister. The response to this letter was good. Then I wrote my parents the letter I had often dreamed of sending. The reaction was shock, and it will remain so for a long time. My parents may never see that by doing this I have a completely new regard for myself and through this a whole new commitment to them. A friend remarked to me. 'Coming out is valuable to the person coming out, but such tedium for those around him.' After the parental (quasi-non) response, I am in agreement with him. I did it for me."

For 25% of the men, the family reaction was highly negative:

"My mother belongs to a fundamentalist Christian church. In May of 1977, after a separation of nearly seven years, I went home to visit and repair the bridges. Since she lives back East and the chances of her visiting San Francisco were slight I had not thought of saying anything about being gay. Out of the blue she said to me, 'You don't have to be the way you are—queer!' And then began to quote Leviticus and St. Paul, all out of context of course. I haven't seen or spoken to my mother since then and I will not attempt to establish any contact directly with her again."

"A couple of years after I met Rod, my parents came for a visit. On the last night, my mother went to bed, leaving my father and me alone, talking. The conversation veered onto religion, and I expressed my religious views (heathenish to my father, although I consider myself quite religious). Then the conversation moved to sex. We talked about my ex-wife, we talked about Rod, etc. Then my dad asks casually what two guys could do together. I reply, 'Anything that men and women do together, except in different orifices.' At this my dad gets down on his knees and starts praying for me. Disgusted, I go to bed. After a bit, my dad comes into the bedroom and tells my mother what I had told him, and asks me point-blank if I consider myself a homosexual. I say yes. He tells me, with tears starting to flow, to get myself the best psychiatrist, get myself straightened out, money is no object, etc. I say, wait a minute, I happen to like myself the way I am, I see no reason to change, if I changed I would not be the same person they always loved, etc. He hit me. My mother literally jumped on his back when he started for me, raking his face with her fingernails. He grabs his coat and leaves.

"I figure he'll call my sister in Florida, so I try to forewarn her. I say, 'Daddy just asked me if I were homosexual and I couldn't lie to him.' She says, 'Goddam him, why couldn't he leave his mouth shut?' I have my mother talk to her, then I call my ex-wife and have my mother talk to *her*. My parents met at the airport the next morning and did not speak to each other all the way back to Kentucky. This incident was the catalyst for their divorce a year later.

"About two months after this happened, my dad called me. He said he wanted me to know he loved me and that I was still his son, and to forgive him for the things he said that night. I am on good terms with my parents, but they still avoid the fact that I'm gay."

"I have told my wife, and my two teenaged children are aware of my gayness. My wife's reaction has been one of questioning why this should happen to her, and I am working with her to help her understand this. My son has threatened to destroy me 'personally and professionally' if I am gay, and my fourteen-year-old daughter sees gayness as 'gross.' By being open with my gayness, I expect my marriage to be terminated and to lose my relationship with my children. I hope that some time in the future, we can again be meaningful friends."

"I told my aged father I was gay seven years ago. He had to look it up in the dictionary (since, in his upbringing, it is unthinkable). He was astonished and probably dreadfully shocked. It served no purpose; most likely I should not have distressed him so."

"I worried when our daughters reached puberty about their knowing, and this is a long and still puzzling matter of considerable importance. I am fearful that it may have been a factor in the suicide of our youngest daughter, beautiful, talented, intelligent beyond enduring this world."

"When my parents first found out, they took me to a psychiatrist. How I and they survived that experience I don't know. He made me feel mentally ill and doubt my every thought, and he made them feel guilty, as though they had done something to 'warp' me. I could write a book about this experience alone."

"Mother and I haven't talked about it since when she found some letters which she stole from me and took from the mailbox and which she threatened to blackmail my lover with who was a schoolteacher. She knows if she'd admit it to herself."

"I told them when I was fifteen years old but they would not believe it. I spent eighteen days in a mental hospital for observation for homosexuality when I was sixteen, only to be released as going through a phase."

"I was caught with a buddy by my parents when I was a teenager. Then I was sent off to a state hospital. They gave me shock treatments to make me not gay. I had a lover in the hospital who was there as a child molester but I thought he was OK and besides the guy he had sex with was seventeen and wanted to. My lover in the hospital killed himself and then I tried to do it too, but they caught me. Now I'm out but I can't get a job and I'm on welfare. Everyone has made me feel that being gay is horrible but I'm trying to feel better about it."

Nearly half the men in this survey have not told their family. Most of these have kept their feelings to themselves out of fear:

"To them being gay is a mortal sin and I would surely go to hell. They would be very disappointed in me, and I couldn't stand the thought of that. If they knew I was gay that would be all they'd think about. I'd cease to be a part of the family; instead I'd be the gay person."

"I am happily married, with a lovely family. The knowledge would destroy this."

"I dare not tell anyone. My mother has had a lot of trouble in her life, especially with my brother being that way. I want a wife and about six kids. That's my dream and my mother's. Because I don't consider myself totally gay."

"When I was involved in the 'normal' experimentation of puberty, I had an encounter with a neighbor and was 'caught' by my father. My mother said, 'If I ever found out that you were one of them, I'd put a knife through your heart while you were sleeping!' My oldest brother, a wildcat trucker, would shoot me (his threat) were I ever to 'disgrace' the family."

"I think it would be too hard for them to be able to understand my being gay. They would think it happened overnight, whereas it had been taking place under their noses all my life."

"My mother would work up a coronary (which she does on command) and my father, if not shooting me, would disown me and consider me a 'defective' child, as if I were retarded or crippled or blind."

"I am afraid of my father's recriminations. We all know he would kill someone—we just don't know who."

"Recently, my father, to whom I am very close, heard that one of his favorite singers is a lesbian. He threw out all of her records."

"My mother is old and has a bad heart, and she thinks that homosexuality is the worst sin there is, worse than murder even. She thinks Sodom and Gomorrah were destroyed because they tolerated homosexuality. One of my brothers feels the same way. Another brother feels homosexuals should be castrated. I would never tell my family that I am gay. But I would never deny it, either."

"My family? They're stupid 'orange sucker' types. Haters —anti-gay. No chance of telling an element like that. I won't even tell them I'm a Democrat!"

Some men are content not to tell their family:

"They're very religious people living in the South. It would cause them more grief than happiness, especially if their friends found out. Just because I can handle it doesn't mean they can, and I think it's a lot of nonsense for gays to feel they *have* to tell their parents. It's my life, not my parents'."

"We maintain a polite fiction, and avoid discussing it. When I visit, I often take friends with me, and it is always arranged that we sleep together and are left in privacy. The unstated signals I've received over the years say, in effect, that they are accepting, but prefer not to discuss my sexual life one way or the other. It seems fairly civilized to me."

"I do not feel that I have to. My heterosexual brothers did not have to explain what they sexually thought. They wouldn't hate or disown me, so I have no fear of that. I would regret any anguish it would cause my folks because they tend to worry about social injustice and to have a son susceptible to that would affect them and I simply want them to not worry because I'm doing fine."

"I feel it is better for me to keep it to myself than to chance giving several others an emotional problem that they might not be able to handle.'

Others are unhappy that they do not feel able to reveal themselves:

"I would like to tell my parents because in hiding it, I have built a wall against them that keeps us from getting close. Now that I am self-supporting, my attention goes to them, not to any aid they could provide. But we just can't get it together, and I feel my being in the closet is why. All my friends know, and nobody has really freaked out on me. I guess I am just too scared."

"At times I would like to have an advocate—even a paid advocate—go around to my close relatives and tell them that I am gay and elicit their responses and how they would like to interact with me in the future. This sounds so goddam cowardly; but it is the feeling that I have. Of course I realize that no one is likely to step forward and accept that role; so I'll have to play that part myself, which I am trying to do. I would like to get the matter out of the way in as low-key and nonthreatening a way as I can rather than have the whole goddam business explode in their faces and mine at some time in the future."

"I want to discuss it so that they understand how happy I am and how normal, and so that my lover will be 'family' rather than 'friend.' "

"I want to be able to share with them my gay friends and associates who are some of the most beautiful people I know. I want them to feel like they haven't failed as parents and to not try to find out where they went wrong. I want them to overcome the fear of the word 'homosexuality' and realize that sharing and caring are the only things that matter. That I am a real person with feelings and emotions, not a pervert engaging in some sort of dark existence."

"I haven't told my family yet. For years, there was no question of doing so. *I* didn't accept it. It never occurred to me that other people could, certainly not my parents. But then I read Laura Z. Hobson's *Consenting Adult*. More than any other factor, that book helped me come to terms with being gay. If you had told me I needed or wanted sympathy, understanding, or compassion, I would have sneered with macho pride. When Ms. Hobson offered it, I realized that I had never known I had any right to it—and that I needed it more than anything in the world. She took me more deeply than I had ever gone through the agony of being gay—but then took me out of it. To gay pride. A concept I had always scorned.

"And that book convinced me to tell my parents, especially my mom. I haven't yet, only because I'm still living at home. And though I expect eventual acceptance, I don't expect it immediately, and I don't want to live here through the initial stages. So I will tell them—gradually, gently, with help from Ms. Hobson's book, as soon as I move out—in a month or so."

Do you ever pretend to be straight? When? Why? How do you feel about it?

Most gay men are assumed to be straight by the nongay people they associate with. The aforementioned Mervin Field poll asked a cross section of Californians if they knew anyone gay. Statewide, 51% said they did not, and the total was as high as 64% in areas outside large cities.* While the 49% of the people in California who said they did know someone gay is considerably larger than it might have been ten years ago, it is probable that a large number of those people who say they know no one gay actually do, but are unaware of that person's homosexuality.

This is indicated by the fact that 58% of the men in this survey pretend to be straight: Thirty-one percent say they do so some of the time, 27% report they do so almost all the time. In addition, among the 40% who state they "never pretend to be straight," a large number indicate that they "also don't pretend to be gay"—meaning that they do not display their preferences, but act in a way most natural to them. "I do not act straight *or* gay," one man wrote. "I'm just myself. My personality is there for all to see, and they can make their own assumptions, if they're interested, about my sexuality." It is to be assumed that a large number of these men are also considered straight by their associates.

Most of the men responding to this question seem to believe in "situational ethics": They pretend to be straight under certain conditions—at work, with family, among heterosexuals whom they feel would not accept them:

"I put on a 'straight' face because my work requires me to—I have seen *too many* homosexuals fired or fail to get advancement because they 'flaunted'—or even made known—their lifestyle. I don't *like* the necessity to do so, but I still feel it's a must for working with the public, and that if I didn't it would cost me in my ability to hold and/or get a decent job."

"At work, I'm still in the closet. I wish I could come out, but I'm afraid. In the past, I worked in offices, and it seems that there were always a few sexually frustrated women around or women looking for a husband so they could stop

* Los Angeles *Times*, August 12, 1977.

working and be supported. They can be very aggressive. It would have been good to tell them I'm gay. That way it wouldn't have been so awkward. I always had to find excuses for not going with them."

"I live the dual role. I look straight and in the staff room talk about rugby, soccer, and pussy. None of my colleagues knows that I am gay. I do not discuss gaiety (??!) in class or staff room; the kids think I'm straight and I try to perpetuate this image because life would be hell on earth, I'm sure, were I to come right out, and it pisses me off that I am this way; being hypocritical about *my*, my very own and none of anyone else's fucking business, life."

" 'Straight' is almost always assumed. If asked directly, the only people I would lie to are conservative relatives and utter strangers who might be carrying guns."

"I don't pretend to be straight in the sense of saying that I am—lying. But I do, in the sense of not correcting people's assumption that I am straight. I don't say 'she' instead of 'he'—I carefully avoid all reference to gender. I say 'date' or 'lover' or 'they' or 'we.' If I am asked if I think a certain woman is sexy, I say she isn't my type. True, but not the whole truth. I would not deny being gay anymore, but I would answer with a joke, or evade it. For instance, to a direct question on preference, I would say, 'I'm citro-sexual. I get off on oranges.' Or: 'Is that a proposition?' Or: 'Give me a kiss and I'll tell you.' Once, when I was rubbing the sore neck of a (straight) guy I work with, another guy who works there saw it and said, 'How come you two are always touching and hugging? You a couple of faggots?' I said, 'You're just jealous.' Everybody laughed and nothing more was said."

"When I'm with a group of newly met gay men, I try to play straight. I find guys are attracted to me to see if they can get me in the rack. It's all a game but I don't play it too long—people get upset."

"My straight friends have no inkling as to my sexual preference. If any nongay should ask me if I were gay I would deny it. I pass as a straight in any crowd, and I wouldn't like it any other way. A guy in a gay bar in Seattle gave me a hard time because he thought I was straight. I hate to use the word 'butch' but that describes my outgoing appearance and actions. People call me that in the gay bar so often that I'm beginning to hate the word. I feel as if I'm stigmatized. I just feel that I'm a masculine gay male."

"I would deny my homosexuality if asked. I have to pretend I'm straight at work, school, etc. But I don't like putting on this mask when there develop situations which I don't like to be put in. Take for instance, I'm at a straight bar with friends and the inevitable happens. The guys are trying to pick up some girls. I have to go along. Plus there have been situations when I had to go to bed with girls after dates. It's expected that I do. When it comes to having sex with girls, no, I don't like pretending to be straight."

"Other than in auditioning for an acting job for a producer who doesn't know my work, I generally ceased to pretend I was straight the first day I heard Anita Bryant speak out. I hate the pretense with producers, but I don't want to have to go to bed with the gay ones and the straight ones are often too stupid to believe that a gay actor could be macho enough to make straight shows work, particularly as a leading man or a star—which is what I'm doing."

"I dislike playing straight at work because some of our clients' kids who are gay are being sent off to treatment centers or learning centers to 'correct' their behavior rather than being worked with toward acceptance of themselves."

"I pretend to be straight on my job. When you think about it, because of prejudice by straights, most gay people spend eight hours a day pretending to be someone they are not, eight hours a day sleeping, and only eight hours being themselves out of twenty-four hours. What a shame and what a waste! And all because of the Anita Bryants of the world."

"One should always pretend to be straight on certain occasions. Intelligent society demands it, and even though a business contact may know your sexual preference is different, there is no need to cause aggravation by overplaying one's role. Heterosexuals rarely do, why should gays?"

"Sure I pretend to be straight sometimes—why not? My closet has a swinging door."

"I pretend to be straight at work. I enjoy the secrecy of it. I'm sure many suspect that I'm gay, but they can't confirm it. I enjoy that little secret of mine."

"When certain people come to visit the house, we pretend that my lover has a bed in his room that he *uses*."

"Late at night on the subway when a gang of kids gets on the train—I try to 'look' straight. Written down that sounds dumb because who's to say what straight *looks* like?"

Some of the men indicated that they pretend to be straight almost all the time:

"I pretend to be straight more or less all of the time. Being a closet queen is essentially all I was ever trained to be. If I didn't, I would lose my job, my family, the respect of friends. I am the same person twenty-four hours a day, but I have been well trained that it is tolerable to be homosexual only if you do nothing homosexual. One does not erase forty-plus years of training overnight. How do I feel about it? I find my weekly two beers in a gay bar speaking to no one and lasting about twenty minutes a grand vacation! Having been trained that this is the way 'life is,' I don't resent it half so much as I probably should."

"I pretend to be straight at all times because of this god-dam fucked-up society I have to live in. However, I am 100% gay inside my head and under the covers (or wherever). Why? Because I don't want a less-than-honorable discharge. I don't like the hypocrisy I am forced to engage in and it really screws up my head to the extent that while I am indeed very hot inside, I am, in many ways, 'the last wallflower.' "

"When I first realized I was 'different,' I began to watch every movement, every inflection to make sure nothing effeminate slipped. Yet I couldn't help it. (I am not effeminate, but I am aware of the so-called 'feminine' traits in my makeup.) I recognized whenever it slipped by and hoped desperately that others didn't. In growing, I have tried to accept that part of me, integrate it into the rest, and be myself. It is difficult. Even more difficult is judging how much openness about sexual preference is honesty and how much is exhibitionism."

"I pretend to be straight all the time because I worry and want to be accepted by everyone. I also enjoy the ego trip of having women approach me and being rejected by me. It's not a fair or healthy role on my part, but I feel women are spoiled by men and need to be shown that they *too* should experience rejection. I also put on the straight role because I'm still not sure how society, family, friends, or God feel about homosexuality. Sometimes I'm ashamed and frightened by my gayness."

"I do not want my children to find out about my gayness—at least not yet. One gay father in my community did come out publicly and it was his children who suffered. No thanks."

"Living in this neighborhood you have to play it straight. I don't mind it too much, as I hate nellies and I like my lover to play it straight. What we do in the bedroom is our thing. I hate necking and kissing in public; it is repulsive to me."

"I pretend every day to be straight, because that is the only way that I could live or work in this small town that I find so otherwise satisfying. There is only one person in this town that I ever had a sex relationship with, and I have not run into him again directly for years. He has since married and had children and we just never get to speak."

"I don't have that many gay friends and I figure that straight friends are better than no friends at all. And what they don't know won't hurt them."

"Most people think I am straight. This is a matter of self-protection, including the rather trivial matter of trying to appear straight just to avoid having to spend time and energy helping casual acquaintances adjust to my gayness. After all, why the hell do I have to educate every store clerk to accept me or any other gay person? Unfortunately, I think that there are still many times—too many times—when I just cannot be myself without suffering either personal rejection or objective losses (loss of business, loss of equal treatment in court, loss of equal treatment in everyday business transactions). I am coldly furious about having to cover up my gayness. Making it tolerable for gay persons and their nongay friends to live openly is a very vexing problem."

"I do not feel particularly good about denying a part of me that is so rewarding and satisfying. When people around me are sharing their home lives and good times it is a little frustrating to have to sit in silence."

"I must always pretend to be straight to protect myself from being 'burnt at the stake' by my community. People here are very hidebound about homosexuality. I hate role-playing. It's a real drag carrying a skeleton around with you. Bigotry has no place in my lifestyle, especially since gayness is *not* a sin. Therefore, I sometimes feel nauseous inside because I'm being a hypocrite."

Some of the men indicated that while they do not currently pretend to be straight, they did at one time:

"I used to pretend I was straight—complete with girlfriends (who knew that I was gay) to act as excuses and dates. Not anymore. I'm done with closets and disguises, and it's not so much that I'm proud or arrogant about being gay,

I'm almost indifferent. Like having brown hair or being right-handed."

"In past years I did act the part of a raving heterosexual, and not convincingly. I was not proud of these masques and was terrified constantly I would be proven a liar and a queer. I was in the army at the time. From this time until a year ago I developed the technique of hiding and got so good at it I nearly lost myself. It was an emotional rip-off. My wife Carol has helped to make it so much easier to be myself that I no longer hide. There are situations better avoided or infused with silence. I am not militant but when intimidated I no longer hide."

"I have pretended to be straight. I have tried to be straight. Sometimes I almost had myself convinced that I *was* straight. When young I thought that my gayness was a disease that could be cured by the right environments. I had a twenty-year career in the military service. Concurrently I married and raised a family. It was *hell!!* I felt my whole life was a hypocrisy. When I got out of the service and my children were grown I came completely out of my closet and ended the lie of marriage. I feel fine about it now."

"Pretending to be straight for so long was one of the madder aspects of my life. But like the recovered insane I know the anatomy of madness now."

40% of the men said that they do not pretend to be straight; many indicated that they are openly and honestly gay; others stated that they do not lie about it if asked:

"I am myself at the job, at home, among friends. I feel that people who pretend to be what they are not usually end up losing."

"I don't volunteer the fact that I'm gay unless I'm asked, which hasn't happened too often. With most people, the conversation rarely moves to sex or sex lives. Nor, I think, do most people want to talk about sex today. But I have discussed sex with people who ask me about it. If they have the wisdom to be able to ask, then I dignify their wisdom with the truth. Being gay and letting everybody know about it isn't necessarily my way of being. I consider it worthwhile only when it matters to me that my friends understand about sex generally and my homosexuality in particular."

"People are free to draw whatever conclusions they wish about my sexual preferences. I don't flaunt my homosexuality, but neither do I make any effort to conceal it. If I'm at a straight party and someone makes a fag joke, I make my situation known immediately. It almost always embarrasses them and makes them think twice."

"In a way, I 'pretend to be gay' more often. By which I mean, when I'm with a bunch of people who all just assume I'm straight (which all straight people do—if you don't really camp it up, they'll give you the benefit of the doubt), I delight in pretending to be gay, because they always think I'm kidding. So I can say anything I want, and they're sure I don't mean it."

"It's the *other* people who seem to pretend I'm straight or want to play the game that way. I don't like to because I have no pangs over being gay and don't care who knows. The only way to get gays their rights and full acceptance and recognition in society is to live what you are, and not hide it or be ashamed. To know and understand and live your values and worth as an individual."

"I try to keep away from situations where I feel I 'have' to *act* straight. When the company president comes by and sees a 'real fox of a young lady' and asks me, 'Wouldn't you just love to eat that little jewel out?', in general I mostly have trouble *not laughing*."

"One of my gay male friends and I always say hello and goodbye with a kiss on the lips—on the street, at the airport, wherever—and I've never gotten any flack about it. Most people don't notice, can't believe their eyes, or really seem to envy that freedom."

Other men who indicated that they do not pretend to be straight stated that they do not try to act any particular way, that they try at all times to simply "be themselves":

"I'm not sure what is meant by 'pretend' to be straight. Does one manifest gayness when shoveling snow, grocery shopping, changing a tire, or working on the job? I'm myself."

"I do not pretend to be anything other than a human being. I am at all times myself. I doubt that most people who know me think one way or the other about my sexual preference. I try to be a fully realized human being."

"Straight-acting except out of necessity is a betrayal of one's gay brothers and sisters. On the other hand, camping it up except in a gay environment is in bad taste and irresponsible. One should behave honestly, unashamed of gayness and certainly not hypocritical toward it, but also not proclaiming that gayness is one's most important trait."

"Life out in the country is a lot different than in a city. There are so few people around, the question never comes up about gay or not. After a hard day on the tractor, or working cattle or sheep, all a fellow wants is a good shower, a good steak, and to relax. When things are not too hectic, you and a buddy can have sex. It's no big deal."

"It's not so much a matter of pretending, as it is just the fact that I don't come across as gay, so most people just assume I'm straight—I'm just being myself. Passing for straight (without even trying) has its advantages and disadvantages: I don't put people off, I don't get beat up in alleys, etc., but there are times when I wish it were a little more obvious to people—especially certain people. I think sometimes other gay guys just assume I'm straight, and I miss out on some opportunities."

"I am against the concept of 'acting' straight or gay and try to do neither. I never talk about fictional girlfriends—in fact, I talk very little about my private life. The bank is four-fifths women and they always make allusions which I ignore. I avoid the men when I hear them talking about women. I find it despicable that some gays feel they have to show that they're gay. What the hell does being gay have to do with mannerisms, mincing, and being effeminate, or being straight with hulking, flexing, and bullying? It's a matter of being one's self in the true sense of the word."

PART TWO:
GAY MALE
SEXUALITY

How often do you have sex? How important is sex in your life?

To the majority of men in this survey, sex is extremely important, and they engage in it frequently. Twenty-one percent reported they have sex once or twice a week, 17% say it is three or four times a week, and 16% engage in sex at least once every day.

Many of these men have an exceptionally free attitude toward sex. Because society's view of their sexual preferences has forced them to live outside the mainstream, they are not often bound by traditional sexual mores.

Most of the men view sex on two distinct levels. On the one hand, it is a recreational activity, something to be indulged in for physical pleasure, expression of affection, communication with others, fulfillment of a biological need. On the other, it has the spiritual importance as an expression of love which has always been presented to most people as the only way sex is acceptable. Most of the men in this survey indicate that the latter is quite special and reserved for special people—but the former is not denigrated. Many do not view any sex—whether engaged in as an expression of love or purely for pleasure—as in any way dirty, deserving of reproach, or sinful. They view all sex as a sharing of affection and physical sensations with another human being which has nothing inherent in it to cause guilt. Such views, so often drummed into them by society, parents, and "experts," have been rejected by these men.

Sex is a very important element in most respondents' lives:

"I have sex as often as I can get it, sometimes four times a day. If I don't have sex with anyone on any day I always resort to masturbation, and that can also sometimes be three times a night. I suppose, without thinking about it, sex is important in my life. I thoroughly enjoy it, and I guess it is important or I would not be masturbating when I don't have sex with someone."

"I have sex with men irregularly, about twice a month on

63

the average. It is important to me. It is bread and butter to keep me alive."

"I have sex with another person very seldom, maybe two or three times a year. It must be very important as most of my spare thoughts concern some form of imagined sex."

"We have sex about four or five times a week at my option, his, or both. It's essential to cement what we've said to one another through the day, or clear up problems. I'd never want him to think I'm not available."

"Sex is still extremely important in my life. I consider it compensation for the injustices society has wished on us."

"My lover and I have sex on an average of twice a week. I consider it extremely important. I broke up with my first lover of nine years mostly because we had no sex whatsoever. If we had had sex once or twice a month, I believe I would have stayed with him."

"Sex is an important element in my total lifestyle and person. I view sex as a recreation, a sport if you wish. I have sex frequently with many different partners in addition to my lover. I view sex within the same framework as people view tennis, golf, or skiing. It's fun and I enjoy the physicalness. I treat my partners as players in the same sport and only want partners who view it in the same way. I don't want or need a bunch of heavy emotional overtones to the actual act of sex. If I want affection and tenderness, I stay home. If I need less affection and more raw physicalness from sex, I go out and get it."

"Sex is the most important activity in my life. To engage in sexual intercourse with a compatible man is the most beautiful act in all creation. To fuck and to be fucked is the supreme ecstasy. All else is secondary. I think fuck is a beautiful four-letter word. I equate it with the most beautiful four-letter word in our language—*love*."

"Sex is quite important to me. So much so that when I'm horny my behavior tends to be irrational unless the urge is satisfied."

"I sometimes think that my functioning and enjoyment of other aspects of my life—job, friendships, my house, daily tasks—are dependent on my satisfaction with my sex life."

"It's important to me mentally, like on a scale of one to ten it's about an eight. I get edgy, restless, and way too horny if I let it go for very long. When I'm training real heavy I will quit for weeks as the sex drive could be transferred into strength. Of course if I go too long without sex I will ejaculate during an exercise—usually something abdominal or weighted pull-ups. This is also as important to me as regular sex, since the orgasm is different yet a real ball-buster."

"I consider sex to be the one truly wonderful aspect of life. If I were not able to have sex I would not wish to live."

"At forty-five I can't say the powerful old desires are there. Instead there is a joy because I'm participating in the Dance of Life. Sex is very important to me; it makes me feel I'm still part of the fabric of life."

"Sex comes just after breathing and quite a bit before eating."

"Sex is quite important to me because it allows me to express physically what words are inadequate for."

"Sex is a beautiful gift of God, when done in love."

"When I am without a lover it seems more important than otherwise. I sort of use it as an excuse to meet other people since I'm basically a very shy person."

"For me, it is not an obsession but more like a rhythm in my daily life."

"It is extremely important. At my age it has become less of a physical demand and more a mental/emotional requirement to hold, hug, and love someone with free sexual expression."

"Sex is very important in my life. It is my life: I paint it, I write it, I act it."

"Sex is very important to me and it's a good release for me. I control my sexual drives by personal moral standards which are very high. I just believe having sex is the most intimate thing in my life and I only share that with men I care a hell of a lot about!"

Some men see sex as an indication of their worth as people:

"I enjoy sex on a purely physical level, but it is probably more important as an affirmation that I am real and alive and attractive to someone else."

"Sex provides me with reassurance that I'm capable of pleasing a partner. Having someone attracted to me provides my ego with the moral support it consistently demands."

"Sex is the only way I can feel attractive and desirable."

"Gay sex is important to me because I have not felt accepted and a good person in my heterosexual marriage. By having sex with men, I feel defined as a whole and good person. My relationship with the men with whom I have had sex has been one where there is mutual appreciation of each other, whether for the moment or the possibility of continued friendship. My gayness, and gay sex, is an important part of defining myself as a worthwhile person."

"Sex is more important to me as a gay person than it probably is to others. By that I mean, when I'm having sex with another man, it's a beautiful sharing, the most wonderful expression of my homosexual nature. I've always been told that being homosexual is rotten and thus I'm rotten for being a homosexual. It's gotten so that I sometimes wonder if they're right. But when I'm *having* gay sex it's so beautiful that I know they must be wrong—I feel good about myself!"

Some men feel that sex holds too important a place in their lives:

"I've thought that I could be on my deathbed and still be up for one more orgasm. My obsessive need for sexual intimacy has sometimes caused me problems: I was terribly offended when someone I was seeing didn't want to have sex with me as often as I did with him. I always took it as a rejection; usually it was simply that our appetites differed. But it often put a real strain on the relationship."

"When I'm upset, I tend to seek out sex even more. I know that I'm giving in to physical urges I should have under control."

"I was trying to get sex from early morning to late in the evening and then starting all over again. What stopped that was that after doing that for about a year I finally caught hepatitis, which nearly killed me. It taught me something."

"Sex is so important to me that I started going outside my marriage to have sex with men when my wife and I were unable to share the kind of sex that fulfills me. By normal heterosexual standards, we had a great sex life. What she didn't know was that my needs were far more than we were satisfying. Oral sex is critical to me, but to her oral sex is dirty. Variety of positions, locations, and atmospheres is essential to me. She is uncomfortable with variety and many locations. Men satisfy my sexual requirements completely. Yet it is so important that our marriage is teetering because of it."

"I believe life would be so much easier for all of us if we were all asexual. Just thinking about it occupies too, too many of my waking (and sleeping) moments. We are all, as Mailer said, *prisoners* of sex."

Other men describe their sexual urges as no more important than other aspects of their lives:

"Sexual activity varies in my life. First of all, I don't find that I have to have sex a certain number of times per week or per month. I only go to bed with men in whom I am interested in more ways than simply as a bed partner. For me, sex is but one of many ways in which I can demonstrate my feelings to those I care for deeply."

"I think about sex much more than I participate in sex, but isn't that true of everyone? Seeing an attractive man on the subway will make me think sex, so I guess you could say it is important. I don't, however, live and breathe merely for sex—there are a lot of other things I enjoy."

"Sex is only a small part of what I consider important in my life. My work, my hobbies of ham radio and photography, scouting work, other volunteer work, etc. are a part of life, too. Too many gays, I think, center their whole life around sex—and this helps enhance the public stereotype of sex maniacs, etc. There is more to a personal relationship than just sex."

"In a relationship, sex is only a part of it. Different people place different emphasis on sex in a match—to me, it is akin to mortar holding a big pile of bricks together, or the frosting on a cake. A meaningful relationship cannot exist on sex alone—and it cannot last without it. To me, sex is sharing. If it is only for physical release—hell, a hand job will do that."

"Having sex is not the *main* concern in my life and sex should not be considered the most important thing in life. God, family, and friends should head the list."

Some respondents say that sex is not important to them:

"I don't go out looking for sex, rather I go out with friends to dance, party, and have fun. If sex happens, it happens. If not, fine—I'm having fun."

"Sex for the sake of sex has a tendency to be boring. Sex doesn't play a very important role in my life. It accents any relationship but it is not purely necessary for a relationship. A relationship based solely on sex cannot last very long, and after the sexual attraction between the two parties is over then so is the relationship. But then, I guess that is why one-night stands exist."

"The idea of sex is what is important. My lover and I

hardly ever have it anymore, but we certainly don't love each other any the less. I am a totally sexual being, but 'having' sex is not very important."

"I have sex every now and then. My brain has always been the number-one organ that had to be stimulated."

"I have gone long periods without sex and been absolutely none the worse for wear."

Do you enjoy one-night stands?

A high level of sexual availability* is a major component of most gay men's lives. Sexual activity is easily found if desired, and there is often a large number of sexual partners with whom a gay man can express his sexuality.

It seems, on the surface, to be a gay phenomenon—indicating to some the freedom and pleasures of the gay lifestyle, to others the decadence and moral turpitude inherent in homosexuality. In reality, it is far more the result of the fact that there are two *men* involved than that the men are homosexual.

Before the advent of the sexual revolution changed this in many parts of the country, it had traditionally been men who were conditioned to be sexually aggressive, to take the initiative in sexual matters. The goal of the male was to get the female into bed as soon as possible, and the goal of the female was to stay out of it as long as possible, preferably until after marriage. A teenage boy involved in sexual activity was admired and envied by his peers: a teenage girl so involved was most often considered "bad." While these attitudes have changed dramatically in the last fifteen years, they still affect many adults who were raised on them.

Thus, two males sexually attracted to each other have a great deal in common: an innate sexual aggressiveness, a less repressive sexual upbringing than women, and the desire to get the other into bed as soon as possible. The result, more often than not, is a sexual encounter which takes place after very little coyness, game-playing, and formality.

Another reason for the usually rapid expression of any sexual attraction between two men is that, in our society, that is

* The word "promiscuity" is being avoided here because it suggests indiscriminate and random choice of partners; a gay man's sexual relationships, no matter how frequent, need be neither.

often the *only* way in which they can express their attraction to each other. Heterosexuals usually work up to sexual encounters by dating; it is, however, frequently impossible for two men to do so—and it is certainly impossible for them to hold hands or cuddle in public; they cannot dance together except in totally gay environments, and they must completely hide their feelings for each other in most situations. Their sexual desires are not given subliminal outlets and, thus repressed, are far more difficult to contain when the opportunity for sex presents itself.

For many men as well, sexual encounters are a highly social activity. They are a way to meet people, to make friends, and certainly a way to find a lover. In those respects one-night stands are often a necessity. It is thus not surprising that over 90% of the men in this survey have had one-night stands with varying frequency. That they are a large part of the gay scene, therefore, is clear. But what do gay people really think about such activities? The reaction is mixed.

52% of the men find one-night stands enjoyable:

"I see nothing inherently 'wrong' or unfulfilling in one-night stands unless one expects them to be more than what they are. I always feel some measure of love and caring for anyone I have pleasurable sexual relations with. Living itself is to some extent a one-night stand. All good things come to an end at some point; and in the case of one-night stands, that end comes rather soon."

"The people I know whose hearts are set on lifelong relationships are the loneliest people I know. You don't start out with love. You start out with sex. With any luck, you build to love. But don't bet any money on it."

"An occasional new and interesting friend can be exciting and fun and, as we all know, a 'trick' or one-night stand is our unique cultural means of getting better acquainted."

"I do enjoy one-night stands and once I got over the fantasy that Sir Galahad was lurking behind every towel at the local bath, I enjoyed them much more. When I'm in the right mood, and the partner is pleasing, good, instant sex can be marvelous. I had to work through some hang-ups about promiscuity, and I did it by realizing that the common societal heterosexual role model (which is in big trouble on its own turf) simply doesn't belong to us. I say this with the proviso that a quickie, no matter how good, cannot, for me, compare with the sexual communication in a love relationship. But then, why should it?"

"Until I'm finished with school I will enjoy one-night stands. In my heart I'm a romantic and sentimental and have a strong desire to live as one with another man. A few years from now I'll sweep some handsome little prince off his feet, build that vine-covered cottage on the side of the hill, and live happily ever after. However, for these few years during which I'm devoting total energy to obtaining an education, it's a choice between my left hand, my right hand, or some passing dude, strictly to get my rocks off so I can stop the distraction of daydreaming and get back to the books."

"Some of the most meaningful person-to-person relationships I've had have been with one-night stands—probably because there's an investment but for the moment; no months of expensive time together, no leisure time spent in each other's presence, no emotional expense to *justify* the sharing of sex and intimacy."

Many men spoke of the pleasurable variety found in a large number of sexual partners:

"I feel that 'one-nighters' are good for curing sexual hang-ups. You meet a variety of guys who are into a variety of scenes, and I believe in trying out any scene before forming an opinion. And I can get a wide range of sexual views with casual pickups."

"It is a fast thrill, exciting and different. Each person is different and the way they fuck is different also. And sometimes it is just that difference that makes you see how much you have at home."

"I enjoy one-night stands for one reason. The first time is usually the most exciting. It also gives me a feeling of getting something good every time I go home with someone new. Like winning a contest."

"The reason I enjoy one-night stands is, I feel I am aware of people's differences and preferences and can pick up on little things that they might throw out. Where if I have sex with one person I fall into a rut. I know what they enjoy, what is a turn-on, etc. With a new partner you are more aware of what is exciting. Also for me, I admire bodies. It doesn't have to be a gorgeous example of a bodybuilder or anything like that. I just enjoy being close to different bodies and this is always exciting for me."

"Having a lot of different partners keeps me on my toes sexually, and I'm always learning something new from someone. Not just sexually, but in all kinds of areas."

Many other men stated they enjoyed one-night stands because of the opportunity it gave them to meet people:

"Almost every close friend I have is a former sexual intimate of mine, and some of those were indeed one-night stands. The sexual or romantic aspects of our attraction didn't pan out, but there was enough commonality for a friendship to develop. Also, I have acquaintances among prior tricks who are interesting, influential, or whatever. Tricking is, in point of fact, a social endeavor."

"I enjoy the fact that most people can relax and enjoy the time you spend together, while treating each other with kindness and respect, even though you know you probably will not see each other again. I like the fact that you can share a moment in someone's else's life and leave with only good feelings."

"Sex is great fun, and if a partner thinks so too, we might repeat the encounter. After a few such repetitions, friendship grows and might involve partying or whatever. My one-night stands are all informed early in the game, however, that I have a lover and a very secure relationship."

"It usually is a way to widen one's circle of friends, especially if you live out of town. They are sexual outlets, but if you aren't receptive a good thing will never get started."

"I like to meet different people, and find out a little of what makes them 'tick.' There are people out there—people with vibrant ideas and personalities; people doing things. To get to know them is refreshing, and gives focus to the things I am trying to accomplish."

30% of the respondents report that, although they engage in one-night stands, they do not find them enjoyable:

"I suppose the main reason I don't like it is because I don't know if we've done it for a sexual outlet or for a potential start of a relationship. Also, it's *very* easy to get hurt, especially if you're as sensitive as me."

"I really like to get to know a person—even sexually. I find there is not too much you can do in one night. Almost every man I have been in bed with, I have felt I have been 'in love' with him . . . though most of the time I felt the opposite the next morning."

"I do not go in for pickup pick-me-ups. I am quasi-Victorian about sex. I don't jump into the sack with just anybody. There has to be some natural progression to lovemaking. It may sound odd, but that even pertains to my lovemaking with usually straight men, of whom there have been two. Those men were married, one with children, and sex just became an extension of our closeness over a period of time. Neither of the men went nuts, nor left his wife, and we are still close and sound friends."

"I do not enjoy one-night stands at all. I feel as if I am prostituting myself."

"If I am into one-nighters, it's usually at a point when I am out of touch with myself."

"One-night stands do not appeal to me. I like the idea that sex is something to share with someone extra special."

"I do not enjoy one-night stands, except when they're happening. In other words, when I have sex with someone, I don't intend for it to be a one-night stand—but they usually are. If a man is good enough to go to bed with once, he should be good enough more than once."

Most of the men opposed to one-night stands stated that they are meaningless, unfulfilling exercises:

"At one time I did enjoy them but not now as I'm getting older. I see a lot of phony people and insincerity in the bars and sometimes it turns me off. I think to myself—I'd rather go home and masturbate than go through this phony ritual. I have been having sex in bars in dark corners. But it's not fulfilling. I guess I do it because I'm horny and I know there's no possibility of a relationship and I'm not relating to that person on a mental basis. I feel very disgusted and disappointed after it's over. And I am usually hornier after I've reached orgasm than before."

"It's been over a year since I had sex with another person. It used to be several times a week. It takes too much time and effort to go cruising, and the rejection is just too painful."

"I hate one-night stands. If I know or hear that a person has a reputation for this, I often find myself avoiding them. I'm into being human and respecting others and myself. I don't desire to be just a number or cattle, nor one who's known as an easy lay. If I consent to a date, or an evening spent with someone, it's because he's interesting enough to get my attention—and, yes, even a potential for being a lover. If not that, at least a good friend."

"It's too frustrating. I don't like not being able to get to know people and I'm too reticent with a complete stranger; I don't let myself go. I satisfy neither myself nor my partner in a 'quickie.' "

"I feel that we place too much emphasis on sex, not just the person as he is. We don't have to have sex with everyone who comes along. I'm tired of being treated as a sex object, and I'm sure you feel the same way. I have a mind, a personality, my own thoughts, good points as well as faults. I read once where we 'fuck first, talk later.' Unfortunately, I feel this to be true. I would rather date a person first, get to know him better before I find if we are sexually compatible."

"Too often the basic scenario—one of a set of perhaps a dozen—is unenlivened and seems all too familiar, merely mechanical repetition. I find that kind of performance boring."

"Since I have been with my lover there haven't been any one-night stands; when I was single I did not invite or enjoy them as I tend to try to touch emotionally as well as physically and it's very hard to do with a transient. When I was single I did consider each partner a potential relationship. Even if I saw a pickup as having only sexual possibilities (that is after trying unsuccessfully to relate to him) I felt sure I would see him again and again, never really grasping the meaning of a one-night stand. I'd give out my number and honestly expect to hear from these people again."

"You have to spend time and money searching; you risk contracting contagious diseases; and you risk wasted psychological energy. You may lose interest in the person between the time you meet and the time you begin sex. If so, what do you tell him—'Forget it, I'm no longer interested'?"

"Earlier in my life I sought them just to prove that I was attractive to *somebody*. Having done that, I am looking for a relationship and I will never take the initiative to have sex with anyone unless I would wish it to be an ongoing relationship. The fact that it usually turns out to be a one-night stand anyway is due to the other person's decision and therefore one-night stands mean rejection."

"There is always a guilty feeling inside when you know

that you are faking the love you make. And that's what one-night stands are all about."

"People who sleep around like that, to me, are irresponsible and guilt-ridden and incapable of truly loving."

Are one-night stands purely sexual outlets or do you consider each partner a potential relationship?

Most of the men in this survey said that they view every individual as a possible relationship, whether as a lover or as a friend. Most of the men who viewed one-night stands as solely sexual outlets were those who have lovers and for whom one-night stands are thus "extracurricular" activities.

"One night stands always start out as a potential relationship—because that is really what I'm looking for. But they usually wind up as purely sexual outlets. Occasionally, but rarely, I go out looking for just a sexual outlet. But mostly, I want to meet someone whom I can truly love and spend my life with."

"I had sex often as a teenager, as often as possible, in fact; always with school friends. It was purely a physical release. Until I fell in love at age twenty-six, I hadn't even realized that actual *love* could be part of a homosexual act. In the few times that I had sex with anyone after that time and until I met the lover I'm living with, everything was in hope of finding something permanent."

"One-night stands are all I know. I consider a *glance on the street* a potential relationship."

"If people turn out to be as nice as their first impression, I'd like to see them again, but it doesn't upset me if I don't. Each partner *is* a relationship. To worry about when it's going to end is self-defeating."

"No, they're not purely sexual. I do like to get to know the person first. No matter how great a person's technique is, he turns me off if he won't converse during sex. Not just dirty talk but communication. I like to use all five senses. I'm not intent on having a relationship but I'm always open to one if it should develop. But even a 'one-night stand' with the right person can be a rewarding relationship."

"When I was a bachelor, I used to evaluate each trick as 'lover potential,' but if I were (God forbid!) suddenly thrown back into the market I would de-emphasize this part of the search effort and look around for a companion among people whom I already knew and liked. Still, it can't be denied that six years ago I took home a sexy trick from the College Commons and he's still around."

"I never go home with someone with the intention of never seeing that person again: everyone is a potential friend."

"I can think of very few times that sex has been purely a sexual release. I have usually formed some kind of relationship with the men I have met."

Other men are quite content to keep their one-night stands as solely sexual encounters:

"I enjoy one-night stands but in the past few years I usually avoid them unless it is for immediate sex. The reason is that if I don't become emotionally involved with the other person then I can enjoy them purely as a fantasy. Often if I get to know much about the person I find I'm turned off because they don't come anywhere near the fantasy I've created for/about them. I guess I'm afraid of having sex be the basis for forming a lasting relationship. My first lover and I fell into that trap. We enjoyed sex with each other so much that it was the basis of our relationship. It isn't enough."

"They are mostly sexual outlets. If I met someone I felt I could care for, I probably wouldn't go to bed with him right away. I really feel there is less of a chance for a permanent relationship if you go to bed right at first meeting rather than if you take time to find out more important things about one another."

"I have sex with heterosexual males more often than with homosexual ones, and sex, therefore, can't be the basis for a relationship."

"I enjoy one-night stands usually as purely sexual appreciation of another's body. The anonymity and temporary nature of these allow me to be a lot looser in my sexual expression."

"They can be very exciting and refreshing, pure sex—a change of pace which recharges the sexual batteries. Turns me on to my lover. I can't leave him alone after I've had someone else."

"When I first came out I felt that I needed to go out to the bars and baths to find a lover, but I soon found that I should let nature take its course and meet men to have a good time and pleasurable releases with no real expectations."

"Tricking is fun, not only for the sexual act, but also because someone demonstrates an attraction to you. It's a real ego booster to have someone try to invite you home. Although I always was interested in a lasting relationship, I was never turned off by someone that would obviously not be compatible in a stable relationship. Don't straight women have sex with men who they do not rate as a potential husband?"

"I enjoy the cruising game in a bar. It's ego-gratifying to get a good cruise. It's sometimes enough just to know I *could* have had a good-looking guy on my terms."

"When I trick, a potential relationship is the farthest thing from my mind. But I still give to my men. No one is a sex machine. Everyone is a person to be cared about—even if for only one night."

Do you enjoy affection during sex?

A belief many people have about homosexual activity is that it is quick, furtive, often rough, and always without love. Some of the men in this survey (as in a quote a few pages back) stated that they themselves at one time had no idea that love could enter into a homosexual act. Homosexuality was seen as a purely sexual phenomenon—an idea given widespread credence by the publication in 1969 of David Reuben's *Everything You Always Wanted to Know About Sex*, a best seller read by millions. At one point, Reuben quotes "one homosexual" describing an encounter between two men in adjoining stalls at a bowling-alley washroom, in which one man sucks the other's penis. At the end of this anecdote, Reuben adds, "No feeling, no sentiment, no nothing." Then, in the question-and-answer format of the book, he asks himself, "Are all homosexual contacts as impersonal as that?" To which he replies, "No. Most are much more impersonal." A few lines later, he asks, "Surely there must be more to homosexuality." Reply: "There are dozens of variations but they all have this in common: the primary interest is the penis, not the person."*

The responses to this question which follow refute Reuben's contentions. Ninety percent of the men in this survey state that they prefer affection to accompany sex. Most

* David Reuben, *Everything You've Always Wanted to Know About Sex* (New York: David McKay Co., 1969), p. 133.

men indicated that to them, "having sex" is at least an act of sharing and affection, at best an act of love.

Although many men said that sexual activity mainly oriented to orgasm was often quite enjoyable, most felt strongly that affection must be present to some degree in the act:

"I cannot imagine sex without affection. Whether it be with a regular partner, someone I know reasonably well and care for, or a new partner, one who I am merely attracted to initially on a physical level, I nevertheless feel a tie to the person."

"Affection during sex is the *most* important thing I can think of. It is very unrewarding to find yourself in bed with a guy who only wants to get himself off and that's it. I like to take my time and involve myself in plenty of affectionate foreplay and soul-kissing, stroking and petting, hugging and body contact. I especially like to kiss the dude on the eyelids just to let him know he's something special."

"Without affection I would feel like a piece of sausage. I've had men who don't want or won't show affection. Their lives compared to mine are horribly empty. One told me that he couldn't do it because he had let his romantic spirit carry him away once and he had regretted it. That's sad. Not everyone will take advantage of a sincere heart."

"I enjoy kissing my partner for the symbolism involved. I expect a man who has sex with me to kiss me on the mouth freely and to kiss my neck and ears and nipples and other parts of my head and torso; this is also a convenient test of whether the person is really gay or not. I avoid sex with persons who do not kiss other men."

"Nothing turns me off quicker during sex than someone who doesn't want to kiss me. That either means that he's not turned on by me or that he just wants to get his rocks off. Either way, I don't like it. A man has to show that he *likes* me, not that I'm just good for an orgasm."

"Sometimes, a one-night stand can provide more affection than what might be derived from a long-term relationship with an essentially self-serving person."

"Affection, every time. I think it's a natural concomitant with sex, and that unless one is an asshole, each person should share a little affection before and after sex. I was recently at the baths in Denver, and was struck by the great amount of affection showered on other people (including me) before, after, and during sex."

"I enjoy giving myself in love through affection and thoroughly enjoy receiving it in return. To me it heightens the physical joy of orgasm. You build up anticipation for the act, and then in performance of the act you reap the pleasure of the buildup. With proper attendance to the needs of the other partner, each can achieve a rather ecstatic state of pure physical joy and fulfillment ending in a sense of gratitude for the mutual participation in sex."

"I think affection is what sex is about. Otherwise why waste time meeting people? Why not just buy an 'autosuck'?"

"On occasion, I've even forgone orgasm. Sex is fun, and to get all the benefits you have to talk to each other, and that invariably brings about a warmth that can become affection. Otherwise, it's just mutual masturbation—which ain't bad, either. But as long as there's another person attached to the other penis you might as well enjoy that, too."

"Affection is a must during sex. I like to be touched, I like to give and receive. Even though I may only be with a partner for ten minutes, I really get into the person for the entire ten minutes. Affection for me includes firm touching, eye contact, exploring the body, verbal grunts and moans, staying with the person through his orgasm and mine, and helping the person tone down after his climax."

"I love petting, etc. However, I can 'play the masculine game' for those guys who need it rough and only want raw sex. That can even be a turn-on. However, strictly speaking, I love caressing, etc. Worthwhile sex is not a five-minute deal."

"Affection is the greatest part! Orgasm is almost an anticlimax for me. My ecstasy occurs during heavy affection scenes, some of which last for four hours. Orgasm is almost a disappointment because it's over."

"Sex with another man isn't just to achieve orgasm. With me it's a highly masculine rite of communication. Orgasm is the catharsis of this communication."

"The three guys I have come the closest to falling in love with were the most affectionate."

"Good sex is affection. I always feel affectionate when engaging in sex—even when I used to suck cock through glory holes."

"I enjoy the person I'm with and I give them my emotions, my feelings. I like to think that I am capable of giving a little bit of myself. So few people care about each other that I feel I should be honest with that person if for just one time. (I also realize that sex is more enjoyable if I try to be the best sex that person has ever had, so that he will be interested perhaps in a repeat.)"

"The old business of impersonality in a relationship is for shit."

"For me, sex without affection isn't sex at all. The processes of achieving orgasm are usually over so fast that, without a lot of affection, they are not worth the effort. I have found that a lot of men who think they are straight really turn on when I start the affection. Maybe women don't know how to make love to a man. I do."

Some men indicate that while they do enjoy affection during sex, they can also enjoy sexual activity without it:

"Some men are almost completely heterosexual, so these types I don't require affection from. I can still enjoy them sexually because I can find affection elsewhere."

"This all depends on who I'm in bed with. With my lover I enjoy much affection, but with most others it is just to have an orgasm."

"Sometimes there is affection during sex, yet even when that is absent, I am not necessarily trying to simply achieve an orgasm. I am more often than not involved in a sexual dream, in which I am cast in a role, and my aim is to 'furnish' a believable fantasy for my partner. This is filled with physical sensations that in themselves are orgasmic."

"I enjoy affection most of the time with tricks, mainly because men have feelings and emotions which are part of sensuality, and it isn't like a dog sticking it in and pulling it out and moving on to the next one. But there are times when I want merely that, which is really kind of like masturbating with the help of someone's mouth or hand."

"Sometimes affection is actually fulfilling in itself and orgasm is just a side effect. But there are other times where the orgasm is everything. Sometimes I get so horny that affection just gets in the way."

Very few (47 out of 1,038) men indicated that they do not want affection during sex. Most of these men were older (over 50) and products of a far more repressive and guilt-

ridden environment. This is clear from a number of their responses:

"I want no affection at all—hypocritical to me. Get on with it, and quit fooling around. I don't know why, but it is imperative that the affair must never go further than the purely sexual relationship—and that very cut and dried."

"I was never handled as a child, and apparently violently rejected any form of overaffection, such as kissing—which was and still is to me a dirty and unnecessary affectation. Means nothing—only done because it is apparently an expected action, and for no other logical reason, that I can see. I still do not like to be touched except exclusively in the sexual area—and prefer not to have to reciprocate."

"When I was a kid, it was OK to do anything sexual with other boys—except kiss them. If you wanted to kiss them, then you weren't just having fun or fooling around until you could find a girl, you were *queer*. Unfortunately, I have never been able to get over that feeling."

"I'm scared that if I let myself *make love* to another man that it will mean I'm totally gay—and I'm not sure that's what I want."

"I've never thought about this until now, but no, I don't like affection. I see sex as strictly getting my rocks off. I guess somewhere in the back of my mind I think of really getting it on with a man as dirty and queer—but just getting sucked off or fucking a guy, I'm only having my manly urges satisfied. I think maybe that's something I should work on."

Do you enjoy giving fellatio?

Of all sexual activities between men, fellatio is the most prevalent. It is the sexual act most closely associated with male homosexuality, as the epithet "cocksucker" would indicate. Fellatio is also the most common act in encounters between gay men and heterosexuals, with the straight man usually allowing himself to be fellated without reciprocation.

Some psychological theories have been presented to try to explain the popularity of fellatio among gay men. Most of these center around the idea that in performing fellatio, a homosexual man is attempting to draw from his partner some measure of the masculinity he feels he lacks. Others feel that fellatio is a form of worship of the male sex organ as the symbol of masculinity and virility. Both views were expressed by some respondents in this study. Others mentioned the importance of giving their partners pleasure and of defying conventional moral attitudes.

It is evident from the responses to this question that fellatio is extremely popular with gay men, and that it is so for a wide variety of reasons. 98.9% of the men have engaged in it, and of those, 88% indicated that they enjoy it, and another 3% said they sometimes enjoy it. Only 7% of the men reported that they did not enjoy giving fellatio.

Many of the men who enjoy giving fellatio do so on a physical level:

"I find the penis to be a fascinating mechanical wonder. The miracle of erection never ceases to amaze me. I am very sensitive to touch and, when aroused, every part of my body becomes an erogenous zone. My mouth of course is a center of sexual response. It is probably the great variety of sensations that I enjoy most—the hardness and strength of a stiff cock rubbing against my lips and tongue, the slight fleshiness of its skin and thick veins, the smoothness of the glans, the slightly musky odor and taste of clean healthy organs. When I fellate a man, I don't limit my attention to his penis. I also like to take his testicles in my mouth and to suck and lick his inner thighs and anus."

"All the years of growing up in a closet, I got my only kicks from seeing the bulge in men's pants and to be finally in a position of fellatio is the ultimate in pleasure, to smell the man-smell close, to feel the touch of the skin, to feel the entire shape, each contour change gives a pleasurable warmth in my groin. The sight up close, the color, the touch of it in my hand, on my skin, particularly the skin of my face, then the skin of my lips, the feel of it entering my lips and touching my tongue, touching everywhere in my mouth, the accentuation of that touch as it moves in and out through my lips, sending a tingling that goes all up and down my spine. Then finally feeling the tip of the glans in my throat and I know that I am giving pleasure."

"I like to suck probably more than anything. Quite often when I see a man who is sexually attractive to me, I think about how I would like to suck his cock, kiss him, and feel his body. I like to prolong fellatio. I love to suck a cock because it is the bodily center of love. For two men to expose their nakedness to each other and rub cocks, touch and handle cocks and to put my mouth on their cock and vice versa, is just very beautiful to me."

"I enjoy kissing a man's sex organ and making it hard. I like its proud stance and its 'cockiness.' "

"Giving fellatio is as natural as drinking mother's milk. This intimacy with another man's body is tremendously gratifying."

"Every cock has its own taste and texture and sensitivities. I enjoy exploring them all."

"I think it most intimate and close and a matter of extreme mutual trust. One could cause inestimable damage in a moment, even death, so there *must* be a trust there."

"I enjoy the variety of stimulation I can provide orally; warmer and wetter than by hand. I can also watch my partner's face and pick up on whatever's turning him on. The tongue is a remarkably erotic part of my body."

"I dislike an extremely large penis, one that gags or chokes me; but I especially enjoy taking a penis to the hilt. I really enjoy it when my partner cups my head in his hands and pulls me into his crotch. This thrills me, deeply so."

"I love that musty odor, the salty taste of orgasm, and the muscular contractions of the orgasm."

"I have a chance to run my hands all over the body while I'm doing it to my partner, and God! how he loves the way I do it and what I do with my hands! I feel warm when my partner likes what I do, for I know I am satisfying him, and that's what sex is all about—satisfaction, right?"

"I know how good it feels to come off that way and so I feel good about having given another guy so much pleasure. I think it's a tremendous way to feel another person's sexuality. You can't experience it with a female. Also one gets the pleasure of receiving the object of the guy's orgasm."

Many other men derive the greatest pleasure from fellatio emotionally:

"It is a very spiritual thing, very intimate. Fellatio has many implications, a lot of thoughts run through your mind about taking this man's sperm into your body, kissing his most mystical part, and so on."

"I like the feeling of power it gives me. Talk about having

a guy by the balls! If you give a guy a good blow job, you can make a slave out of him. On the other hand, it is also a way of showing him how much you care. After all, in our society, being called a cocksucker is one of the greatest insults; yet you would do that to please him."

"I always feel I am draining a bit of male power from my partner's body to mine."

"I find that when a man orgasms, I feel closer to him. I'm devouring a part of his body that holds the key to life in it."

"I like the feeling of trust that the other man gives me, entrusting his most important and vulnerable part to me. And I like also the feeling of worship that sometimes comes over me. The very position and terms suggest that—kneeling before someone, going down, etc."

"Since I view the cock as the distinguishing organ of a man, I feel like I am coming 'in touch' with the 'heart' of his masculinity."

"When I suck someone, I get off on the idea that I'm devouring or raping my partner."

"Besides this act being a physical expression of an emotional bond, there is also a great attraction in the fact that society condemns it so fiercely. It is absolutely taboo for a man to take another man's cock into his mouth. By doing so and sucking it dry, I feel I am defying all of society's false principles, values, and prejudices."

"What physical organ has the mystique, the mystical qualities, the mythology of the phallus? What organ is valued more by either men or women? What is a man's most treasured possession? To me, to be able to be close enough to another man's phallus to suck it, and having one of my own, is the epitome of masculinity."

"I'm not sure but perhaps I'm more turned on by the fact that my partner allows the act to be performed than actually performing it."

"It makes me feel like I'm giving a guy's most fantastic muscle what it likes best, and that makes me feel very good, very self-confident."

"I get a feeling of pleasure, a feeling of knowing I am giving my partner pleasure. A personal feeling of pride in being able to serve. This act is everything."

Many men say that their satisfaction in performing fellatio comes from the fact that they are giving their partner pleasure:

"If I am happy with my partner of the moment, I desire to please him as much as possible and make him glad he has met me. I get a full degree of emotional satisfaction while making another man happy and satisfied."

"I enjoy giving fellatio since I feel that I am able to give something of pleasure to another person. The other person enjoying receiving it is important to me. It is also one way to know that I have brought my partner to completion. It is pretty hard to simulate orgasm in fellatio."

"I adore giving fellatio, either as foreplay or as the main sexual act. I find it exciting to know that because my head is buried into a guy's thighs, I am able to make him tremble and shudder and moan. I like feeling his leg muscles tense and relax in rhythm, and feeling him squirm with pleasure. There are those who think that giving fellatio is an act of submission. Is it really? Who is actually in control of what?"

"I don't seek out performing fellatio, but if the man I'm with indicates he wants it, I'll do it. Then when I hear him moan with pleasure and I realize how much I'm giving him, I love doing it and could go on all night."

"I have been sucked off, so I know what it can feel like, so I thrill knowing that I am achieving this for somebody else's cock. I am a very good cocksucker."

"I feel that when you suck the penis of somebody you really care for, you are making love to him in the best possible way. To me, there is something if not violent at least forceful and dominant about fucking, and it isn't possible to have the nuance and sensuality one can achieve through fellatio. When I suck my lover's cock I can show him in a hundred ways how much I love him. In our everyday life, I try to please him and make him happy and keep him satisfied, etc. He does the same for me. Fellatio affords us the opportunity to do that in the most intimate and pleasurable way possible. My lover knows when I suck him that I'm trying my damnedest to give him as much pleasure and satisfaction as I possibly can. His pleasure is the goal, but of course I get tremendous pleasure out of pleasing him. Isn't that what lovemaking is all about?"

"Emotionally, I feel it does more for the other person than for me. I don't mind being of service especially since most partners have loved it so much."

"I love sucking my lover. He enjoys it so much. I try to make love to his penis rather than just mechanically sucking it. I give it every little sensual thrill I can come up with.

Once he looked at me while I was doing it and said, 'Baby, you're the best.' I felt such pride and happiness I couldn't describe it to you."

A few men indicated that they do not enjoy performing fellatio:

"I dislike the 'dirtiness' of it. I have a lot of childhood indoctrination about cleanliness. I was brought up to think of genitals as dirty."

"I only blow another as a favor to him. I dislike it physically and emotionally. I'm too fastidious for that!"

"It's horribly boring because it's a repeated movement."

"It seems too far away from your partner—too impersonal, too 'ordinary.' I like face-to-face, not just that one part of a body."

"I tend to gag, and feel inadequate because I'm not good at it. I prefer it to be a part of foreplay, and not the main sexual act. That way it's not so much pressure. I guess what I really don't like about it (aside from the physical discomfort) is that it's the only sexual act that is entirely up to me how it goes."

"My hygienic training is so strong that I am repelled by the idea of putting a penis in my throat. And I hate the taste of cum."

Do you enjoy having your partner ejaculate in your mouth?

A large majority of men report that they do enjoy this:

"I think that's one of the main purposes. I like its taste (with rare exceptions) and like to feel that I've made the partner feel fulfilled and happy. You might call it a 'reward' for the effort you've put into the act."

"Without this, it's not emotionally complete."

"There's a feeling of having *done* something. I can look at a cock I've sucked off with a feeling of pride. Has it become a part of me?"

"I find it exceptionally stimulating because I know my lover is being satisfied—I frequently come to orgasm when it is happening, without masturbation."

"It blows my mind what a mysterious, potent, secretive liquid this is, the beginning of life and creation, a beautiful million-times-multiplied sacrifice to the creator. The first taste is strange, but the religious mystery takes over later and one can get excited about any taste."

"It's an act of possession as I see it. Semen has a tremendous symbolism in our culture, and making love, reaching orgasm, and doing something with the semen is all wrapped up in having a strong sexual and human relationship and cementing it by literally giving of yourself in lovemaking."

"How much more private and intimate a 'gift' could one receive from another for whom he feels something? From his innermost recesses, the seed of life so uniquely his own. Evidence of the extreme pleasure you have provided him—and to have and hold a little bit of him afterward, in your own body."

"I like the taste of cum. It's grrrrreat tiger! They should make a drink that tastes like it."

"The Greeks believed that this seed produced intelligence. That's a hot fantasy."

"Unless my partner gets off there is a sense of incompleteness. It makes me feel like I have the seed of superman if my partner is a real turn-on."

"I know that I can make him happy in this small way and prevent the loss of the most vital part of his manhood."

"I enjoy swallowing semen. It's silly to drive a guy all the way to orgasm and then be afraid of a little protein. How anticlimactic!"

"I like the sense of having something denied in upbringing and something that not everyone can enjoy."

"I like to swallow the semen. It tastes good, it excites me. It gets the person 'off' even more—which makes him like you more."

"I like a guy coming into my mouth. I know he's happy and functional. No taste is too bitter any more."

"I really enjoy taking the semen of another man which is the gift from him to me that very few people ever get the opportunity to have. I guess it is that I am good enough to penetrate this man's barrier and have the whole man that other guys can't get and I am good enough to qualify to taste his semen."

Nearly 15% of the men said they did not enjoy having their partner ejaculate in their mouths. Most of these objected to the taste and consistency:

"I think come tastes just awful. Everything about fellatio is fine except that. Emotionally, I think it would be nice to take a guy's come but I just can't handle the taste. Sorry."

"Whenever I have come in my mouth its texture reminds me of raw eggs. It makes me nauseous."

"I like the idea of having a guy come in my mouth but I only did it once and I promptly threw up."

"I very much dislike having my partner ejaculate in my mouth. It makes me sick. Not always literally, but I just don't like it. I don't like the taste, or the feeling. All during fellatio (when I'm giving), I fear it, and I tense up for it, and I dread it. This is why I don't like giving fellatio."

"With the number of men who smoke, a prevalence that my roommate and I have found is bitter semen. I can 'taste' it if my partner has used amyl, pot, booze, beer, or tobacco."

Other men dislike it for other reasons:

"Physically, I choke. Emotionally, it's degrading to me."

"It's more of a mental problem than a physical one. I guess I don't like the odor of come."

"I guess I can't help thinking I'm going to catch something from it."

"I get no particular thrill out of it. In fact, sometimes I'm a little irritated realizing that's the end of that. Also, as I can take it all the way down the throat, I often fear they will cum into my lungs and I'll drown. And what would the neighbors say?"

Do you enjoy receiving fellatio?

90% of the men in this survey answered this question affirmatively. The forty-three men (4%) who said they did not offered a wide range of explanations:

"I don't particularly like receiving fellatio, because I don't very much enjoy being passive."

"I do not really abhor the physical sensation, but it is difficult for me to reach orgasm this way. For many years I have preferred a totally passive role where I give rather than get."

"I have a very thick cock and 80% are scrapers and it hurts."

"I do not get an erection when engaged in sex, and I always tell a trick that I am not going to have an erection. It's my problem, not his. Maybe the second or third time around with him, but never the first. This makes the guy feel bad. Since I am concerned about the other guy's feelings, I don't score often. It hurts them, their pride. Which is why I prefer 'trade.' "

"I am there to please—not to be pleased."

"I simply have no oral sexual urges—active or passive. I realize I am fairly unusual in this but this questionnaire is a chance to be totally truthful."

"I don't particularly enjoy fellatio. Physically I believe my cock is very tender and gets sore if fellatio is not performed just right; I also feel the base of my cock is a very erogenous zone and does not get the attention it needs during most fellatio sessions. Emotionally, I miss having that person up where I can see him (eye to eye) and hug him and kiss him."

"I find it extremely hard to relax and enjoy it because my head is so conditioned to feeling guilty about sex that I still get all 'uptight' even though I try hard not to."

"I do not like to be sucked. I always felt like I was being paid, like I had to reach orgasm to get my money. I can barely keep a hard-on. It's strange."

"I feel too much like I am getting pleasure from my partner, but not giving any in return."

Many of the 90% who say they enjoy being fellated do so because of the physical pleasure involved:

"Receiving fellatio is better than intercourse. The mouth used as a sexual organ can produce a variety of stimulus that is unsurpassed by any stimulation that I have ever had on my penis."

"Getting sucked off gives me my most intense and gratifying pleasure. My orgasm becomes a completely overwhelming experience. It is as if my entire body has become a sex organ. Anywhere my lover touches it is cock."

"I enjoy the physical sensations—the warmth of my partner's mouth, the softness; the firm pressure of his lips around my cock as he pulls me toward climax. As I do for my partner, I enjoy the feeling of being taken through aftershocks after orgasm."

"When done well it is the most pleasurable sensation of the sexual experience. I can relax my entire body and focus my mind totally to that one sensation. In other forms of sex I am diverted by other feelings and movements and the pleasure is not as strong."

"It gives me great pleasure to know that another man desires my penis and is willing to take it into his mouth. I feel that by sucking on my penis he activates a field of energy within me and I can actually feel the energy flow with my semen through my penis and into his mouth."

"I like the wetness and warmth of a receptive mouth. Someone experienced in the art of fellatio can produce sensations impossible to obtain from an anus, or thighs or hands. I like the feeling that someone is really trying to please me rather than just passively letting me do my thing, as in intercourse. I do get offended when a guy does not want me to come in his mouth and I usually don't let him get away with that. I sometimes get a little nasty because if I am close to orgasm and he attempts to pull away I will grab him by the hair and thrust wildly into him until I am done. Later I'll wind up kissing him and asking forgiveness."

"It's the wildest feeling I know! Also, it's a way to get to orgasm with almost no effort at all on your own part. Which is a switch from any other way, where you must exert some effort to cause orgasm."

"I enjoy receiving fellatio when the emphasis is on sensation and builds steadily and unhurriedly toward the climax. A good cocksucker knows from experience when to slow down and when to speed up for maximum effect. He knows how to combine swirls of the tongue, up and down movement of his head, and so forth, alternating them to modulate sensations in different parts of his lover's penis. Receiving fellatio is learning how to relax your body and be given to, which is an important lesson in allowing the other person to give. The feeling of cumming in someone's mouth for me is one of unparalled ecstasy like no other. I feel the greatest sense of trust and abandoning myself to the other person and later share a deep sense of a mutual secret."

"I love the sensations of a hot mouth and warm tongue on my cock. It also has a very relaxing effect on me. I feel as though I'm drifting through clouds while I'm being sucked. I'd have to say I enjoy this sex act more than any other."

Others felt that emotional satisfaction with the act was foremost:

"It is great to know that some good-looking stud wants my cock and I want his. We both know that all barriers are broken down and we can have each other totally and satisfy each other's physical desires."

"I feel more masculine, maybe egotistical to the point of being worshiped or served."

"My psychological reactions when I'm getting sucked are the opposite of what they are when I'm sucking someone: I feel superior and very sexy—'Here's this cute guy and he wants to suck my cock because he thinks I'm hot'—it's a real big turn-on."

"It makes me feel like I'm being worshiped for being a man."

"What I like about it most is the 'forbidden' quality it has. Sexual organs are, as a rule, hidden from the public eye, and I find it very stimulating to have someone sucking on my 'forbidden fruit.' "

"I'm flattered and love to know that my partner cares enough to let me come in his mouth."

"When there is a good feeling of interplay with my partner then I get a big kick out of him fellating me because I see this as a sign of generosity and caring and wanting to do rather than just receive and I usually respond to that with enthusiasm toward doing what I think that he would like."

"The mouth is the part of the body which we all depend on for communication. Simply, words of love are said through the mouth. Therefore, for my partner to place his mouth around my penis is a great thrill."

"When I was a teenager, I wanted to have sex with my friends, but all they would let me do was suck them, and somehow I felt (thought it was never said) that I was less of a man because of it. Now, I have sex with people who want to suck me and it makes me feel good about myself. Sometimes I fantasize that *I'm* one of the hot dudes I used to do in high school."

"Until recently, I had to fight against the fucked-up notion that gay people aren't 'real men.' Well, I know *I'm* a real man, because if another gay guy wants to suck my cock, I must be a man—and a hot one at that!"

Do you enjoy '69' (mutual fellatio)?

The practice of '69', in which two men fellate each other at the same time, is enjoyed by half the men in this survey:

"To my feeling the 69 position is the ultimate in sensual pleasure and sharing. My penis is less sensitive in this position and I can enjoy the feel of another man's penis in my mouth at the same time my own penis is being pleasurably stimulated. Also I can have more body contact with the other man, stroking his body, fondling his testicles and buttocks."

"I just love 69 because it gives you everything you want to do at once."

"69 is fun, because one is active and passive at once, one's superior or inferior feelings are all mixed up, it is such a fun physical constellation and is so terribly naughty."

"There is something miraculous about having a cock in your mouth while someone's mouth is enveloping your own cock. One becomes someone else, just as that someone else is becoming you. It is the infinity position, the snake eating its tail. Eternity."

"I love the union of the bodies in 69 and once and with a *very special* friend we both went through the full course and came simultaneously. Bells rang, sparks flew, rockets burst. It was a supremely unique rush of ecstasy and we just lay there together, completely engaged, drained of all strength, so satisfied, so close, so warm, and so much in love."

"I prefer 69 because I may get bored if I have nothing to do."

"69 is the most meaningful of all sexual acts."

"The reason I like 69 best is that there is no role-playing when you do it. No one is dominant, nor submissive; no one is too good to do *that* to you; both partners are receiving equal pleasure, both are trying to please the other. To me, 69 is the most egalitarian sexual act possible—and as such, the most pure homosexual act there can be."

Other men find the act less than satisfying, especially in a physical sense:

"If we are both sucking each other I don't like it because I can't concentrate on either activity. It spreads my desires too thin."

"69 never works out. It's awkward and it's difficult to either feel or do a good job."

"The strain of being involved in both is too distracting. Besides, mutual orgasm can be one of the most detrimental things in causing sexual problems in a relationship, be it gay or nongay."

"I don't like 69 because I can't split my mind between being aware of the other person enough to give him good head, while trying to relax enough to enjoy being sucked. I never come this way and it takes 'hours' to get anywhere with the other guy. It seems too much like a technical emphasis to me, not enough on the emotions. But it is an interesting concept and very kinky to watch or think about. It has its place."

"69 is all right in its place. However, I don't think its place is in a serious relationship."

"It is less satisfying because the tongue can reach only the top of the glans, not the more sensitive underside, during 69."

"I enjoy alternating, rather than 69, because to really make a person 'feel it', you have to *concentrate* your *whole* attention upon it, and be *aware* of all the little nuances of feeling he is experiencing, and use these as guidelines to increase his pleasure. This is sometimes difficult when you are both doing it simultaneously. In other words, it is better not to have your attention divided or diverted."

"I don't usually enjoy 69. The psychologies conflict. I get in one head to give head and another head to get head."

"I am usually the first to come—and it is very difficult for me to continue to hold my partner on the 'Cloud 9 of sexual ecstasy' when I am already back on terra firma. I think that if both partners could ejaculate at the same time, then the love experience could be very rewarding."

"69 tends to disturb me. It almost seems like a race. 'Who is gonna come first?' It simply is not relaxed enough for me to enjoy."

Do you enjoy anal intercourse?

Among the men in this survey, anal intercourse is neither as popular nor as prevalent as fellatio. But more than three-quarters of the respondents (76%) do enjoy it, and only 12% indicated that they do not. Anal intercourse was frequently mentioned as the most intimate act between men, the sexual activity holding the most emotional impact. Quite a few men indicated that they do not engage in anal intercourse unless their feelings for the partner are particularly strong. A majority of those who do not enjoy this activity experience too much discomfort for it to be pleasurable; many of these men expressed regret at this and wrote that they find the idea of anal intercourse very pleasant. It is a measure of the spiritual intimacy the act connotes that many men who find it physically uncomfortable nonetheless engage in it—and enjoy it for what they perceive as its importance in the expression of love between men.

Many men see anal intercourse as a spiritual bonding between men:

"I think it's the ultimate in giving oneself to a partner, whether you're giving or receiving. I think it's the best way to be completely intimate with the other guy; you're *in* him, about as far as anyone can get, he is accepting you, as much as he can take. How much closer can you get?"

"It is the most personal physical relationship one man can have with another and it makes me feel more responsive to another's needs and desires than any other form of sex. It can be an incredible high for two people who care for each other."

"I won't go so far as to say that I think it's the only real sex between two men, but deep down inside I think so. It's a true union of two people. It's as close as you can get, I think."

"When on top, one is in total possession of his partner, and when on bottom, you are totally possessed. What could be more perfect?"

"My body has to adjust to the penetration. It is this physical and mental adjustment where pain gradually gives way to pleasure with each penetration that causes more and more of my 'being,' or my 'psyche' or my 'self' to get caught up in the most excruciating, unrelenting, and sublime pleasure that I know of. I even wonder sometimes if a woman enjoys this kind of pleasure when she is getting fucked by a man."

"In my limited experience, it seems men like to fuck more than anything. It seems to give them the greatest pleasure and I feel the most appreciated because of that. Being a dancer, I've come to distinguish good pain from bad pain."

"How clever to use the anus and rectum in this way. The anus intrigues me, it is the most secret part of the body. Only in extraordinary positions can one see it at all."

"To me it is the sexual way of expressing love. I can read a person's heart and mind by the way they screw."

"The combination of emotional domination-submission and the closeness it provides between the two people, mixed with the animal sensations and orgasm, are almost inseparable."

"The emotional character of it permits my partner to keep his masculine identity and perform almost as though he were with a woman. I suppose it is the ultimate act (for me) in acting out a same-sex act, yet keeping the ingredients of my partner's heterosexuality intact. I know that sounds a little screwed up, but the doctors I've mentioned it to don't seem to think it is so far out."

"It's a great way to express the masculine and feminine parts of your personality. When you're on top, you're performing the traditional male role, and you feel that way. When you're on bottom, it's the other way around. I think it's a very healthy thing. There would definitely be much less hostility, warfare, and aggression in this world if more men were getting fucked."

Others' enjoyment of the act was primarily physical:

"What I enjoy about intercourse is that it is not limited to a part of the body the way fellatio is. When I have intercourse, my entire body is rubbing against his entire body. It is not just a penis going in and out of a hole; it is thighs rubbing against thighs, feet against feet, torso against torso."

"To me anal intercourse is one of the most satisfying feelings in the world. In all my life I have never had anything I enjoyed as much. I like it because of the way it makes me feel."

"A male ass is a beautiful thing, or can be. I find the sight of a man's ass completely thrilling. I like the way the hair is arranged; I like its musculature, the shapes it can take, the ways it can flex. I like having my ass appreciated, and take advantage of its looks to show it off in tight jeans or shorts. Anal intercourse is a natural concomitant of such appreciation."

"I like the feel of him close to me, and I like the feel of his penis inside me—especially when he comes. It is technique that really makes it all worthwhile, and proper lubrication and foreplay."

"I can't explain why, but it is such a complete feeling and I want more and more and longer and longer. I cannot always be sure when my partner is ejaculating by the feeling within me, but I can tell by his actions, breathing, moaning, etc., and I want to be sure that he is also being satisfied."

Several men stated that they had to learn to like anal intercourse:

"One night I asked a friend with whom I had had oral sex many times to fuck me, so that I could know what that kind of sex was like, too, since so many of my friends seemed to enjoy it. He said, 'OK, turn over on your belly,' and I complied. He penetrated in such a way that I experienced excruciating pain. I tried to get him to withdraw, but he would not. When I struggled to get out from under him, the pain increased tremendously. Finally, I gritted my teeth and let him finish. A few days later I began to have a discharge. He had bruised my prostate, and the pain when the doctor began to massage my swollen prostate was so great I collapsed. I was under treatment for most of a year. For a long time I would not let anyone try it again. Then one night I was in bed with an older man, who penetrated me (with me lying on my side) without my knowing that he even planned to until he was inside me. He did it so gently that I felt no pain, and even some enjoyment. From that time on I occasionally let myself be penetrated with me lying on my side. Then I met someone who really turned me on, someone I was willing to try anything with. He wanted me on my back so we were copulating face to face. He would begin by rimming, then fellatio while he got his penis into position to penetrate; then by the time he had kissed his way up my body, he was all the way in, and I felt nothing but pleasure. He taught me how to enjoy being screwed."

"Up until about a year ago, I was strictly an 'on top' man, because of my emotional fears concerning my masculinity and my physical inability to relax. After a lot of careful practice and comforting and compassion from Jack, I am now able to relax and enjoy the passive role with him. It means a lot to me to be able to 'give' of myself to him and I think we are both able to enjoy and experience the whole realm of intercourse. I consider anal intercourse the ultimate sexual experience, with the only possible drawback being highly unlikely physical damage."

"When I was still seeing girls, I often had trouble getting an erection when it came time for intercourse. I guess it was part of a fear that I wouldn't be able to perform well or something. Then, when I was with a guy and he wanted me to fuck him, the same thing happened. It was horribly embarrassing. Most guys just said forget it, which was bad enough, but one guy muttered 'strange' and made me feel awful. It certainly didn't help the situation any. Then I met a guy who wound up being my lover, and he made me feel that it was OK if we didn't fuck. He said, 'I'll be satisfied if you just hold me.' Well, that romanticism so turned me on that I got an instant erection, and boy did I 'perform'! He loved to get fucked, and was so good at it that I developed a great love for doing it, and now have no problem whatsoever fucking someone I really care for. We're no longer together, but I'll always love him for that."

12% of the respondents report that they do not enjoy the act:

"I have a tendency to come too quickly when I'm screwing someone. I have less control over my buildup and I feel like I'm just being very perfunctory and mechanical."

"It causes me pain. Plus, just when the pain is over and I begin to enjoy it, they stop."

"When I'm being fucked I feel the person is very impersonal and is trying to have a heterosexual fantasy. Few people are really understanding when you say no!"

"More than any other homosexual act, it seems to function in lieu of vaginal intercourse. I'd prefer to have sex with a woman, which achieves the same result with much less discomfort."

"I am very tight and entry is always painful to me. When I fuck another, I always feel dirty afterward—presumably an overemotional reaction to contact with excrement in the rectum. My experience in the area is limited: I do not seek anal intercourse out. I will occasionally submit to it if I like the guy and he wants it badly and he has been good to me."

"My mind always ends up picturing what we must look like physically, and the picture amuses me enough that I have laughed out loud—much to the distress of the top man. The act just doesn't turn me on."

"I have noticed that I will only let certain men fuck me. Those who I feel pretty comfortable with. I find fucking a very close, intimate thing that needs time, understanding, patience, and gentleness. I don't really enjoy getting fucked that much."

"I don't understand it. I mean, there is a certain anger that can be dispelled by plugging somebody, but since I don't enjoy being on the receiving end, I can't get into being the giver."

"It hurts when I try to be fucked and I am distracted by all kinds of confusing emotions when I try to penetrate a man (or a woman). I lose my erection. Intellectually, I tell myself I am rejecting the hated dominating image of straight men (a feminist argument), while recognizing the satisfying fantasy of taking in a part of another person, the merging of the bodies. Being gay I can take or leave fucking. If I were straight, I'd have severe impotence hang-ups."

"If I am fucking, I lose my hard-on frequently before I come. If I am being fucked, I frequently feel abused and dominated."

"Because of my large build, other males seem to expect me to fuck them, and I resent that because I prefer fellatio. It is my experience that more gay men are into anal intercourse than fellatio, which may be one of the reasons I enjoy heterosexual males, who seem to prefer receiving fellatio."

During anal intercourse, are you usually 'top' or 'bottom' man? If both, what determines which it will be—your partner, your mood, or what?

The responses to this question indicate that homosexual men are very versatile in their sexual self-image. Three-quarters of the men said that they had acted as both top and bottom man* in the course of their sexual lives and more than half alternate freely between the two at the present time. Most of the men see this flexibility as an ideal situation.

51% of the men said that they alternate between 'top' and 'bottom':

"I have been on top as often as on bottom. My partner and mood definitely determine which position I will assume.

* For the sake of simplicity, "top man" in this section means the anal penetrator, and "bottom man" the penetrated, although that, of course, is not always the case.

There are times when I want the weight of a man on me and to feel the fullness of his cock inside me. There are other times when I want to feel the tightness of his anus around my cock. It's strictly mood—I'm flexible and creative."

"Usually my partner and I take our turn on top. We usually decide our 'plan of action' together. If someone wants to be fucked, but doesn't care to reciprocate, that's fine with me. However, if someone wants to fuck me then I insist on fucking him."

"I'm both. Why limit yourself? The determination is done by a very complex thought process which I do not understand; it will vary from minute to minute and from partner to partner. I enjoy thoroughly fucking someone and then being fucked by him. I see no real domination here, but a mutuality that makes two people closer. If you really enjoy someone, you want to do everything with, to, and for him that is possible."

"I like to achieve orgasm as top man first and then after a few minutes of rest, let my partner take the top position for his own pleasure and orgasm. If being the top man is the only way the partner can or will operate, it's okay and I will usually masturbate myself and try to achieve orgasm along with my top buddy."

"Often I work out aggressions or hostilities while on top. Being on bottom is more of a shared experience with the person I am with, while top positions are more for when I'm only into a one-sided thing (*my* side) such as at the baths."

"My partner's mood is as important a factor as mine. Reciprocity is a great advantage that male sex has over male-female sex; thus I would not make it with a man who limits himself to being strictly bottom or strictly top."

"Top or bottom depends on my partner. If he is dominant then I let him decide. If he is passive then it depends on my mood. If we are both passive at the same time, it's disaster."

"I'm automatically the top unless the man is big, with a big cock, butch, and I'm in the mood to be 'taken advantage of.'"

"I do not enjoy being solely active or solely passive. For me, sex is sharing, exploring, learning, feeling. It is not at all satisfying for me if I must play a role or limit my activities. Futhermore, I am usually not comfortable with a man who is solely active or passive."

"I like a man who is loose enough in his gay behavior to be happy to both fuck and be fucked. I would not want a long-term relationship in which I never had the opportunity to do anything but be fucked by my partner. I want someone who is more open, playful, fun, laid-back, accommodating than the 'specialist' who won't do this and won't do that. After all, who needs all of the specialization anyway?"

"Whether I'm on top or bottom usually depends on my partner. I consider fucking someone an act of domination—not necessarily angry or forceful, but dominant. If I'm in bed with some massive bruiser, I want him to fuck me. I would feel somehow inadequate fucking him. If the guy's fairly average, it could go either way; and if he's somewhat feminine, I would want to fuck him. (I was very insulted once when a beautiful but somewhat effeminate young man wanted to fuck me.)"

"With young men these days, say in their twenties or thirties, there seems to be no conception of role-playing on their parts. They simply do everything, apply no labels, and still consider themselves equal in every way. I like this attitude. It strikes me as being realistic and far more wholesome than the role-playing I knew when I was much younger."

"What determines it? The person, what he would rather do, how I'm attracted to him—like is his ass so delicious I just *have* to fuck him; mood certainly—there are times when I just have to be fucked. All kinds of reasons, all of the moment. I just find it less frequent than fellatio because it isn't as easy to accomplish—it takes more space, longer time, sometimes you need creams and towels, etc."

"I'm always top man with my lover, and I enjoy it. I'm always bottom man with others."

"I'm usually top man. In fact, the only person I'm ever bottom man for is my lover. I'll let him do that to me because I love him."

23% of the men report that they are usually bottom man:

"I enjoy the bottom position more. When I'm top, I work to please my partner. It is more like heterosexual intercourse, which has been a matter of trying to prove myself as a person of value. Being the recipient is new and provides pleasure for my partner and me."

"I strongly avoid any partner who wants to be the bottom man. I can't even raise an erection if someone wants me to fuck them."

"Since I like straight kids, I usually end up on the bottom."

"My size hints to my partners that I like getting fucked. On more than one occasion, a stranger has picked me up and said, 'You want me to fuck you.' No question, a declarative statement."

"I am usually bottom during anal sex. I am normally sure which role will be played before agreeing to have sex. When cruising, I wear a dark-blue bandana in my right hip pocket; in this town, 95% of gay people know what it means, so a verbal discussion of roles is not necessary. Some of my friends feel this symbol-wearing is limiting, and takes some of the mystery out of an encounter. I can understand that, but I am really looking for anal intercourse *only*, so it seems to me I am being fair and thoughtful of potential partners by making my sexual interests obvious. It saves them, and me, time and disappointment."

"More often than not, I am usually bottom man without having been asked. I tend to have a passive personality at times, and combined with my being young-looking (read 'vulnerable'), skinny, and small, it is too often taken for granted that my place is on the bottom, which I resent."

"I am usually bottom man during anal intercourse primarily because (1) I really enjoy being fucked, I like to feel my partner in me, and sex is infinitely enhanced when I realize my partner is feeling great, and (2) frankly, my penis is rather large, and most men are afraid of pain or damage they suspect I might inflict."

"I enjoy getting screwed more than I do screwing. The main reason for that is that for me when I am screwing someone it is just one sensation—all in my penis. But if I am getting screwed, then I can enjoy all the sensations from that, from around my penis, my nipples, my armpits, my feet, my legs, etc."

"Sometimes, with a particular partner, you reject the bottom 'role' (ouch on use of that word); sometimes, the top. I nearly always enjoy the bottom when I'm feeling 'slutty,' and when feeling slutty I have few if any inhibitions. Sex is more satisfying, generally speaking."

"I like being the bottom man because it makes me feel sexy and desirable. I feel submissive—there to give this man pleasure."

"A sense of security accompanies my being bottom man— being able to please my partner is important to me."

19% said that they are usually top man:

"I have a terrible and complex macho hang-up. If the dude is super butch I can really dig kneeling at his feet and giving him head, but the idea of giving him my butt to bone turns me off. There's nothing that determines I'm on top—that's just the way it happens. One exception: a guy I knew for about six months didn't take my no for an answer and just rolled me over and did it. I liked it OK but I wasn't wild about it. All others give up when I first indicate I don't care to be on the bottom."

"My gay friends seem to have a hang-up about the passive role. Some equate this to the 'woman's position' and tease other men about their being 'a lady.' "

"The top man can really enjoy the experience selfishly. I've never seen a top man have any more interest in the act than responding to his own urges—perhaps properly."

"It's not that I'm against the passive role, but simply I've never learned to relax enough and relinquish enough control to enjoy the passive role. My partners here must be really into the passive role, enjoy it and want it, because I derive no pleasure out of attempting to force or prod someone into the act."

"When I'm on top, I feel good about myself. I feel dominant and masculine and aggressive. I feel like a hot stud who this guy wants to fuck him silly."

"I am really confused on the issue because, even though I prefer to be dominant, total submission in a partner turns me off. Basically, I suppose I am a great believer in equality, but only with someone that I really love. I have only been bottom man once or twice—and briefly at that. In both cases, I knew that my partners had suffered so much rejection in the recent past that I didn't want to refuse their requests for fear of driving them deeper into depression. I don't, however, understand why men would seek to be submissive in an impersonal situation, although, Lord knows, I certainly am grateful to them."

Do your emotions differ when you're on top from when you're on the bottom?

64% of the men who have experienced both to any extent said their emotions were different:

"On the bottom, I usually feel relaxed, happy, and very content, willing to submit to my partner's pleasure. As top man, I feel as if I'm in control, as if I have a great deal of power, and that my partner ought to give me free reign for the time I'm within him. Strangely, I usually feel greater affection for my partner when I'm on top."

"When I'm doing the screwing I feel as if I *have* to have a climax. If I don't I think I've hurt the guy's feelings. When I'm getting screwed, I do my best to help him reach climax. If he doesn't, I feel like I wasn't good enough."

"When I'm on top I feel I am farther away from the guy (relationship-wise) than when I'm on bottom."

"Once a man wanted me to penetrate him, and I had this incredible feeling of power—that he was relinquishing the position of superiority—especially since he had wanted to fuck me but I had not wanted him to."

"I go on top to please a partner. I assume the bottom to please me."

"When I am on top I feel strong, in command, and like a mighty stallion. When I see and feel that I am giving pleasure to him, then I feel proud and revel in the sensuous feeling that I am a great lover—that just inspires me further and he senses and enjoys it even more. When I am on the bottom for a man that I feel deeply about, I feel very lovable and am delighted that I am turning him on so. I also feel vulnerable for some reason. I feel like saying, 'Hey fella, I hope you realize that I am giving you my most valued treasure—access to my ass—and I am only doing it because I trust you and feel deeply about you and want to make you happy too. I am forgetting all of my inhibitions and laying myself open for you to make love to me.'"

"I feel like I have to perform when I'm on top. That I have to prove myself a man. This I don't like. On bottom I can just lie back and *be* a man."

"When I am bottom man I tend to worry that my partner will think less of me for 'giving in,' and also that he will expect the same every time he is with me. Or worse yet that he will talk and everyone I meet will expect the same."

"When I'm on top, I feel very butch and when on bottom I feel like a woman."

"When I'm on the bottom my lover is making a sexual statement—I love you, I'll take care of you, be at ease with life, all is well. When I'm on top it is just sexual frolics and fun."

"When on the bottom I get really tense and often bound up. I never know what to expect. I often feel that the guy is just getting his 'piece' and that's it. I can't perform that way. I'm not a machine and I'm also alive. On top I sometimes have trouble coordinating movements. I would like to be better at all this, but when you're with different men all the time, they're not willing to help or be patient, they just want to get it on."

"When I am on top, I am in full control because then I am the 'all-penetrating male'! I am the man. And it is my responsibility to gently impale my partner without hurting him and give him that thrust of ultimate peace. I treat my partner as I would a woman when he is in that vulnerable position. I kiss him. I whisper words of endearment. When I am on my back with my legs thrown over the shoulders of my partner, I am in that wonderful position of the vulnerable woman. In my younger years I preferred being bottom man; but now that I am older I enjoy being top man. I recently had relationships with two ex-married men, with children; and both insisted that I take the part of top man. I thought it would be the opposite, but it didn't work out that way."

"Getting fucked is to feel submissive somewhere inside your brain; on top is the opposite. Anyone who denies that lies. Both are wonderful, I think. We need both. At least I do."

"On top I feel a bond and duty to satisfy the recipient in his sexual need more than my own sexual release and gratification."

"On top I am likely to feel more aggressive and rough. On bottom I think I feel willingly helpless and conquered, but also accommodating, as if I am really the one who is getting the best of it. I think being gay and having anal intercourse is one of the most liberating experiences a human being can have—you find out what it is like to have simultaneous female and male sexual experiences; you have empathy for others who are not built the way you are."

"On top, there is the sense of power and control—perhaps machismo-like. On bottom, there is the sense of being taken care of, of being loved, of giving of myself, something of a sense of weakness, which in a man who makes a big production of being strong and self-sufficient, is a nice change of pace where I can just let go and not worry about it, manhood-wise."

20% of the men experience no emotional difference in either position:

"I don't really get into this domination trip in anal intercourse. I don't think the top man is more masculine or anything. I think no matter how it works out I feel very close to the other person, very much one with him."

"Both times I try to please. I found out a long time ago that if I try to please I usually get more pleasure myself."

"My emotions are the same. I don't feel that being on the bottom is a 'put-down.' I'm secure enough in my masculinity to like it."

"I always feel tenderness, gratitude, warmth, and a desire to share and give of myself."

"I don't feel any more or less manly being either end. Does a football player feel more masculine because he is on the offensive team? A defensive player less manly? Does a lineman feel less important because he is not a back or an end scoring touchdowns? I doubt it. All are equal and all are necessary. It takes more than one person or one type of person to make things happen in the world."

What is it like for you to be anally penetrated by a penis? What do you experience physically? Emotionally?

The sensation of being anally penetrated by a penis is one that most men have never experienced. While it is possible that a majority of men have experienced fellating another man (most often, of course, in childhood experimentation), anal intercourse is quite often "the last taboo," something few young boys are either willing to try or physically able to handle. What is it about this act which makes it so physically and emotionally pleasurable for so many gay men? The responses to this question give us some very interesting answers:

"Well, the best way I guess to put it is, when you feel the penis at your anus, and it slowly and easily enters your body, it just feels so good and you have such a desire to have it enter all the way, and then as your partner starts his movements you just want to hold it in there as tight as you can and help him to have his climax, and when he does you feel so filled.

Then you have the desire to leave his penis in you as long as possible."

"Penetration takes two distinct forms. One is the slow passionate penetration that causes no pain. The other is the quicker and more painful insertion. The former is like having another man inside you. With my small build I can wriggle and have all of me massaged. There is an intense transfer of energy. I feel most like a man during intercourse—in a sexual mode. The latter is an attempt that likely will not be repeated by that individual."

"I experience a moment or two of tightness and pain when the guy first makes his entry. I usually ask him to try a few small strokes and then wait until I tell him to plunge in the rest of the way. By then the nerves in my anus and the stimulation of my prostate gland have taken over; I really want him in me then. When he does go in all the way, it is a wonderful, full sensation—a warm, tingling feeling. Emotionally and physically, I feel on fire and full of desire for a man when he fucks me up the ass."

"I prefer being on my back, legs raised, facing my partner. While I can occasionally reach climax without manipulation, I usually masturbate to orgasm and can frequently time my orgasm to match my partner's. The physical experience is very, well, filling and pleasurable."

"There is a very fine line here between what constitutes a painful or a pleasing sensation. I know what is pleasurable for me is often painful for others. I have had partners who tell me they do not see how I can stand it because they could not. But the emotional and psychological factors are most important here. My attitude toward what I am doing and with whom I am doing it is all important. That is why I cannot ball with someone to whom I am not physically turned on. It would be too painful."

"The initial entry hurts a little, but once he's in, it feels like a moment of pleasure stretched over a long time. I mean, for instance—when someone touches your hand or your leg, briefly, the first time, there's a moment of special pleasure. If you take that kind of moment's pleasure and stretch it for several minutes, that's what having someone inside you is like. Then, if you can get in just the right position and his penis rubs on your prostate gland, it's not just a moment of pleasure stretched, its *the* moment of pleasure—orgasm— stretched. It's as if you were coming for several times as long as it's possible to come. The words that occur to me are 'being driven up the wall.' The feeling is a mixture of anxiety and something good."

"There's a funny thing about being fucked—someone else's cock can look pretty inconsequential when you're holding it in your hand but when it goes up your ass it seems to increase tenfold. The pain occurs right at the entrance of the anus but deep inside it feels wonderful!"

"What is it like to be 'anally penetrated by a penis?' How would you describe Heaven? How would you describe a rose to a blind person, or the Mahler Second Symphony to a deaf person?"

"Some initial discomfort, always, followed by a sensation of pleasurable fullness and a sensation of being overcome, overpowered, and possessed. Essentially being anally penetrated is a far greater emotional experience for me than a physical one. I do not have an orgasm as a result of it."

"From time to time I suck off somebody who asks me what that stuff tastes like. I tell him there is only one way to find out. Taste it. I feel the same way about being fucked. It is impossible to describe. But if you refuse to get fucked, you are denying yourself a certain heaven."

"It's the most wonderful feeling ever. It feels like he is filling a gap in my soul."

"I feel gratitude for the pleasure he gives me and self-satisfaction from knowing that I am giving him great pleasure. I also feel very powerful because I have him at my mercy and at the same time I feel vulnerable because I know I want and need him as much as he does me."

"The pleasure is indescribable. My cock feels like it is constantly cumming, and my balls feel tingly. My intestines feel like orgasm internally. Emotionally I feel like one person with my lover."

"Getting fucked properly is an involved procedure, and when performed well is mostly a painless experience. When the stroke builds properly I feel orgasmic rushes shooting upward through my spine as the cock hits my deepest part. Emotionally I 'give up' a little at a time until at its peak I am a 'slave' to the unending thrust of the almighty cock. I want to give myself totally to whatever my partner wants of me. When I come it is all over my body. I feel grateful, and fulfilled."

"I get an erection that seems to almost burst and a high degree of sensation inside the penis shaft, in the balls, inner thighs, and a general higher sensation all around. The penis itself responds heavily to a light touch. Emotionally, I feel like a stud ready to shoot the load of all times due to the increased sensation."

"I feel free and cosmic and a little triumphantly defiant of those who would put down what I'm doing."

"For me, being screwed satisfies a need that nothing else fills."

"I feel like I am letting off tension and sometimes I feel like I'm enduring something that is unimaginable to others."

"I gain a deep sense of satisfaction from the inclusion of a part of my partner in my body for his pleasure. I feel a deep sense of love flowing from his body and surging from the penetration upward into my body, very much like being bathed in light and enraptured in love. I am receiving physically, yet spiritually, his body extension and giving him both physical and emotional pleasure coupled with spritual love in return. At the ejaculation of my partner I sense a deep flowing sense of fulfillment."

"Full anal penetration by a hard cock is truly a wonderful sensation. The warm smooth penis and the in-and-out motion along with the throbbing and pulsing deep inside my anus bring joy to me and a deep feeling of intimacy and emotional love."

"I have a feeling of someone powerful controlling me and taking us together to a wonderful orgasm."

"I know why females like to have a penis inside them. It fills you up and you feel a part of his body has slipped inside you. The sensations are very intense. I lose my physical and emotional separateness."

"When I am penetrated I feel what love, lust, and passion represent. Only novels try to put that in words. When I penetrate another man I feel much the same way. Only if you practice both sides can you be really *good* at either. I firmly believe that."

"It's like . . . openness, trust, wonder at what somebody is doing to you. It's a very satisfying body feeling, not just the asshole. It's a fantastic embrace, very total, the ultimate embrace for which all others are symbolic. In a sense, the guy is fucking your body from his viewpoint, but fucking your emotions from yours."

"Penetration is always a surprise, no matter what foreplay has occurred. It's a rush of pleasure, with just enough discomfort to keep it interesting. I suppose it's comparable to a woman losing her virginity—and yet I have the same experience every time."

"It's sexually arousing, my nerve endings seem to crave that pain. Feeling a big cock inside is indescribable. Emotionally, I feel I'm underscoring my partner's masculinity. The more he rams it in, the harder he does it, the more satisfaction I feel, and a kind of proof of his manhood."

"The sensation is very alien because you suddenly discover a very new source of tactile sensation—*strong* tactile sensation—and you never even knew it existed. Better, once you've relaxed (which, if you're well lubricated, stops any minor discomfort), the area sends out pleasure signals in waves."

"I can feel when my partner is ready to come and I like to think that I am helping him to feel good by any movement I can cause in my ass. Emotionally I feel good knowing someone is attracted enough to me to want to fuck me."

"Physically, it feels as if I am grabbing my partner and holding him inside me. Like we are one body. I feel very erotically stimulated, like all I want is more. Emotionally, I feel completely fulfilled—like I really belong. I wish I could have his entire body mesh with mine and we could become one person."

"Near the end when the fucking becomes very frantic is when it is best. Sometimes I feel the other guy come inside me and the sensation of that is like a mental orgasm."

"I feel like it (the penis) is something that has been missing all my life, and it feels so good, like it was meant to be there. I think it's healthful to be put in your place somewhere—sort of in between dominance and submissiveness."

"I guess it's sort of like having a full stomach. It's very satisfying."

When you are anally penetrated, does your orgasm feel different? How?

The responses to this question indicate that gay men may be the most orgasmic of human beings—not only in the number of orgasms achieved, but in the variety of orgasms possible.

Men in these responses spoke not only of heightened penile orgasm created by the rubbing of their partner's penis against their prostate gland, but also of anal orgasm, of general orgasm impossible to fix at any one location, continual orgasm which lasts throughout the sexual act, and of penile orgasm achieved without any contact being made with the penis either by themselves or their partners.

In light of what is commonly believed about the limits of male orgasmic capability, these replies seem to show that when a man denies himself a variety of sexual experiences, he is cutting himself off from a potential new world of physical and emotional pleasures. One of the respondents summed up his feelings on this by writing, "I feel sorry for any man who hasn't been fucked."

Most men report that their orgasms are more powerful and feel better when they are being anally penetrated:

There are definite physiological reasons for this. The prostate is a gland located just beneath the bladder and directly next to the anal canal. Its function is to supply the seminal fluid—that milky liquid which carries the sperm cells out of the penis during ejaculation. During anal intercourse, the rubbing of the penis against the wall of the anal canal massages the prostate, frequently causing it to produce a larger amount of seminal fluid and heightening the physical sensations characteristic of orgasm:

"Whenever I come while being screwed my orgasm feels so much better than at any other time. The indescribable, delicious feeling orgasm brings is just magnified, increased, better. It is incomparable."

"When I orgasm during anal penetration, to say that it feels different is putting it mildly. It's like comparing a little Cessna to a Boeing 747."

"My orgasm is more intense if it occurs while I'm being anally penetrated. I shudder and convulse with the intensity of my pleasure in a manner that does not occur with masturbation, or when I'm being sucked."

"It is a greater climax that sends me climbing up the walls with pleasure and I feel that it is only when having an orgasm while being screwed that my sexual fulfillment is total."

"If I have an orgasm while penetrated, the orgasm is more intense and more expansive than if only my penis is involved. The greatest orgasms of all have been those when I have been fucked and blown at the same time, with both of us climaxing at the same time."

"The orgasm reached during intercourse is completely different. It is slower and longer. It isn't the frantic hit-the-ceiling orgasm of strictly fellatio or masturbation but rather a complete release of the body into complete nirvana."

"I feel as if my entire body is coming apart. It is a much more forceful orgasm—almost convulsive! I feel like I want it to go on forever. I usually try to keep the penis in me as long after we orgasm as possible."

"I always come more after being fucked, and the sensation of orgasm is more intense because sexual stimulation has been coming from somewhere other than my penis. So the feelings are more sudden and unexpected."

"I prefer to have the guy fuck me independent of my coming. The exception is when he is lying down and I sit on his cock and then control the speed, angle, and depth of his penis in me while I masturbate at the same time. In such cases I build to an absolute mindblowing climax that can go on for ten minutes and leave me weak and unable to walk or stand up."

"It feels like my partner's penis is a part of mine. The orgasm feels like the cum is running from his body through mine and out my penis."

"I'd say there's a 300% difference, the orgasm itself is tripled—I always come more and I always shoot farther."

"When I'm getting fucked, the orgasm is magnified in so many ways—it lasts longer, it feels stronger, that wonderful sensation in your penis is heightened. The first time it happened, I couldn't believe it—it was even better than the first orgasm I'd ever had!"

Some men report orgasms quite apart from the penis:

"I seem to orgasm internally, if that's possible, while being fucked."

"When anally penetrated I experience multiple orgasms—feelings from my head to my toes. The sensations that I feel are far different from that of my penis. I have at times felt that they are very similar to a woman."

"It's a much more powerful orgasm. It's not shooting off but I go through all kinds of emotional orgasms also. I can have as many as three or four orgasms before I shoot a load that is the most powerful. It takes control of my whole body and makes me do things I couldn't do if I weren't being fucked."

"The orgasm is stronger because there are more sensations,

and the brain loses track of neat explanations as to what's happening. When the brain stops insisting that everything be labeled, the body takes over and revels in the resulting physical explosion."

"Sometimes I feel as though I'm having an anal orgasm. The pleasure is so great and builds steadily until I think I've come—but I haven't, at least not through my penis. The first time it happened I practically passed out—I couldn't believe it."

"I have a series of mini-orgasms all through my lower body before I have an actual orgasm with ejaculation and all. This only happens when I'm being fucked."

"Orgasm produced by anal penetration is a different sensation. It comes from your very soul—which leads me to believe that the prostate and the soul are synonymous."

Can you reach orgasm without direct stimulation of your penis?

We have seen that it is possible for some men to experience orgasm in other parts of the body than the penis. Other men in this survey reported that while being anally penetrated, they are able to achieve penile orgasm without masturbation and, in some cases, without ever touching the penis:

"If the cock is long enough, it rubs against the prostate, which is unbelievably stimulating and gets me so excited that when I come off it becomes a double pleasure: having that feeling in my ass and in my cock. I have gotten so stimulated by being fucked that I've been able to reach orgasm without ever touching my cock. Those times are as special as wet dreams."

"Sometimes, when anal intercourse follows heavy foreplay, orgasm can happen without any stimulation. That orgasm tends to be volcanic."

"I can come without jacking off if I'm being screwed. It's forced out from the inside rather than pulling it up by friction on the outside."

"I would say this depends a lot on the size of my partner's penis and how violent he is in his thrusts. A very large penis and very violent thrusts will cause me to climax without any direct stimulation at all."

"When I am getting fucked, it is the other guy's ride. I like to get into what he is feeling and giving him the best. That way I very often come without trying because I am focused elsewhere and therefore relax enough to allow for it."

"Sometimes the guy just fucks the come out of me. Banging against my prostate it just makes me come and the ejaculation is very, very powerful and shoots across the room."

"I don't have to touch my penis at all if the one on top gets me off enough."

"If the curve of my partner's penis is just right, it hits my prostate gland, releasing the semen. I have had ejaculations in this manner without even having an erection."

"Once my lover and I were screwing, he inside me, and when he came I, too, experienced an anal orgasm if there is such a thing. I almost passed out and it felt so fabulous. That has happened only once. (How sad!)"

"Sometimes, when I'm really into my partner and the sex is going well and everything is just right, I can come just by being screwed. To me, that's an indication that I was right— this evening is truly special. To describe what such a thing feels like is impossible. Emotionally, I always think when it happens that I'm the luckiest person in the world—being a man and experiencing what a woman must. Strangely, when it happens, I feel by far the most masculine."

Do you ever go to the baths?

The baths are a uniquely gay phenomenon; there is nothing comparable to them in the straight world. A heterosexual man seeking sexual activity with a woman who is not an acquaintance must either pay his way into a brothel or massage parlor or employ the services of a call girl. A straight woman in the same situation will most often engage a call boy. But at the baths, gay men can, for an admission price not often over $5, walk into a sexual fantasyland in which both activities and partners are quite varied and plentiful. Bath houses are legal in states without anti-sodomy laws. In those states with such laws still on the books, they are usually left alone by local law-enforcement officials since they are regarded as private clubs.

Among the men participating in this survey, 54% report that they do not go to the baths at all, 9% say they go infrequently, and 35% attend with regularity. Twenty percent of the men who do not currently attend indicate that they have gone in the past, and the rest (44% of the total) have never been inside a gay bathhouse.

Most of the men who attend regularly have very positive feelings about the baths:

"I like to go to the baths at least once a week. I think they are a marvelous institution. Imagine, instant sex without any hassle, all for a few dollars; it is the best value in sex or almost anything else in the world. There is a great variety, you can see what you're getting; there is also as much or as little privacy as you wish. It's a great relaxing place."

"I go about once a month. I am hornier than hell and I want to meet a variety of new people. I feel like acting out the voyeur role for a while, looking at a variety of beautiful bodies and either fantasizing or getting it on with someone that I feel I would enjoy and that would enjoy me, playing around in the steam room or pool or the gloryhole room. After a five- or six-hour session, I am very relaxed, having gotten it on with two or three different men. Mentally and physically I am drained, and am ready to reenter the normal conservative world I live in outside the baths."

"I go to the baths occasionally, but not to have a full sexual experience. I guess I go for the tease, and to watch the men in the buff; to feel free, to chat with a naked fellow now and then. The biggest reason, curiously enough, is the steam, in an atmosphere of gay companionship which I find very restful and relaxing."

"I prefer to have a partner I can spend a long time with and perhaps have subsequent dates with, but a good orgy can be fun at times (especially in the steam room—the feel of a good slippery orgy is not easy to duplicate at home!)."

"I like the camaraderie of baths, and the nearly instant gratification."

"I like to work out on some of the gym equipment and use the steam or sauna or the Jacuzzi. One of the baths shows gay movies in the TV room and admittance to the baths (and the movies) is cheaper than going to an adult movie. I seldom have sex unless I like the person and then it usually is oral or maybe a jack-off session. I have gone anal in the Jacuzzi—wild feeling, especially if you're in front of the water jet."

"I enjoy the honesty of the whole thing. I came out at the

baths when I was sixteen, because I couldn't get into any of the bars. I enjoy seeing other naked/semi-naked men walking around. It doesn't seem to have the potential letdown the bars do. I mean, you can spend hours in a bar wasting your time and money, perhaps meet someone who wants to go home, but then you still have no idea how he looks under his clothes, what he likes to do, and pow, you've blown the whole evening. If I'm going out to find a sex partner I want it to be more of a 'sure thing.' At the baths, if you feel that you are not quite 'getting on' with the other person, you can excuse yourself and go find someone else. It's also more conducive to conversation and relaxation."

"I go both for sexual release and to meet someone for a possible relationship. I often enjoy group sex at the baths. A truly good (friendly) orgy seems like a symbol of universal marriage. And even the experience of having sex with one another while others are having sex there too is enormously satisfying. It enhances my own pleasure and I suppose lends sanction to what I, like all other gays (of my generation at any rate), cannot help but feel a little guilty about, no matter how intellectually liberated we are."

"I am much freer there in making initial contact with people. The dim light that makes it impossible to look someone else directly in the eye is helpful. The initial contact can be impersonal and the rejection, if any, is impersonal. Once actually engaging in sexual activity, however, I do not believe that my conduct (or 'role') is any different than in more private sex. Another advantage is talking to partners in the small rooms. Hearing other men's stories, or part of them, is fascinating. People are often very frank about their lives at the baths. It must be the combination of the utmost intimacy with the notion that you need not have any further relationship, which relaxes many men. Lying in a cubicle with one man and thinking of that row of cubicles all filled with men making love and talking quietly is a beautiful and rather proetic experience."

"Once, I ended up in a TV room watching television. I did, that is, until I was invited to join the groping party that was beside me. I'm shy, and didn't want to. Finally a cute marine asked me if I'd like to join him. So I did, and we spent one of the nicest nights together I can ever remember. We never did have sex, mainly kissed and talked all night. Then in the morning he was gone and I never saw him again."

"I like the atmosphere, the Fellini-esque hard-core sex

feeling in the baths. It turns me on a lot to just walk around and see what's happening. Even at the baths I still look at most partners as potential relationships—so it's not totally anonymous."

"I'm less inhibited at the baths, and get involved in activities that I can't express at home with my lover. I go out of my way to please people at the baths—do anything they want within reason—rather than fulfilling my own desires."

"My reasons for going to the baths are complex and difficult to articulate without making a total ass of myself. My first trip there was to drown my sorrows after being rejected by a man who had obsessed my every waking hour for months. It ended with uncontrollable sobbing and retching in the television room. After that, my reasons for going became masochistic-narcissistic. I used to be very conceited about my appearance and would go to the baths for the humiliation of being lost in a horde of beautiful people on a busy night. In that situation, one cute number more or less is irrelevant."

"The baths have been very good to me. On my third visit there, I met my lover and we have been together four years. Now, we both go to the baths, separately, as a sort of mini-vacation from our relationship, which tends to refresh us and make our togetherness so much nicer. Neither of us feels threatened because the baths are the best place for casual, anonymous sex, if that's what you want."

Of the 567 respondents who do not currently go to the baths, 20% have gone in the past and found the experience unpleasant:

"They're too dark for my eyes to see in there. And my first experience (at the old Everard in New York) was depressing beyond words—all that pure raw sex in the gloom—just not my bag."

"I go to the baths rarely. I am in my mid-fifties and too heavy and never was handsome. The young crowd in the baths are unlikely to respond to me, and the older ones there are usually, in my experience, after the chicken. The baths seem to have little for me. I usually end up fellating one or more who will accept me."

"When I'm really horny and desperate, the baths always come in handy. After each time I go there, I leave the place swearing never to go back again, it makes me feel so low."

"I went twice, once in Atlanta and once in Houston. I

hated the whole scene. The sex is too casual. I want a relationship."

"I've had all kinds of sex in baths, some of it very good
indeed, but as I sit here thinking about it I really can't get
very worked up about any of it. To me, the mood has to be
special—not routine—and it certainly can't compare to having someone real at home."

"I've been to the baths once out of curiosity and found
myself being fondled by five men, of different sizes, shapes,
and ages, and was appalled. It was very upsetting to me because each one wanted to be accepted and only one would
get chosen. I found it humiliating, for them, and felt very
uncomfortable."

"I have found that most gays share my low esteem for the
baths. Even the ones who extol their virtues would rather ignore my presence in the baths and approach me the next day
in the more 'respectable' atmosphere of a bar if they are really interested in getting to know me. My interpretation of that
kind of behavior is that it is not considered 'nice' to meet a
person at the baths."

"I usually ended up there through sexual frustration, lack
of success somewhere else when I really wanted to get laid. I
spent most of my time at the baths looking for a desirable
(to me) partner and trying to evade the grasp of nearly
everyone else there."

"I have been to the baths maybe a half-dozen times, looking for something that I know is not there. Maybe I get so
horny that this is necessary. However, after a varied amount
of sex I leave unsatisfied."

44% of the men have never been to the baths:

"I think that's a disgusting, dreadful thing to do."

"I want to have at least one new experience to fall back
on. I'm also a bit afraid that I'll like it too much and that I
won't be able to leave."

"A bath to me is so impersonal that it constitutes merely a
sexual release. There's more to sex than that."

"At the baths, I feel like a sex object, not a human being."

"From what I've heard about the baths, they leave a lot to
be desired because people aren't sociable enough. How can I
have sex with someone who won't tell me his name?"

"I've never been to the baths, but I would expect them to
be pretty grimy."

"I have never been to the baths but I will one day, when I gather the courage to go there. I am scared to go there for I really do not know what happens there and I do not know anyone that has been there."

"I wouldn't feel comfortable there with the open nudity and open sex. I don't think a lasting relationship could be found there."

"I am too self-conscious about what I feel is a rather dull body and penis. I suppose there might be someone in such a place that might like my looks, but I feel I would be let down too often before that happened."

Do you ever have sex in restrooms or other public places?

Seventy-three percent of the men in this survey responded negatively to this question; 12% indicated that they frequently have sex in public places (which also included parks and theaters, among others), and another 12% said that they occasionally do.

Why do some gay men engage in sex in such places? The most frequently mentioned reason was that restrooms are (or were at one time) the only place that they knew of to have sex with, and sometimes even to meet, other gay men. And some of these men, having started this activity at an early age, found the habit difficult to break. Others described the activity as exciting, because the physiological reaction of their body to the possibility of getting caught was quite similar to their bodily reactions during arousal. This situation tended to increase their state of excitement and thus their enjoyment.

Some men stated that restrooms are the only places in which gay men can have sex or meet other gay men:

"I'm seventeen and it's almost impossible for me to meet men. None of my friends are into gay sex; I can't get into bars or baths, and I don't know where the cruisy sections of town are. Once I walked into a restroom and this real fox of a guy kept watching me while I went. I started to get excited and was embarrassed and scared and turned on, all at the same time. When this guy saw my hard-on he touched it and I've never been so thrilled in my life. This is what I had dreamed of. The surroundings disappeared, and we could have been in the most beautiful spot on earth. I was having sex with a man at last."

"Often it is the *only* outlet for teenage males and they are afraid to go elsewhere or come to your home. They are seeking immediate response and have no interest in any sort of relationship—in fact they don't want you to know who they are or anything about them. It is unfortunate that restrooms are used this way but I feel it is a response to the kind of suppression homosexuals have to endure, i.e. a lack of public acceptance of homosexual encounters in more conventional ways. A heterosexual male can approach a woman in almost any situation, but the homosexual must rely on clandestine meetings where the situation allows an exchange of 'signs.' Restrooms lend themselves well to this."

"I have sex in restrooms often. Usually, it's fellatio. If it's not in my own area, I don't feel bad about it. I just wish there was some other way."

"Most of my sexual experiences take place there because it's about the only place to go around here. I usually have oral sex. I would not like to get caught, not that I'm ashamed, but I don't like for people to see me in sexual activities."

"I've had sex in restrooms many times, because I lived at home with my parents and neither of us had any place private to go. It always consists of fellatio. As to getting caught, it's very easy to hear someone coming in. If a guy did walk in on us, what could he do? I can't imagine most guys calling a cop. Chances are he would do absolutely nothing. If it was a cop, well, obviously that's a worry."

"I do it because of lack of time or another place to go. I'm usually oral–passive. I won't take the active part because then I can't watch for someone who might walk in. When I'm on the receiving end I'm very alert and have never been caught in twenty-five years."

"It's usually the only place available, and time is a factor. He usually has to be home for dinner with the wife and kids."

"I have sex in tearooms and other public places because it's fun. Dangerous, but fun. When I was a teenager, restrooms were the only place I knew that gay men met. It became a way of life, perhaps even addictive. I think about getting caught and use reasonable precautions, but as long as the elements of fun are in the tearooms and parks, I will continue to check them out. There is a price to pay if I am caught (and I have been caught) but for me the fun is well worth the risk. A few times I was caught and the price I paid was to have sex with the person who caught me. You can imagine how upset I was (smiles)."

Some men find the quick availability of sex attractive:

"The main reason I have sex in public places is because they're accessible and it fits into a busy schedule. I most often engage in fellatio. I feel public sex can be exotic and exciting at times. I try to be cautious, but give little thought to getting 'caught.' In my state, entrapment and general police harassment are somewhat passé."

"I am an expert tearoom boy by now, but I only go when I am really hot and want relief *now*, or when I don't know anywhere else to go."

"I go about once a week for quick sexual release. I really don't even think about getting caught until I leave and I'm scared shitless!"

"The reason I have sex in restrooms/public places is that it is an immediate fantasy realization. Often, if the situation isn't acted upon immediately it will not arise again elsewhere—it's a now or never situation."

"I work downtown, so john sex is easily available near the office. It's oral sex—I wouldn't even attempt fucking in a john. I try to minimize the risk by (almost) always letting the other guy make the first move."

"It has its own particular kind of excitement, coming, I suppose, from the element of the forbidden. I don't think anyone should ever pass up what could be a delightful opportunity, but I would check out the circumstances very carefully. As for deliberately hanging out, cruising, etc.—that's out."

"The reason I like it is that no games are played. People are frequenting those places with sex in mind, so it erases a lot of mental fatigue."

"Sex in T-rooms is more blatantly immediate and honest—we don't have to 'fit in' to each other's life in order to have a place there. Vice Squad officers should all be lined up and shot!"

"I don't go out with the intention of cruising tearooms, but sometimes when I'm in one things will happen. I'm not sure why sex there sometimes appeals to me, probably the availability and quickness of the sex. I also like the domination of having some guy on his knees sucking me off. I never do it to others unless they're super hot. I've met three very nice, very sexy guys in tearooms who I got to know, so it's not a total loss relationship-wise. I would be mortified if I ever got caught. I don't think the idea of getting caught appeals to me, even subconsciously. I do it in spite of the danger. I don't know why there's such police harassment of tearooms. I've never been involved with someone that didn't stop as soon as we heard the door open. I've never been seen by anyone I didn't want to see me. And nine out of ten guys who walk into a tearoom either couldn't care less what's going on or want to join in."

"I am increasingly attracted to the thought of having sex in tearooms, particularly in 'likely' places, like college libraries. I don't know if the fear of getting caught is a turn-on. I think the turn-on is the thought of doing it quick with a total stranger."

Some men find such activity exciting:

"I do it whenever I'm around a campus. It's real exciting to make it in the john with young jocks who probably don't have gay sex anywhere else."

"There's something very exciting about having sex with a hot number in an area where someone might walk in at any minute. It's kind of urgent and intense. Maybe the adrenalin that flows because of the fear helps make you sexually excited. I do know that I'm rarely ever as turned on as I am in that situation."

"You can't get a much more masculine atmosphere than a men's room, and the people in there who are available for sex are usually much more butch than other places. It's just a very hot thought, and just as hot in reality."

"The last time I had sex in public was in a restroom and it came as a complete surprise. I was in a restroom without doors, having gone there to take an urgent dump. Suddenly, this number appeared, unzipped his pants, and showed me a beautiful cock. He says, 'You want it?' I opened my mouth for an answer. It was a dangerous situation because the restroom was in a very popular and crowded shopping center. It was all over so quickly I hardly knew what happened. I did know it tasted good. The idea of getting caught in such a situation is mind-boggling, but so is the excitement."

"It's exciting because of the location. You meet a wider variety of people than in other places. Besides, I've had some of my best sex scenes there, and met some really groovy people. There's not much game-playing or messing around with small talk that's always uncomfortable and hard for me anyway. I met my lover in the subway in New York, in the restroom. It was in the 23rd Street stop—on our lunch hour!"

Some men have had sex in a variety of other public places as well:

"I have had sex in restrooms, in parked cars, in moving cars, outside standing next to a car at a drive-in, under a bridge, on a boat, in a park, on the street, in a bar, in a train station, in a library, on a Xerox copier (which was running), in the lobby where I work, on the balcony, in the pool at my high school, under the bleachers, and on the street again (it was one of my best casual encounters). I do it mainly because it is exciting, stimulates the adrenalin, you know. At first I was worried about getting caught, but I never have been, since I choose the location and time very carefully."

"The only public place I have ever had sex is in the park, very late at night. This does not happen often, only during the summer, weather permitting. One can have any kind of sex there, from the most impersonal to very affectionate. Usually sex tends to be rather wild in the bushes. People are not very inhibited, and will do exactly what they feel like doing. Getting caught would be horrible of course but if I were really scared about getting caught, I probably would go elsewhere for sex. I'm sure the 'possibility' of getting caught adds some excitement to this act that also seems sort of 'nasty.' It's fun because it's so easy to obtain."

"I have contacted sex partners by leaving my phone number in a restroom. I've never actually had sex in a restroom. Once, at the university, I flirted with a gorgeous guy in the hall late one day and we ended up having sex in an empty classroom. (We locked the door.) I don't know what would've happened if we'd been caught. Since we weren't caught I just don't worry about it. At the time I was enjoying it too much to worry, so that's that."

"Sex is a beautiful thing for people to do together but there's not much atmosphere for beauty in a smelly shit-house: I abstain. On a field of clover under a hot sun, or a soft bed of fallen leaves in a cool valley, more beauty is found than in my bedroom, and this I've done many times but not nearly often enough. We usually make love as we would anywhere else rather than 'have' some particular 'kind of sex.' About getting caught, I would feel the same as getting 'caught' having a hamburger at McDonald's. I would be rather indignant with some fool being indignant over it. Assuming he's not holding a gun on me, I'd jump up and flatten his nosy face."

"I have never had sex in a restroom, although I have occasionally made the initial contact in the johns for later sex at home. Why? Why not? The stuff is there. Riverside Park, which is just across the street from my apartment and extends for seven narrow miles, used to be a wonderful place to make out any time of the day or night, year-round. By day, I usually brought the contact home. Nights, the action usually took place in the park, mostly sucking. I once shared in an orgy of about fifty men, mostly Latin butch types in their twenties and thirties, who were tongue-sucking while masturbating each other or doing belly-to-belly grinds. I am sure that if I pointed out to these guys that they were doing something homosexual, I would have my teeth knocked out. So I never mentioned it—I just enjoyed. Maybe other people need games, I don't. Getting caught? I would dread it, naturally."

"I have had sex in restrooms, park areas, theaters, movie houses, alleys, etc., but this is not too often now that I am older. I might still have it in such places if the opportunity would arise, but it seems to happen less often. I was never 'caught.' I have been observed, but by a person who was there and 'in sympathy' or at least understanding of the situation. If I were caught, I think it would make one feel very bad—if not suicidal. Society should not make this such a crime."

"I had mutual fellatio with a marine on board a TWA 747 at 40,000 feet above Iowa or Missouri once. Nobody was the wiser! We did it in the restroom. The restrooms on those 747s are so big, nobody notices if two people enter the same room."

"I've had sex in public places if you consider having sex while driving on the highway or parked at a drive-in movie, etc., public. Why? Because we liked it. Getting caught would be nasty—but to see us would have involved invasion of our privacy."

"I do love to ball outdoors and do wherever I can. But this

is in isolated mountain or desert areas, not places where I might be seen. That isn't the point—it's the sun, the wind, the air, the isolation that provides the romantic thrill."

"Never had sex in a restroom, but I've had sex in lots of public places, particularly a large park. There's no escape from a bathroom stall if you've picked the wrong customer or the vice come around. The park is patrolled with ludicrous frequency but I can always slip off in the opposite direction. Sex in the park has a couple of big advantages over cruising in bars. It's free. It's far less time-consuming. And it's less game-oriented. Offer, acceptance, act. As opposed to hours of eye contact, meaningless conversation, exchanging drinks, taking the bus to his place, and then finding he isn't compatible."

Nearly three-quarters of the men do not have sex in public places:

"I don't believe in it. It can be embarrassing. I've never run into it myself, but I guess it is fairly common. I am for sex with whoever the individual wants, but sex in a public place can shock too many people. It's hard enough for the world to accept gay sex. Let's face it, it will be almost impossible for the world to accept public sex. I think when sex goes public, it is cheapened. It becomes too common and loses its meaning, becoming a mechanical thing, involving little true feeling."

"I've never had sex in a restroom or other public place, although was once tempted by an erection being fondled at a urinal next to me. I'm not really sure I would enjoy it, if for no reason other than the fear of being seen or caught. It somehow seems silly."

"I don't consider an act of love appropriately placed in a restroom! I wonder if it isn't an act of contempt (both self and other) on the part of those who engage in such activities."

"I never do as I'm not sure of the cleanliness of the prospective partner. I most certainly would not like to get caught, and if I were to get caught, I would feel I deserved it."

"Never had the opportunity. But I would be petrified about getting caught. This kind of sex is socially even less acceptable than bedroom gay sex. With some justification, I suppose. But it's a shame that gays have to be forced to places like this to find each other."

"The risk is too frightening and the whole sleazy atmosphere really turns me off. In fact I am turned off when I have to use a public restroom to go to the bathroom."

"When I stayed at the Y in New York there was a great deal of restroom sex. It seemed to me to take very natural acts and get off on them in a smut kind of way. It struck me as boys being dirty and taking it seriously. Men being boys."

"For me sex is a private thing. The restroom runaround makes sex too cheap. I'm looking for a relationship, not quickie sex."

"I think that is the kind of irresponsible behavior that only fuels Bryant and Briggs. In a gay bar or theater is one thing, but in a regular public place, including the park, having sex infringes upon the rights of others."

"This kind of activity can be devastating to all gays and will add to our 'demoralization.' "

"It is dirty, filthy, and disgusting."

"No, never! I do not think this is a part of the gay world. All such activity should be prohibited just as man-to-woman fucking on a public park bench should be banned. There is a place for everything."

"I stay away from restrooms and other public places when it comes to sex. I am an animal, but I am not just an animal. I don't find a shit-and-piss atmosphere particularly erotic. I don't care particularly one way or the other if other persons have sex in tearooms; and I don't want anyone arresting such persons or otherwise harming them. But as for me, I would prefer a more luxurious atmosphere for love and sex."

"I think worst of all would be my own loss of self-respect for doing it. Sex in a restroom is to the one-night stand as the one-night stand is to a real loving relationship. It's irrelevant."

"I have never had a sexual encounter in a public place and I never will. The whole concept is disgusting and offensive to me. Public places are just that—for the use of the general public. For any individual to think they have the right to do whatever they want in public is asinine. Gays who get caught deserve the consequences just as straights would. One thing that really angers me is to use a restroom in any large department store here in L.A. and be forced to deal with a bunch of men attempting to lure me into their 'cheap thrills.' "

Some of the men who do not have sex in public report that they used to:

"I used to think it had no class. Then I got into it at the university as all sorts of neat people went there and there were no cops. I still couldn't get into regular public restrooms, but then I discovered I had the capacity and courage to do anything if I used poppers. So then I got into it. So then I got into jail. Now I think it has no class."

"My first homosexual experience was in a restroom, and for months, almost years, I thought that's where everybody did it. The first time a guy asked me to leave the restroom and go to bed with him I thought he was crazy. I don't go anymore. It's available in too many other safer places now."

"A few years ago I did often frequent such places. I felt cheap, dirty, and used, but where else could I go? The type of sex was always mutual masturbation. I felt terrified when the idea of getting caught entered my mind. I could just see my name in the papers for having been arrested."

"No 'public sex' in about twenty years. I was then quite young and in the service. I went to restrooms almost daily for a period of almost two years—because it was the simplest place to find sexual outlets and because I couldn't take a lover while in the service. It was almost exclusively giving fellatio—occasionally getting it or on very rare occasions getting screwed. I did not consider getting caught."

"I confess in the early days I did and got caught by the police. I'm glad my relatives had died before it happened. I think it is very wrong to have sex in public. I'm ashamed that there was ever a time when I did."

"I have been caught four times over some years and feel very angry as in two cases there was no one in the restroom but me and the officer who was there to extort money with an erection; in one case the officer drove me to a secluded place (after all kinds of threats), unzipped, and said it was no trick, he was just horny. The fourth time I wasn't really caught, just stopped by a store detective who said he suspected the john was being used by homos. I told him homos were some of his best customers. It is very dangerous in this state."

"I don't have sex in restrooms—fear. Sex in restrooms was my first experience as a youngster. I was always passive then and went often, even though it laid immense guilt feelings on me. I could not stay away."

"My homosexual experiences practically started in the public johns. In some ways, that's unfortunate; screwed my head around for a while. I would often go to a place here on campus where someone had cut a big hole in the partition between two of the stalls, and would engage in fellatio (giving and getting, though mostly the former) and occasional mutual masturbation by kneeling down where the partition stopped. Never been caught, fortunately."

"I tried them years ago, even the gloryholes, until once I saw a penis shoved through the hole and there was a big ugly sore on it. That finished me for good. Leave them to the cockroaches."

Do you engage in any unusual sexual activities—fist-fucking (active or passive), sadism and masochism, bondage and discipline, humiliation, watersports (sex involving urination), scat (sex involving defecation)? Others? How often do you engage in these? What do you think of them?

How many gay men are involved in what has become known as "kinky" sex? Is such activity an integral part of the gay scene? Why do those people who engage in these activities do so, and how frequently? What are the extents to which these people go—is there a great deal of brutality and pain in such acts, or is it just a form of game playing?

Over 70% of the men in this survey report that they never engage in any of these activities. The percentages of those who do are as follows (most of these respondents mentioned more than one activity):

Watersports: 18.5%
S&M: 15.7%
Active fist-fucking: 14.5%
Bondage and discipline: 12.4%
Humiliation: 8.3%
Passive fist-fucking: 8.2%
Scat: 3.0%
Others: 1.8%
Activity not specified: 1.2%

Many of the men indicated that they engage in some of these activities infrequently, usually at the behest of another. Very few said that such activity was a way of life for them; rather they saw occasional activity of this sort as adding spice to their sex lives.

It is important to an understanding of these figures to stress that although some of these activities might suggest the infliction of great pain and suffering, that is rarely the case. Many men spoke of "limits" and "just enough pain to heighten sexual pleasure." The heavy dominance and submission inherent in some of these activities were seen by most men not as violent, but as part of a scenario, a way to realize fantasies and therefore add to the sexual experience. These activities are viewed by most gay men as fun, not as brutality.

Of the nearly 30% of the men in this survey who engage in one or more of these activities, most find them pleasurable:

"I enjoy being fist-fucked—but only by one who knows what he is doing. My lover really gets turned on when I tie him up and fuck him real hard and use a dildo on him. I'm sure most straights would like the same things—probably fantasize about them but are too inhibited."

"I would estimate four-fifths of my encounters involve some of these trips; almost all with my lover do. This kind of activity requires empathy, practice, good judgment, creativity, and trust. Being able to do it is tremendously liberating. Being into S&M puts one in a strained relationship with gays who aren't comfortable, just as being gay puts one into a strained relationship with straights who aren't comfortable."

"The only one of these activities in which I've engaged is fist-fucking another guy. I must say that I find it kind of a turn-on, being so deep inside him, and realizing how much pleasure he received. I've never seen such a powerful orgasm."

"Bondage without discipline is one of my activities. I try to engage in this at least once a week. My lover is not particularly interested in this. I think it very exciting and pleasurable, but also 'strange' (I don't berate myself however for wanting this type of outlet). I would like to have an explanation for wanting it and enjoying it, but simply accept it as a part of the whole sexual experience."

"I have engaged in all except humiliation. I participate in fist-fucking fairly often. It is an incredibly exciting thing if one of you is in the right (drugged) mood. I still prefer fucking to fist-fucking: a fist does not come, a cock does. These variations are exciting occasionally, boring and too much trouble on a regular basis."

"I don't actively seek to engage in sadism. If someone just happens to want to be spanked, I'm happy to do it but I never suggest it myself. I really love the masochism, discipline end of it, though. I must have a certain type of man to administer it. He must have a hairy chest—the more the better. A beard is a real plus although I like heavy face stubble just as much. I like him to be older than I am, and the shorter his hair the better. I think of him as a father figure. I like to be cussed out and criticized, especially for my appearance. (I really am not bad looking.) Then I like to be stripped, spanked, and fucked—but always hugged and loved in the end. These desires are natural to me and I see nothing wrong with them. I only engage in these activities about once every three or four months but I fantasize about them often."

"I find that I often engage in heavy sex to get over anger, frustration. It helps like a good drunk does for other people."

"I engage in watersports rather infrequently, possibly because it is so messy. I feel it is fun, and really not perverted, like I'm sure many think it must be. I don't feel guilty, or that I am doing anything wrong. If you're willing to let someone come in your mouth, or on you, how much different is that than letting someone urinate in your mouth, or on you?"

"Sometimes I urinate on myself and occasionally have had someone else do it to me. That soft, warm liquid feels nice."

"The only activity listed that I ever engaged in was watersports, in which I pissed on my partner. We both enjoyed the act. Another activity I enjoy is to have someone lick my ass. I feel my anal opening is very sensitive, and I am excited by having someone's tongue run over it."

"I do enjoy kissing and sucking a clean ass and having my own ass licked the same way. It can be very exciting to masturbate while a guy licks your ass. Basically, anything anyone wants to do and does is OK with me, as long as it's not forced. I consider myself a very liberated sexual individual and would probably try anything reasonable once. If I didn't like it, I wouldn't go back to it."

"I am not into being fist-fucked, but if my partner wants to be fist-fucked and so turns me on, I oblige. When I get into it, I always position myself in front of my partner so that he can see my face. Talking is a major part of this art as well as body gestures. I make a ritual out of preparing my fist for penetration while making sure he is comfortable and has all the assistance (such as poppers, Crisco) he needs. The ritual is slow and builds as progress is made. I start with a finger and progress from there. I always use my left hand (rings removed and nails cleaned, trimmed low and filed). Once all my fingers have been inserted I begin to imagine my own arm from the elbow down to be an extension of my own cock. Before inserting my thumb, I tend to linger in this position—moving in and out of my partner's ass, opening him up, and psychologically preparing him and myself through conversation restricted to language appropriate for him and the occasion. Once my thumb is in, I usually feel some pain getting my knuckes in his awaiting cavity. But if we are both in the right head set, the mighty hand enters. When I am sure he is comfortable with my hand inside him, I close my fingers into a fist and continue my fantasy of my arm being an extension of my cock. I move in a fucking motion and either play with my partner's balls, his nipples, my nipples, or my own cock. The point here is that the right hand should be as active as the left. When my partner's climax has been reached, I allow him to evacuate me at his leisure."

"Being fist-fucked is like being fucked by the biggest cock ever. Every sensation is heightened. A good fist-fucker can give you feelings inside your ass that no cock could possibly. The orgasm is incredible."

"I had my first fist last week. It was the most incredible experience I have ever had. It lasted about two and a half hours. It happened sort of by surprise but it was my choice. I'm not into S&M. I once went into a bath in New York City and some guy wanted me to beat him up. I left, thought 'How strange.' "

"All, but with the right people. They involve trust and emotional involvement. I know some psychologists will find reasons for them but if they give pleasure to both, why not? My head is on straight enough to know that I find just pleasure in them, nothing more or less."

"I'm into S&M—a lot. Ditto B&D, watersports, scat, pain, etc. About one-third of our sex has some of the above. I think they're beautiful, exciting, mystical, and *very human*. I approve of *me*, in other words."

"The only fetish I'm pretty obsessive about is watersports, and I love the idea even though I rarely have the opportunity with the 'right person.' It seems most sexy to me when the individual is rather atypically turned on to it, meaning some 'nice person' rather than a big brute. So I would say there have been maybe six occasions when it has been 'right' and I would certainly love to do more, but I won't ever insist."

"I think all these things, within the limits of reason, are probably beneficial in some way as far as relieving aggressions, etc. If a person is left with more than sore nipples or the result of a good ass spanking, then I think caution is advised. Continuous activity of this sort with someone you have a relationship with I think has the potential of doing great psychological and emotional harm. The passive partner becomes demotivated and indecisive. I think it's healthier to do these things with strangers."

"I have occasionally gotten into one or two of these things. What usually happens is, my partner will suggest it and I'll be hesitant. But he'll talk me into it and once I get over my apprehensions and tenseness, I start to enjoy it. There are certain things I draw the line at, though, and I will only do those other things if someone else suggests them. I see it as one more aspect of the variety of sex you can have with different partners."

"The statistics you get from the answers to this question will probably be misleading. By this I mean that most people think of S&M and B&D and that stuff as cruel, brutal, painful, and harmful. But I know lots of men into these things and it's none of that. It's mostly a game, with only enough pain inflicted physically to heighten sexual pleasure. Emotionally, I'd bet that everyone has at one time or another fantasized about being roughly dominated by someone very sexy. In stuff like B&D, guys are just acting out their fantasies. If they both get off on it, and no one really gets hurt, what's wrong with it?"

"I think the reason I ever let myself even try any of this stuff was because of all the bullshit I'd been fed about gay sex. Everyone thought it was wrong, disgusting, that it was horrible and God would strike you dead if you kissed or sucked another man. It wasn't any of those things, it was beautiful. So I figured everyone who was aghast at things like S&M must be wrong, too. So I tried it and guess what? They were!"

"Sadism and masochism—usually, but to a very mild extent. I think any sexual act involves both, and we can always take it to a degree comfortable to both partners. B&D, yes—but when it gets into abuse or humiliation, I stop identifying sexually. I don't find any need for it, but have found it an exciting game. I can act serious, and fantasize, but can never really take it seriously."

"Whenever I do them, I don't feel bad. Just nasty—remember when you first started finding out about sex, it was all nasty then."

"Sometimes I get into B&D and S&M and sometimes some sex games. I like to be beaten, bitten, scratched, and whipped sometimes. I don't all the time. It's a really good way to release lots of energy. Sometimes my body just surges with an extra energy that's useless to me so I must vent it. Sometimes I like to be bound and disciplined for energy release. I also like to be brought to the brink of orgasm while bound and then left alone. It is very rewarding and very intense when you finally are allowed to orgasm."

"I do enjoy spanking and military discipline in moderation. I fulfill my military-discipline fantasy mostly by wearing parts of military uniforms or by cruising and making it with someone in the military. Being an ex-marine of four years, I know just where to look for Uncle Sam's boys and how to make an approach. I don't know how I got turned on to spanking and being spanked, but I have found very few men not turned on to a few whacks on the buns or unwilling to return the thrill if introduced at the right moment. I use only my hands and am turned off by the use of belts or other aids."

"Bondage to me is a foreign country. But I can still understand how a guy and a girl or two guys might get into it. I agree with Albert Ellis: anything two (or more) people do together is normal—as long as all participate willingly."

"When you have a lover I believe you should engage in numerous sexual activities. The same old blow job every night gets awfully boring. Sometimes I tie George up (which he loves). Sometimes I make him lick my boots. Other times I strap him gently with a yardstick. We find these things add a lot to our sex life."

"My opinion when younger was that this was all sort of 'far out,' but now I begin to understand these particular desires and interests. I have gotten into watersports and scat with *both* male and female partners."

"I've been involved in S&M for about seven months, and have had six or seven scenes. I think it is healthier for me to do these things than to do nothing and just fantasize about them."

"The only far-out thing I go in for is enemas. I can be on

either end, but I prefer giving them. The interest comes from giving enemas and seeing how long the recipient can hold them. Even though I know better, I still think of this as a perversion. There aren't many guys who will let you give them enemas."

"I feel that S&M is the epitome of masculine sex. Besides, partners can penetrate each other's minds in ways that ordinary sex can't. I am, however, very much against abuse, crassness, and outright brutality. When I am the dominant partner, I make it clear beforehand that I am not going to do anything to hurt him, that we are only playing a game. Sex of this type has to be mutually agreed upon beforehand. S&M is beneficial to both partners if handled correctly. It helps me to get rid of frustrations, and I feel happier after such sessions—whether I have been submissive or dominant. I have no use for exclusive sadists—I feel that most of them have sex problems. On the other hand, I have the greatest respect for role switchers (like myself)—only a real man can dish it out *and* take it. I have a slight pity for masochists, and usually encourage them to also switch roles and take the dominant role."

"I guess there's something so 'forbidden' about it which turns me on. It's all emotional. As is most of this stuff. That's where the real turn-on comes."

"I prefer S&M or 'raunch' over any kind of sexual activity, and seek out partners of like interest whenever I can. These can be very enjoyable, the very best kind of sexual relationship. They achieve an intimacy which is impossible on any other level."

Many men said that they have highly negative feelings about these activities, both those who have experienced them and those who have not:

"I don't engage in any of these and have no wish to. They are not forms of *lovemaking*. They are violent and signs of neurotic behavior."

"No. No. No. No. No. No. No. Ugh! Who knows what new thrill I'd need?"

"This is unclean, unhealthy, and vile. I don't deny that my feeling toward those who participate in such activities is that of distrust, horror, and fear."

"Occasionally I'll meet someone who wants to be humiliated and I'll go along to some extent playing the role of the big macho straight punk, but I really dig hugging and kissing a lot and that usually turns him off so it's a one-nighter only."

"I think all of these things you mention are idiotic, sickening, silly, insane, or some combination of the above!"

"I consider these to be activities engaged in by persons whose sex drive has become numbed because of age or promiscuity. They seem to require increasingly large doses of unusual sex to get the same sort of climax they used to achieve when they were young."

"I have never tried any of them. I feel that they are simply alternatives for avoiding an emotional sexual experience. I feel that people should be allowed to indulge in whatever kind of sex practices they wish as long as nothing is harmed in the process. My personal opinion is that somewhere along the way, these people who must participate in these depraved sex scenes have been depraved themselves. Anyone who must be humiliated in front of his partner in order to achieve orgasm can never have a healthy sexual relationship."

"I don't engage in any of the activities listed, or analingus either. The subjects are weird, kinky. I don't know anyone who practices them. There is no connection between them and love or sex in my mind."

"I don't do anything outside of fellatio, anal intercourse, and masturbation—that's it. I feel that is very normal gay lifestyle. But those so-called others are all a bunch of crap to me. To me that's not the real gay life, those people are from another world or sickie. I don't count them as gay people nor would have anything to do with any of them—no wonder society and the laws are against us. I feel it's people like them that ruin the gay name and what gay really means."

"They're OK for them that like it. I prefer regular sex. I don't really approve of fist-fucking because I think it could be rather dangerous. And I worry about what people's assholes will be like after forty years of fist-fucking."

"I am repelled by these activities, though I keep this view to myself unless questioned. Just because I don't enjoy something doesn't mean it's wrong."

"I think this stuff is an extension of the fucked-upness of being gay. If gays weren't persecuted so much a lot of this bullshit wouldn't exist."

"I am rather conventional when it comes to sex. I believe that sex should be tender and loving. In my book, that rules out pain and abuse. In my early teens, I was always top man.

After fucking a guy, I would feel revulsion and anger toward him. I would then humiliate him and even strike him if he tried to touch me. The reason for this is now obvious to me. I wanted him as much as he wanted me but I had been raised to believe that this was depraved and sinful so I hated my friend for inspiring these feelings in me. I was cured of that easily enough. One day, when I was sixteen, I was horny as usual and I was trying to get my friend aroused. He wasn't in the mood but he warned me that if I managed to arouse him he would fuck me. He was strong enough to carry out his threat, so when he did become aroused, he raped me. I loved it. Since then, I have always treated my sex partners as equals."

"I am lukewarm to hostile on these activities, since they tend to involve degrading or humiliating the other person. In my normal life at work and in my relationships with people outside work, I like to support, encourage, and build up people. These types of sexual activities go counter to that for me."

"I think these people need two doctors. One to help fix their heads, and one to fix their bodies."

"I have heard too many stories about people injured or permanently disabled by such activity, most of the times accidentally. If you don't leave yourself open to risk, nothing will happen to you."

"I have engaged in the active role in fist-fucking. I don't like it because there is a detachment involved that seems to have nothing whatsoever to do with sex. I do not like masochism because often some sort of pain is involved. If the sex isn't warm and affectionate, it doesn't do a thing for me. Pissing on somebody isn't sex. It's pissing on somebody."

"I have heard of people having orgasms while being hanged to death, but orgasm is not important enough to me that I will 'cut off my nose to spite my face,' so to speak."

"Humiliation? No way! Isn't that what we're fighting?"

"This is the kind of sex that helps keep the yoke on gays."

"There have been a few isolated incidents in the past, stemming from a 1961 evening in Berkeley during which someone prevailed upon me (when I was very drunk) to urinate in his mouth. And I remember not being disgusted but instead thinking: 'How sad that he has come to the point where the ordinary joys of sex won't do anymore.' Like being unable to go to bed without a sex toy or achieve climax without poppers. All these things have their place, but when they

become an obsession—when you are literally unable to function without them—then I think you're in trouble. Also, the
human psyche is a complex mechanism and one needs to be
wary about opening certain doors which, like Pandora's box,
once opened can never be closed."

"I do not engage in any of the activities listed, and I am
not tolerant about them. I do not consider them a part of the
gay world at all."

"The only one I might engage in is humiliation, which
impresses me as an acting out of the usual opprobrium one
lives with each day. Perhaps it would exorcise the ghost, but
only momentarily. I probably would be afraid of the backlash
reaction afterwards."

"I have too much respect for myself to allow it to occur to
me and I would want to respect my partner too much to do it
to him."

"I've always found the activities described as being quite
revolting. I see it as being degrading to both parties involved:
one feels so superior that he must denigrate the other to the
point of filth; the other feels so inferior that this is all he's
worth. At that point I think mental instability is involved."

"I don't engage in any of these activities. They repel me
and seem abnormal. One must be really jaded to indulge in
fist-fucking, etc. All sexual acts are holy as far as I am concerned when they are engaged in by two consenting adults.
But fist-fucking and the like are truly perversions. I consider
myself a normal gay male who likes to suck and be sucked,
fuck and be fucked. I guess I'm old-fashioned."

Do you ever use drugs, sex toys, or pornography during sex? How do they enhance your sexual experience?

Pornography is the most prevalently utilized sexual aid by
the men in this survey. 50.6% said they used it, either during
sex with a partner or when masturbating:

"I thoroughly enjoy looking at pictures of my ideal men or
men in interesting sexual poses while I masturbate. Without
this, I would have difficulty, at times, getting an erection."

"My lover and I both enjoy looking at pictures of handsome, well-built men. We made love once while watching a
film. He was high on grass and said it was very special. I en-

joyed it, of course; I always enjoy sex with him. The film didn't add to *my* enjoyment—his added excitement did."

"I am a porn collector. I have invested well over $1,000 in it. Mostly I like the 8"x10" picture books. I must have 100 of them. I wish the government would legalize porn so that the Mafia would be forced out of the business—there would be competition, and prices would fall. The models should be getting most of the dough, not the pornographers. I like to masturbate while looking at the pornography. I spend too much time doing this, in fact. Again, a prisoner of sex."

"Although I find porno stimulating when I'm alone, it seems like a waste of time to look at photos when you've got a real man lying next to you."

"My lover and I collect male porno movies and find them stimulating during sex together. After all, it's been twenty-eight years."

"I read pornography while masturbating, but these images of foot-long cocks coming twenty times are so absurd there's no turn-on. More inspiring are pictures of men sticking their asses out as far as they'll go, but they are hard to come by. I wonder why?"

"I never use pornography when I'm having sex with someone (why bother?) but I love it when I masturbate. I don't like pictures, I like to read hot sexual stories. I guess they're more surprising and hold your interest more than your own tired old fantasies, and you can picture yourself as the hero. It gets me very excited and then jacking off is almost as good as sex with somebody."

"I write my own pornographic stories. I put all the elements in them that I know turn me on, then I don't look at them for months. When I want to read one, I've forgotten what's in it, and it's like reading it for the first time. It's a surefire method."

42.8% of the men use some kind of drug during sex. This statistic includes all drugs mentioned, including marijuana, amyl nitrate, uppers, downers, etc.

"The only drug I use is marijuana, but not specifically for sex. But I must say that some of my most favorite sex has happened when my partner and I were stoned."

"The only thing I use during sex is marijuana. That is because I like them both, so doing both at the same time is logical."

"I use poppers. It seems to be instantly uninhibiting to my body, my muscles. Like melting without any loss of energy or vitality."

"Grass and sex are a mellowed-out trip that's slow and dreamy; orgasm with poppers can send you right through the roof."

"I only use amyl. I like the floating sensation, the way it makes your cock hard as a rock and the total lack of inhibition it creates. It heightens my pleasure tremendously."

"I use amyl as often as possible. It has an incredible effect on me. It makes me totally uninhibited and terribly horny. I usually don't like getting fucked because it hurts too much at first, but amyl makes me so horny that the pain is bearable. It also allows you to float away, so that the pain seems duller. Then when you want to focus in on orgasm, it has the opposite effect—it makes your orgasm ten times stronger. The stuff really is a miracle product."

"I will usually use drugs during sex with a new partner whether he does or not, since I am usually more concerned with my excitement and finding out what his pleasure is, with as little inhibition as possible, than I am with a partner whom I know how to excite."

"Sometimes I use poppers, which I like because of the way they intensify things. It also helps me to seduce my lover because he doesn't always want to have sex as much as I do."

"I use poppers frequently. They seem to black out everything but that cock and my mouth or ass."

"I have used hashish, marijuana, and psilocibin during mutual sex. The drugs, which are organic only, helped relax us and helped us reach deep in our selves to overcome any distinctions and helped us express all those strong to gentle, named and unnamed feelings that we might only experience individually."

33.4% of the men use various sex 'toys':

"I use cock rings and dildoes. These toys in the right hands enhance the sex by giving the two people something to play with besides each other."

"I use only a small vibrator capsule which slips into the anus. It gently massages the prostate—feels good and hastens ejaculation."

"Cock rings on occasion. I don't know what they do for me. I seem to get a harder hard-on."

"A cock ring helps keep it all going longer. Why use them? 'Cause it's fun and isn't that what sex is all about? Sex that isn't fun is not worth the trouble. I don't use anything all the time but it can be a nice change if the time, place, and partner are right."

"I think a cock ring's better function is during cruising. It makes your basket more noticeable. False advertising? Not really, if it is all really you. Besides, size queens deserve to be deceived!"

"I like to shove a dildo up the ass of a butch-acting guy as it makes me feel so dominant. I prefer this to screwing him; it turns me on."

"Tit clamps allow me to use my hands in other places. Dildoes are much easier on me both ways. If they're in me I can control the penetration. In others—I usually come fast, so it allows me to satisfy them if they like to get fucked a lot."

"Cock rings are a great turn-on for me. I like the feel of a cock ring when I am ready to orgasm. It seems to help push the ejaculation to greater heights. I like the butch look of a guy wearing a cock ring."

"I use a dildo to masturbate with. I put the dildo up my ass and move it in and out with one hand while masturbating with the other hand. That way, I can have an orgasm that's as good and as powerful as the one I have when I'm getting fucked."

"I find that a dildo helps to loosen me up so that there isn't as much pain when my lover enters me. He can fuck me much harder and he enjoys it more than if we have to struggle through my getting used to him first."

"I never was able to give a good blow job because I would always gag and I thought that was something that always had to happen. But then I heard that you could practice relaxing your gag reflex or something like that. So rather than practice on someone I got a dildo and used it. Now I can take a cock as deep as it will go. I feel much more confident about my ability to please my partners now."

"I got an Accu-Jac through an ad in a magazine. It's this machine that jerks you off and it feels like a warm mouth. I have to admit it sure has made masturbation time a whole lot more fun."

"I got my tits pierced recently and I have tit rings there now. It's simply incredible when my lover gently twists them while he's sucking me off. There seems to be a current of electricity running right from my tits to my cock and it feels incredible. My orgasm is always so much better when he does that."

40% of the men do not use anything during sex, and many are opposed to such use:

"Porno leaves me feeling very cheap. The idea of having to use anything seems to me a sign that sex has lost its spontaneity."

"I don't like amyl during sex. It gives me a form of sensate paralysis and I am unable to respond with my body to my partner. It instantly drains my energy into myself and I am unable to participate mentally or physically with my partner."

"I have had sex when high on cocaine and freaked on acid, LSD. In both cases your mind is too out of touch with your body for sex to be in the least pleasurable."

"I have absolutely no use for drugs. I've never used them. I think all drugs do is harm you, and that people who do use them are just abusing their body. I think that is one reason people on drugs seem to age so fast."

"I *occasionally* smoke pot prior to or during sex but see no difference in the enjoyment. I am opposed to other drugs and especially liquor. Nothing is more disgusting than trying to make it with someone who is drunk."

"Things like cock rings and dildoes are a real turn-off. If a man can't keep it up unless he's wearing a cock ring, he's not much of a man and not very attractive to me. And I certainly don't want a fake cock up my ass when I can get the real, beautiful thing."

"Curiously, I like amyl on any occasion *but* during sex. It tends to anesthetize me and give whatever I'm doing an air of unreality."

"I am opposed to the use of drugs; and I feel strongly about this. I don't know if I am opposed to marijuana; I haven't tried it (can you believe that? It's true in my case. I am intending to use marijuana sometime soon just to see what it's like.) I think that the more powerful drugs should be avoided for two reasons: one, is reality really so bad that one cannot face it without resorting to drugs and other screens against it? And two, should I develop a fatal progressive condition, like cancer, I would want to get the maximum relief from pain from whatever medication might be prescribed—which might not be the case if I have built up any tolerances or chemical dependencies in advance of any

such unfortunate terminal illness. I would hope that gay
people would stay away from drugs as much as possible. It is,
in my estimation, a cop-out to substitute drugs for the personal and social struggle one should face and work through
to be truly liberated and alive."

"I have noticed lately that many guys I have been to bed
with seem to need amyl to keep it hard or to keep sex going.
Two guys that I went to bed with fairly steadily and wanted
a relationship with me I dropped because they were hooked
on or need amyl during sex. That to me seems like or reminds me of my alcoholic mother who needed booze. It's a
turn-off for me."

Do you ever get aroused by uniforms and leather? By garments, odors, and the like? What is it about them that arouses you?

Fifty-nine percent of the men answered no to this question,
Twenty-five percent indicated that they find uniforms sexually
exciting, and 18% felt that way about leather. Seventeen percent found certain garments highly erotic, and 18% said the
same about odors.

Most of the men who replied affirmatively said that their
appreciation of these things was not fetishistic, but rather a
sexual stimulus which was most often determined primarily
by the man and how much his innate attractiveness was enhanced by a certain garment. Many men stressed that an
unattractive man could not be made attractive by the addition of a uniform or leather.

**Most of the men who find these things arousing do so be-
cause they heighten masculinity and sexuality:**

"I like men. Likely, if they are in leather, a uniform,
and/or have a masculine odor, their masculinity is enhanced.
If in the beginning they haven't got that maleness, no matter
how much leather they add it doesn't do a thing. But if they
have got that maleness and then add such tough masculine
apparel, then it is a turn-on."

"I always loved the old 'sailor suit.' Sailors always seemed
to exude sex to me. Don't know why. I think it was because
they were always supposed to be horny from being at sea.

I've never seen anyone in a suit and tie who could arouse me. The same person in blue jeans might put a chill down my back, but suited I'd not look twice."

"Quite often a black leather razor strap in a barber shop will arouse me to the point of near embarrassment. This fascination still has me curious about myself but it has been with me since small boyhood. I think I associate black leather with manhood of which I seem not to have too much in my own personality."

"The leather fetish goes back to my early teens, before I had any of the associations with leather that I now have mentally. When I was about thirteen I put on my brother-in-law's leather jacket, inside out, and jacked off to the most tremendous orgasm I had ever had till then. I still recall it vividly. The leather odor when warm, its texture under the hand, its sheen in dim light, its slap against a buttock—all turn me on."

"I don't consider myself a fetishist, because I don't *need* uniforms or leather to turn me on. They just add to the enjoyment."

"I get off on my lover's uniform and shoes. I love to press his uniform and see him in it. I like to feel his holster and gun. It goes about that far. Once, we fucked while he was going to work and he was in uniform. I was very aroused. He feels no arousal by it at all."

"To me a uniform is a definite sign of power, strength, and dominance. Instant arousal."

"I love *boots*, not the silly fashion dress ones, but real construction, cowboy *heavy* ones."

"I am turned on to levis, flannel shirts, tight-fitting T-shirts, tube socks (white), and work shoes. Although these are gay stereotype garments, they represent (in fact or fiction) my current image of being masculine."

"Tight denim and army greens are very exciting. Denim's effect is probably due to its tightness, which accentuates all the best features of a man's body (his ass, thighs, and crotch). The effect of the army fatigues is more difficult to ascertain, though soldiers are the epitome of masculinity. As a teenager, nearly all of my fantasies were populated by soldiers."

"As for the uniforms, I think it is the taboo nature of gay sex within institutions like the police department that makes the men in uniforms specifically exciting—like, I must be incredibly attractive if he gets turned on by me because he is risking so much by doing this."

"Leather gets me hot because when I reached puberty all the hot guys were greasers and bikers and juvenile delinquents and I got very fixated on that and those were the guys that I fantasized about and Elvis *was* sexy in those days or everyone wouldn't have tried to emulate him and Marlon Brando and those guys so there is something innately sexy about that look and it turns me on."

"Swimming trunks or shorts (underwear) of someone who is attractive arouse me when I put them on—if I know the person. When I put them on, I become them and have their attractiveness. It also seems that the person is in me and I'm in them."

"The cop, lumberjack, telephone lineman really turn me on. I think it's the idea that I can't have them that turns me on."

"I enjoy going to our local cowboy bars, and often dress as a cowboy. I think that this is also one of my fantasies, that I have often accomplished. I am really aroused by the idea of a cowboy, and the representation I have seen in the media."

"A military uniform is a symbol of masculinity and male prowess—especially when a cute young soldier is in it."

"I find the odor of manly sweat highly exciting. I love to have sex with a man who has worked up a sweat doing some heavy work."

"The odor of a locker room sends me into erotic fantasyland. Sometimes a pair of sweaty sweatsocks will be enough to do the trick."

"My lover doesn't know it, but sometimes when he's not around I'll smell his underwear. It's very exciting and brings back sexual memories."

"Once when I had to leave someone I cared a great deal about, he gave me a green parka that he had had a long time. It had 'his' smell on it. For months afterwards when I missed him so terribly I used to hold it close to me and I would remember being close to him. Even now, three years later, I can put my face in it and get butterflies in my stomach."

Other men are opposed to uniforms and leather:

"I hate leather. Especially black leather. I can't understand all those crazy people in these black outfits, or this stupid subculture. I have no idea what they are talking about. They are laughable to say the least."

"Uniforms and leather and the generally lardy creeps who wear them are repulsive superficially to me, so that even when I discover that the man clad in leather is a nice, warm human being I still am not turned on or likely to be turned on to him."

"Being a police officer and wearing a uniform myself, this is a rather humorous question—the answer is no concerning all parts of this question."

"After a war in Central Europe, uniforms and leather arouse my hatred and anger and murderous instinct."

"Generally 'dressing up' does not turn me on. In some cases I think it is a turn-off when a fat middle-aged man walks into a bar in full leather drag that is so tight he can't move. I would probably be attracted to the fat middle-aged man if he were wearing something less outrageous and tried to just be himself."

"Part of me would like to get into a group leather fantasy, but the other half would be off to one side laughing like crazy, which is really a terrible thing to say. In America, you can apparently do anything with sex but laugh at it."

"The 'butch drag' syndrome puzzles me. Ask any of those guys what they think of drag queens and they'll probably tell you they can't stand guys who pretend to be women. So why is it that they have to 'pretend' to be men?"

Have you ever paid or been paid for sex? Why? How did you feel about it?

22.5% of the men have paid for sex. Most of these feel the experience was a positive one:

"I have paid and felt good about it because I am then reasonably certain to get the kind of sex—and orgasm—I enjoy. I consider the hustler a partner who delivers a needed service, the absolute equal of the client. Mostly I enjoy his company as well as the sex."

"I believe that I'm still reasonably attractive—but I'm also fifty-five—and while I once enjoyed standing around bars looking for a sex partner, it's not that easy any more. There's nothing like being twenty-one. Paying for it doesn't bother me, although if you indulge too much it could be very expensive. The hustler (model) has a service to sell (rent) and you want to buy—and if you hit it off, why not? There's one sexy devil in San Francisco who I try to spend at least one evening with on every visit. He's not cheap, but does give me as much (if not more) affection and hot imaginative action than someone you might have struck it up with from a bar—and who doesn't charge. This kid and I have managed to develop a rather fond relationship over the past three years. I used the word kid—he's actually twenty-eight."

"I have paid for sex a few times. I wanted to have a bondage 'scene.' I didn't like to pay the high prices, but I was glad to have been able to have fantasies actually take place."

"It was the only way to get a certain person. I had a great time and the price was less than I've spent for a good meal. I felt good about it."

"I paid for sex three times, because the boys were uncommonly beautiful hustlers. A wise old gay once said to me, 'You always pay for love, and money is the least expensive medium of exchange.' "

"My sex experiences as an adult have all been paid for, even when the partner was not supposedly a hustler. I paid because it was easy and I was attracted to the person and I could call the shots. I love hustler types."

"Yes, twice. Because he was beautiful and I liked the way he came on to me. The idea of it—the first time—was exciting. Plus it gives me a feeling of power and freedom I don't have with a straight pickup. I feel freer to ask him to do or try things I couldn't ask another unless I knew him very well. He was one of the best lays I've ever had. He made me feel as beautiful to him as he was to me. He went out of his way to please me and satisfy me. I felt good about it and his head seems to be together so I don't feel that I'm hurting him. On the contrary."

"With a heterosexual male it is often the only way they could have sex without feeling guilty about the act. If they were paid I presume they could feel they weren't being homosexual. I know this because I've paid as little as two dollars to a male to whom this was an insignificant amount of money. If I have the money I don't mind paying for sex. It's purely for pleasure and I pay for most other forms of entertainment."

"My first two gay experiences were with hustlers. It was the only way I knew at the time to have sex with a guy. I was dying for the experience but didn't know of gay bars in Baltimore and knew no one gay. I gladly paid for the experience. If I were rich I would pay now if someone really turned me on and I couldn't get together with him otherwise. I find nothing wrong about hustling, though I think it should be legalized and controlled from criminal elements."

"I'm older and never was a beauty. The only way I can have sex now is by paying young hustlers for it. I certainly don't feel badly because they need me as much (if not more) than I need them. My money keeps them in clothes and food. I also show them affection and caring. Many of these young men have left miserable homes, and this is the only way they know to get any affection, much less make a living. I really wonder why there's so much opposition to prostitution. No one is getting hurt. Sexual tensions are getting released this way rather than through force, the boys are involved (for the most part) in loving rather than burglary. Maybe it's the fact that there is often criminal elements involved in prostitution. This is only because it is illegal—the guys and girls need protection from the police and thus get involved with shady characters. They're certainly not criminals themselves, and those who do get involved in illicit activity weren't that way to begin with, they were exposed to it. Isn't it ironic that the police harassment of prostitutes leads to criminal activity? Prostitution need be no more socially damaging than having a plumber over to fix your sink."

"When I was a teenager I was crazy about an older boy and the only way he'd let me do anything was if I gave him fifty cents. I used up all my allowance money on him for months. I was so stuck on him I didn't care."

Some of the men who have paid for sex feel bad about it:

"I have paid for sex, only because I was in love with the guy, and the only way I could get him in bed was to put money in his hand or buy him something that he wanted. I was blindly in love and couldn't see that he was just using me."

"I have paid for sex twice, both times to get at the body of boys I had seen dance at the Gaiety Burlesk in New York. The experience was brief, unsatisfying, and humiliating. I will not do it again. For sex to be satisfying to me it must be mutually desired. The hustler desires the money, not the sexual experience, and that turns me off."

"Yes, because I wasn't having any luck scoring and/or that was the only way I could get the hunk I was after. I dislike paying intensely, but when a man reaches forty-seven, straight or otherwise, sometimes it is necessary to make compromises. I don't start out looking for a hustler, but often after the act there is this song and dance about how bad things are and buddy, can you spare a dime, that sort of approach. I know sometimes it's coming, but what the hell, if I am horny and the sex object is hunky enough, that's what money is for."

"I've paid for sex three times just to try to figure out why and how someone could get their heads into such a place as to accept money for what is readily available for free. Neither public nor paid sex is my bag. I can simply say that while some things I'll never get used to at least I should know about them."

"About six years ago I went through a period of practically specializing in hustlers, whom I used to contact through their ads. I met some pleasant guys that way, but it was ultimately frustrating because I could never feel really wanted for longer than a couple of hours at a time."

"I always hate myself when I pay for sex. You'll notice the words suggest an ongoing process. It always seems to be the same scenario: I spot a gorgeous, hunky boy on the street. He's so beautiful that my first thought is, he'll never want to have sex with someone like me unless I pay him. So I mention money early on, so that even if he isn't a hustler I don't know if he would have come with me without money (almost everybody will accept proffered money). Then, nine times out of ten, the guy turns out to be dumb or self-centered or uncaring, and I realize he's really beneath me, I hate myself for placing so much emphasis on physical beauty and for having such low self-esteem in the first place. So the experience turns out to be highly negative. Unfortunately, I never learn because soon the process starts all over again. Perplexing, and sad."

22.2% of the men in this survey have been paid to have sex. Slightly more than half felt good about the experience:

"From the time I was thirteen until I was approximately seventeen, I made myself available to men who were willing to pay for sex. I don't think what I was doing was wrong simply because I never demanded payment for having sex with a man; if they thought they wanted to pay I accepted it. I knew what I was and I enjoyed the things I was doing."

"Once I was paid because I was offered money by a man I would have gone with for free and I wanted to find out what it felt like. I felt no different. Just twenty dollars richer."

"I am eighteen and hustle. To start out with, 80% of juvenile hustlers are wanted by the law and have no means of support or ID to get employment. Hustling is good for both the people (the john) and the hustler. They both come out happy. A gay person is the best friend a person can have. They're not aggressive or violent. They will do anything they can for a friend. If there wasn't gay people, your runaway kids or delinquents would be sleeping in the street, starving, wearing grubby clothes. You people out there, I get your whole viewpoint. I know because I'm one of your kids writing this. I'm not gay, but I hustle for a living. You people think these kids are sexually abused. No one is. Think real hard."

"If the person has the money and is that anxious to have sex with me that he will pay, I make sure he enjoys himself. (It has never happened with a woman but I assume I would feel the same)."

"When I was in graduate school, starving to death, I turned a few tricks. I rather enjoyed it. Most of the guys were nice and I would have done it with them for nothing under other circumstances. I never felt cheap, or used or degraded. Sex degrades you only if you let it."

"Once I was paid $20 by a man who wanted to suck me off, but I came so quickly I gave half of it back to him. It felt fine to me; I was turned on by the fact that he wanted me so badly that he was willing to pay for it. Too turned on, I guess."

"I got paid once, not because I asked but because this guy wanted it that way. So who was I to deny someone his pleasure?"

"I have never paid for sex nor been paid for it. The thought revolts me in either case. (Since typing this I accepted $20 for sex. I wasn't so revolted. Fred and I went out to dinner with it.)"

Some of the men who have been paid for sex have negative feelings about it:

"I have taken money for sex but only when I was very young—and the guy was trying to make sure I'd see him again. I hated myself and spent the money on food—quickly."

"I hustled for a while in Denver. Initially it was exhilarating, a challenge, easy money. But after four to five months, I found that I was no longer enjoying it. It was jading the experiences I had for pleasure, was making me lonely and unhappy (there are some very unfortunate men paying for sex) and was limiting my life in other areas. After this I worked in New York City for a man who set up encounters for me. (For a cut, of course.) This eliminated much of the risk, as well as my getting involved with weirdos, and I enjoyed some fine times, but eventually felt that I needed a permanent relationship with someone who appreciated more than my body."

"I have been a male prostitute. Most (about 99%) of my clients were very unattractive to me and for many it was the only way they could find a sexual partner. I only met two men during this period who I would have had sex with under normal conditions. One was a young man who had no idea how to meet another man and I told him how to go about it and had a great time in bed with him. He would have turned many heads in a gay bar. The other man I enjoyed having sex with was very attractive but he was unable to go to gay bars because he was in business and couldn't afford to be recognized by anyone as being homosexual. I didn't like being paid usually because I was often asked to do things that turned me right off. Most clients wanted to be fucked which I don't enjoy much anyway."

"I have been paid for sex when I was first coming out and I didn't want to admit to myself that I was gay. I told myself that I was doing it only for the money, not for pleasure. And most of these encounters were not pleasurable."

"I've been paid to have sex. That was when I was in college and let a man pick me up in a car. I'm certain I asked for money to assuage my guilt. I didn't need the money but it was an easy way to lie to myself that what I had done was all right. I was deluding myself of course."

"I hustled as a young man. At the time it was kind of exciting and flattering that people wanted to pay money for me (I tricked with men and women). But as I got a little older I began to realize that most of these people were not interested in me as a person, just as a body. And, worse yet, that I had nothing to offer the world except my body. So I started to hate it and even got nasty to some of my clients a few times. I started to save my money, went back to school, and now I'm earning a good living, have a wonderful lover, and feel good about myself. I'm glad I got out of that."

64.4% of the men have neither paid nor been paid for sex. Some, simply because they never had the opportunity. Others, because they are opposed to such activity:

"I would never pay to have sex. My partner would really be just interested in my money, not in me as a person. Anyone who offered to pay me for sex I would feel also would be just interested in my body, not me as a person. This is why I care to have nothing to do with prostitution. If I were so 'hot' or 'horny' but could not find anyone to have sex with besides prostitutes, I could always masturbate and have sex fantasies as I jack off."

"I was romantically involved for seven months with a hustler (I didn't find out till the end of our relationship). I feel that for a person to sell himself is a terrible way to make a living. It is degrading."

"There were a couple of times when I should have expected money because it would have confirmed my 'being used,' except I was loathe to admit it to myself."

"Somehow, I think sex should be fun and not commercial. On the other hand, there is the argument that marriages are really paid sex arrangements and that one pays one way or the other for any relationship. The baths are really a form of paying for sex and so is going to a bar, having a few drinks for the privilege of meeting someone. I can't quite get it together on the pay business—maybe I'm just stingy. I guess I would feel if I had to pay directly that I just 'don't have it anymore.' Part of the fun of picking up someone is the flattery of being wanted, of being considered attractive."

"While Lee was living here and I spent $6,000 on him in one way or another, was he paid? Perhaps that is when I feel that I was used, when I let myself dwell on it. My friends say that I was used, but I don't want to believe them."

"I often drive by the meat market on East 53rd street and look over the merchandise. I have gone with the intention of buying and have been propositioned by some pretty attractive boys but I can't bring myself to do it. I think it is degrading.

I have been offered money for sexual favors but I think too much of myself to go for money."

"Why buy the cow when the milk's free? With all the available people in this town, I think it's sad that someone would have to buy sex."

"I have a policy against it. I can't see paying for sex when so much of it is for free. I would not feel very desirable if the only reason someone were having sex with me was that I had paid him. Once I picked up a hitchhiker who was a hustler but I didn't know it. I asked to take him home and he asked for money. I told him no and said, 'I would rather feel that you had sex with me because you really wanted to.' He said OK and I felt great!"

"I don't want to feel that I have to pay for it. But if I had a lot of money, I'd give some to hustlers to show them that someone cares about them, without having to have sex."

"I think this most disgusting, repugnant to me. Like buying love. How could there be any feeling there? There are too many nice people about who would like to share, and *sharing* is the name of the game for me."

"If I were to hustle, I could take money much easier from women than from men. I enjoy sex with men but there would be no pleasure for me in sex with women, therefore I could justify being paid for it. I guess I'm lucky I don't need money."

"I have been offered money for sex but, although the temptation was great, I refused it. I was unemployed at the time and at a low point in my self-esteem. I didn't refuse the offers because of any moral considerations, but rather because to accept would be simply an affirmation of the feeling that sex and a body were all I could offer to the world. Now I know why hustlers can never look anybody in the eye: prostitution is the ultimate in self-hate."

"I don't like thinking about paying or being paid for sex. Every sex act is an act of love. I hope."

Is the size of a man's penis (including your own) important to you? Why or why not?

"I like 'em big. I guess it's the same as a straight guy liking big breasts on a woman. It's more sexually powerful."

"I love big cocks, but hardness is more important. The

body the cock belongs to is also important. A queen with the biggest cock in the world will not turn me on."

"I find that the size of a man's organ has always intrigued me. *The bigger the better*! I feel that the size of a man's organ denotes virility and strength."

"Since the dick is the center of the sex act, the larger the better."

"Size is unimportant to both of us. I suppose personally, size is a hand-me-down of the past where one's masculinity is associated with size; that's a lot of bullshit as we all know."

"Penis size is not important. I am only put off by guys with small cocks who want to pretend they don't have one! If I desired a partner without one, I'd be bisexual."

"You can't measure love or the size of a man's heart by the size of his penis. Love is still love whether the penis is one inch or ten inches."

"A person's body is much more important than his penis size. If a person is good looking with a small penis, I for one am not going to turn him down. I don't go to bed with a penis, I go to bed with a man."

Response to this question was about evenly split between "very important" and "unimportant." 36.7% stated that penis size (i.e., largeness) in others was "very important," 20.5 indicated that it was "somewhat important," and to 41.6% it was "unimportant."

Many men, including those for whom size in their partner was unimportant, were quite concerned with the size of their own penis. Almost all worried that it was too small; men with penis sizes from under five inches to over eight inches expressed a desire to have a larger organ. Some men report that they are embarrassed by the size of their penis, or that they are turned off by others unless they meet a certain standard.

The majority of the men in this survey wrote that while penis size is important, it is not the be-all and end-all of sexuality:

"Certainly not! I'll bet 90% of the respondents say that. Well, it is important. I have a rather large cock and am glad I do. My lover is enormous and I'm glad of that. I always get turned on by a guy with a big basket. But, I also remember that some of the best sex I ever had was with a man who was considered below average. A case of not what you've got but what you do with it. It's an emotional thing."

"Penis size is important because the mythology, history, and mystique is fantastically consistent in the area of penis size and its relationship to the man. I know it isn't accurate but it is interesting. I wouldn't turn down a potential relationship because of it."

"The size of a man's cock is not important, although I will admit to feeling good if my cock is larger than my partner's, or if my partner's cock is exceptionally large. But his overall performance in bed is the important thing."

"The size of the penis is important. I'd be lying if I didn't say it was. But it's of relative importance. If the man has qualities like tenderness and warm affection, the penis becomes a secondary thing. I think also that the shape of the penis is many times more important than its size. There are small cocks I've seen and experienced that were fabulous tools because of the physical beauty of them. Most guys with huge cocks—at least those I've tricked with—have problems getting it up and keeping it there; I have seen men with small cocks get beautiful erections and seem to keep them forever. Most of the time I wish mine was larger (it's seven inches if that matters) but the endowment is hard to change. I guess we're never content with what we have."

"I would rather have a larger penis because I still end up thinking that I would be that much more attractive to many more men if it were larger. I see that sort of attraction very visible in the activities at the baths, but then once the contact is made and the affair develops, I do not think that the penis size is important at all."

"A big, fat hot cock is so good to suck and/or sit on, and to fuck *with*, too. I'm glad mine is big. But it ain't terribly important in one's relationship. People tend to compensate."

"It's important, but not too much. It's got to be large enough to do something with. (I have run into a person whose cock was only one inch long when erect—not a child, either.) More important, I try to avoid people with overly large, more than eight or nine inches, cocks. A phobia, I suppose. I'm perfectly satisfied with my own six and a half inches, and most all the ones I've run into. There's more important things than size, such as cleanliness and shape."

"I must admit I'm turned on by a larger-than-average hang. However, I'm not attracted to the penis alone—if the man doesn't turn me on, no penis is going to do it by itself. I have had a lot of average or even smallish dudes that were super. A big hang is a stereotype—the guy can do no wrong with a piece like that. Which I realize is a fantasy and in no way related to reality. But who says sex has to be rational?"

"For a one-night stand the size of the penis is very important. However, after a few times with the person the size has nothing to do with it."

"I often say no, then go about fantasizing having a huge cock. It's definitely not important in whomever I'm with. I guess I'd like to be well hung 'cause there's so much made of it (ads, porno, and cruising). It would make an otherwise plain person stand out (no pun intended). It's almost like having a great build—something that would make you appealing."

"Any male homosexual who says penis size is not important is lying, though I do not consider myself a 'size queen.' Sure, I like for my partner to have a big cock (circumference is more important to me than length), but it is not the primary consideration. I cruise bodies and faces first."

For some men, penis size is of considerable importance:

"I hit puberty very early, a year or so before most kids my age started, and absolutely reveled in the attention and envy I got because of what they saw as a gigantic penis. It wasn't until later in high school that I came to realize six and three-quarters inches wasn't all that spectacular. But I'd be lying if I said I wouldn't just as soon have maintained that brief advantage. It felt good. I admit I'm attracted and turned on by large organs. I suspect that part of the reason I'm so attracted to blacks is because of the reputation they have for being so well endowed."

"I think penis envy is stupid—but I have it as much as the next fellow. I find a large cock fascinating although I can't service an enormous one skillfully. I would say that mine is average in size and my only regret is that I don't have a bigger basket when I don't have an erection."

"The larger it is, the more beautiful it is. If mine was two inches longer, I could suck myself. What an experience that would be!"

"I like a nice piece of meat. I'm happy with mine. It's important. Small cocks—poor baby—are not exciting sexually no matter how hard I try."

"I had never thought about it until I heard the term 'size

queen' (I resent derogatory terms to describe gay tastes), but a large cock (six to nine inches) is always more appealing. I have a seven-inch cock and have never felt inadequate but I do get a tinge of jealousy when I see someone with a larger cock."

"I notice guys that are hung don't have so many hang-ups."

Some men prefer large sexual organs for physical pleasure:

"The size and shape are important because of what he or you are capable of doing—like more unique positions, for one. Also the shape affects the amount and type of sensations you can create or experience."

"A big cock in my partner brings me more sexual pleasure. You can do more with it orally, it feels good and full in your hand, and you can really feel it when you're being anally penetrated."

"I have to have a fairly large penis inside me when I'm being fucked because a small one tends to jab me and causes a great deal of pain."

"When I get screwed, I like to know that I'm getting screwed."

"If his is bigger, I get fucked. If not, he gets fucked whether he wants to or not."

"If I'm fucked by a smallish dick I can hardly feel it. It becomes just an attempt on my part to satisfy my partner, and I get very little pleasure out of it. A big one inside me, on the other hand, can bring me to roaring orgasm and total satisfaction."

For some men, the size of their own penis is particularly important:

"The size of my own penis has caused me considerable anguish in the past and is one of the reasons that I have doubted my own masculinity. It's three inches long when it's flaccid (six to seven inches when erect, though!). There's supposed to be this big cultural 'thing' that says that you're not a man unless you have an eight- or nine-inch cock when flaccid, which I've always resented as an ignorant and stupid attitude, but that's 'the world' for you! That attitude is especially prevalent among gays. Back in high school, when I undressed for PE, these guys who thought they were real 'macho' would laugh at me when they saw the size of my cock, adding to my consternation."

"The big ones attract the most attention and you are more sought. This I do not have so I feel put down because I know I am good and sexy."

"I never was large in the flaccid state and was forever embarrassed, felt less than whole, had terrible penis envy. I am fine and average erect, but you can't just walk around erect. It's always been difficult for me to piss in a public urinal. Military service was hell!"

"Mine is very important. I feel very inferior in almost all respects except for the size of my penis. Somehow because of the size of it, it will make up for other qualities I am lacking."

"I wish my penis were smaller. It's so big that most guys refuse to let me fuck them (which I love to do) and lots of guys can't do much with it orally. I used to think it was a blessing. Now I'm starting to think it's a curse."

"My penis is very small and it has been the dominant factor in my life since puberty. I've been trying to compensate for it in every other area—athletics, bodybuilding, career accomplishments. I've had so many men obviously lose interest in me because of it that I was practically suicidal. Then I decided that any guy who would toss me over because of my cock size wasn't worth it in the first place. It's a good rationale, and probably very true, but deep down inside, being rejected by any number of men for this reason hurts, deeply."

Many men consider penis size of little importance:

"Size means nothing to me, as I'm initially attracted to someone from his neat outward appearance, conversational ability, levels of interest, etc. These qualities mean so much more than penis size which signifies nothing."

"My own penis is longer and thicker than average, but that does not make me feel superior to others with smaller penises. Size is not particularly important to me; as a matter of fact, I am turned on by larger muscular men with small penises."

"If I had to choose, I would say average size is preferred; too large can be painful for either anal or oral sex (also, awkward); too small can also be awkward for various sexual activities. Neither condition is a major obstacle. My own size (moderately large) is of relatively little importance to me. I can graciously accept moderate admiration from a trick; however, I do become uncomfortable when a trick is overly obsessed with a Priapus."

"As sex is not the primary objective when I meet someone, penis size is not important. Too many men think with their cocks, anyway."

"It used to be important and I stared at big cocks whenever I saw them and felt very inferior that mine wasn't bigger. Gradually I have become indifferent to it. I always found the very big numbers very hard to deal with in the mouth and the anus and often not very aesthetic in terms of the whole body. The rest of the body has such great fascination that the cock is not all-important and indeed certain small pricks that I have contemplated lately have struck me as very beautiful."

"Big cocks do not always mean big action. I refer to this as the phallic phallusy."

"Cock size isn't important, just as long as he has one."

"Physically, I look at a man's body and face before I think of noticing his crotch. In contact, it is not the first place I explore."

"For me, it is how well the other guy's head is put on. If he knows where he is at, I don't care if he has one inch."

"My high school friend, the class stud, always acted like he had a two-foot cock, and couldn't do anything with anyone smaller unless he was forced to. But at our first meeting, I found that his cock was only slightly longer than mine, about six inches, and about the same width. We had a rather remarkable relationship, too. Another 'stud' friend was more concerned about his ten inches than I was about my own. But we taught each other a few things about what to do with what you've got, and did well after that. I don't believe cock size is a problem unless a man believes it is. Then all it takes is a sensitive and loving partner to bring out the best."

"I like the story told by a friend (perhaps an old one, and in his case certainly an apocryphal one): one night he found a cock so big, all he could do was hug it all night long, bathing it in his tears."

"Generally one with a monster knows that is his stock in trade, and could be easily self-centered—which aspect encourages me to just admire in passing. If he might indicate warmth and friendliness—well, how nice, and that really becomes the important thing then."

"I get turned on by things like a man's eyes, his face, his

general body type. I'd look at a man's buns and his legs before I'd look at his penis."

"I have known some men to be psychically crippled by the knowledge that they have small penises. This is so sad and unnecessary. They usually were the nicest and most attractive of people. I have wanted some of them for lovers only to have this 'problem' of theirs get in the way—manifesting itself as uncertainty, impotence, insecurity, and a lot of other compulsions. I like all sizes."

How would you define masculinity?

"Masculinity is virility, courage, strength, muscles, a prick and balls."

"Masculinity is being a man. Walking like a man, not swishing. Talking like a man, not lisping. Acting like a man, not getting into a flap at the slightest provocation. But more—it is being able to be forceful, to take command. I suppose masculinity is a state of mind."

"Masculinity is physical. It is a combination of a harder sort of body, body hair, a deep voice, a flat chest, narrow hips, and of course—a cock."

"My first reaction was to answer, 'Having a cock is masculine,' but I think that it is really more a matter of the mind. I feel masculine, therefore I am."

"Masculinity to me is robust and brawny manliness. Males boot-tough and wolf-mean personify masculinity in my way of thinking."

"Masculinity—virile, neat in appearance, conservative in dress, aware, alert, considerate, sense of humor, tenderness, and a capacity for love."

"It's being proud you're a man. It's being sure of yourself. It's being able to laugh at yourself. It's being able to respect yourself and what you are trying to do with your life. It's being openminded and willing to change, being fairly secure with your judgments, and not walking like my mother."

"Masculinity is to me an overall appearance—style of clothing, and lack of affected mannerisms and speech. Those who accentuate their macho image I am very suspicious of— Methinks, thou protesteth too much."

"Masculinity cannot possibly be defined in words or phrases applicable to generalities. There is no question, in my opinion, that some characteristics of both masculinity and femininity work in tandem to produce the element of attractiveness in all people."

"Being masculine is standing up for your God-given rights."

"Leather. That's how I define masculinity."

"It means having a 'masculine' job (construction, pilot, doctor, lawyer) as opposed to a less masculine job (secretary, salesman)."

"Being masculine, to me, certainly means much more than the mere possession of 'balls' and/or the aggressiveness of so-called 'he-men'. I think being masculine truly is being strong and decisive but also kind and tender and loving and tolerant. Jesus Christ, as I understand Him, was the epitome of masculinity."

"To be masculine is to have a cock and balls between one's legs. Period."

"Masculinity means *male*, *manhood*. It means the ability to penetrate, to create, to make, to build. It is strength plus tenderness plus intelligence. A prize fighter or a football player is not necessarily masculine in my book. That's a throwback to something primitive, brutal. That turns me off. A poet is masculine. Any man who fathers anything is masculine. He can father a child, a poem, a philosophy, a building, or an elegant ball gown. As long as he is making it, he is a man. As long as he protects it, provides for it, and fights for it, he is indeed masculine."

"Masculinity is being straight."

"Every man I've heard define masculinity managed to include in that definition everything he liked or enjoyed, and excluded all the things he personally didn't care for. And so each man ended up the prime example of his own idea of manhood. It's too easy a trap to fall into. I think the word is in a lot of ways self-explanatory. Its opposite is femininity. Anything that is acknowledged to be feminine cannot, by definition, also be masculine—however acceptable it may be in a man. We cannot define words simply by what we *want* them to be—they are what they are. As dark is the absence of light, and cold is the absence of heat, masculinity is the absence of femininity—and vice-versa."

"I would say that Golda Meir is masculine."

This question was often cited as the most difficult of the entire group of fifty-five, and it must have been, judging from the diversity of the responses. Clearly, the concept of what constitutes masculinity is a highly individual thing, varying from person to person as well as from culture to culture and from era to era. It may well be that there is no universally acceptable definition of masculinity. The dictionary is of little help: "Of or pertaining to men or boys; male."*

It is evident from most of the responses, however, that gay men attach a much looser definition to the term than most. For many of the respondents, our culture's apparent acceptance of masculinity as a rigid set of mannerisms, actions, and interests was seen as oppressive and damaging: "what we are supposed to be like but aren't." A new concept of masculinity emerges from the replies which follow, one that has little to do with America's traditional ideas on the subject. Many of the men see masculinity primarily as "being yourself," stating that feeling secure about who and what you are is masculine. More than that, many of these men feel that the very concepts of masculinity and femininity are damaging to individual expression and human development and that they should be done away with:

"The term 'masculinity' is so abused, overworked, and emotion-laden that I personally dislike using it. Masculinity is a socially derived term that is subject to definition and refinement depending on what society in time and space is used as a reference point. To me, it does not originate from nature as does the term 'maleness.'"

"In its classical definition, I suspect it's harmful to mental health. It would seem that being masculine is taking pride in one's maleness while slighting one's humanity. For me masculine is shooting ducks in the fall, playing baseball, and proudly announcing that your male children are reading *Playboy* at age six. I reject it all. I suppose masculinity could be a positive concept (maybe) but it seems to be merely a way of dividing the men from the boys from the women."

"Masculinity and femininity are overused, overemphasized, and misunderstood. I, too, think I've been duped by the traditional myths. Rosie Grier is anything but feminine, but he knits (or something like that). Knitting is not considered a masculine activity. It seems like masculinity/femininity criteria have been based upon activities/vocations/avocations. I define myself as masculine, but I can sew, cook, dance (bal-

* *American Heritage Dictionary* (New York: American Heritage and Houghton Mifflin Co.), 1969.

let to disco), but also can lift weights and overhaul an engine. Maybe 'strong' or 'delicate' don't offend me as much."

"I don't define masculinity. It's only a word man made up to hide himself in."

"In terms of human emotions, there is little real difference between masculinity and femininity, except for the limitations placed on each by society's standards and expectations. Man feels the same emotions as woman. He can feel love, joy, delight, happiness, bliss, melancholy, sorrow, grief, shock, trauma, fear, panic, hatred, etc. But he is restricted both in the emotions he can display to fellow humans and the degree of display. Woman may vent any and all of the emotions without restraint."

"I personally see this 'macho' thing as really sick. If a child has a flair for drawing, it is wrong to force this child to abandon the drawing and go outside and play ball, where he does not excel."

"I think masculinity, as such, is a myth just as much as 'macho' is a myth. I think people fall into a trap when they believe in such stereotypes. Besides, the traditional definitions of masculinity and femininity are fading away. It's now considered more masculine to be tender and sensitive. Gays who fall into the 'macho' trap are living an anachronism. As long as people continue to abide by ill-defined roles, terms like masculinity and femininity will persist."

Do you consider yourself masculine?

Most of the men in this survey expressed disapproval of highly effeminate men, as well as effeminate affectation in men not usually given to it. The majority of the respondents (75%) do consider themselves masculine, some within a traditional framework and others within the looser definition of masculinity discussed in answer to the previous question. The men in this survey overwhelmingly take pride in their genital maleness and their ability to perform with their penis. Many men expressed the view that sexuality acted out between two men is the epitome of masculinity.

The men who answered this question affirmatively gave a wide variety of reasons, again reflecting the divergent views of what constitutes masculinity:

"Although I am not an athlete, I certainly consider myself masculine. It is really a matter of degree, I think. Some men are more masculine than I am, and I am more masculine than some men. I daresay that I enjoy the performance of my cock and balls as much as the next man."

"I consider myself masculine now, although I did not *before* I came out seven years ago. My sexual performance may have been affected in the early days of my gayhood. I would not have wanted to be on the receiving end. Now that I'm more comfortable with myself, my likes and dislikes, I'm less concerned about taking the woman's role or man's role."

"Yes, I consider myself masculine. Masculinity to me is men loving men. What better way to show you're a man than to touch, feel, and care about another man? It doesn't mean super strong, super macho, super stud, at least for me. It means caring, in short."

"Gay men like men, right? If they wanted womanly people, they would date women. When another man cruises me, picks me up, makes love to me or loves me, I feel as though I'm as masculine as you can get."

"I am masculine enough on the surface (noneffeminate) to be able to live in the world without being suspect. My inner life abounds in feelings and emotions, gloriously intertwined in terms of male and female expression."

"I am 'masculine' in the sense that I enjoy the things men are supposed to like. I played football in high school and I'm an avid hockey fan. I hunt and fish if that means anything. I do not feel uncomfortable in my occupation (RN), generally considered a female occupation, and always conduct myself in a masculine manner."

"I do not subscribe to the accepted American definition of the unemotional jock. As a child I considered myself 'feminine.' After I entered a heterosexual marriage and fathered two sons, I felt 'masculine.' Despite this equivocation I still consider myself 'masculine' now that I am back in the gay world."

"When my last boss left the company, I felt so strongly about him as a boss and friend that I called my group of thirty employees together to tell them of his forthcoming departure. Halfway through my speech about what a loss he was for the company, I suddenly broke down and cried in front of all of them. For a minute I panicked and felt like a kid who was weak. But then I told them through my tears that I was not ashamed to show how much I felt about my friend and boss. Afterwards, several of the employees told me privately that they were delighted and impressed to see a man, especially one who had the reputation of being so strong, cry in public and show his true feelings so openly, and particularly about another man. I also now find straight men developing quite strong emotions and feelings about me. Yes, I now feel masculine!"

"First, I know the trappings of masculinity are taught nearly from the beginning of understanding to the child as his inherited role. Certainly, I, as male, have learned to behave in acceptable male behavior patterns. In my view it takes great courage and grand defiance to alter or deny cultural heritage to be and act comfortably with yourself and others. So few men really question the condition of masculinity in their lives, and accept as axiom that men are men with appropriate lusts for women, war, and government. To behave otherwise, or to show an acceptance of a different order of priorities, and to 'get away with it' will reward the perpetrator with undying enmity from some and confusion from others. Masculinity has some pretty hefty guard rails around it, and the gay movement has torn some of them away, putting in question the validity of many postures long held sacrosanct."

Some of the men report that they do not consider themselves to be masculine:

"On occasions I have been complimented on my masculinity (a compliment which always tends to make me uneasy). I generally respond to such a compliment by saying, 'Thanks.' Nevertheless, I do feel that within me there is this screaming queen that is dying to come out."

"Masculinity to me is the part of a person that makes the person strive for their goals. In other words, it's in everybody. Yes, there are times that I strive for my goals, but basically I am feminine."

"There is no greater joy to me than to meet a man with a deep voice, who dresses like a man and acts like a man, who is proud and confident of himself. I would like to feel I was masculine, but inside I *know* I lean strongly to the feminine side."

"I am not as butch as I would like. I would, granted one wish, want to be a super hunk type, sort of rough, but not crude."

Many of the men answering this question would prefer not to label themselves one way or the other:

"I think of myself as a man, but I make little effort to cultivate 'masculine' traits if they do not come naturally."

"I'm not too big on any macho concepts, and I haven't really fallen for any of the cigarette ads. In the inevitable contrast with the feminine, I guess masculine means tough and hard. I'm not too masculine in this respect, but I do fully identify myself as a man, and for all my feminine qualities, there's a lot about me that's masculine. Too masculine, in the bad sense, maybe. That is, I have too great a control over my emotions. I don't let myself cry when I should, and I stifle my natural impulses."

"I do not consider myself 'masculine,' nor do I consider myself 'feminine.' I suppose I have some qualities which one might describe as 'masculine,' and others one might consider 'effeminate' or 'feminine.' It is these latter that I value the most highly!"

"Given only two choices, fit the mold (masculinity or femininity) or be a pariah, I am a pariah. Unfortunately, as noble as this sounds, I am not nearly brave enough to tell society to fuck off (I'm a little too sensitive to physical abuse). So I am tenuously clothed in masculinity, which, thank God, I can take off and hang up in the closet."

"I am not too spectacular an example of the totally masculine man. I am of average height, slightly overweight, a bit nearsighted, very soft-voiced, and have never been a sportsman. I'm into art, music, and literature. But while I have many qualities which I acknowledge are considered to be feminine, I sincerely don't think I'm effeminate. I accept myself with the particular blend of masculine and feminine which is a part of me, but I would never consider myself an ideal of anything, nor would I judge others as to masculinity or femininity by how they compared to me."

"I'm 'macho' enough to pass as straight, but I don't work on projecting a 'butch' image. I don't put down anyone for being effeminate. Our culture has terribly limiting sex roles. I'm not sure what true 'masculinity' is. One social-science study reports that men who feel most confident and at ease with their 'masculine' sex roles are the ones most likely to switch and play the passive partner in anal intercourse. What does this do to the definition of a 'queen'? Gays spend altogether too much time worrying about whether they're masculine or feminine. People, biologically and psychologically, are mixtures of both. I like it that way."

PART THREE: RELATIONSHIPS

How would you characterize your emotional involvements with men? For example, are you usually like buddies, like father and son, or what?

The egalitarian nature of most male homosexual partnerships is by far the dominant theme emerging from the responses to this question. Rather than role-playing, 65% of the men characterize their relationships as "buddies," "brothers," or "equals." In addition, another 14.6% report that the general tone their relationship takes "depends" on their partner—his age, his social status, his education, his wealth, his personality, etc.—and that they are flexible in how they relate to other men. Just 7% of the respondents see their relationships in terms of specific roles such as father-son, master-slave, etc.

It is also clear from these answers that gay relationships are just as loving and meaningful as their straight counterparts. A great deal of feeling comes through in these answers, and in those about lovers which follow. Where gay relationships may be said to differ is in the frequent camaraderie between partners, quite apart from sexual attraction. One respondent summed this idea up when he wrote, "My involvements are as friends. It's just like having a best buddy—with the extra element of sex added."

This was the dominant theme expressed in these answers. For many men, having a best friend with whom they could share everything—including sex—was the epitome of a human relationship:

"I like a man who is a friend—someone who shares trust and warmth and caring for each other. I like to feel needed and appreciated and I would hope the other guy would also. Sex, for me, is a lot of touching and feeling and getting close to someone—not just something quick."

"It is very important to me that any man I'm romantically involved with be my friend. This 'buddy-ship' means a lot to me because when I was in junior high and high school I was a misfit, an outcast. I was made fun of, I never got on teams, I

167

didn't have a single male friend. Now that I've gotten my act together and my emotional world doesn't set me apart from my peers I make it a point to play sports, go on camping trips, go fishing, etc. with guys—all the things I longed to do as a kid but couldn't. I could never play a role. If a man doesn't want me as first and foremost his friend, then I'm not interested."

"My involvement with other men is always like we are buddies, or at least that's what I strive for. Since adolescence I have been thrilled by the act of putting my arm around another man's shoulders. I very much want to have a man-to-man relationship with my friend and I value this element of masculinity and athletic-type buddyship very much. I like seeing two guys together—whether they are straight or gay. I believe masculinity can be realized as readily through another man as it can through a woman."

"What I like about my relationships with gay men (and a few straight friends as well) is the relaxed intimacy, the lack of competitiveness that marks many straight male relationships, the ability to admit weaknesses and fears without the problem of letting the other dominate—in general the lack of role-playing."

"Relationships I have preferred have usually been along the buddy-buddy line. Sort of a friendship, but with an extra added dimension (and that's emotional, not just sexual). Lately, I've been giving a lot of thought to whether I want a permanent relationship with anybody at this point in my life, and the only thing I know for sure is that I'd want it to be that kind of relationship—friendship at the core, with an extra layer of love."

"I would characterize my emotional involvements with men as caring, loving, joyful, serious. I guess I cannot compare it to other relationships such as father-son or brother-brother since I find it to be very different from other relationships. It is a finely combined intellectual, emotional, and physical interplay, both fulfilling and exciting."

"My emotional involvement with anyone is solely with the intent of learning all about that individual; since each of us is purported to be 'unique' in our own way. I explore the depths of their minds in search of those qualities which may or may not complement mine; and thus may or may not prompt me to 'attach' myself to them. Each new introduction makes life's pursuit of happiness a never-ending, all times learning experience."

"I am totally wrapped up in him, what he does, his ideas, goals and plans in life, and past life experiences. We are buddies."

"I try to treat each guy I spend time with as a potential lover. I try to be caring, loving, and affectionate and treat him as a human being."

"We are close and intimate friends. A man is someone with whom I share life's pleasures and pains, assist in any way I can (while not asking anything in return unless in dire need), go places and do things with, share confidences with; and general enjoyment unique only to these relationships."

"I have to be able to relate to them in my general activities. Therefore, usually any real involvement (emotional or otherwise) only gets underway if I can find more in that person than physical attraction."

Many men felt strongly about maintaining equality in their relationships:

"In order for me to even begin an emotional involvement, I must be able to respect a man for his thoughts, his achievements, his integrity, his values, and his view of life. I must be, indeed demand to be, respected for the same things. From such a respect may issue a fine balance of emotions, and from such a balance one can feel when to be a 'giver' and when to be a 'taker' emotionally, and a pleasant symbiosis can be the result—based on independence and personal integrity."

"I don't see either person as superior to the other, or dominant, but rather as equals trying to share time together, somehow adding to each other's life, giving each new learning experiences in life that will better each person involved."

"I have a lover with whom I have lived for two and a half years. Our relationship is one of equality. There is no real role-playing. Both in bed and around the house we each play a full variety of roles."

"In each of my relationships there have been various degrees of dominance, but only the ones that are more or less a sharing as equals survive into a good many years."

"The men I become involved with (and stay involved with) are totally free towards me and my behavior, and are totally equal to me in their behavior. I am me, and they are who they are, and we love each other (sexually or not—who cares?)."

"I suppose the easiest way to characterize my relationships is that of married straights. As a matter of fact, in my present relationship we use the term 'wiband.' It is half of *wi*fe and half of hus*band*; we are each a wiband, thus equal in the relationship, and we also avoid one being exclusively male or female as in husband and wife."

"I prefer relationships that have some kind of equality as a basis. I do not like to play father, though I'm getting to the age where I may appeal to certain younger men in that light. It has been a great disappointment, to say the least, that relationships usually end up with one member dominant and the other, if not passive, at least upstaged."

"I never or very rarely play roles in a relationship unless it is clearly understood to be in fun. We are foremost two men, unique individuals who love each other and like each other as much as we can."

Many men find it difficult to categorize their relationships because they vary from person to person, and sometimes vary within a relationship:

"My emotional relationships with men are enormously varied, not only from man to man, but within my relationship with each man I know. The ideal for me is the relationship I would call 'soul mates.' This, I suppose, is a spiritual variation of what you call buddies, but buddies is somehow too macho a word for me. As for familial terms, well, yes, father and son, but also son and father when the situation calls for it (50/50); brothers, too, and sisters, and I have to admit there's a whole lot of mother in me."

"With one lover, it definitely was a father-son relationship because I provided financial support and was in many ways a teacher and therefore something of a father figure. With another lover, there was a sense of being buddies; with still another, almost of being 'sisters' (the third brought out the 'queen' in me)."

"The one and only time I had a lover, I was his buddy, his father, his mother, his brother, his nurse, his minister, etc. etc. I most prefer, though, to have a man who is able to take care of himself, but when he needs me, I'm there to give whatever I can."

"I have always let my emotional involvements with other men and boys take on their own character. I become whatever the other person wants me to be. Sometimes I am a buddy, sometimes I am a father, sometimes I am a woman. I find my greatest pleasure in giving pleasure to the other person, making no demands of any kind whatsoever. I have found that the looser I hold a sex partner, the longer I hold him."

"The type of relationship depends on the age of the partner. I prefer a relationship that is one of equals. Sometimes when a person is between twenty and thirty I find that I have or can develop a fatherly instinct towards him. When it does happen, it normally dampens the sex relationship inasmuch as I then have the feeling that I am 'taking advantage' of him. I feel the only significant relationship is one that is freely entered into by each party and one to which each party contributes."

"I like it when the interaction is so fluid it cannot be characterized."

"No human being is all one thing or all another. Each one of our personalities is made up of a myriad of emotions. I like it best when each one of my 'mini-personalities' gets to take over and do its thing. It makes me feel like a much more rounded individual, and that's good."

Some men find any kind of relationship with another man a difficult proposition:

"My 'emotional involvements' usually consist of nothing more than one-night stands, a state that displeases me. I am thirty-four and have been married (to a woman) for ten years. The ideal 'buddy relationship' I have been desiring for years has never materialized."

"For the last two or three years, there hasn't been much involvement, just pleasant conversation and sex. When I was younger, I looked for father figures, but though they were older men, I never found what I was looking for. They were more lost than I."

"For the most part I am very remote around men in general. I inspire a kind of loyalty from men but rarely am able to let them get close to me. They will tell me their most intimate secrets but I tell very little of myself."

"My emotional relationships with other men seem to be somewhat like being a pair of romantic lemmings—involved and caring, but knowing in the back of our minds that the odds of overcoming the apparent gay destiny of relationship failures are probably low. As much as one might like to think that he is not subject to societal laws and roles, the fact is that embroilment in that sort of thing is part of the temporal existence known as life."

"I always want to be more emotionally involved with my friends, both male and female, than I usually am. I feel a need to be close friends, to feel an exchange of love. I rarely achieve it, however. I only have my lover and my wife who fit the description."

"My emotional involvements have been mainly with straight men all my life, but they would not know how I felt toward them. My history of gay sex life kept since 1939 is full of more action with straights than with gays. As a loner and one-night-stander, emotion plays little part in sex. Emotion plays more with those I admire and don't have sex with."

"I fell desperately in love with one college roommate, but it was unknown to him and unfulfilled and represented several years of pure agony, especially as we became separated."

"The last three emotional involvements I had ended in sexual rejection of me by my lover. The primary reason this happened is because, as the relationship continued, they started to relate to me more as a substitute father and less as a lover. There was no significant age difference in any of the relationships. This is not what I am looking for in a relationship and I am currently undergoing psychotherapy to find out what I have been doing wrong."

Some men have seen changes in their ability to relate:

"For many years any emotional involvement was an anathema to me since I mistakenly associated such involvement only with pain and suffering. Coming from an alcoholic family probably had much to do with this mistaken early impression. My early emotional involvements with men were few and shallow mainly because I was paranoid that my true sexual preference would be discovered. Now my emotional involvement is with my lover and while much emotional growth is necessary I at least am able to feel and express my emotions which had been repressed for years. I am no longer afraid of emotional involvement and would say that the relationship between my lover and myself could be best characterized as two men sharing equally the pleasure, pain, joy, and sorrow of our lives together."

"There has always been a fear of discovery and rejection by straight men, therefore close relationships have been difficult to establish. Relationships with women as friends have been easier to establish. Since I came out close relationships with men have been easier to establish because of less fear of rejection."

"I have been by earlier emotional 'overboards' and I'm much more careful now. Realistically, how the hell can someone allow that they are 'in love' with you thirty seconds after meeting you? It's BS. Let's face it, I'm no spring chicken—I'm forty-five and fairly well settled—I enjoy sex but a friend lasts longer."

"I used to be a little girl, clinging vine looking for that great big wonderful supportive he-man my mother structured me into looking for. Then I discovered my own strengths. I can't really stereotype my relationships now; we're just two people relating from our own strengths and weaknesses."

"As a young man, I consciously sought the approval of older men, via sex, achievement, or whatever means possible. As an older man, I still seek that approval, incongruous as it may seem, but I seek it from strong, mature males. Sex is no longer a tool to achieve that result."

"My involvements with men are very emotional. I tend to become totally taken up with the affection I feel for the particular one. The great tragedy is that for a good half of my life I did not even have the vocabulary nor social approbation to make sense out of what was and still is the strongest emotion of my life. Now, thank God, I feel good about my attractions to men. I think they are beautiful—the emotions, I mean. And men in general are beautiful, too."

For some gay men, the most satisfying relationship is platonic:

"I have a number of gay friends with whom I have not had sex, and probably never will. We're 'buddies' and enjoy being together—socially, for dinner, for movies or sports events, camping and fishing. I like—or dislike—a person for what he is. I'm selective in my continuing relationships and find myself turned off by bar butterflies and downright 'whores'—how shallow."

"I have three very close friends. My relationship with them is what one would call 'brotherly.' I am currently living with two of these people and we have never had sex, or really even thought of it, although we gleefully share tales of the previous night's experiences."

"Of all the men I've been involved with, I don't love anyone as much as my best friend, with whom I've never had sex. It is truly a spiritual love. We have so much in common and care so much about each other that we don't want to spoil it by having sex. Both of us think that after we've been through years of muck and heartache and broken love affairs, we'll settle down with each other and get old together."

Some men do characterize their relationships in terms of particular roles. Some of these were father-son:

"My emotional involvements are all father-son because at my age and in my situation (late forties, professor) I simply can't manage to be a buddy to the kind of boy I like. To make matters worse, I like independent, self-assured kids (right now, I'm keeping—without sex—a champion athlete) to whom I can, at most, be a mentor. Kids I enjoy sex with usually bore me silly. What I suspect I want is a beautiful, intelligent son I can fuck."

"My emotional involvements with men have always been composed of friendship, love, concern, and erotic attraction. I should also add that I have always felt a strong desire to look after someone else's well-being because I derive great satisfaction from seeing another person happy and knowing that that happiness is partly attributable to me. Sometimes the situation requires that I play the father role and sometimes it requires that I play the son role. I find both of them equally satisfying, but I do not like to remain in the same role all the time. Basically, I rejoice in the idea of being needed by another male."

"My lover is much younger than I and we both love our families very much. When my lover and I started living together, one of my sons became very suspicious and made several snide remarks. Later in the year we attended a family reunion (mine) in Louisiana and all my relatives accepted him as a good friend of my son's. This gave us the idea for adoption, so we immediately started the legal wheels turning and I legally adopted him and had his name changed to mine. Most of his and my relatives accept him as my son."

"I usually call my tricks and lovers daddy, even though they are a great deal younger than I. Basically, I think I always have been in love with my father. I tend to be attracted to men who have traits similar to his."

"A few times I have fallen in love with a father image. In real life I have an older brother and a father who I never liked or loved, but who I got in the habit of obeying and being protected by."

"I play the role of the father, someone who's older, someone to lean on, someone they can count on for financial support. I would just like to have one lasting relationship based on buddies. Sons grow up and move on to lives of their own, but buddies *can* last forever."

A few of the men described sexual roles such as man/woman and slave/master:

"It is like a man and a woman, with me in the woman's role. In most things other than of a sexual nature I am very masculine and independent. I can do harder physical labor than those I have relationships with—I can run faster, hike farther and longer, carry more weight, am more independent, etc. But in my mind I characterize myself as in the dependent, more feminine role. I am also a better cook and an easier housekeeper."

"I guess I would sincerely have to say my emotional involvements with men are on a master-slave basis, although I would not want a cruel man for a 'master' or partner. I like to admire the other man tremendously and look up to him, and I seem to enjoy a little domination. Please understand, I am not into sadomasochism in the true sense, but I enjoy a touch of it."

Some men do not care how other men relate to them:

"I want a lover so badly I really wouldn't care what role he wanted me to play (short of anything violent or painful). I'm very flexible—I think you have to be to get a lover."

"I just want to be loved."

Some of the men described their relationships to heterosexual men:

"I have a very difficult time establishing a friendship with heterosexual men. None of the men I would consider my good friends are straight. When I am confronted with a situation which could possibly lead to a simple friendship, I can recognize apprehension and anxiety directly related to the amount of sexual feeling I have for the man. I usually find myself mentally squaring off with every man as a bedfellow, overlooking him as a person."

"My deepest emotional involvement with another man has been with my apartment-mate, who is straight, but knew of my gayness before living with me. Our relationship goes beyond buddies, sharing all aspects of our lives except sex. His presence and continued acceptance during my coming out smoothed the road so that I never lost self-respect or felt guilt."

"I have three people who I consider true friends—only one of whom is gay. I suppose that we, whenever we are together, can tune into the same wavelengths so that we can, in effect, become the other person. I suppose we are in love, and we have verbalized that to each other, but we are too close to each other for a physical relationship."

"I have a very hard time dealing with my heterosexual friends, my best friend in particular. He's my best friend because I like his qualities, qualities I want to find in a lover. While I accept the friendship for what it is, I have a deep longing that it could be something more for me."

"Friendships with straight men are difficult. I tend to hold back and I am not really myself. I always fear that any offer of close and sincere friendship might be misinterpreted as meaning 'too much.' With rare exceptions I have never admitted I'm gay to straight friends, which causes further strain."

Do you have a lover? When and how did you meet?

Forty-one percent of the men report that they have a lover. The definition of this word, however, varied somewhat. Some men described their lover as someone whom they see more than others; some indicated having several lovers; most of the men who answered yes to this question either share a home with or devote a large majority of their time to this person.

The men with lovers met their lovers in a wide variety of ways. It used to be that one of the few places gay men could meet each other was a gay bar or, occasionally, a private party given by a gay acquaintance. Now, with gay men so much more open about their orientation, they can meet practically anywhere. In addition to gay bars, dating services, and baths, places mentioned where respondents met their lovers include "a pen-pal club," "through business," "hitchhiking," "at our gym," "on bicycles," "on the bus," "at church," "in school," and "at a political dinner."

Some of the initial meetings were highly interesting:

"We met May 15, 1975. I was nineteen at the time, a sophomore at Oregon State University. I had never met a gay person before but had wanted to find out about gays and to try gay sex. I was very naive, and did not know how or where gays met, so I decided that maybe gay people or people like myself who suspected they were gay would check out books in the school library on the subject. So I browsed through the books and noticed this guy's name in the check-out card in several books. I looked his name up in the student guide and wondered what a business student would be doing checking books on homosexuality. So I wrote him an anonymous note telling him about myself, and asking him if he was interested, to leave a note in one book in particular. Several days later, I returned to the library and found he had left a note. We did this back and forth and gradually I built up enough courage to write him my name and address, which eventually led up to us meeting in person on May 15. We liked each other right away, fell in love, and have been together ever since!"

"I met my lover through my wife's brother. He was his roommate during college. We lived together for a year and a half."

"My lover and I met through my supervisor at work. Her boyfriend and my lover both drive buses. He was in the same hospital room that she was at. She told me he was from New York and I went to give him my regards, thinking he'd have no visitors. After several months of writing and visiting, I moved to New York City to be with him."

"He's my neighbor. We met three years ago. In June 1977 I came home drunk from a party and went to his house, instead of home. That night, our relationship as lovers began. We don't live together, but he does live about thirty feet away. I'm very happy with this because we see each other often. His wife and two children suspect nothing."

"I was unloading redwood planters from a van for a friend at a busy urban-center plant shop. He walked around the corner of the van and turned around and there he was. A policeman. It was his regular area to patrol and he knew about the plant-shop owner and he asked about the planters and then about who I was. We started to talk. I asked him if he could come over for supper sometime. We have been lovers now two years December 16. Needless to say, he came over. We live together because I would be worried if he didn't come home and touch base . . . he has a dangerous job."

"This question involves a rather complicated answer since in fact I have two lovers. Jim #1 I met on Grant Avenue here in San Francisco. We do live together. I was window shopping, not looking where I was going, and kicked his cane away. We both fell. We've been together ever since. We are both very happy about the sharing. For the first time in our lives we have a *home*. We've been together two and a half years. Our relationship was solemnized with a Holy Union performed at the Metropolitan Community Church in L.A. on August 28, 1976.

"Jim #2 (their first names are the same) I met at the 'tubs.' We waltzed around each other for almost a year, each afraid to approach the other. Finally one night I decided, 'What the hell, he can't do any more than tell me to bug off!' He didn't and it's beautiful! That was seventeen months ago. He lives alone. While some of our friends have trouble dealing with our threesome, we do not. We have found our separate relationships are enhanced due to our relationships to each other."

"We met seven years ago. I was a friend of his mother, who wanted to get me into bed. I met her sons and fell in love with one of them."

"We met at Disneyland, where we both were employed. As I would have to pass his booth when I would go on a break, I would stop and talk with him. One day I had to find out if he was gay or not, so I broke the ice by asking him where he goes on Saturday nights. He named a few straight bars and then I said that I also went out and mentioned some of the local gay bars. He then mentioned that he had been to some of them, too. After work that night, we went to the local gay bar and later to his house. This started a long and lasting relationship."

"We were introduced at a small dinner party given by a member of my church. The straight couple who introduced us—now in their seventies—have remained close friends, almost like surrogate parents for both of us."

"After tiring of bars and baths and not being able to find a lover in them, I put an ad in the *Berkeley Barb*. My lover was one of those to answer it and we started going together. I had doubted this method would work, but since it has proved successful for me, I'd recommend it for other gays who also want lovers."

Some relationships have lasted an unusually long period of time:

"We met almost twenty-eight years ago in a little New York bar that was half gay/half straight. We began living together in a new apartment about eight months later and stayed there until we moved to California, where we built a home of our own where we have lived for twenty-one years. Yes, I'm happy with the 'living together' and can't imagine ever being alone again, although with life expectancy being what it is, it's inevitable that one of us is going to have to bury the other."

"For the past twenty years we have shared an apartment and for eighteen have been co-owners of a co-op apartment. It is how I always wanted it but for the first several years my partner was afraid to commit himself, afraid that living with me would limit his sexual options, afraid that being younger, I would tire of him. From rooms near each other in a residence club, I was the first to take an apartment, to which he came for most evening meals and in which he spent weekends. I feel now that this is a good arrangement, instead of rushing into 'playing house' as I call it, as soon as some do. I most decidedly am happy living with him and at our present ages, don't feel I could settle for anything else."

"We met December 23, 1955, at a party thrown by mutual friends. I was 'hit by lightning' as the Europeans say—love at first sight! At our second meeting (before any sex) I showed him an apartment I wanted us to share, and incredibly enough, he agreed to live with me. Even after twenty-two years our love and affection for each other is strong—perhaps stronger than when we first met, because we now have more shared experiences."

"We met December 26, 1953, in the restroom of a movie-burlesque theater. I refused to have anything to do with him there or to go with him to a cheap hotel. I thought him to be a member of the vice squad, a Baptist minister, or a very successful businessman. He was the latter. He invited me to a gay bar and there we were properly introduced by a mutual friend. I invited him to my apartment. He hesitated to accompany me there when I told him that one of my gay 'sisters' was staying with me for a few days. He thought that my friend and I might set him up to rob him. I was rather scroungy in dirty jeans and scuffed shoes and my hair was long and a ragged mess. I was poor but rather proud. He was impressed with a few antiques in my almost empty apartment. When I showed him one of my poems in a famous literary magazine, he fell like a ton of bricks. We do not live together, but we mutually own a very lovely house in Dallas. I'm happy with this arrangement because I like to be alone a great deal."

"Met him August 5, 1933. Our families were friends but we were not aware of each other's homosexuality until we met at a gay beach. Yes we live together and are very happy. Frankly it is the only way for lovers to live if they are sincere lovers."

Most respondents who have lovers live with them:

"We have been together for nearly six years. We were introduced by a mutual acquaintance. We live together in a house we are buying together. I am extremely happy with this . . . for so many reasons I couldn't begin to name them all. Just the ease and comfort of our life together is plenty of reason to be happy. I never would have believed it could happen to me. We have enough common interests that there's always something to share, and enough diversity that conversation never gets boring. Our lives, our outlooks, and our interests are constantly expanding. We're both better people— and more complete—together than we ever could have been apart."

"It has been said, 'You don't go to the baths looking for a lover.' I wasn't looking, but that's where my lover and I met. We live together and have for four years in almost idyllic compatibility. Having been married for thirteen years to a woman in almost complete incompatibility, I know whereof I speak, and not just from sexual standpoints."

"Living together with my lover has been a fantastic growth experience for me. He is older and much more academic than I; with that comes the people who surround him and their variety. Each of these encounters is usually so varied, so diverse it really allows me to experience life with more than just my two eyes. After six years, am I still happy with living with my lover? Yes, because he still stimulates my mind and turns me on sexually."

"Our relationship works very well, I feel, because we are both in our mid-thirties, are mature and have had various relationships with other men and have learned how to live with a partner. We have a warm regard and love for each other and try to comfort and take care of one another."

"We met in a bar about three and a half years ago. We live together and are buying a house and restoring it and have lived together for about two years now and it is going quite well. I consider myself quite lucky and have never been happier in my life. A lasting relationship is of utmost importance to me. Someone with whom I can share things and really know the meaning and purpose of human life."

"We began seeing each other very hesitantly, neither of us really being out. It was a month before we broached our mutual gayness, and two months before we slept together. We live together, and I am very happy with this because I feel that to be in love really ideally means sharing as much of life as possible. This is what having a lover means to me."

"It's nice to have someone to stand by you and do things with; we have a lot of common interests and we do almost everything together. I enjoy having a nice peaceful home life where we can talk and just be together. We go out now and then, but not as often as when we were both single."

"I am happy with our relationship, because we get along so well together and I don't have to go scrounging around for sex."

"I prefer to think of Denis as my mate rather than just my lover. We met through a pen-pal club in July 1977. At the present we live together with my mother until we save up enough money to get our own place. I'm as happy as I have ever been. My life is completely new because I love him more than anything or anyone."

Quite a few of the men in this survey have lovers with whom they do not live. In many cases, this is a matter of choice:

"I met my lover two and a half years ago while cruising the Promenade in Brooklyn Heights. He was actively cruising; I was just recovering from a quick trick. We don't live together—a situation that is practical, if anything. He's very disorganized and often explosive. I work at home and need calm and order. There are also problems of privacy: I need a sense of my own place; other than family, I've never lived with anyone."

"The main reason we have not moved in together is that financially it would be a hardship (re New York's rent-control laws) and our current inexpensive rents allow many luxuries (travel, concerts, etc.) we would have to cut back on if we found a place together . . . we are equally at home in each other's place and share our lives together totally, including finances."

"I currently have a lover twenty-five years younger than I am. He used to deliver newspapers to my door when he was sixteen or seventeen, and I thought he was the most beautiful thing I had ever seen. Over two years ago we struck up a serious acquaintanceship and we started going out together. He became interested in the gay lifestyle and admitted that he had been attracted to men as well as women since he was ten years old. Finally we became lovers. We do not live together. We both agree this is best, because we are both so very much alike, very independent, and we care so much for each other we only want to be at our 'best' when we meet. Nothing kills 'love' more quickly than spending the night with someone who 'breaks wind' or having to use the bathroom right after someone had a bowel movement and left an odor, etc. So we get together when we both agree that we feel and look great!"

"There are a number of reasons I felt separate households are best for the present, but primarily it is because I have a lot of work to do at home, and prefer not to have the temptation to fall into long-established patterns of behavior—cooking, doping, etc.—that are very time-consuming and pleasant, but relatively nonproductive."

Some of the men don't live with their male lover because one or the other of them is married to a woman:

"I have a lover of some eleven years' standing. We are long-distance lovers as he lives in Los Angeles and I in Oakland. He is deeply closeted with a wife who is completely unaware of his homosexuality. We have a constant correspondence and manage to get together for a weekend about once a quarter."

"We do not live together at present due to the fact that he has a wife and has not dissolved the marriage yet, although he is in the process. I am very happy with the relationship. I still have fears about the 'this is another burn' syndrome because of a past relationship and since my profession facilitates seeing many failing relationships. I fear that pain. However, this other person is aware of the difficulty of getting gay relationships off the ground and wants to give it a hell of a try. That is one reason for having a prolonged dating and courtship period and for me not to meddle in or rush the marriage problems he is undergoing at present. I think that has a very strengthening force in the formation of the relationship."

"I have a friend who I make it with often. We have been making it since we were about thirteen. We love each other but we are not in love. In fact, he is married and has five kids. We met in seventh grade, discovered sex together, and have been lovers ever since."

"I would love to live with my lover, but since we both have families, this is out. I would leave my family to live with him but he is too deeply closeted for such a move. The thing such a move would bring to me is that I would have a constant exchange of sex and love. I have love but not sex with my spouse. The ideal situation, of course, would be a trio with my lover and my wife."

Others find societal and family pressure too great to establish such a relationship:

"My lover and I met during new student orientation week about three months ago at the seminary we attend. I had been attracted to him and during a dorm party I sat next to him and allowed our hands to touch. He picked up the signal and we went to my room for sex. Instead of having sex, we made love and within the week had told each other we were in love. Since our school is not positive toward gays, we are not yet able to live together 'officially' in the dorms. Yet he has spent most of the evenings these three months in my room because I do not have a double room. We joke about his having to periodically 'dust off' his sheets so his suite-mate will not notice the collection. This school does not allow two people of the same sex to rent a school-owned apartment (due to their gross homophobia) but we as members of a semi-underground faculty-student committee are attempting to change school policy. Ironically, for next year, we will be able to request each other as roommates."

"Tom and I met at our job. We work for the federal government, and not only can we not live together but we hardly even acknowledge each other in the halls. We're positive that if they knew we were gay we'd be fired. It's a terribly depressing situation and has created a terrible strain in our relationship. We've talked about getting less sensitive jobs but that's almost impossible for a variety of reasons. So we do the best we can, which ain't much."

"My lover and I are in the air force, and as you might suspect it's pretty damn difficult to be lovers when you're in the AF, much less live together. We would both like nothing better than to live together as a couple in base housing, but I don't suppose that will ever happen. To make matters worse, my lover wants to make this his career. I'm hoping I can talk him out of it."

"We met at a party. We do not live together. If I did live with him I would be very happy. I would cook and clean for him. I can't move out now because I'm only sixteen."

"My lover and I could never live together because we're both policemen. It's bad enough we're not married, and keep to ourselves. I'm pretty sure some of the guys suspect that we're gay. We usually don't acknowledge each other on duty unless we absolutely have to. It's a real shitty state of affairs and we both hate it."

"I couldn't live with Tom because in this hick town everybody knows everybody else's business. Christ, we have to leave town separately to get together!"

Of those men who do not have lovers, many had such a relationship but it did not last:

"We met at the YMCA in the fall of 1973. We lived together the entire three years. We were happy, but we spent too much time together and consequently became too emotionally dependent on each other. We shut out the rest of the world, so to speak."

"I might find someone who I'll love as much as I love Robert, but I know I'll never find anyone I'll love more. I love him with all my capacity. Robert and I did live together for a summer and we were extremely happy. While living in the apartment an intimacy grew between us that was unlike anything I've ever known. At the end of the summer, I moved back to the city where I had been attending college. I had a substantial music scholarship there and a situation advantageous to both my education and my career. The city was too far away for Robert and I to visit each other. We could only write and talk on the phone. I consider my moving to be the biggest mistake of my life. I'll never forgive myself for putting my desire for a college degree above my love for Robert. Before the end of the school year he had found someone else. My being there may not have prevented that but even if it hadn't I would have had a few more months of the happiest time of my life."

"The lover I had at nineteen fell in love with this street character I'd done. He arranged with my stage director to take me to a night spot and that's how we met. After four years of pain, he finally told me that he was not in love with me but the character I did."

"We were happy and unhappy at the same time. What I mean is that we had mutual respect and admiration for one another but not too much in common—not to mention that it was the first relationship for both of us and we were making mistakes right and left. Also, we were sexually incompatible—I being much more sexual than he. The added frustration about that was that we both feel very strongly about a monogamous relationship. Hence, I felt I was becoming a virgin all over again. I cared too much for him to have sex with others."

"I let him pick me up in the park. He was twenty-six. Incredibly, he was a one-in-a-million sincere man who became my friend and lover for three years. It was the relationship gays seek—and I got him on my very first shot. But since it was my first shot, I had no idea that he was rare. And I treated him very badly, mostly because I was totally unaccepting of myself as gay at the time. I projected all of my self-hatred there, despite the fact that I was drawn to him. I never told him he was my first lover, and I made up a sexual history for myself. He taught me some self-acceptance and let me see a gay who was good and intelligent and masculine and decent—the first one I ever knew existed. For a time, he was in love with me. But because I didn't recognize the concept of gay love, I didn't return it or even fully realize it was being offered. By the time I was ready for it, he was fed up with my 'problems' and coldness and no longer loved me. We stopped being even friends. But I still love him."

What is it about your lover that made you fall in love with him?

Dr. Irving Bieber, a gay sexuality researcher and originator of the famous "close-binding mother/distant father" theory to explain homosexual development, wrote in 1965: "Despite the distortions and elaborate projections of the adult homosexual partnership," one of its primary goals remains that of sexual gratification."*

However, the findings of this survey indicate that sexual considerations play no more than a typically important role in most "adult homosexual partnerships." Rather than being the primary consideration in pairings of any duration, sex is most often cited as of only relative importance. In fact, when sex *was* the primary reason for a gay relationship, the respondents frequently report that it did not last.

Although the relationships of most of the respondents began through sexual attraction, falling in love had more to do with other aspects of their partner's personality than his sexuality:

"My lover is my best friend. We view many things in the same way. We are different in other ways, but they always seem to be complementary. He understands me and we are supportive of one another—we act as mirrors so we can both grow and through that growth come to love one another in a deeper, more meaningful way (although at this point, it is still more than I have ever known or shared with another)."

"As for my lover's particular attributes, I find him warm, sensitive and kind. He allows me my independence as I allow him his. He's loving and generous, interested in my work and progress, undemanding of my time. I like knowing he's around, I like his excitements, and I can sympathize with his disappointments and despairs. I like him when he's funny and when he's serious. I like to watch him when he's sleeping. I love his mind. Well, hell, I just love everything about him."

"I did not fall in love with him immediately and only after we gradually came to know each other did love enter the picture. Although I love him for many sundry reasons I suppose his character is one of the most important. He tolerates my temper and peculiarities with unusual calm; he also appreciates my love and efforts to a very great extent; he's true to himself, not ever wearing a facade, and he appreciates so many of the little things in life as I do."

"He is a gentleman. He treats me like I'm special by his consideration, understanding and warm sexual love. He is masculine and sturdy and I can relate to that also. He demonstrated to me a lot of common sense, fair play and

* Irving Bieber, "Clinical Aspects of Male Homosexuality," in *Sexual Inversion*, ed. Judd Marmor (New York: Basic Books, 1965), pp. 254–55.

good manners. He offered me security and it all adds up to love."

"I didn't like him at first. But he seemed to offer me unconditional love. He saw things in me I didn't and made me grow."

"It was mostly his response and attraction to me. I guess I am the type who has to know that he is wanted for something other than sex to formulate a relationship and feel secure that another guy wants me."

"I fell in love with him because he fell in love with me. Because he called me from Israel one morning to say hello. Because he made me feel his feelings just by looking at me."

"I think you fall in love with someone for a million reasons. In my case, my lover makes me feel warm inside. He can be strong and forceful, then terribly vulnerable. He is one of the most sensitive people I've ever met, and his efforts sometimes to hide that are very touching. He loves his family with all his heart. He also loves me, and he's the first man I've ever been involved with who has given me confidence that the relationship is going to last. He's loyal, and I know I can be myself with him and that making a mistake or a series of mistakes won't send him off to greener pastures. He's wonderfully affectionate and makes me feel loved."

Mutual need was a contributing factor to love in some cases:

"We were the same age, each with a family, each gay (and married). His married life was a disaster. My marriage was at a terminal standstill and I was deeply closeted with my homosexuality. We were good for each other at that particular time in our lives."

"He lacked schooling, experience, and refinement, but he was sincere and strong-willed if he wanted to be. I wanted to help him learn and grow. Here was the big brother coming out in me. This was the first time I ever experienced this type of relationship."

"The type of guy I usually fall for is someone younger than me, good-looking, slender and lonely. Most of my loves have come from broken homes and have parents who can't find the time to let the guy know they love him."

"We were both emotional wrecks because our previous relationships had failed and we were convinced that relationships were impossible in the gay world. It was almost a self-fulfilling prophecy because our fear of being hurt again kept

us at a distance for a long time. But we needed each other
and an emotional attachment so much that we finally came
together. So far, it's working."

In several instances physical attraction led to emotional commitment:

"I was attracted to him immediately, on a physical level,
because he is beautiful. But I began to love him when, after
many conversations and exchanges of letters, I found that our
interests and outlooks were so similar. Best of all, he seemed
to like me very much as a *person* rather than just admiring
what I can do. And he seemed to need what I had to offer in
return: affection and companionship. We both declared our
love for each other, hesitantly and fearfully, before there had
been any physical contact between us at all."

"I fell in love with him at first, purely physically. I loved
his looks and build, his smile and voice, and his big eager
cock. That was years ago. Now I love a tender, sensitive,
sometimes confused person. I worry about his health, and
nurse him when necessary. I cook dinners for him, give him
presents, go places with him. I do not criticize or try to
change him. I love him."

"I was first attracted to his physical appearance, but I soon
became more interested in his mind and emotions. In fact, I
believe that I fell in love with his mind first because our early
sexual experiences turned out rather poorly. I realized that
despite this we had a great deal in common, but also that
some of his interests were almost foreign to me and vice
versa. I was excited by the prospect of learning new things
from him and being able to teach him new things."

**Of course, some relationships were founded on and thrive on
physicality:**

"When I met this guy, he impressed me in a lot of ways.
Mature, very masculine, good-looking, intelligent, fun. In
other words, he was like a fantasy. He is every bit a man, six
feet one, blond, very blue eyes. A big mustache. He has a
natural build, hunky, hairy, hung. Our sex was fantastic and
uninhibited. I enjoyed being with him—he was a perfect
buddy. We did everything together—worked on our cars,
drank, went to movies, played racquetball, you name it. It

was really great being with him and I eventually loved him. It came easy."

"Even though we're opposite in everything from fine arts to politics, the sex and emotional high we get from each other is fabulous. In the months we've been together, the sex has become increasingly better instead of dying down, and that, for me, says a lot for male sexuality."

"I fell in love with him because he is tall, slim, blond, very good-looking, blue eyes with long eyelashes, dimples in his cheeks, he has a beautiful perfect body and is amply endowed. (Needless to say, I am the envy of many gay people.)"

"I liked his looks, thoughtfulness, honesty, patience. Of course, he's well hung, and I'm not sure I would even have gotten to know him if he wasn't."

"He helped me to sexually rediscover my body. I had only been able to climax once before my lover and that was when I was first touched by another guy years ago. From that time on I figured that my role in gay life was to get the other guy off—my needs were only secondary and didn't matter. My lover changed all that."

Other men saw their relationships fail because they were based on sex:

"I fell in love with my lover because of his body. That's the reason we broke up. It turned out to be the only thing I really loved about him."

"Physical attraction played a major part, that's probably why none of my love affairs lasted more than three months."

"My last lover and I broke up because the only thing we had going for us was sex. It was the best sex I've ever had. He turned me on like no one, we did everything to each other as often as possible. But once we got out of bed we barely had anything to say to each other. That tired old saying 'Man does not live by bed alone' sure applied in this case. It wasn't enough to keep us together, that's for sure."

Do you and/or your lover have sex with others?

While sexual considerations seem relatively unimportant as reasons for enduring gay relationships, sex—as we have seen—*is* an important part of gay men's lives. Perhaps the area in which gay relationships differ the most from heterosexual ones is "open marriages." 74% of the men who have lovers state that they, their lover, or both of them have sex outside their primary relationship. Most of these men (65%) feel very positive about this. They view such outside sex as recreation, and see it either as not affecting their partnership or actually enhancing it.

In most cases, both partners are aware of and approve these outside encounters and would bristle at the suggestion that such activity indicates a lack of true commitment to their lover:

"If anything, having sex with others makes our love for each other stronger. We are honest about it with each other—I know when he goes out, he knows when I go out. The only condition we ever put on it is that neither of us takes a trick into 'our' bed—that is the holy sanctity. Tricking out makes us appreciate each other and what we have together."

"I think that I am a better lover after I've had a 'promiscuous' sex affair. After having sex with a stranger, I come back to my lover and appreciate and love him more than ever."

"Both George and I have agreed not to ruin our relationship with monogamy. Our sex is just too great to let it be spoiled with artificial rules. He has had two sex experiences with others since we met. I pretend to be annoyed because he wants me to but in reality I am not jealous at all. It is kind of exciting to go with a man that other men want."

"In the relationships we have known, and which were supposed to be so monogamous, it seems that the attitude prevails that 'monogamy is great—but for you only.' This leads to mistrust, bitterness, watchfulness, and accusations when none of it is at all necessary. Those who would impose monogamy must be so terribly unsure of themselves as persons of value. Are they afraid that the partner would find someone else more appealing? If that's going to happen, it will just happen. With an open relationship, one is forced to do something in order to remain interesting to a chosen lover; one must progress in some direction. Without such progress, there is nothing for the lover to keep an interest in. Fresh approaches, sexually or otherwise, do not generate from a closed unit. Input—sexually, intellectually, or just friendly—generates output of the same type in an expanding proportion, and our relationship has grown because of this."

"As a man who was venomously jealous in my heterosexual relationships, I am astounded by its complete absence in this relationship. If circumstances offer him an opportunity to explore, I am the second person to benefit from the exploration. I am less inclined to try new things, yet sensuous dalliances and friendly exchanges do not disturb my primary commitment."

"'Variety is the spice of life.' Most relationships I don't think work out without it. I see things in others that I want to share and be a part of. That doesn't by any stretch of the imagination mean that I love my lover any less. I think that it just helps to make me a more complete person and, by extension, us a more complete couple."

"I have been very active sexually throughout my lifetime and no single man could fulfill all my desires, even now. I think it is ridiculous, and also frustrating, for gay men to attempt a monogamous relationship unless they are without sexual desires at all. The fact that my lover is sexually attractive to others and has widespread sexual interests makes him all the more attractive in my eyes."

"We have an agreement that sex with others is OK as long as it's not hidden. We both have learned that our relationship is a good deal more than a hot fuck, and it would take more than a dynamite body to come between us."

"From the very first my partner and I have had sex with others. I realized even in the first flush of romance that my eyes were always going to wander if good-looking men came into view, and that sleeping with others had nothing to do with my love for him. In thirty-two years or so I have probably done more sleeping around than my partner but have never for a moment been in love with anybody else nor fancied myself so."

Many of the men who have "open relationships" feel that sexual activity outside a primary relationship is a very natural state of affairs:

"I am neither jealous nor possessive. I believe that intelligent and mature persons are capable of loving more than one person, each in differing degrees and for different reasons. The male of any species essentially is sexually omnivorous, and monogamy is a stern, and usually unrealistic, condition to impose on a relationship."

"We had both come from other relationships, he a wife

and me a girlfriend and a lover (which was tearing me apart). We vowed right from the start that we would not restrict each other's sexual expression. That was decided from the standpoint of knowing that, at least in the case of men and men, both parties 'cheat' anyway (probably a male characteristic), so let's not look upon that urge as something that would disintegrate the relationship. Rather let's see it as a logical extension of our sexuality, which, in the final scheme of things, is not as important as, say, how much we helped each other when it counted. The result? A ten-year relationship, five of which were creatively (songwriting) and physically exciting and satisfying, and five of which have decreased sexually to the platonic in the last three years, and grown beyond all limits to the abiding love of beloved friends and confidants."

"I think it is unrealistic to expect two men to have only each other as sex partners forever, and be satisfied with that. Men by their nature are promiscuous. People think of homosexuals as being promiscuous, but it is really a male phenomenon. If it's true that 'gays' are promiscuous, why are lesbians so nonpromiscuous? I believe that heterosexual men would love to be as promiscuous as homosexuals, but there are not enough promiscuous women. We have found that this has not hurt our relationship (as so many people believe it must). I think the important part of tricking out is being honest with your lover. Relationships go bad in many cases not because there was an outside sex experience (or several or many) but because the people involved were not honest with each other. I do know some people who I believe are in love with their lover, but claim that if they ever found out their lover had tricked out, that would automatically be grounds to terminate the relationship. I cannot understand such an attitude."

"We tend to combine all the worst aspects of heterosexual monogamy in our idealized model of what a gay relationship should be. With marriages in America failing at an ever-faster rate, why should we model gay relationships after an idealized heterosexual model of relationships?"

Some men find outside sex necessary for their well-being:

"We feel that monogamy for the male is physically impossible and if you try and enforce it you have either deceit or else so much energy is dissipated in trying to comply that the relationship will not last unless both parties have an abnormally low sex drive."

"I don't particularly feel comfortable with the fact that I am married and have sex outside my marriage. However, my emotional and physical needs for relationships with men are so strong that I can't deny them now as I did in the past. Denying them almost killed me. If my wife were to give me an ultimatum to either give up my sexual relationships outside the marriage or lose her, I am afraid we would have to separate. I love her and leaving her would be shattering for me. I would prefer to be monogamous and I am sure I would be again if my sexual needs were met by one person. They are not by my wife."

"When I had a lover, I had sex with others, he did not. I explained to him that it was something I had to do, because he didn't always want sex; I was not long out of the closet and still saw a lot of men I liked, etc. I also felt there was no *one* person who could give someone everything they want, and while one person supplies a great deal of needs and wants, they can't have everything to offer. I told him that he was the most important man in my life and meant more to me than anyone, and that there was a special place in my heart for him that no one could violate. But still there was a part of me that I felt I could share with others in a sexual way. He didn't understand too much, as he had been drilled in old-fashioned ways."

"Sometimes I feel guilty, but I do it because I didn't really start having sex until I was well into my twenties. At this point I am not seeing many other guys so I suppose I'm beginning to feel comfortable with myself."

A few men have sex with others only in the company of their lover:

"Both me and my lover have sex with other men, but only together. This way, there is no competition, the chance that one might be getting more than his share. We both like to have a lot of sexual partners, and when we started going together, we decided this is the best way. We started within two weeks of establishing our relationship, and have continued, on and off, for as long as we have been together. We plan to continue until sex no longer interests us—hopefully never. We especially like three-ways, although we have been in orgies of over twenty. We also go to the baths, and participate in group sex. It seems that neither of us ever stops cruising."

"My lover and I used to be terribly jealous when the other would go out. So we decided that we could only have three ways. It works out fine. We enjoy a new person livening up our sex, and many people like to be the third man with a couple because they get paid an awful lot of attention to, being the new face! We've never had the problem of one of us getting most of the attention. It works out pretty good, knock wood."

Nearly a quarter of the men who are involved in open relationships are unhappy about it. Most of these, and others who have been in such relationships, view outside sexual activity as destructive to a primary relationship:

"While we were together I wanted sex and lots of it with only him and he wanted sex with me but also with anybody else that so interested him and that was many people. In theory I could deal with this. After a lot of it I became automatically ill, anxious, depressed, jealous, and insecure. This finally broke us up. I am better at dealing with my jealousy now, partly by acknowledging it and partly by having established myself as a more complete and self-sufficient person. But I'm still not sure I could buy an open-ended relationship with a lover for any great length of time as it tends to break down whatever stability you are trying to build. I always have this abstract 'one-ness' I am trying to create."

"I don't like tricking out because I'm afraid of getting attached to another when I am deeply in love with the one I have."

"We both had occasional outside sex. He because he liked and wanted it, I because I wanted to be like him. The trouble over promiscuity was one of the major factors in breaking up the relationship. It's not that I disapprove of promiscuity, but that I have always been unable to handle it emotionally when my lover wants—and gets—sex elsewhere."

"My lover was having sex with others, which wouldn't have bothered me if he had been honest with me about it. I feel that an understanding concerning 'outside' sex must be reached in a relationship and our failure to do that early in our relationship resulted in our breakup."

"My lover wanted us to have an open relationship. I wasn't thrilled by the prospect, but I could accept it. It allowed me freedom too, after all. What I couldn't accept was that he was constantly trying to pick other people up when we would go out together. I got so sick of it (it was terribly humiliating) that I finally told him to get lost."

"Tricking out is OK as long as I'm the one who's doing it. I mean, I know I love my lover and this is just a way to get my rocks off quickly in a somewhat different way. But when my lover does it I have fits of anxiety and depression and insecurity. And even when I do it, although the sex itself might be good, I always feel empty and guilty when it's over. I wish that my sex drive wasn't so strong."

"My lover says he needs sexual variety and that it doesn't mean anything because I'm the only one he loves and will ever love. I believe him, but I don't understand why he needs to trick out if he really does love me. But I don't make a federal case out of it because I'm afraid that if I do I'll scare him away."

The remainder of the men answering this question (24%) described their relationship as monogamous. Nearly three-quarters of them were content with this:

"Our relationship is monogamous by choice. This is not a stifling situation. We've talked about this a great deal and both feel that we satisfy each other sexually. It *is* a fact that I'm more highly sexed than Mike, but it would be incomprehensible for me to look elsewhere for satisfaction. I equate sex with love; I don't and can't love anyone as intimately as I love Mike. To have sex with someone is to share a very personal part of oneself. And my allegiance is with my lover. Period."

"I am basically a monogamous person and I am quite comfortable with it. Many of my gay friends feel that my attitude towards monogamy is stifling but I just happen to value and find interest in one-to-one relationships. I see more potential for personal growth and explorations in monogamous relationships—that is, for myself."

"We are both rather 'faithful' creatures essentially. Why bother with someone else, when you've got it all with one! And we keep discovering things about each other which make us care even more for each other, so love is a process of constantly growing and expanding."

"If I cannot satisfy my lover sexually, I feel I cannot satisfy him otherwise in our total relationship. Thus, I am strictly monogamous and will remain so."

"I could not want to be united in any way with a moral weakling. I would not want to have such a person as a friend or acquaintance. Monogamy is a sacrament which adds to the depth, joy, and fullness of sex and sanctifies it."

Some men see promiscuity as a threat to their relationship:

"I feel that in theory there is nothing wrong with an open relationship, and if a couple can make this work, fine. I have seen, however, the jealousy and strain such an option can place upon people. In a number of relationships I've seen dashed on the rocks, this has been a contributing if not a main disruptive factor. As someone once quipped, 'Open marriages would work if you could repeal the Law of Jealousy.'"

"Though of course we each are occasionally attracted on a physical level to someone else, neither of us is willing to risk the relationship we have for a one-night stand. I know he would try to be understanding, as I would, but we're both a little jealous—I because of the attention his looks bring and he for the attention my work brings me. We've accepted our homosexuality; but haven't because of it abandoned all concept of faith and morality."

"If you love someone, you shouldn't allow yourself any temptation, because it's real easy to have your head turned by some beautiful number. I'm susceptible to that, unfortunately, so I keep away and it keeps us together and that keeps me truly happy."

"No, we do not have sex with others. We have agreed that if we feel we want to have a trick, we'll simply be honest about it and tell each other. Our main fear is not that we'll split, but that we'll contract a disease. This latter fear is keeping us monogamous. But the more I think about it, the more the idea of a trick with somebody else revolts me."

Some couples are basically monogamous, but are flexible about it:

"We see monogamy as an ideal that is important to our goal of a stable, durable, and lasting relationship. However, like most ideals put into practice, monogamy may hinder the same objective it was established for. Although we don't expect to have to break from a monogamous style very often, we plan to talk it over in advance, trying to analyze the need and effect that it might have on our relationship. I suspect that an understanding with the third party would be important so that he isn't deceived into believing that this sexual encounter has potential for becoming a 'lover' relationship. I would be comfortable with an occasional break in an otherwise monogamous relationship under these circumstances."

"We have sex with others only when we are apart, never when we can be together. You could say it is a silent awareness that does not intrude on what we have. He feels guilty about it, but we both recognize that being possessive and demanding is the quick road to hell in a relationship. We simply have agreed that when we are together, we are *together* and no one outside can disturb that."

Would you like a lover?

Eighty-eight percent of the respondents who do not have a lover answered yes to this question. Sharing their lives with another man is clearly very important to gay men, and quite independent of their sexual views. Men who enjoy one-night stands and sexual variety as well as those who prefer to have sex only with someone they love would like to have a primary relationship with one man.

The reasons expressed for wanting a lover reflected very natural human emotions:

"It would be wonderful to have someone warm and tender with whom to share your most inner thoughts and feelings and begin and end each day in his embrace—someone to really care for and who would care for you."

"I wish I could somehow be involved most of the time. You see, I love men: love relating to them, emoting with them, sharing with them and growing with them. As rare as these goings-on occur, I constantly desire being 'involved.' I'm an incurable romantic by nature so love and emotional involvement are my thing. Romance!"

"I would like to have a relationship with someone with whom I could share more than sex."

"I've spent a lot of time alone—almost emotionally destitute. There are times when I'm so wound out because there isn't a man in my life like my buddies and close personal friends that I withdraw and hate. Fortunately those times are brief. Touching in itself, just a contact with a thigh or shoulder or back, sends my head off into the wind. I don't like sleeping alone all the time."

"A lover, a lover, my kingdom for a lover! Man was put here to share all his life with others, to share all the loving, caring, needing, and dreams with someone special. We all need someone to love and love us in return. That's human nature, whether some of us want to admit it or not. As the song goes, 'No man is an island.'"

Some men see such a relationship as providing them with security and stability:

"The most important thing such a relationship could bring is the knowledge that someone loves and needs me as I would love and need him. It would be a stabilizing force in my life and give me a sense of security that I can indeed handle the many responsibilities such a relationship entails."

"My life has little solidity right now. I have sex with a lot of different people, and I'm responsible to no one. I liked that for a long time. But now I want to settle down, to be special to someone and to have someone in particular to think and worry about. In short, I want to be in love."

"I am terribly insecure, and I hasten to add that this is not *because* I am gay. I feel that a lover would give me some security, some sense of being truly needed, someone who would believe in me and I in him, and together we face the world with chins and third fingers raised on high!"

"I want to share my life with someone. I want a lasting relationship. I think sex gets better with one person over a period of time. And because affection—not just sex—is very important to me, how can one have much affection for a parade of partners?"

"I think the greatest benefit a lover might bring would be to cut down the number of my sexual contacts, decreasing disease possibilities and freeing my 'cruising' time for more productive endeavors."

"A male lover could bring me a ground wire into being, a whole new way to look at things—new energies, insight, security, hope, sharing, personal growth, also pain, hurt, sorrow. This may sound romantic but hell, I'm a homespun Okie and spiritual. I can't have it any other way. I would be destroyed any other way."

"I have found that it is easier for me to withstand the prejudices and pressures of our heterosexist society if I know that out there stands a man who is willing to fight the battle alongside me and who gives a damn about how I feel."

Some men felt that a lover would give them companionship—a sense of family:

"I miss physical closeness and I would like to have someone to go places with and to play games with and to talk to. I wouldn't even care if he slept with me, I'd just like his company."

"Living by oneself, married only to your job, really gets to be a drag and oftentimes depressing. Everyone needs someone to love and feel close to. There should be a bond of emotion. I'm not one who feels sex is all that important. Sex is fine but I'm not gay because of the sex end of it. A relationship would bring security, same interests and just enjoyment of each other's company."

"I see having a lover as the ultimate way of expressing one's gayness. I am a sharing person by nature and would willingly give my love to a man who would want to share my life."

"I need someone to share the good and the bad with. I want someone to lean on when I need help and I want to be needed as well. It's essential for my home to be comprised of more than one person. The concept of coming home to loved ones appeals to me."

"I would like to have a lover and live with him. I grew up in Middle America, and though I don't expect to father a family of my own, I am a believer in the family unit, even if that's just me and someone I love."

Some of the men felt that having a lover would better them as people:

"The most important thing a love relationship brings, in my opinion, is that you are stretched as a person. In other words, you have a reason for attempting to be and to grow and to widen in certain directions—and most importantly, to *give*—that single living doesn't ordinarily produce (unless you have a massive ego, and then that brings its own problems). If you try to be open and vulnerable, and the communication is good and honest, you also have, as it were, a mirror image in which you can see and measure yourself in terms of the other's reaction—both strengths and weaknesses.

If you trust and respect him, your lover can almost serve as that outside eye all good actors must have. Richard Burton once said, 'Unless you love someone, nothing makes any sense.' I agree."

"To me, a lover relationship is comparable to a heterosexual marriage; you want to love, be loved, and share with that person for the rest of your life, and his. For me, I feel I would gain a lot from having a lover; different types of security, such as emotional, physical, social, financial, etc. Being gay can be a very lonely life, and for a lot of gays, including myself, it is. Having a lover affords us the alternative to the cruising and bar games. I think that having a lover would make me a total person."

11.4% of the men answering this question said they would not like to have a lover. For most of these, their freedom was more important:

"At this time in my life, I would rather be alone. I've been living in San Francisco for eight years now and have always been in a relationship. This is the first time I have been free and noncommitted. Relationships are nice but sometimes can be too demanding."

"I have made my own lifestyle and am sufficiently crotchety to be happy in my independence. I recognize the pleasures of living with another man from previous relationships—shared household duties, usually more healthy routines as to eating, sleeping, exercise habits, having the other guy to lean on emotionally, sometimes financially, etc. However, the loss of my own freedom is too high a price to pay."

"I've weathered a number of relationships, homosexual and heterosexual, and I want to use my energies toward realizing some dreams that have been somewhat aborted because of the demands of the relationships I've had. When I want sex I find it (if I'm looking for men) or it finds me (if I'm looking for women). Wouldn't want to live with either. For now I feel fairly contented living alone. My father and mother went from their parents' homes to their home. When my mother died, my father had never lived alone, even once, in his life. He died three years later, at age sixty-seven. Had he learned how to live alone he'd have survived in a much happier state for a much longer time. It's good training to live alone."

"I dislike the word lover. I prefer roommate, friend. I don't want to belong to one person, and I don't want one person to belong to me."

"It might be nice to have someone that you could relate to on most if not all things. Why is it necessary that one have a lover? Can't one just have close friendships? I don't think I would enjoy being tied down to one person sexually. I think the relationship (lover) would bring a closeness or a feeling of being wanted or needed. I think you can also get this without being involved sexually with a person."

There were other reasons expressed by those who do not want a lover:

"A lover would be impossible for me because I want to remain married."

"I'm afraid that I could not handle the questions which would arise from neighbors and friends if I had another man living with me. But I'm worried about getting old alone."

"I know as a practical matter that with my straight public image it is inconceivable. If I had a lover I would want to be totally involved and since I can't I guess I am rationalizing myself into saying this is the way I want it."

"I couldn't allow myself to have a lover because I'm a teacher in a small town and if I saw any man as much as I would want to see my lover, there would surely be gossip and I'd probably wind up losing my job. So I have to have a series of unfulfilling encounters in the nearest big city. I can't afford to leave here now and it's driving me crazy."

"I can't take this question seriously and seldom consider the possibility of having a lover. Loving is extremely rare in gay life and I cringe at the number of recent books on the subject. There isn't enough loving among gay men to warrant a paragraph, much less a book. The typical faggot is interested in sex, not love; he's collecting 'numbers,' constantly looking for a trick hotter than the last one."

"Perhaps I'm looking in the wrong places, but it seems too many live up to the stereotype of 'size queen' etc. I have yet to meet someone who's interested in my mind, my work or studies. Until I find such a person, I have no desire for a lover."

"It is very difficult to find a gay male with a Christian view of sex as opposed to the general view which is one of guilt, or hedonism."

"Living in places like Los Angeles, New York, and San

Francisco, there is so much sex around, I don't feel I need a lover. And I get enough emotional fulfillment from my friends and career."

Would you want to live with your lover?

59% of the men who want a lover would like to live with him:

"I live alone at the moment and I feel a lack of someone to share my mental highs and lows with and also a longing to share someone else's highs and lows. To share a person's life, I would have to be living with that person. The uncertainties involved with not living together would, as far as I can see, not make for a good lover relationship. I would hate to rush over to his apartment after just getting a raise or something and find him not there and not really know where he is."

"I would like to live with someone because I want to share and I want others to share with me. I want to say listen to the adagio from Bruckner's Eighth with me and I want to be told, 'You must read this book, it'll do things to your mind.' Anyone who grows up gay and didn't live all his life in Greenwich Village has got to experience the dichotomy of what you want and what television tells you is in store for you. Ideally then, living with someone could bridge the gap between what I want intellectually and what I want emotionally."

"I would want to live with my partner in an arrangement that is mutually sustaining and in which responsibilities are shared and decisions made by both. I think such a commitment would be healthy and lead to a very mature and adult way of life."

"The only way I know I could truly express my love and hope to fulfill his needs is with the intimate relationship that only living *together* can bring about. A relationship that is built on love, trust, and mutual and self-respect. Sounds rather like a marriage doesn't it? Exactly!"

"The reason I would want to live with any lover in my mature years is that some of our best times are quiet ones at home, reading passages from newspapers or books to each other. This sort of moment would be hard to come by if we lived apart. Lying in bed remembering funny things that happened at parties and laughing over them is something else we would be less likely to do if just snatching hours or days together."

31% of the men who desire a lover would not want to live with him:

"I think seeing a lover on an occasional basis is much more stimulating than being with him day and night. It tends to become commonplace and less exciting. I would like to have occasional sex but it is not primary."

"I want to have someone around that I can share things with. But I wouldn't want to live with my lover because I feel that when you live apart, you spend your time together because you want to, not because you have to."

"Love should happen—from moment to moment—and shouldn't be arranged or agreed upon. I would want to live *amongst* as many lovers as possible."

"The only kind of lover I would like at this time is someone I see only occasionally—say once a week or once every two weeks. It would have to be someone rather broad-minded who could appreciate my 'situation': I am married and soon to be a father. I am certain beyond any doubt that I am a bisexual, to the degree that I have rejected the argument that saying you're bi is just a copout for a gay."

"I have lived with lovers and I find that living together destroys those unique individual qualities that first attracted me to him and are really the basis of a relationship. I do not plan on living with someone again."

"I would very much still like a lover or lovers. I don't necessarily want to 'get married,' however, and am very critical of that manner of imitating hetero relationships and lifestyles. I acknowledge that I ought to be able to get along as a complete human being just by myself but would certainly like to have the attention of someone who was able to be a caring partner."

Do you prefer men younger, older, or the same age as yourself?

Many people believe that homosexuals have an inordinate interest in sexual relations with children. Anita Bryant speaks of gays "recruiting" children to homosexuality. In 1977, a Los Angeles Police Department sergeant stated on the television program *Sixty Minutes* that 70% of L.A. child molestations were homosexual in nature. At the insistence of the American Civil Liberties Union, LAPD Chief Daryl Gates looked into the matter and made an apology before a Police Commission hearing when it was discovered that, in actuality, 78% of such cases were heterosexual.*

The *Sixty Minutes* program, of course, was viewed by many more people than those who heard Chief Gates' apology, and the "child molester" tag is one still applied to homosexuals by many. In this survey, age preference was quite clearly delineated: 61% of the men under twenty-five preferred older partners; 49% of the men between the ages of twenty-five and forty preferred men the same age as themselves; and 56% of men over forty preferred younger men. Many of the men who indicated that they prefer younger men stressed "over eighteen." A few professed interest in teenage boys; just one was interested in anyone under fourteen. All of these men made the point, perhaps defensively, that they would never have sex with anyone who did not want to have sex with them.

28.3% of all respondents, mostly the younger men, prefer older men:

"I'm twenty-two years old. I prefer men older than myself. I enjoy feeling like I'm the younger brother, or the student, and they are leading the way. Older men are more in control and lead the way better and I feel more comfortable around them. I feel better about myself having sex with an older man."

"I'm twenty-three and prefer older men (under forty but over twenty-five). They seem to be over the 'tramp' period and they enjoy sex more and I enjoy it with someone who's been around and can show me new things."

"I am twenty-three. Most of my relationships have been with older men. In one sense, I think this is because these are the images I grew up with. This is what they give you in ads and in pornography—and if that is what you're exposed to when you're forming your sexual tastes, this is what turns you on. I also find that older guys are usually into younger guys, so it works two ways."

"I am nineteen years old, college junior, pursuing two majors. It's hard for me to prefer younger men, since I would no doubt be called guilty of 'recruiting' (gasp!!!). Most of the men my age are freshmen or sophomores in their first semester, and few have any notion of what life is all about, or even

* Los Angeles *Times,* July 12, 1978.

any notion of what they really are. I guess I'd have to say I like older men, older than I am."

"I am twenty-three. I prefer men older than I because I can benefit from their experience and emotional maturity. From casual observation, long-lasting relationships don't occur until after one or both men are over thirty. I think that says something. I still have to 'date around' before I'll catch up to the position straights have reached after high school. With good models, I'll reach that stage more easily."

"I'm almost twenty-five. I prefer older men, though have been with younger. I have always felt more mature than those my own age, and I feel a relationship would work out better with a mature man. Also, I feel a deep inner warmth and comfort at the idea of being wanted and held by an older man—father fixation? I like the idea of entering the life of a man who is established and stable, and not still lurching around for what he wants, because I feel definite about my career plans, and I become impatient with those my own age or older or younger who are not."

"I am twenty-six. I definitely prefer older men; the older I get the more I appreciate older and older men. Recently I had sex with someone who at first looked to be in his thirties. I began to realize that he was much older than that, he just kept himself in good shape and looked really good. I never asked him his age but I'm sure he was in his fifties. This realization made me become much more aroused. It was definitely a turn-on to think that I was having sex with someone almost twice my age, someone who was doing this even before I was born. Older men are good at sex (or can be) because they have had so much more experience than someone who is say twenty-one. Unfortunately it is not very common that people want to have sex with older men. I think partly because there is a stigma that old is bad. Unfortunately, many older men let themselves go to pot. I think this is what people think of as old. They equate old with out-of-shape, flabby, etc. If more older men stayed in shape and looked good they might find that younger people (like myself) have nothing against 'old,' it's the falling apart that is a turn-off."

39.7% of the respondents prefer men in their own age group:

"I am thirty-eight. I prefer men somewhere in my age bracket. But what I strongly demand is that they be *emotion-*

ally mature as I am. I have no use for 'chickens,' even though they have a youthful look, which 'turns on' or excites many older men sexually. 'Chickens' are just too immature, generally irresponsible, and don't know where their head is at."

"Thirty-nine. The same age or a *little* younger. They know what they like and are good at it. Their emotions are stable, too—less 'You're good sex, I'm in love' stuff."

"I am twenty years and six months old. I prefer my partners to be between sixteen and twenty-five. Very seldom do I have sex with anyone older than twenty-five. However, when I was twelve I liked twelve-year-olds. When I was sixteen I liked sixteen-year-olds. So maybe as I grow older, my age preference will grow, too."

"I'm twenty-three years old and I prefer someone my own age because I don't want to have the edge on someone else's life experience or vice versa. I want to discover together."

"I am fifty-six this year. I prefer to talk to people my own age or older. Will have sex with younger individuals if they act like they really want it. I have no real rapport with anyone ten years younger than I am."

"I am thirty-two. I like them usually the same age or a little older. I don't see what all the excitement about teenagers is. Usually they're mixed up or you can't talk to them about anything and they're afraid to have you fuck them. And older than forty, the bodies usually start to go."

"Age fifty-one. Prefer same age or a little younger. I find so many guys my age have written themselves off as being old. Sure the body doesn't move as fast or as accurate, but if the mind is young then life is exciting. That is how I feel—eternally young, but mature."

"At forty I still prefer men the same age, as has always been the case. While the beauty of the young eighteen-to-twenty-five is often legendary, the reality is I have much more chance of developing and sustaining relationships with my contemporaries."

"I'm thirty-four, prefer same age or older. There's more substance to men over thirty-five, or at least thirty. Under that, the kids are hung up on themselves too much, into clothes, making themselves beautiful, etc. The outside man ought to look good. But the inner man is much more interesting."

"My age is forty-five. I feel most comfortable with men my own age because they would share the problems of reduced sex drive and other minor afflictions of aging. They can be more sympathetic to me, and I can be responsive to their needs. Younger guys are good if you like getting fucked, because they are more virile and ready to go than men my own age. But for prolonged companionship, I prefer my own age group."

Younger men were favored by 27.4%, mostly the older respondents:

"I am thirty-six. I find that I am more comfortable mentally, emotionally, and physically with younger men. We seem to identify with each other easier. I also suspect that being with younger men also superficially makes me fill the 'senior' role since I usually have had more experience with work, travel, and human relationships than they have. Since I tend to be somewhat dominant and aggressive, this age difference helps support me in my usual role."

"I am thirty years old and prefer younger men. I feel that for me it has something to do with the fact that as a child I was always treated as an adult and never allowed to be a child even though I was not the oldest. My father was gone most of the time and my mother made me responsible for my three brothers. It is also tied up in my concern to want to make it easier for younger kids."

"I'm forty-two. Generally younger. Something to do with idealizing youth, vitality, beauty. My fantasies are of teenagers and young men, perhaps because although I had regular sex with classmates in high school, I didn't have regular sex after that until I was in my late twenties—I had mostly adolescent memories to fall back on."

"I'm thirty-two and prefer teenagers, or men in their twenties. It isn't insignificant that my lover, though nearly thirty, looks and acts much younger. Why do I prefer youth to age in sex when in all other life areas I prefer age? I entertain the fantasy that youth will be less jaded, more artless, more open to experiment, fresher."

"I am thirty-nine. I like men in their twenties who are growing, making decisions about their life and maturing into men."

"I'm seventy-one. I am turned off by older men. Turned on by and seek younger, twenty-one to thirty-five."

"I'm twenty-eight. I prefer my own age or a little younger, from about twenty-four up. I've learned a lot in the last few years. I think that the typical seventeen-year-old blond California surfer is the epitome of beauty and desirability (and very often available, I've found!). But I've come to realize the utter insanity of pursuing them for any kind of relationship. I've never met one who had his head together or could talk about anything but rock 'n' roll and surfing. Personality and intellect has come to be more important to me than it once was. I guess it's just a process of maturing. When I felt down on myself, I sought out types who were totally unlike me (I was an unattractive, unpopular bookworm at seventeen). Now that I've come to like and respect myself, I realize I have it all over those little cuties, and a lot of other people my own age seem to think so, too."

"I am twenty-three. I prefer someone in the sixteen-to-forty-six bracket I suppose (I've not the experience to eliminate any particular group). Sexually lately my fantasies have been primarily with teenage boys. I think this may be because I remember how horny I was in my teens and how I wished someone would use me sexually (such as the present me)."

"I am forty-five. Younger. I seem and look much younger than I am. I do not want to be old, I do not feel old, and I see no reason to be old until it is necessary, which, God knows, will be soon enough."

"I'm fifty-five. I prefer younger men—and I don't mean children. Mid-twenties to mid-forties is just fine. A younger partner is both flattering and more stimulating. For a brief time one can pretend to be younger yourself."

"I am twenty-nine and prefer younger guys. To explain why I could only resort to the aesthetic consensus that the young male is the most beautiful of human figures. I would like to be the man to my lover that I wish I had when I was his age."

"I am forty-five years old. I prefer men slightly or quite a bit younger than myself but *never* 'chicken.' Quite truthfully I suppose because I feel at times I'm over the hill with a downhill tailwind and younger men, at least for a few moments, give me the illusion of being not quite so far gone. Besides most men I know (or have known) my own age seem and act a lot older than I do and feel—they come once and pass out! And that is usually when I'm just getting up a full head of steam. Younger guys can make it at least twice and I've known a few that have made it six and seven times in one eight-to-ten hour night. That, my friend, one doesn't easily forget!"

"I am sixty. My partner excepted, I definitely have never

cared for older men, wanted them the same age. I am not interested in the really youthful, but twenty-eight or forty-eight is already a lot younger than I now am. When I was twenty-eight I wouldn't have touched anyone forty-eight nor even been very polite to them."

"I am forty-eight. I prefer younger men (my current lover is twenty-three), not because I am hung up on youth, but because people my age have let their faces and bodies go to wrinkles and potbellies. Even as a child, I have taken superb care of myself, so now at the age of forty-eight people guess my age invariably around twenty-six to twenty-eight. It takes time, care and exercise, but is worth it. However, any man at any age who has kept himself fit would be acceptable. Older men have a more 'mature' outlook, more experience, expect less, think more of 'you' than of their own satisfaction, and demand less attention and flattery."

A few of the men said they preferred teenagers, or commented on the issue of gays and children:

"I have the feeling that I'm not an average homosexual simply because I find so many gay men uninteresting. I'm into chicken and I know that most of the gay men I know aren't. I worked as a child-care worker for three years and perhaps it helped me realize how great kids are. Many gay men have no real meaningful contact with children and adolescents and that's unfortunate."

"I can't close without some comment on pederasty. Many—I suspect most—pederasts know from experience that adolescent boys have a huge capacity for sexual enjoyment. They know, too, that boys who have not been taught to fear homosexuality (or have lost that fear) can be wonderful, playful, happy lovers. They know further that early homosexual experience is totally irrelevant to later psychosexual development—unless the experience is traumatized by hysterical parents or police. The pitiful cases, paraded on television these days, of 'boy prostitutes' are beside the point; those kids are almost all refugees from loathsome home environments.

"Pederasts know also that they are the objects of very widespread hate and fear. No other group in America is more brutally victimized, and it is in large measure this victimization that leads to 'kiddie porn' (as a release of bottled sexual energy through fantasy) and boy prostitution through pimps (the 'chicken hawks' who do indeed victimize children for profit). In societies that freely acknowledge the attractiveness of boys, boys are respected and loved, as they should be, by their parents, and allowed their sexual freedom."

"There are a couple of kids in my school class that I am fairly certain are gay. And yet, they are not going to expose themselves to the possible torment of saying they are and finding that I'm not sympathetic—and I'm not going to expose myself and find out that I misjudged them and it gets spread around the school. Yet, if we could only discuss the matter freely we could both have a less paranoid life and they could benefit from my understanding and support."

"I'm particularly fond of boys, especially between the ages of twelve and sixteen but often extending either above or below these ages. My emotional involvement is usually *very* loving/adoring, with sexual interests subjugated to the emotional love of the young man. A lot of these kids are from broken families and are crying desperately for a loving adult."

"Having had so much sex with other boys when I was a boy, I find I can still enjoy a boy. When my work takes me on the road to smaller cities and towns, I make out with boys fabulously. I am always amazed by their prevalence, their readiness, their skills, their enthusiasm. In a rural area of this country, I once picked up a teenaged hitchhiker heading for another part of the country. He spent four days with me in a motel. The kid was incredibly insatiable."

"This 'Save Our Children' stuff is so much bullshit. First of all, it's a cliché by now that gays do very little child molesting compared to wonderful straights. And I always think, 'What's wrong with a child having sex?' If he or she is old enough to want it, he or she is old enough to get it. It's the old Victorian thing that sex is bad, and we must protect our children from this dirty, horrible thing until we just can't do so anymore. Is eighteen a magic age whereby everything becomes handle-able? I really think that if more adolescents were able to freely express their very strong sexuality, they would grow up so well adjusted and happy, the world would be a far different—and far better—place."

The remainder of the respondents report that age is of little importance to them:

"I am thirty-four years old, and actually have no preference with regards to the age of my partner. The thing I look for in a partner is a mature aptitude and outlook on life and the ability to carry himself as a responsible person. I have had affairs with men the same age as myself, older men, and one loving relationship with a fourteen-year-old boy that lasted nearly fourteen months."

"Fifty-six. I prefer any age if the person is interesting and vital. One of the sillier aspects of American society is the worshipful adulation of youth. Working with them in pleasant circumstances I am also aware of the natural callowness of young people."

"I'm now in my fifties. I once thought at thirty-five I was 'getting old'—so why not have fun with *everybody*—young and old alike? I enjoy it—so do they."

"Good encounters and emotional/sexual vibes projecting from two males should not have an age-factor linkage. We ol' gays do need to keep ourselves in shape, though, since appearance and grace enter into our physical imagery."

"I am thirty-five. For a long time society (I think it was society) led me to believe that unblemished beauty and youth were equal to sex. For a long time now I have appreciated maturity of body and mind. Some gray hair turns me on. As far as age goes—anyone over twenty-six and under sixty."

"I am in my mid-fifties and prefer mature men as friends and sex partners. I don't get on well with the very young. They seem to need parenting and I have used up my parenting on my own children. There is more of a feeling of equality and mutual pleasure with men in my age group. I feel more relaxed and comfortable. Age range from the thirties to the sixties or older."

"Forty-four. No preference and, I must add, a good deal of wariness because I have reached a point where younger men are attracted to me, for various reasons, and I think one of the saddest sights imaginable is to watch a mature person making a fool of himself chasing younger people. Bad scene."

"Twenty-four. I have had terrific relationships with a seventeen-year-old, a twenty-four-year-old, and a thirty-six-year-old. They were all different. The seventeen-year-old was aggressive and volcanic. The twenty-four-year-old was curious and quiet. The thirty-six-year-old was practically a genius. I feel I learned things every year of my life, and I don't believe that my partner need be of any particular age."

PART FOUR: WOMEN

Do you have sex with women? How often? How does it differ for you from gay sex?

Nearly 40% of the men indicate that they have had sexual relations with women,* and 45% of these still engage in sex with women as well as with men. Most of the men who do not have sex with women pointed out that they have nothing against women. Many wrote that they appreciate and love them as friends, others indicated that they could appreciate womanly beauty and, in some cases, sexuality. But they also noted no sexual arousal whatsoever from women. Quite a few of those men who have had sexual relations with women in the past but no longer do report that they found such encounters unfulfilling, that there was "something missing" in them which they could find only in sex with men.

A substantial percentage (17.3%) of the respondents currently have sex with women. It might be argued that these men are not homosexual but bisexual. However, this survey was intended clearly for gay men, was distributed among gay men and reproduced in gay publications. It is thus significant that such a large number of men who sufficiently consider themselves gay to respond to this survey have sexual relations with women.

There are a number of reasons why these men enjoy sex with women:

"For me, a woman sort of serves as a resting place between men. I can make love to them, and yet not get truly involved."

"I have sex with a woman once or twice a week. Physically, I think sex with a woman is superior to sex with a man in most cases. The woman's vagina is designed to accom-

---

* Because of the wording of this question, it is probable that a number of the men who answered simply "no" have had sex with women in the past. Thus this figure may in fact be quite conservative.

modate and stimulate a penis far better than either a mouth or even a tight asshole. Consequently, the amount of pure sensation a woman can provide is greater than a male normally provides. Mentally, though, sex with a man, for me, is more satisfying than with a woman. I always come away from a homosexual experience more content and gratified."

"I have a real love affair with a twice-divorced sweetheart. It doesn't differ much physically. Emotionally, I feel more 'right' and approved."

"I have sex with women as often as possible. It differs in that women are easier to bed down with than gay men. They don't sit on barstools and wait for the grooviest number to show—then get frantic at closing time."

"Straight sex I found does a lot to build up your 'masculine' self-image."

"It's getting less frequent. The last time was a year ago. The time before that six months. It doesn't differ greatly from the head I'm in when I'm fucking a man and I'm in the 'top' position."

"Sex with a woman is quite different for me than sex with a man. I am very much turned on to their bodies—especially their genitals—and I love their passiveness in bed. If I could stand the idea of family life I would probably be straight, but my childhood was so miserable I'm just plain not interested in reliving all the hell I went through."

"Sex with my wife is not as intense, as traumatic, and the earth doesn't quite shake. Sex with women I can take or leave, but sex with men I got to have. On the other hand, my relationship with my wife has been emotionally deep, beautiful, and very satisfying, the only such sexual relationship I've had in my life, and it gives our sex a special glow which is very strong and pleasing and a turn-on, which I haven't had with men yet."

"I had one female encounter which lasted for six months, and still does occasionally now. It was most enjoyable (there is a definite emotional involvement on both our parts) and was a whole new world, though I wouldn't like a steady diet of it."

"I do have sex with women, and if I can find the right woman, sex can be very good. Women are improving in their sexual abilities now, over say thirty years ago. They are now learning the techniques of fellatio and many of them like to be penetrated anally, in fact, prefer it. After all, what better contraceptive can you get; it's handy and rewarding. Many of my friends are bisexual as well and so we often have threesomes, such as a friend and his wife, so that my sex with females is fairly frequent. I find this is a fine arrangement for good wholesome sex. Every sensory nerve is stimulated and satisfied."

"I become very attached to women when we are making love. That is because I love their softness. I tend to have deep abiding relationships when I get involved with women. With men it is more impersonal, more removed and alienated. I'm promiscuous with men, but not at all with women. I like to play house with a woman. The sex usually is more romantic, until a few weeks go by and then a tremendous sense of dominance overcomes me and I feel very powerful and in control. This better suits the personality of a woman. She usually wants to be faithful, knowing that it takes a while to develop good sex and that if she were promiscuous like men, she wouldn't have the fulfilling satisfaction from the 'one-night stand' that she gets from a regular partner. Because I don't want the limitation of a 'relationship' in my life at this point, I avoid all relationships. Occasionally I'll service a woman if I feel relatively safe that she will not 'fall' for me and/or I for her. But I am kept safer from the possibility of involvement by just 'tricking.' "

Many of the men indicated that their sexual experiences with women have not been pleasant or fulfilling encounters:

"I have 'tried' sex with women several times—was even married to one. It just isn't satisfying to me. I do not enjoy 'screwing' as much as I enjoy being screwed—so it's a hopeless thing to go with a woman who doesn't have a penis to put into me."

"I had sex with a woman in January 1977—the first time in fifteen years. I do it rarely because I feel used, threatened, fearful, and seldom sexually or emotionally satisfied."

"I have had sex with women since I was eighteen or nineteen. It has always been poor to OK in reward. There was always something lacking—I didn't know what it was until I 'turned.' My sexual relations with women are steadily decreasing as my relations with men and my acceptance of myself increases."

"I never enjoyed sex with a woman. When I had sex with my wife I was fantasizing my last gay experience. I thought about cocks I had sucked and how guys had sucked me."

"I haven't had sex with a woman for some time. I find it less satisfying than homosexual activity because women tend to be more limited in their sexual attitudes. Men can be dominant or submissive with greater ease than women—in my experience. Also, penises are not generally found among women."

"The last time I had sex with a woman was over fifteen months ago. The biggest difference between gay sex and sex with a woman is that gay sex is less inhibited by social restriction with regards to the standard missionary intercourse position that many people believe is the *only* intercourse position that is *normal*. Gay sex is diverse, without placing certain standards or norms on what sex is acceptable and what is not."

"Having sex with men seems to flow more easily than it does with women. Women seem so serious about sex, whereas men just regard it as good clean fun."

"The sex with women was quite good, I suppose, if there was nothing better. But I performed the actions more out of a sense of duty and affection for the woman than out of any genuine desire. With a man my whole body and mind work totally differently. I understand his body intimately. All my nerves tingle and every inch of me is alive. I make love with my toes and my knees, even. My fingers do not need to be told where to go and what to touch, as they did with women, when I kept thinking what I ought to be doing. Heterosexual activity seems as unnatural to me as gay sex must be for most straight people. If they could understand that what I feel for men is exactly what they feel for women, they might start to understand."

"The only woman that I ever had sex with was my ex-wife. Sex with her always left something lacking. With her, it seemed that it was an obligation, so get it over with quick and go to sleep."

"I have sex with women a few times a year. It is not as emotionally satisfying, though physically enjoyable. I always had great performance fears with women and don't feel sexually comfortable with many."

"I have not had sexual contact with a woman since I broke up with my fiancée in March 1976. I find sex with women harder than men because they fake orgasm, don't tell you if they are enjoying it. Plus I like sucking cock and they don't have one."

"I have had little sex with women since my divorce.

Women seem to be 'mother objects' sexually, and I have a notion (which I will not put to the test) that there is latent violence in my heterosexual feelings—something that does not come into my homosexual feelings."

"I've had sex with women three times in my life with close friends. It was a physical act which I was quite capable of performing, but it was like having sex with my mind turned off. In sex with a man, a large part of the pleasure comes from my head."

"I no longer have sex with women although from age fourteen to twenty-five I did, on the average of four times a year. The last five years of this were obligatory on my part, preserving for myself the illusion that I was bi. Never saw it as more than what I was supposed to be doing, always concentrating on refining my technique and focusing on giving them pleasure and neglecting myself. My experience with women can be compared to the least pleasurable I've had with men, far inferior to sex with most men. Finally, I am able to admit my revulsion about women's bodies."

"I have sex with one woman about three times a week. If she wasn't aggressive I probably wouldn't. I don't crave sex with women until I'm having it. Most women that I've met want me to play a role, and are too passive, and expect me to do everything. I guess they think I'm turned on by just looking at them. Men seem to know me better."

"I haven't had sex with women for about eight years. Not because I disliked it, or because I think it is wrong, but because I never felt anything. I would ejaculate, but not even have an orgasm."

"I did try recently with a girl with the 'I've got what it takes to cure ya' mentality. She failed."

"When I was about seventeen, and still trying to 'cure' myself of my nature, I thought that if I once had that supremely ecstatic experience, fucking a girl, everything would change for me. As chance would have it, a college girl I met at a party took a shine to me. She also took birth-control pills, and soon we were fucking regularly. The first time I came after about thirty seconds, I was so excited. In time I guess I got to be a better lover for her, but for me it was always a big put-on. I pretended to feel passion such as I'd read about in books, but I felt really hollow inside. After a while I began to feel really trapped by this girl; she was very nice, but she began to be really attached to me, and while this was good for my ego, it became a real drag. Finally I told her that I really was turned on by guys, and she didn't bat an eye—'Oh, my brother's gay; I don't mind.' She was really great, and I'll always be grateful to her for giving me an experience I had to have before I could really understand my sexuality."

"I now have a lover who when making love is the most wonderful thing in the world. The feeling is there. I've never had that feeling with my wife. She always demanded, 'Sex! I want to get off and now!' Now, is that love or feelings? To me, no."

"My only experiences were while in the navy and overseas. There is just not the same satisfaction. I guess I like to satisfy someone whom I would like to identify with—such as a handsome, hunky, young, virile man."

"I had two important affairs with women, one during my thirties and one during my forties. In both cases, they happened because I was on the rebound from a painful involvement with a man and could not face another male-to-male relationship at that point. Sex with women was always a substitute or a temporary refuge from the real thing: sex with men."

Most of the men who do not have sex with women answered this question simply "no." Some, however, did elaborate:

"I have never had sex with a woman. It is because it makes me uptight, not because I dislike women. I would try it but I lack the self-confidence."

"Sexually, women don't turn me on. I have seen several women who had bodies that I admired because they were beautiful bodies but they were not a sexual arousal. Emotionally I have friends who are women and I work with women, and it doesn't affect me one way or the other."

"I've never had sex with a woman. Only a little touchy-feely petting while in my freshman year at college. Though I dated, my being gay and my wanting to come out precluded my enjoying women at that time."

"I did try once. One should, I guess. It was total disaster. I really couldn't get it up. We blamed it on the amount of alcohol I had consumed, but alcohol never got in the way when a man was involved. I really hated the whole thing. I do not hate women, however."

"Never have been able to get it up to have sex with a woman. There was always a blank wall there that I could just not overcome."

"I never have. I used to lie about that because I felt it was manly to sleep with a woman, but now if anyone asks I tell the truth."

"No, and I wish I could. My fanatic religious upbringing so conditioned me that I can't bear to inflict myself on a woman. I was taught that it was cruel and sinful. But nothing was said about doing it with men, thank goodness!"

"I have never gone all the way with a woman. They find me attractive and sometimes at parties I get into some very heavy scenes. I like to get them turned on and then leave them hanging. There are two girls at work to whom it has become a contest to see who gets me into the sack first."

"I did date in my teens, partly from societal pressure, and partly because I told myself that I could *learn* to like girls. I'd buy girl sex magazines and force myself to masturbate while looking at the pictures. I was a pretty confused youngster after sessions of psychotherapy. At the same time, I was engaging in gay sex activities. I promised myself I'd quit and told myself I wasn't really 'queer.' I never enjoyed dating girls and loved making it with guys. I read a lot and especially liked W. Somerset Maugham. I used to read through his journals in the library. At seventeen, I came upon his comment that the tragedy of his life was that he had tried to convince himself that he was basically a heterosexual who had homosexual inclinations, while in reality the opposite was true. It dawned on me that I was in very much the same boat. I thought it was better to accept myself than to lead a tortured life. I quit dating girls. I've often been grateful to Maugham for that."

Are you now (or have you ever been) married to a woman?

Five percent of the men are currently married to a woman, and an additional 12% were heterosexually married at some time in their lives.

Most of the men who used to be married found it a negative experience:

"I was married from 1963 to 1970 and was divorced when my wife learned I was gay. I knew I was gay at the time of my marriage but also enjoyed sex with women. I view my marriage as a disaster and the only good that came from it was my kids, who are the most important thing in my life right now."

"I was married two years. She divorced me because of it. She hated me, but we are now good friends—that took five years to do. I told her before we were married but she didn't believe it. Thought she could cure me."

"I was married to a woman for six months. It was the thing to do when I felt a need to be socially acceptable. That occurred over ten years ago and I have not seen my ex-wife in that time. She does not know I'm gay."

"I was married for five years. She was a great lady but I could not find any satisfaction, emotionally or physically. She was aware of my sexual preference, accepted it in word, but not in mind. She considered me a good lover and could not understand how I could possibly be attracted to men."

"I was married to a woman for two years. It was the right thing to happen at the time but the pain of getting out of that relationship, and free to be in the gay relationship that I'm in now, was taxing on me."

"I hated being married. I had sex with my wife only nine times, all unsatisfactory, although she had three children and two miscarriages. My wife doesn't know I'm gay, nor do my children."

"I was married to a woman at twenty-five and divorced at thirty-six, and feel that a tremendous amount of emotional damage to both of us could have been avoided had I felt an option existed in 1961 to live a gay life. My wife did not discover my homosexuality, I told her—which needless to say was traumatic. Obviously, living with a man for whom she could do nothing sexually was threatening and crushing. Now that we are divorced and she remarried, she is most accepting of my lover and myself, as is her new husband. In fact we will be having Christmas dinner with them."

"I would never do it again. I'm sure she feels contempt and anger for me because she could never accept the fact that I preferred sex with men to her. She hated Robert and was always as hostile as she could be towards him. However, we stayed married for five years because of mutual dependency even though I lived with Robert the last three years of the marriage."

"I got married thinking, at the time, that that was the only way to have a stable home life. I had some pretty rough gay experiences prior to that, never developing to fruition, because of the other person's hang-ups that being gay was 'wrong.' I demanded a stable home life, and not finding it possible with gay people (at the time), I thought a straight relationship would solve that. But the emotional fulfillment was never there."

"I was married for twelve years. My wife did not know. She is very Anita Bryantish about homosexuality. She said all good male cooks are fags. I never cooked during our marriage."

"I was married, but she didn't find out I was gay until after the divorce. I feel that a gay person who marries a woman is asking for trouble and a woman who marries a guy she knows is gay is responsible for whatever happens to her."

5% of the men in this survey are married. Most of these are unhappy about it:

"Finding out about my gay feelings and desires after I was married and had two kids is rough on all four of us. It really sends me on a guilt trip—not so much for my being gay but for what the discovery does to the family. I feel as though I have double-crossed or failed them. It is stupid and I know it but while I accept (finally) my gayness, I also can't shake the guilt feelings. She is aware of my gay activities and hates them. She is trying to accept my need for male relationships but the thought really makes her angry and frustrated and sad. As she said, she only wishes I was interested in another woman, for then she could decide whether or not she wanted to fight for me or leave. She doesn't know how to cope with my gayness. One effect of my telling her is that she now looks at every man (straight, since I don't bring my gay friends into our married world) and wonders if he is gay and whether I am having sex with him. Every man is suspect now. She has become paranoid about other men and me."

"I still share a roof with my wife—and nothing else."

"I think my wife assumes I have gay activities and doesn't particularly approve. She understands, but is basically opposed. We don't discuss it, except that a couple of months ago she said that if I was getting into the gay scene she wants a divorce. I told her a few days later perhaps we should get a divorce. We haven't discussed it since."

"I am married to a wonderful woman. She knew I was homosexual when we got married. She believed—as our generation was taught to believe—that this would cure my homosexuality. It did not. I do not think I would recommend heterosexual marriage for homosexuals. Not so much for what it does to the homosexual but for the limitation it puts on life for the partner. My wife should have married some strapping male and lived a full, rich life. She has settled for me—a compromise she did not have to make. We are very close—we live more as good friends than as lovers. It is not a bad marriage—in the eyes of the world it is a very good marriage. But both of us know that there must be something more to life than this."

"My marriage will probably end during the next several months. My wife's perception is that my gayness destroyed our relationship. My perception is that our relationship has been in difficulty for a long time and I was not able to ask for what I needed. Since she has not been able to meet my needs, and after working for twenty years to make her happy, I am now looking for my own happiness. My wife is aware of my friendship with gay men, and is very fearful that I might be sexually involved—although I have communicated clearly that I *am*, in fact, sexually involved. At one time I thought we could work out coexisting marriage and gay sexuality. It is clear that this is not true as she values monogamous marriage and sees my gayness as the 'worst thing that could happen.'"

"I am afraid. I'm sorry. I made a mistake and feel that I'm just stuck with it."

"I am now married to a woman. She is not aware of my activities. I don't like being married to a woman. I was 'forced' into it by the Mormon Church which I joined only two years prior to marriage. The Mormons, pushing me into marriage, will rot in their graves I hope. Oh, I know—I should have said no, but I felt so sorry for this kid twelve years my junior, who had been tossed out of her home after graduation from high school by a stepmother that makes Cinderella's stepmother as nice as Kate Smith, and I am *not* dramatizing! I have a streak in me that makes me want to help people. I was not clearly thinking, I'm sorry to admit."

Other currently married men feel good about their marriage:

"In a way I am happy because life is a whole lot easier among straight people, and it is good for my family (parents). My wife is not aware of my gay activities at all, but I know she is quite understanding and open-minded towards this subject."

"I feel a stable relationship is necessary and the odds of a stable relationship with a woman are substantially greater than with a man. There are certain characteristics natural to men and others to women. A marriage between a man and a woman is normally a very efficient matching and complementing of those characteristics. My wife is aware of the fact that I am gay but likes to believe I engage in no gay sexual activities. She has no basis for believing it but she finds it easier to ignore distasteful facts than to admit them and face them. My girlfriend is fully aware of my gay activities and does not frown on them in the least."

"I love my wife very much. She is aware of my gay activities. She doesn't accept them, but she accepts me!"

"I have been married to two women for a total of about thirty years. My wife knows of my bisexuality. As she is a nonsexual-type woman, she likes it that I have another outlet for my sexual needs. She is jealous of another woman but not another man."

"My wife ignores it mostly. Sometimes she says, 'You have a need.' She is a tremendous human being! I love her! I cannot imagine life without her, but I cannot imagine it without 'homosex' either. She often says, 'I cannot understand why I don't want to have sex.' In Rome a few years ago she saw my interest in the boys and indicated she wanted me. Afterward she said, 'I feel like a woman again.' Draw your own conclusions."

"I am married. My feelings about it could fill a book. I want my wife because I like her, I respect her, I can have kids with her, and because she distinctly gives me the gorgeous feeling that she is with me for *keeps*! Which you don't get that easily in gay relationships. My wife knows everything about my gay activities. She puts up with them in a nice way—especially since my gay sex activities are very unanonymous."

"I have been married to a fine woman for the past ten years. I needed a hostess for my home and she needed a home and security. I leveled with her about my sexual preferences and this met with her approval. She is kind and friendly to my men friends. I once thought she was fond of women in a sexual way, but it is only platonic. She has a low sex drive and we have sex once a month and she is quite satisfied. Her interests are her home and charity do's. I think I have the best of both worlds."

"I am married (nineteen years in 1978). I feel fine about our marriage now that we are both aware of my homosexuality. I have never been heterosexual and she never lesbian-inclined. So in order to keep our marriage working for us we are constantly in the position of trying to understand each other, our desires, needs, and feelings."

Some of the men who are not married wrote of their feelings about marriage, both pro and con:

"I am extremely grateful for having discovered myself before being trapped by marriage. It would have been unfair not only to me but also to the woman involved. A living lie. In answer to those who argue that unmarried gays are destined to a horrible old age of loneliness: marriage never did ensure a life without loneliness. I've known couples who were more alone than any single person I can think of. Consider the conditions of parents when their children are grown and leave home. Many who argue from this point, I believe, are not looking objectively at family life as it is today. Marriage might offer companionship, but I can have companionship with a lover or my friends—I do not need a legal document tying me to a female body for companionship."

"I would like to have children. Dennis and I have talked about adopting someday but there is still that desire to have at least one of my own, a part of me."

"I used to date girls. Before my last lover left, he said as soon as he got out West he would start going out with girls and that I should do the same. So I gave it a try. I started seeing a girl and before long we were making marriage plans. We were to become engaged at Christmas and to marry the following August. In October I found out she was pregnant by someone else and that was the end of that. It has been over a year and I haven't even danced with a girl since."

"I have been engaged to two women before—we shared a purely platonic relationship. I chicken out because I know that I would never be able to resist other men. Deep down inside I knew that it was a man I wanted anyhow, but I was getting tired of having no one to love me."

"If I ever marry a woman I will tell her that I had gay experiences before I met her; however, I would be marrying her because I loved her, so she needn't feel threatened."

"I used to think that gay men who married women were doing a rotten thing to women. Now I realize they are often as tragic a victim of it as the women are, and that they don't do it to 'exploit' women."

What is it about men that you find more sexually attractive than women?

"The whole male body is sexually attractive to me. The lines which are trim and solid-looking are very appealing. To me women are like uncooked bread dough, soft and unappealing. I guess I would have been a good Greek because I think the male body is a thing of beauty."

"Sexually, men can prove their satisfaction by orgasm, whereas with women, you never know if you're really satisfying them. When having sex with a guy, satisfaction is naturally mutual. No faking."

"It's the fact that their sexual excitement can be seen—an erect penis."

"Aggression. Hard-ons. That glazed-eye look of passion. Typical masculine sexual responses are a real turn-on."

"Older women have a tendency of getting sloppy, overweight, unattractive, and let themselves run down. I dislike so much in the way of cosmetics. Women primp, pluck their eyebrows—they can't be themselves. They have to wear awful 'eyeshadow' (usually overdone), have to fiddle and fool with makeup. Why not be themselves?"

"It's that big bulge between their legs and what we can do with it, which to me provides an excitement and attraction and desire to share a sexual experience that is just not there with a woman."

"The man's body, the cock, are wonderful to me. The woman is a cave, a darkness, a mystery. I don't want to go in there."

"When I make it with a man, we have sex as equals. Everything I can do to him, he can do to me. I know what I like and I attempt to give him the same pleasure. I get pleasure out of knowing from experience what he feels when I do something to him. I believe that the fact each one knows what the other feels increases the pleasure for both of us."

"I like men's chests. They aren't all soft and lumpy. They are hard and firm. I like penises. They are fun to touch and they get hard and big. The testes are fun to hold in your hand. Men's asses are better-shaped than women's and are fun to grab ahold of. I like the odor of a man's body. A man moves nicer and talks with a deep voice."

"I just love the look of men's bodies. They turn me on when they are smooth and muscular. And they can fuck me when a woman can't."

"I do not find men more sexually attractive than women. I find they are sexually attractive in different ways."

"It isn't that men are *more* sexually attractive than women. It's that women are of no desire to me as sexual objects. I have nothing against women and can frequently admire their beauty and appreciate their sexuality. It's just that I have no great desire for their sexuality and can never remember ever having that desire."

"Men feel better physically, through their muscles, and they smell better. Maybe there's an element of familiarity that makes a man more appealing. And besides, so far we don't get pregnant! I can fuck as much as I choose and never hear a word about paternity suits, child support, etc. Sex with men is freer."

"What I don't find sexually attractive about women is all the softness and roundness. One of the things I find sexually attractive about men in general is angularity and hardness. A cock excites me tremendously, a cunt doesn't. A chest is dynamic. Tits are mushy. Men smell better. Men's faces are ... Oh! I could go on and on."

"Perhaps I can explain it by saying for example that I enjoy a man because of the feeling of strength, whereas with a woman, I see them as too soft; and not able to give me the support I need."

"I guess I am basically narcissistic: other men turn me on because I turn me on. Don't get me wrong, I think women are beautiful, but I just don't find them sexually attractive at the moment."

"Men are naturally handsome—most women have to wear makeup and what you're actually seeing is an illusion. Why have an illusion when you can have the real thing?"

"Men are more predictable sexually, more quickly aroused, seem to enjoy sex more often and with greater relish. Men do not have the cloying needs in a relationship that are so typical of women."

"I like the ability of men to be so gentle while being so strong."

"I like men's bodies more. The preference is primarily aesthetic, it seems to me. In other respects—intellect, sensitivity, emotional honesty—women are more attractive to me. But these qualities don't arouse my lust, at least not nearly as much as the physical beauty I find in men."

"It is hard to explain, but I would much rather look at a naked man than a naked woman. I guess this makes gays rather fortunate because we can 'legally' look at other guys in the gym showers all the time. Makes for a nice life."

"Let me answer by saying that the female sex anatomy repels me. I think of it as actually ugly. The frontal views of women in *Playboy* and other magazines upset me. The thought of the sex act with women in revolting to me. Perhaps it has something to do with the fact that as a boy I was subjected to the jokes about a woman's 'pussy' before I had been educated to appreciate sexual union with a woman."

"I'm a homosexual, therefore I like men, and am attracted to things masculine in a person for relationships. No woman has ever been masculine enough for me to find her sexually attractive."

"I have the same body the other fellow does, so I know what he feels when I suck him or lick him or fuck him. I don't have to guess. We go to the bathroom the same way— he doesn't have periods, he doesn't have water-weight gains or moods. He thinks like I do (which is not to demean the way a woman thinks—but I really don't know how a woman thinks because I am not a woman). I think there is less bullshit between a man and a man."

"I feel this question is sort of a useless one—I am attracted to men, so all things essentially male should by definition attract me, and listing them does not explain *why* I am attracted to them, only *that* I am."

What can an emotional relationship with a man offer you that one with a woman cannot?

The replies to the last question were so widely varied that few conclusions could be drawn from them. The responses to this question are also varied, but there is a dominant theme which appears in the majority of them: in an emotional relationship with another man, gay men most value the *empathy* which they share with their partner because both are men. This is much the same feeling discussed in the answers to the

question "How would you characterize your emotional involvements with men?"—the idea that two men romantically
involved are "best friends" taken a few steps farther:

"Other men understand me better than women can. We're
soul mates. Our views are similar. Our interests are similar.
Our problems are similar. We're not emotional dichotomies,
we're the same *species*."

"I believe that a man, simply because he is a man, can understand and cope with my feelings better than a woman
can."

"A man feels the way I feel. He can be my other self, my
best friend, my lover. A man can be to me what a woman is
to a straight man—and more."

"There is a mutual basic understanding that two men can
share that a man and a woman cannot. Plus I do honestly
feel two giving, loving men in a relationship have no limits
and achieve heights no male-female relationships can achieve.
It's hard to describe, but it's like reaching to one's soul."

"It's simply the commonality of male emotional and psy-
chic urges—libido, I guess. This produces recognizable and
direct approaches, outlooks, and actions in comfortable,
relaxed personal relationships and shared interests and activities. This male rapport exists of course in straight society, but
role requirements have warped such relationships to the
locker-room syndrome."

"An understanding of the male sexual urge—in that fucking others need not mean we don't love each other anymore.
Less clouding of realities because of romance."

"I, for some stupid macho reason I suppose, do not feel
comfortable completely unwinding or leaning on a woman
for emotional support. With a gay man, I can support him
and then when I need it, allow myself to be supported by
him. With a man I can really be myself and be open. They
know where I'm coming from and can empathize much easier
than a woman. Sexually I can relax far more and turn my
feelings and fantasies loose with a man."

"Womenfolk get things too 'frilly'—worry too much about
insignificant things. And most are clinging-vine types (or so it
seems). They expect too much financially, want new furniture to keep up with the Jones family. Living with a man, he
has the same problems of keeping debts paid, and shares the
cost of living, and the experiences of living, and their problems are compatible. Womenfolk add to the costs of living all
the time."

"Men bring me pleasure in a body I know and understand better than a woman's. Intimacy and closeness with a human who is 'another me' and not *the other*."

Many of the men replied that they feel less pressure in many different areas when they are involved emotionally with a man:

"I feel more at ease about everything with a man, and I am speaking of a gay man. I feel more myself. I don't feel that there are unrealistic demands or expectations made of me. I'm a free agent. I don't feel I am some kind of possession. If I want to go someplace by myself, even to get a pack of cigarettes at the drugstore, I don't have to offer a lengthy dissertation about it—I just go and come back. My wife had made me feel that I owed her an existence. If I spent too long practicing or writing, she complained that I was uncaring, inattentive, and selfish; that I took her for granted. What she did not understand is that I do not feel that I am anything without my work. I would have nothing to offer anyone if I didn't do it. In living with a man, I am able to do my work, and as a consequence, I have a great deal to offer in terms of love and companionship—*after* the work."

"It offers freedom. There is no family life to worry about. Even though I don't foresee my lover and me breaking up, if we do we don't have to worry about anything but going our separate ways. I basically want to be free; free to do the things that I want to do and not have to consult a woman to find out what she wants to do."

"The relationship with a man affords for me a more comfortable togetherness without the male-female role-playing—I don't have to wait until she goes through the door, I don't have to open the car door, etc. There is a feeling I can do and say anything and he can do anything without thinking about the social graces learned for being with women. I am more relaxed around men."

"A relationship with a woman usually involves the possibility of children. I want to avoid such relationships until I can live with that possibility."

"When I commit myself to a relationship with another man we more or less have a firm understanding what each wants and expects from the other. I do not feel used or threatened or afraid—just a willing participant. Women demand much more emotionally than I have to give them. This leaves me feeling drained, helpless, inadequate, sterile, paranoid, etc.

Most men I've known give me what I want and need, take what they want and need and then we each go about our separate business of living our own lives. Women become tenacious and hang on and demand more and more. Relations with another man offer me considerably more freedom to be myself, to do and act as I want to."

Some men feel that sex is an important element in a gay emotional relationship:

"To me, sexual compatibility is one of the most important factors in a romantic relationship. I could never live with a woman because she would not interest me sexually. I suppose there aren't too many other things a man could offer me in a day-to-day relationship that a woman couldn't—so I'd have to say it's sex."

"I believe, in essence, only women know what turns on another woman and only a man knows what turns on another man. Therefore, a man offers me fulfillment."

"Men offer more availability than women (easier to get intimate with) plus variations I find emotionally satisfying—variations that are impossible with women."

"A man-to-man relationship is one that you can get down to quickly. The games are minimal, if the two of you are really serious. None of this 'will he respect me in the morning?' stuff! Men aren't taught to defend their virtue and 'be nice.' (I am very much a staunch supporter of the feminist movement in this regard—the double standard toward women has got to go!)"

"My climax comes much faster with a woman than with a man, so the pleasure is longer with a man."

"I have found the absence of 'performance' in our homosexual relationship the opening door to genuine sexuality."

Many men simply expressed negative feelings about women, and/or positive feelings about men:

"I cannot describe it, but it's real. I can compare five years with a woman with two with a man and tell you men are more exciting—and gay men especially so. There are all the paradoxes—strength and sensitivity, dominant and submissive, masculine and feminine and so on. It offers me more excitement, more sex, more fun, more growth, more possibilities."

"A woman has emotional needs and I cannot relate to them fully. My wife was very dependent on me for support in all her undertakings. She expected me to take command in all given situations, social, taking care of the house. She would not initiate sex at any time, expected change but would not contribute new ideas. I find men and their independence very refreshing. My lover and I share all—the housework, marketing, cooking, laundry, entertaining. We find doing it together more fun and the mundane tasks get done twice as fast, leaving time for more important matters."

"I am interested in male occupations, interests. The outdoors. Bike runs. Sports. Somehow I suspect that even if I were straight I would not get married. Most straight men I know seem to, once the marriage has progressed, retire to a man's world. It seems that most of the battles between the sexes begin between the sheets. And I can do without that."

"Friendship. Honesty. (No crazy schemes, etc.) Good sex. Besides, girls are expensive, even if you're married to them. Two boys living together and working full time can enjoy much more economic freedom. I know from experience of others."

"I need to feel secure and looked after in a way only a man can do it."

"I think that by training in the WASP culture I am not aware of women's needs. As I have thought of them as sort of a backup to a male-dominated world, they had no significance of their own. I didn't like the idea of being the better or worse half of a male-female relationship."

"I find men are more honest than women. I can never tell if a woman really means what she says. Men are also more willing to share and to give. Men are less selfish in their love. There is also a certain feeling of comradeship between men. I know women married for years whose relationships with their husbands are still nothing more than games. Men seem to know each other intuitively. There is less need for games and more room for an open, loving relationship."

"I have had happier and less demanding relationships with men than with women. Women, in my experience, will not let me be myself, but try to change who I am. The men who have loved me have loved *me*, as I am, and didn't try to rework me into someone who would be their ideal of a person. It's in *My Fair Lady*—'She'll take over the enthralling fun of overhauling *you*.' Most of what I have talked about above are psychological considerations. As far as sex with men goes, contrasted with women, it's more fun and less work."

What are your feelings about lesbianism?

Most of the men in this survey (67.1%) had very positive feelings about gay women:

"I feel a kind of kinship with gay people, whether they are male or female, and lesbians are really my sisters. There's a lesbian bar near where I live, and I sometimes go there when I just want to be around gay people, but am not especially interested in cruising or whatever. I always feel at home there; once the girls realize you're not after their bodies they usually treat you like a friend."

"I feel the same about lesbians as male homosexuality: that it's wonderful, blessed, and a good facet of humanity."

"In general, I find lesbian women to be more stimulating and interesting than heterosexual women."

"I sometimes feel more comfortable with lesbians than I do with other gay men."

"The lesbians I know have impressed me with their being more responsible in relationships than most gay men."

"It is wonderful that two loving women can enjoy themselves in this way. It is a liberating thing for them against the sometimes tyrannical attitude of some men to their women. Women have a great sex drive too, which is just beginning to emerge."

"I think when women love each other emotionally, they are more caring and gentle and understanding than men."

"Right on! I wish more women were. Then maybe they'd leave *us* alone!"

"I never knowingly met any lesbians until I visited a Metropolitan Community Church in June. There were humpy gays all over the place, but they just stared and were standoffish. I felt so out of place, I was about ready to leave when this woman came up to me, greeted me, welcomed me, and started introducing me to the guys around me. The next time I got up the courage to go back, she greeted me again (remembered my name) and I soon realized that the lesbians were the friendly, outgoing people there. The first month I got to know about two dozen lesbians on a first-name basis, but the gays were still standoffish—I think we're all afraid of being rebuffed."

"Lesbians are the only women I like to meet because they don't try to have me."

"They tend to have relationships that are much more stable and long-lasting than those of men. I don't feel this is due to any special capabilities on their part, but due to less pressure on their relationships from society."

"I think lesbians are just fine. They have some harsh opinions about men, but for the most part they are right, because many men, including gay men, are sexist, chauvinists, male supremists, etc. It's definitely there, and it should be broken. Women are equal, they have their rights like any man. I respect women, I respect feminists, and support their causes wholeheartedly. I thought the Women's Convention in Houston was great, and I had a continuous chill throughout my body for thirty seconds when I heard the Lesbian Bill passed."

"I think lesbianism is great. How could I feel any other way?"

"I have lesbian friends and they are very feminine people. I don't know why lesbians have a reputation for being hard, brutal, and mean."

"I could never see why lesbians and gay men couldn't get along, they have so much in common."

"Right on! They have every right to love who they want to love. If I was a woman, I think I'd be a lesbian. Straight men are so obnoxious."

"Some of my best friends are lesbians. I don't think about it often, but I'm sure sex between gay men is much more fun."

"I think if bars were mixed, they would be more socially oriented than sexually oriented because the presence of the opposite sex would make the atmosphere less tense sexually."

"Lesbians will prove to be the strength of all women."

"I think lesbians and gay men should be more united. We know very little about each other's lifestyles. They should get their rights also—custody of their kids, etc."

"Gay men and women should mix more. There are two sexes in the world, and it's not just for fucking purposes, either."

"I don't like straight women generally—they are fake. Lesbians are real human beings. We have a political commonality. We understand our oppression because it's shared."

"The lesbians I know are extremely brave people who live in a society that discriminates against them first as women, then as gays. They deserve much more support than they get from the women's movement and from the gay liberation movement."

"I never thought about it till about a year ago. I've noticed lately that gay women are often fantastically appealing spokespeople for gay rights, whereas men seldom are. I heard a public radio show about gay teachers and the lesbians struck me as happy, pleasant people I would like to know. The men struck me as obnoxious stereotypes. Then I read *Rubyfruit Jungle* and I think that solidified my position. The success of the gay-rights plank at the Women's Conference was the icing on the cake. Hurray for lesbians!"

22.7% of the men had negative feelings about lesbianism:

"I have just begun to meet lesbians and am just now beginning to know them. Currently I am very prejudiced toward them and do not like them. I find them hard, uncaring, and demanding. They try to manipulate and control me excessively and I find I need to back out of confrontation with them or face a collision, as I am very stubborn."

"Socially, I find it is a bad inclination, but I feel the same way about homosexual attractions—in other words, I have been completely *burned* by the Conservative tradition—I have to intellectualize being kind to Jews and Negroes and others who aren't quite in the correct stream of things. This is dreadful prejudice, and I fight it."

"I feel alienated about lesbianism because I don't know *shit* about it. I have very little interest to study lesbianism because I'm not directly affected by it."

"I think it's weird. Isn't that amazing? I think it's very bizarre. I don't know what they do with each other. I don't like their masculinity (don't like feminine men either) and they scare me. They're too tough. Every fucking stereotype!"

"I wish I knew more about it. Since I see nothing attractive in women, I cannot see why other women do. I am really ashamed to admit that I am as benighted about (and as quick to stereotype) lesbians as the average heterosexual."

"I subconsciously loathe and feel threatened by lesbians, even though I politically support their rights."

"Let the ladies love one another, as they should. They dress for each other. They paint their faces and scent themselves for one another. Let a man try to choose a woman's clothes. She will refuse his taste and select what has a value to some other woman's choice. A man is never involved. On the Isle of Lesbos men were cast off cliffs. Sorry Sappho."

"Two penises are better than one. None is simply inconceivable."

"My instinct makes male homosexuality much more natural than the funny behavior of lesbians. Maybe that is because they do not have a good weapon (phallus) and cannot perform the real thrust of sex."

"Sorry, I don't like them. They have the worst traits of both sexes."

"I don't feel threatened by them, but am bored to death with their rhetoric. I would really like to find some that I could relate to. I have never met one that indicated the slightest trust in me or interest in any mutual friendship."

"Why do most of them keep such a double standard? Try to keep a woman out of a men's bar in Chicago and they will scream like hell. But let a guy into one of the three women's bars here in Chicago and it's a different story. They will ask for all sorts of ID if you are not with women they know and even if you are they don't like it. One place has had guys beaten. Of course, the women will give you all kinds of good reasons why men shouldn't come to their bars but in a reverse situation no reason is good enough."

"I guess I'm a little afraid of them. Their masculinity is rarely toned down by the gentleness of a bona-fide man. The femmes I have no problem with."

"I cannot comprehend what they feel. I can understand straight sex more easily because at least *part* of what turns me on is involved."

"I'm probably somewhat jealous because two women can show affection in public much easier than men."

"I have far more in common with straight women—who are attracted to men, as I am."

"I think women are rather selfish and petty and I find they are very bitchy with each other. Thus I cannot bring myself to see the possibility of a loving and physically fulfilling relationship between two women. I do try to understand, although I find it difficult to equate lesbianism with male homosexuality."

"It does not seem to be a very joyful life. I'm sure that my views are clouded by prejudice and stereotypes. Lesbianism exists, it has little if any impact or influence on my life; consequently I see no reason for giving it any consideration. This may seem superficial or careless, but I have no feelings about lesbianism other than the conviction in their right to love whomever they choose without persecution."

Do you ever dress in women's clothing?

Do most gay men enjoy dressing up in the clothing of the opposite sex? Are those who do attempting to be women? Are most transvestites homosexuals?

The answer to each of these questions is no. According to the findings of researchers Prince and Bentler in 1972* and Pomeroy in 1975,** most transvestites are heterosexual men. Often married, they lead "acceptably" masculine lives for the most part. Their cross-dressing offers them a sexual excitement because they are wearing the garments usually worn by the objects of their sexual desire. Usually, this kind of transvestism is engaged in with varying frequency in private.

Many public transvestites, those who wear women's clothes in everyday public situations or as part of a stage presentation, are also heterosexual, but the number of homosexuals in this group is higher than among more "closeted" transvestites. Many of these men enjoy projecting a feminine image to the world part of the time; many see it as a form of acting; others are pre-operative transsexuals. With the exceptions of the transsexuals, most of these men would not rather be women.

Homosexuality and transvestism are in no way synonymous—a fact made clear by the research findings mentioned above, as well as by this study. 86.3% of the men have never dressed in women's clothing, others have not since reaching adulthood. Five percent of the men said that they sometimes dress in women's clothing; most of these said it was for costume parties and at Halloween.

2.6% answered "yes." Many of those men stated that dressing as a woman was fun, "a camp," and, in some cases, a thumbing of their noses at society:

* V. Prince and P. M. Bentler, "Survey of 504 Cases of Transvestism," *Psychological Reports*, 31:903, 1972.
** Wardell Pomeroy, "The Diagnosis and Treatment of Transvestites and Transsexuals," *Journal of Sex and Marital Therapy*, 1:3, 1975.

"Last Halloween I went to a costume party in drag. It was the first time I'd ever tried it. I even shaved off my mustache, a great sacrifice, but I enjoyed it. I was very uptight about that sort of thing for a long time, since I had a prejudice against effeminate men, and was probably afraid that I was one myself. I gradually got over that hang-up, and I'm glad, because going in drag was really fun for me. Some of my old friends didn't recognize me for a long time! I'm not usually at all physically or sexually attracted to men dressed as women, but I'm fascinated by them. I love to be around really campy queens with their good-natured viciousness and their brothel humor."

"I was at a costume party in France, where I was studying, and I did it for two reasons. One was to see what it would be like to be in drag, and the other was to deliberately horrify and repulse some fellow students who were goody-goodies. I was pleased with the result; they were, indeed, horrified. Plus, I was propositioned by a royal personage who was also a student. When he discovered that I was not female, he seemed even more intrigued. Nothing came of it, though, as I had made other arrangements for the evening. I shall always remember that evening with a certain amount of pleasure, if not actual glee."

"I do it for fun, like at Halloween. I like to express the feminine side of my nature. I like to camp without drag when I'm among friends. I *like* my feminine attributes, and enjoy other men who get into drag for reasons similar to my own. I'm not attracted to men who want to *be* women."

"Other than in plays, I have only gone in drag on a couple of Halloweens. It's not a sexual thing for me; it's the elation I get from successfully playing a character part—whether it's a woman or an old man."

"Last Halloween I went as Maggie Smith in *The Prime of Miss Jean Brodie* to Studio One. And the year before, five of my friends and I crashed a Tupperware party in Fullerton, California, dressed as hausfraus. It's to the credit of the salesperson that she continued and only once did her mouth fall open."

4% of the men in this survey report that they used to dress in women's clothing, mostly when they were children:

"I did enjoy it when I was a kid, but so did my brother, and he's straight. I think we have a need to express both our masculine and feminine sides and that one need not fear this need and realize that we can express both without being labeled either butch or femme."

"I did it when I was young, because I thought that was a way to attract men."

"At about thirteen or so I would put on my older sister's clothes—it was the only way I knew of to have a man attracted to me. About a year or so later I learned differently."

"When I was in my early teens, I used to put on my mom's clothes and makeup when my family went out in the evening, and I used to call on our neighbors and ask directions, etc., just for fun. It *was* sort of fun. Of course, they didn't know who I was, or I hope they didn't."

"When I first came out at seventeen and tried to get into the gay world, the only people who were visibly gay were the most effeminate ones, and a lot of these were drag queens. I thought that this was what it meant to be gay, so I got into it. I didn't hate it or anything, but I later discovered that there are a lot of masculine homosexuals, too, and I was then able to express my true nature. People who know me now can't even imagine me ever having been in drag."

"I used to be a drag. Because at that time I thought that was what a faggot was."

Some of the men, although never having dressed in drag, have positive feelings about transvestism and/or transvestites:

"While I am not attracted to men dressed in drag nor do I do it, I respect them for being what they were born to be and not trying to hide it."

"I'm not sexually attracted to transvesites, but I do enjoy their company and I love seeing a good drag show—Charles Pierce, Jim Bailey, etc. I think many transvestites are more courageous than so-called butch guys because they dare to be themselves and risk societal *and* gay disapproval. No gay person should ever put down another gay person."

"I do admire the 'gender fuck' as it's called, implicit in doing drag—the 'put-down' of stereotyped thinking as to what 'masculine' means."

"I've never dressed as a woman; in fact, I'm afraid to. It would probably be a good growing experience for me. I think I would do it with someone else . . . maybe a woman."

"I especially like to see blatant drag—men with hairy

chests, mustaches, etc. It is the ultimate thumbing of the nose at straight society."

"I see a lot of men who I find attractive in drag, but they are usually the ones who don't do it regularly. I would find it very exciting to undress them, and find that man underneath."

"I'm attracted to men dressed as women because it fulfills a fantasy of being fucked by a woman."

The majority of the men, however, have negative feelings on the subject:

"I cringe at the image projected by such men except for two or three notable professional entertainers. I often feel embarrassed by and for the typical 'drag queens' who appear at gay and straight clubs or in any public place. I feel that 'drags' (men and women) in the public eye only serve to reinforce the many negative images straights have of gays in general. Despite these personal feelings, I would not want to be guilty of the same discrimination I accuse others of—'Free to Be You and Me' includes the rights of transsexuals, transvestites, drag queens, et al."

"I find transvestites extremely sad, and when exposed to them on stage nearly always get depressed and want to cry for them."

"I'm not at all attracted to drag queens. I enjoy seeing a good drag when it's all in fun. I get a little uneasy when those involved take it too seriously. Besides, if I wanted a woman I'd go after a real one."

"I sense something 'fake' about guys in drag. It seems to me that they don't belong in women's clothes. Possibly they are trying to be something that they are not, and that I can sense this, which I find repugnant. This is one reason why I never go to drag shows."

"A female impersonator strikes me much the same as plastic flowers—at best, a poor imitation of the real thing. But I realize that transvestism is a real need of some men, and I do not condemn them for it. I'm just as gay as they are."

"For me, the whole point of being a homosexual is that I am a man wanting another man. It has nothing remotely to do with women; if it did, I would seek out women, not men who wear dresses."

"I find this very repulsive and sick. I have often said that there are extremes in the gay world, much to the detriment of more moderate gays. I think we should admit that men who want to be women are sick. Not just because about 100% of the population find them repulsive but because these people are in need of help. It is terrible to want to be something you are not. These pathetic people march around trying to be sexy and are often turned away by more moderate gays. It leaves them, to a large degree, with only the old and lonely, those who want to be supported, and other unfortunates to pick from."

"Drag is the biggest reason gays are hated and ridiculed. The TVs cause gay oppression more than anything else. Far from being attracted to such people, I despise them for what their existence does to gays, and I groan whenever a gay publication gives them any coverage. Every time a guy puts on a dress, it sets gay rights back. When I was a boy, and was told that being gay meant you dressed up like a woman, I was in agony. This kept me from understanding and accepting being gay for several years. I resent being discriminated against because all gays are lumped with the drag queens. No one—not Anita Bryant, not John Briggs, not Ed Davis—has ever hurt gay people or gay rights as much as men who wear dresses. The final irony is that most transvestites are heterosexual."

Would you rather be a woman?

Most of the responses to this question were brief and emphatic. "No way," "Hell, no," and "No damn way—forget it" were typical. The overwhelming majority of respondents (97%) report that they are quite happy with being men and have no doubt about their sexual gender identity. These responses indicate that male homosexuality has very little to do with feeling like, or wanting to be, the opposite sex. Most of these men stressed here that they are men who are attracted to other men, and they profess no desire to change that.

Seven men in this survey did say that they would rather be women, and thirty-five others reported that they used to feel that way:

"Many times I have wished I were a woman. Because as a woman, I feel I could have a better emotional and sexual relationship with a man. Deep down inside, I've always wanted to be a 'home-maker' with a house full of children and a *man* to be sort of a 'slave' to. The kind of woman that Marabelle Morgan writes about in her *Total Woman* book of garbage. I would not have a sex-change operation because I don't feel I could 'face' my family if I did."

"I would rather be a woman. I can't say why—I don't think anybody knows the why about sexual identity. I wanted to have an operation but now I wouldn't—it's too dangerous, complicated, and ultimately unrewarding."

"I'd still be getting a man. I wouldn't be missing anything. I would have a sex-change operation if I had the money. I was going to go through with it, but I thought, What's the use, I can't afford it. But I'd like to, really."

"When I was younger, about fifteen, I wanted to become a girl and from reading about sex-change operations, felt I wanted one. But as I've matured, my outlook on the subject is quite reversed. I like being a man, now that I have fully accepted my own sexuality."

"As a child I wanted to be a girl, but now I don't think I could stand it. I admire people who have had the courage to do it. I don't get sad watching Christine Jorgensen, I love her."

"There was a time (when I was married) that I would have liked to have been a woman—so I could screw all I wanted. But now that I have a gay lover, I am completely satisfied and I no longer have this desire."

"I think I wanted to be a woman when I was fourteen or fifteen or sixteen or so but I also wanted to kill myself then too, and run away from home and be my sister's husband's wife and just die. But since my awareness of my homosexuality and my acceptance of myself, I certainly haven't felt that way. I would not care to have a sex-change operation and I enjoy doing the masculine outdoor things and doing them in the company of men who also enjoy these things."

"I feel I would function more effectively as a woman. I would enjoy dancing, singing, having sex, dressing, living as a woman. If I were a woman and could still have my voice I'd put Barbra Streisand in the poor house. This must sound narcissistic but it's true. I would be a success as a woman."

"As a child, I thought women had it made. It seemed to me that all they had to do was make themselves attractive enough to marry the right man, and they were fixed for life without any of the worries of working or having to support a family. I greatly envied that. It wasn't tied in to sexual desires. I resented the fact that as a boy I was expected to be interested in so many things—sports, hunting, fishing, camping, etc.—that turned me off. I liked color, but back then boys could wear only blue, brown, black, and certain limited shades of green or maroon. Before puberty, if the chance had been offered to become a girl with the snap of a finger, I'd probably have accepted. But when I reached puberty and realized all the great possibilities inherent in what I'd have to give up . . . no way!"

Twelve of the men say they sometimes think it might be preferable to be a woman:

"Sometimes I wish that I were a woman, because I am attracted to men, and if I were a woman, this would be acceptable. Also, the kind of men who are attracted to me tend to be effeminate, and that kind does nothing for me. Straight men seem much more genuinely masculine, but they are attracted to women. I would not go so far as to have a sex change operation."

"I would have no sex-change operation, but if I could be a woman that would be great because I would have no difficulty laying the most gorgeous man in town."

"It would be nice to have what the straight guys really dig, but all the rest of being a woman does not appeal to me. So I suppose the sex change is not for me, although I have fantasized about it a few times. The only part I would like is having intercourse with a man in the way he would like."

"The only reason I would ever want to be a woman is so that I could have that many more men. Undoubtedly I would be the biggest whore or nympho or whatever to get as many cocks as I could if I were a female. I would probably be dead long ago from pure and simple *excess.* I honestly don't think, however, that I would actually want to be a woman. I would prefer to have as much sex as possible with as many men as possible as the man that I am, than to be a woman with all the attendant crap females have to put up with."

The vast majority of the respondents are opposed to the very idea:

"Christ no! I like my cock and I like to fuck. Just because I also like to be fucked does not mean that I wish to be female. I would lose the 'buddy' relationship I have with men which I like and a male straight would not know in many cases how to turn me on as a female. A gay man knows how to turn on another gay man."

"Surgery results only in external changes, in either direction, and it does not change the inner person. There is an intellectual dishonesty in it. Being given a cock that can't harden doesn't make a woman a man. Being given a pussy that can't be entered by a man's cock and won't produce babies doesn't make a man a woman. What these people need is psychotherapy that will help them accept what they are without trying to become something they can never be. I am a man with a capacity of love for men in all ways, and I will not make myself more valuable to a man by having my cock and balls cut off."

"I rather doubt that the sex change is a very satisfactory operation. I'll stick with my seven inches. Any reading I have done on this subject has indicated a lot of unhappiness. We should all make the best of what we have."

"God made me. Why should I change his work?"

"Definitely not! Then I wouldn't be a gay man and feel and experience my gayness for my same sex. How dare you!"

"No. I wouldn't be able to screw a man the way that he could screw me."

"I love my cock. I love being a man loving a man. I would hate having a period or unwanted pregnancies."

"I love everything male, and that includes myself. I am very proud of my body and also quite vain. I will never comprehend how a man can be dissatisfied with being a man. I think the male body is the closest thing to perfection. I have a great body and men find it very attractive, as do women; I have no desire to mutilate it."

"I think it is actually spiritually damaging to change sex."

"I wouldn't want to be a woman in this day and age for several reasons. One is women are oppressed, and the other—I probably couldn't have the guys I wanted. To me, all the best ones are gay!"

"I was born male, feel that I am in every sense of the word a male, and do not wish to change that in any way. I would never consider or have the need for a sex-change operation. This whole question is barely related to homosexuality. Transsexuality and transvestism are different subjects."

"The very idea horrifies me."

"What I have between my legs makes me what I am. I'm happy being the man that I am. To me, my dick is the greatest treasure on earth."

PART FIVE: PROBLEMS

Have you ever been arrested for a sexual activity?

Eight percent of the men in this survey have been arrested at some point in their lives for a sexual activity:

"I was arrested when I was about nineteen. I was hornier than hell and still a virgin. I had pulled my car off on a dark sidestreet in a deserted area. I climbed in the back seat, pulled my pants off, and was jacking off when suddenly a spotlight flooded my car. I tried to get my pants back on but the cops came up and looked in the window before I could get them on. They knew damn well what was going on but they still took me down to jail, booked me, and put me in a cell overnight. What an experience!! The next morning, my parents came down and got me out. I was scared silly from being in the cell all night with all the adults around. When my parents showed up I was so embarrassed I wanted to run away from home.

"Since that time jails terrify me. Then I worried my whole life about what that police record of 'disorderly conduct' would do to my chances for employment, etc. I have since gotten security clearances but that charge still lurks in the back of my mind as something really nasty and evil in my background. Even writing about it here makes me feel nauseated and very uncomfortable. It was pure shit to put someone through that and this for a lifetime just for jacking off in a car with no one around. Those feelings that masturbation was a crime really set me up later when I started having feelings about sex with men. My God, if masturbation is a crime, what can male-male sex, feelings, fantasies be? I suspect that is why I fought my gay feelings so long and with such intensity."

"I was arrested for just touching the outside of a guy's pants in high school. He went to his parents, who in turn went to the police."

"I was arrested once. It cost a fortune. It was in the horrible '50s. The kid was sixteen, but he looked in his twenties. I'll never forget the treatment of the police. Like Nazi Germany. I'm registered as a homosexual, which is shit."

"I've never been arrested for sexual activity but I have been arrested because I was homosexual. I was the doorman at a gay club. Several young street kids tried to crash the place, a fight followed, and the police came. They let the guys go who had beaten up several patrons but I was arrested. I've been told to 'fuck off' by a police officer while working at the same club. I was also stabbed while working at the club. The police made no effort to find the person who stabbed me. I was never questioned by the police although I was on the critical list in the hospital."

"I was once arrested and tried for having sex in public, but it became obvious that the whole thing was manufactured. I received financial aid in paying the lawyer but lost a lot of time and energy dealing with the case. At the time I was very upset and indignant but I learned to compromise and settle for a dismissal of charges."

"I was arrested at the baths in 1971. The place was raided; I was having sex with a guy. I spent three days in jail before bail was set. As a result, I hate cops with such a passion that it's unhealthy. I'm trying to overcome this now."

"I paid $2,500 to get the charge dismissed. I think this was a big rip-off. A bail bondsman in the Valley gave me this lawyer's name as a guy who knew how to get people off. It took ten minutes in court. But I think this lawyer is a scab. I was charged with soliciting a cop in a restroom, which I did not do. I was loitering, perhaps. I have lived in fear of getting caught ever since."

"At eighteen I was arrested for being sucked on in a public restroom. Paid $800 and got off on a misdemeanor. Never had sex in a restroom again!"

"I have been arrested for a sexual activity as the result of a relationship I had with a fourteen-year-old boy who was consenting in every sense of the word and who had lived with me for nearly fourteen months. Even though he was unwilling to testify against me, I was found guilty of Infamous Crimes Against Nature, and was sentenced to life in prison with a possibility of parole after five years. I am still serving this sentence."

"I was arrested by an off-duty cop working for J.C. Penney's in a T-room myself and a married guy were messing around. At first we were booked on a lesser charge, a misdemeanor, and the next day the state changed it to sodomy and months later we were indicted but the case dragged on and on and the cop changed his story sort of—he lied about what he said he saw and what his actions were and we just kept quiet, though the married guy turned on me and tried to blame me for the whole thing. I had bailed out the S.O.B. and then he tried to make a deal. His lawyer had him take a lie-detector test, and mine called me and said, 'You'll be glad to know Mr. S— failed his test with flying colors.' Ah, humanity. Ended, of course, in plea-bargain."

"I propositioned a young fellow I met in a bar and he started beating me and dragged me to a policeman who took me to the station, booked me for 'invitation to sodomy.' I paid the bail the next day and was released. Other than the invitation, nothing happened."

"I've not been arrested directly for being homosexual, but as a youth I was considered an 'incorrigible,' 'delinquent,' and other things which were really for being a homosexual."

"Three times. All were 'tearoom' busts. One was an illegal arrest, since I never did anything but loiter, but was charged with lewd conduct and convicted. Needless to say, these were the worst experiences of my life. After my first arrest (while I was still in the navy), I spent a *month* in L.A. County Jail awaiting trial. I had to wear a little card in my shirt pocket which had my name, serial number, and 'sex perversion' written on it."

"The military found out about me and had me court-martialed. I was discharged with an undesirable discharge. After that they held me in jail for three months waiting for my papers to arrive."

"I was twice placed under arrest on suspicion of being a homosexual. At the age of eighteen, I was arrested in a cafeteria in downtown Los Angeles that was frequented by gays and because I did not have my draft card with me, I was taken to Lincoln Heights jail for being at suspicious premises. I was placed in a common cell, where I was propositioned by various attractive black and white inmates while the policemen watched. I had the sense to turn them down. It was an instructive experience."

"At the age of thirty-two, while working for the U.S. government, I was denounced by a jealous neighbor for giving gay parties. I was placed in the psychiatric ward of the local army hospital and observed for a week, while an agent impersonated me on the phone and tried to entrap various German and American gay friends. There were embarrassing interrogations, but nothing specific was proven. I resigned from my job for the good of the service and went back to college—one of the better decisions of my life."

"I was twenty, and was blowing a soldier in a car in a park. The cop beat me up. I was booked while the soldier was alleged to have been forced. My brother used family influence to get the charge dropped."

"Yes, I was arrested. I lost my job, had a year of psychiatric care, and had to redirect my life. It has been traumatic for ten years."

"It was a matter of meeting a kid down by the river, and making too aggressive an approach. He ran off home and along came the cops, to take me in on a 'statutory rape' charge when all I did was put a hand near his crotch and ask him if he wanted a blow job. Fortunately, my family lawyer made a deal and got me out of the state. For $6,000 in 1963! Almost as bad as blackmail."

Some of the men describe the circumstances surrounding their arrest as entrapment:

"In Arizona, I was in a park and went into the men's room and there was a vice cop in there jacking off with a big hard-on and *he came on to me* and I said, 'Let's go to my place,' and he arrested me and took me to jail. I was out on bail in an hour and the charges were dropped due to lack of evidence the next day."

"I was arrested three times on morals charges; fortunately I had hidden my identification in my tall boots and so gave the vice goons a false name and address (vice squad is an apt name for those fellows). Posted a bond twice for $25 and never went back for trial. All three charges were phony and police entrapment. In London I was having a leisurely piss in a big pissoir in Piccadilly Square. There were a lot of interesting cocks in view, so I took my time and was enjoying the scenery, when two young punk policemen ushered me out to a cute little van, where they interrogated me. I talked them into letting me go as they picked me because I was a well-dressed foreigner, so I threatened to call the Canadian High Commissioner and complain about discrimination against tourists. I used everything in the book, even pulled my glorious wartime career that practically saved the English from the Germans.

"I was also picked up in a Detroit adult movie house; the charge was soliciting. The truth is that I was minding my own business, enjoying the action on the screen and lazily pulling on my own cock, when a young bearded punk sat down beside me. He immediately pulled his little prick out and kept watching me. His equipment was so small compared to those big pieces on the screen that I was entirely turned off, made not the slightest move towards him. He then left and came back a few minutes later with another young punk who flashed a badge and so off to the hoosegow. What a rip-off, in a city that has the highest murder rate in the country and the authorities spend money trying to trick innocent people."

"I saw two men that turned me on. I tried picking them up. I got in their car. I never touched them, we just talked. They kept offering me money. I kept refusing. Finally I said OK, just so I could get in their pants—and I was arrested for soliciting, got a $50 fine and had to spend two weeks in jail. In court I didn't even get a chance to defend myself."

A few men report police activity of a different kind:

"I was in a shopping-center men's room taking a leak and minding my own business. It wasn't very busy, and there was just one other person there, sitting in a stall. I noticed he was playing with himself, and since he was cute, I watched him. He motioned for me to come over, but since I don't go in for that sort of thing, I thought better of it and started to leave. He yelled, 'Hey!' and jumped up, flashing a policeman's badge. My heart was in my throat. He started getting real rough and abusive with me, and when I protested that I hadn't done anything he told me to shut up. He told me I was under arrest, then said, 'Listen, faggot, you get on your knees and suck this cock and I might consider letting you go.' I knew immediately I had no hope any other way, and a 50-50 chance if I followed his instructions. So I did it. To his credit—I suppose—he let me go."

"Once I was in a park and this guy came up to me and pulled out his dick. I started to blow him and he was obviously enjoying it, even ran his fingers through my hair and moaned with pleasure. Then we heard a rustle, his body stiffened, and he called out, 'I got one of 'em, Joe.' His partner and he arrested me and it took me a lot of time and money to get out of it."

"While out of town about a year ago, a guy and I met in a movie booth in a bookstore and were taken out by the police.

The cops checked our IDs, lectured, threatened, and never arrested us. Why they let us go I don't know. The true impact of it hit me later when I thought of how that could have affected my record and my future. It's interesting to note that it didn't take an arrest to teach me a lesson. I'm grateful to the two cops for that and I wish the LAPD could use that as a guideline."

"I was picked up in Australia for sunbathing in the nude on a deserted beach, by two Sydney policemen who I think were 'queer bashers.' I was taken to a cell, stripped, and handcuffed to the bed while the two enjoyed themselves masturbating me and themselves. I was finally let go with a warning that if I said anything about it, I would be beaten all over with a rubber truncheon. Being relatively young at the time, I did nothing about it. Today, it would be a different thing."

Have you ever had any of your rights denied you because you are gay?

Eighteen percent of the men in this survey either know or suspect that they have suffered discrimination. Most of these instances have been in the area of employment:

"I was forced to leave my job when 'homosexual tendencies' showed up on my honorable discharge. They threatened to ruin my life and see to it that the record followed me all my life if I didn't resign. I resigned!"

"Years ago, my boss called me in his office to tell me that the promotion I had expected was going to one of my employees instead of me, as the other man was married. Since I was unmarried, he said, I was 'suspect.' I demanded to know what I might be suspected of. He said, 'Well, you know,' and made an unmistakable motion of his hand. I was really mad and in the following argument got him to admit that I was much better qualified for the job, and he also used the word 'queer' to tell me what I might be suspected of."

"I suspect that my opportunities to teach may have been restricted because I was not married. I had seventy-three interviews in surburban New York, New Jersey, and Connecticut, seventy-two of which came to naught."

"I have lost promotion within the company where I work. They will find another reason not to promote you—like saying, 'You don't get along with your peers.' They cannot prove this and therefore say that is the reason that you were not promoted, instead of saying, 'We disapprove of your lifestyle, therefore we will not promote you.' "

"I could not get a job for almost a year because my last employer found out I was gay and gave me bad references, which I didn't know about—even though I had a good job rating."

"During my last year in college, I confided in the placement counselor that I was gay. Because of this, I wasn't allowed to see the recruiters from business, government, and graduate schools. As a result of this, I groped around blindly for jobs, without knowing what I was qualified for or what was good to try for. I have been to organizations and told them what happened, but they did nothing and offered me no good advice. I have been out of school for nearly four years, and time is running out for me to do anything with my life."

"I was fired from a job after two years because I admitted that I was gay. It hurt deeply."

"My right to honesty (if there is such a right) was denied me while I was in the service. Otherwise, if I had not surrendered this 'right,' I would have had to sacrifice my right to employment in the military service, and I was desperate for a job then. So, you can guess which right I gave up."

"I suspect that I have been denied promotion at the hospital for being openly gay, but that is their problem since they keep hiring incompetent people to do a job I am more than capable of handling successfully. I actually get much amusement out of it."

"I have had my rights denied me for being gay. I have been fired from three jobs in the past, because they 'thought' I 'might be gay.' One job was for a major railroad. I held it for over five years, then an ultra-Catholic Freight Traffic Manager was installed, went on a witch-hunt, and I was dismissed on a framed charge not related to sex. I went to the labor union, and the union man told me it was really because I was gay that I had been fired. They had no *proof*, but they just wanted to terrorize and force even deeper into the closet the other railroad clerks and stenographers, 95% of whom are gay, too! Fortunately, my articles began to sell then, so I was able to survive!"

"Once when I was about nineteen I missed the overtures of my boss and I was fired on a minuscule pretext. I found this out two or three years after the fact. I found this experience very disturbing at the time as I never thought of work and sex at the same time."

"Only once have I been discriminated against for being gay. When I applied for a job in Virginia, I was given a lie-detector test as part of the application. One of the questions was 'Have you had any homosexual activity after age eighteen?' Since I had, I said yes. Even answering the question yes, I still did not get the job."

Some of the men feel they've had their rights denied them in other areas:

"In New York, all homosexual sex is against the law. Each time my lover and I make love, we commit a felony. We have no legal recourse. In the sense that we cannot legally seek redress in the presence of this injustice, our civil rights are denied us."

"I have been denied the use of public accommodations— on one occasion, I was denied service in a restaurant with a group of other gays."

"My lover and I were discriminated against when we attempted to purchase a townhouse together. There were several complexes whose owners were reluctant to sell to two unmarried men. When we finally decided to purchase the townhouse we live in now, my old bank turned us down for a joint mortgage loan. Fortunately we were able to find a bank that was agreeable to the loan. I feel that the bank denial of the loan was the most overt discrimination we faced because we both have good credit ratings, good income, and sufficient savings."

"I've had my rights denied me because I'm gay when I was robbed by a trick. Because I knew the investigation would be nonexistent, I didn't even press charges. I denied them to myself, only because I was sure my complaint would wind up in the wastebasket."

"I can't claim tax advantages straights enjoy because I cannot claim legal marriage."

"I was kicked out of the air force, if you call that being denied a right. I can't imagine now why the hell I ever joined. A woman tried to blackmail me—much later, I mean—but I went to a lawyer and took care of that."

"I am involved in civil litigation in which my gayness will be brought before judge and jury by my opponents. This is scaring the hell out of me. I have gone to rather great and expensive lengths to keep the gay business away from the jury if not the judge but I don't know if I will prevail over my wily and well-heeled opponents. This is another of the real-world, objective loss situations I have had to face as a gay person in America. I am mad as hell about it; but, with the weak legal protections of gay rights and rights to privacy and minority rights in general that exist in this country, I don't know what more I can do other than to become violent or become completely passive. The legal problems of gay persons, especially those of us who are trying to hang on to property we have and are trying to move forward financially, are very severe. And to think that the U.S. House of Representatives would actually vote to deny Legal Aid funds to homosexual persons! Can you imagine anything more cruel or bizarre? That's *really* queer."

"I have lost two jobs because I was gay when there was nothing else interfering with the work. I also just lost a discrimination lawsuit and have to pay off $1,000 to the school I was attending. Seems real strange, being an alternative-education college, but it is real and happening to me."

"Recently I had a problem with the phone company because they questioned my paying my roommate's bill. They even called my neighbors to ask what our relationship was. Also, I cannot be openly gay and pursue my educational profession."

"In 1945 I was denied entrance to a fundamentalist theological seminary when a religious prof to whom I had turned for counsel revealed my confidences. In 1953 I was asked to resign from a teaching position in a fundamentalist college when a gay acquaintance who could no longer keep a job because of anonymous revelations to his employers went to a prominent minister of my denomination and named me among others as homosexual on the faculty.

"In 1954 my lover was court-martialed out of the service because of his homosexuality. Someone had reported him to the FBI more than a year earlier as a Communist. Though he was exonerated of those charges, the investigation brought out his gayness. Since we had lived together several years before he went into the service, the FBI built up a dossier on me, too. In 1960, using information from that dossier, an agent of one of the service intelligance agencies came to my apartment to ask me about a former roommate. I managed to evade his queries and thought I was all right until some weeks later another agent came to my place of employment.

"He made it clear that he knew all about my previous involvements and scared the hell out of me. When I would balk at telling him anything about my former roommate, the agent would raise his voice so that he could be heard by colleagues near me, and in this fashion forced me to admit that I had had sexual relations with the former roommate."

"I believe my whole life has been altered and diminished because as a homosexual I've had to live in real or anticipated fear. Fear of physical violence, fear of blackmail of one kind or another, fear of ridicule, fear of being denied my right to live a peaceful, loving life as I see it. My right to decent employment is still denied because homosexuals are not hired for the type of positions for which I am qualified. To the government, whether I work for them directly or indirectly, I am a security risk. Perhaps a distinction between rights and liberties is too fine a line to draw here but I am not really at liberty to be a Big Brother, to get too friendly with children, to be as affectionate as I wish with other males, to lead a fully open life as a gay person."

The rest of the men who answered this question affirmatively feel that their rights have been denied them simply because they cannot be openly, happily gay:

"I am denied the right to the 'pursuit of happiness' by being forced to remain partially in the closet. The older I grow, the more stifled I feel by the restrictions of my lifestyle. I am not as free as straights to show affection to a lover."

"The only right that has been denied me is the right to express my feelings toward someone I care for in public without ridicule or uneasiness. By this I mean holding hands with a guy in public or kissing my lover goodbye at the airport, which I have done and found hostile eyes watching us as we parted."

"Once, holding hands with another man on a main street of Brooklyn, the two of us were pelted with stones, rocks, and bottles by a group of teenagers."

"All gays suffer because of the prejudice directed against us. The California legislature recently passed a law forbidding gay marriages and the economic benefits that gays might thereby derive. That's ironic because I've often heard straights put down gays because they are promiscuous (and straights aren't?) and now they seek to deny gay unions, which they claim are immoral. What do these confused straights want?"

"I have denied myself rights. I have not attempted many things because I was sure I would be scorned."

"I have been denied respectability."

"The fact that I can't tell the world I'm gay is an infringement of my rights."

"I'm denied the right to flirt without wondering if I am going to get a fist in the mouth."

"I feel I was denied a natural right to grow up open, proud, and happy. I should not have had to live in the kind of fear I lived in constantly. No child should have to live in fear."

Have you ever had any form of sexually transmitted disease?

That there is an epidemic among gay men of venereal diseases and other sexually related health problems is strongly supported by the results of this survey. Forty-four percent of the men have had some form of venereal disease, and 53% have had body lice or "crabs." Twelve percent have had scabies, another form of body mite.

Obviously, the amount of sexual activity and the variety of partners enjoyed by many gay men contribute to the spread of such diseases. In many cases, symptoms are masked, and the individual is not aware he has the disease until a close associate develops it, or until he goes for a routine checkup. Also, men can transmit venereal diseases between the time they themselves are exposed to them and the time the first symptoms appear. Thus, many men cannot cease sexual activity in time to avoid spreading the disease to others.*

Another factor in the spread of at least one form of VD, gonorrhea, is that many strains of the disease are becoming resistant to such common antibiotics as penicillin and tetracycline. Often an infected man takes these drugs, thinks he is cured, returns to sexual activity, and continues to spread the disease because the drug has not been totally effective. Researchers are attempting to develop new and more powerful

* Hans Neumann, *The Straight Story on V.D.* (New York: Warner Paperback Library, 1973).

drugs to combat venereal diseases. Free VD clinics have been opening in most major cities and have helped a great deal in keeping the incidence of the disease from going even higher.

Some of the men who have contracted venereal disease took the experience in stride:

"I've only had crabs, caught in an L.A. baths. I was embarrassed, but it was so funny. I felt very human."

"I've had crabs—hasn't everybody? Crabs are sort of funny. I had a roommate (no sex) who was always getting crabs. Finally, he took to dousing himself with A-200 whenever he tricked. Eventually, I got them from a trick and knew what they were and marched into a drugstore and said to a clerk, 'I need something for crabs.' He did a double-take, but got me the A-200."

"I had gonorrhea during the last war, when the treatment was straight torture (before sulfa). At the time I and other men were almost proud of it: a badge of masculinity, practically."

"I had gonorrhea once—anally, and didn't know it. A friend called and told me and I quickly informed all my contacts. It was just an annoyance—an 'occupational hazard.' I don't think it's the wrath of God—just a bad joke on His part."

"If a partner of mine came to me and said that he had a form of VD, it wouldn't make me mad. It's something that anyone could get."

"Fortunately, I have a very understanding straight doctor, whose reaction to VD is, 'It is just like any other disease, except you have more fun getting it.' I go regularly for a checkup now."

"My only feelings have been to get them taken care of as soon as possible. No guilt, but some trepidation about lectures from unenlightened doctors (I've had two about 'casual sex')."

"When I had it, I was terrified to tell anyone that I had had sex with, for fear that they'd hate me and never want to see me again. Well, I knew that I had to tell them, so I did. They were all, to a man, real cool about it and thanked me for letting me know rather than sticking them with it. I felt pretty foolish about my fears."

"My feelings about contracting VD are rather neutral—get it treated and get it over with without anyone laying a morality trip on you."

"Any of the things you mention is no reason for embarrassment. Do people apologize for having a cold?"

Most of the men, however, found the experience highly unpleasant:

"I had crabs once. I felt very cheap and 'untouchable' and I wanted to die."

"I've been embarrassed when someone else discovered the crabs and herpes on me before I did. Otherwise, it's just a bummer waiting for treatment to take effect, knowing I can't have sex even if some new opportunity presents itself."

"The threat of diseases is one of the most powerful arguments for monogamy."

"You just can't fuck around a lot, especially with other men, and not end up with some form of VD at some point. I had crabs so bad one time that my lover and I had to move out of the house we were renting, the place was so infested. I feel that VD is one of the great drawbacks to having fun. You pay the piper."

"I had crabs. It freaked me out. I threatened the guy that gave them to me. I told him he should be shot."

"I invariably get crabs whenever I go to the baths—whether I engage in any sexual activities or not. The first time it happened, I thought I had sunk to the depths of degradation. Now I just keep a bottle of pediculicide handy. I also contracted an extremely severe case of hepatitis over the summer. Aside from being bored to death by the bed rest and being grounded during the entire summer, I was furious with the entire gay community for accepting as an occupational hazard the selfishness and lack of consideration manifested by anybody who would so wantonly indulge his sex, knowing full well that he was transmitting a debilitating disease. If I ever run into that tacky queen again, I will have no compunction about reading his beads in public at the top of my lungs, even with his wife and kids present."

"There are two awful aspects to it. One is telling someone you're seeing that they may have to get themselves to a doctor. The second is a general fear and disgust of any form of illness/disease."

"I used to be a hustler. It was an occupational hazard and

a real drag. I got a terrible form of gonorrhea and was ill for a long time. Once I had it anally and didn't even know it. It's embarrassing and terrible."

"I have had syphilis, gonorrhea, and hepatitis. I had serious secondary syphilis and almost went deaf. Without a good MD who correctly diagnosed my case and put me on a very careful therapy of drugs, I would have had very, very bad complications."

"I wish to Christ that a person could be treated completely anonymously for VD, so one would not dread presenting himself for treatment. Can't society be enlightened enough even for this? A human being should be able to get diagnosis and treatment for VD freely. I am not worried about the cost. I just want complete anonymity."

"One of the reasons there is so much VD in my small town is that everyone who has it is terrified to go to the doctor because then he'll know they're gay. Also, a lot of guys I know weren't treated for gonorrhea because the doc never thought to look in their rectum. There have to be more VD clinics with enlightened doctors before the spread of this will stop."

"I recently had an operation for the treatment of venereal warts in my rectum, which, because I didn't have a clue as to what was wrong, developed an abscess and a fistula. The pain defied description. I would be horrified to get syphilis or hepatitis or rectal warts again. My fear is such that I've decided to be a bit more discriminating about who I go home with and how often. For this reason, and others, I'd prefer to have a lover."

"I've had VD a few times, non-specific urethritis a few times, crabs also. Too many times for one year if you ask me. And usually at a time when it is virtually impossible to have contracted it from another person. I believe it is all mental, something I create myself through fear and anxiety. I don't like it, of course—but I think each time it teaches me a lesson, and helps me slow down and take inventory of my actions and feelings."

"Crabs, gonorrhea, herpes, and syphilis. And all in the same year! I felt like the black hole of Calcutta. In fact the syph still shows in my blood. I still can't believe I contracted it. Compared to some people I know, I'm Bambi, and yet they never had anything."

"I have had syphilis once. At the time I was quite disturbed about it because my doctor told my parents without my consent and I had some other physical ailments. I was fairly ignorant about VD, although not as ignorant as the doctor. It took me a long time to get over the emotional trauma induced by the doctor and my parents."

"Yes to VD and crabs. Terror! the first time. Careful from that time forward. Thank God we have progressed, as a culture, to the point of having City Clinic. As a side note: my wife and I suspected VD and as I am the promiscuous one we went to the City Clinic together. It was an odd experience, but brought a reality into our lives that we needed."

"I've had gonorrhea several times, syphilis never (knock wood), scabies twice, crabs a number of times. Other homosexual 'venereal' diseases: hepatitis four times (now chronic), amoebic dysentery several times, giardiasis once. I felt resentful of the persons who do not care enough about themselves or others to see a doctor when symptoms present themselves, and who do not call you to tell you they have a problem and may have passed it to you. Of course, when you don't exchange phone numbers, there is no hope."

"I had crabs once. I was repulsed. It happened while I was at the university—from sleeping with a runaway street kid. I was too embarrassed to ask for help, so I used the print shop's many diluted acids, solvents, etc. to inadvertently remove at least one layer of skin and, eventually, the crabs, too."

"The first time, I was really upset. It happened just two years ago, and I had always prided myself on having been promiscuous for years and years, and still 'unspoiled.' I deluded myself into thinking I had a natural immunity. Ha!"

Have you ever been in the military? Did you have any gay experiences there?

The responses to this question are included in the "Problems" section of this book because homosexuality and the military would appear to be incompatible at best. Indeed, for many of the 35% of the men in this survey who have served in the military, dealing with their sexual preferences while in the service was a tremendous struggle.

Many others, however, report a surprising amount of tolerance, acceptance, and even encouragement of homosexuality in various branches of the armed services. All of it unofficial, of course, and much of it underground—but nonetheless extending, at times, into the highest levels.

64% of the 360 respondents who have served in the military experienced homosexual activity while there, and most of these feel positive about their service:

"I was in the army for three years and all my sexual encounters were gay. They were my friends, my roommates, several officers, lawyers, and many others. I was playing the field and took advantage of the great opportunity Uncle Sam provided me."

'I met my first lover in the service. It lasted six months. After that it seemed that everyone I met was gay—or straight but wanted sex with a guy."

"I was in the army and it was like being in a candy store. No sex with immediate companions, but the time off in foreign parts was great. It was sort of exciting to see one's officers cruising the other end of the parks. They probably saw me. I had many ranks, services, and other nationals, and natives."

"Usually I would have been drinking with 'the guys'—and one or more of us would leave the group to go home or elsewhere and we'd end up having sex. Once I blew four of my buddies on the way to another bar about ten miles from the one we'd just left. None of us ever mentioned this afterward as if it had not happened but I remember it all quite vividly and feel sure they all did too. None were opposed and all seemed to enjoy it but it was never repeated. In fact, we drifted slowly apart from that time."

"I was in the air force from 1943 to 1946. I had my first love affair there, with a nice guy who was twenty-six and had been in the army for three years and transferred over to the air force. We were on the same shift at a radar site on an island and had a lot of time off and not much to do but swim, play ball, and fish. We were building a boat one day and he said, 'I'm gay. And I think that I'm in love with you.' All I knew was that I liked him more than I had ever liked anyone in my life. He was fun to be around and do things with, he was a hell of a guy. I can say that this was the happiest time of my life, now that I look back on it. He was killed three years later."

"During basic training, all of us who were not circumcised were instructed to report to the base hospital for the operation. The surgeon was a very young doctor, and I soon found out that he was gay, because I reacted every time he touched me. Following the operation he was the one who removed the stitches personally, and gently massaged me back into production. Everyone else received the rough treatment from the orderly."

"I was in the Army during WW II, and I had numerous sexual experiences with other servicemen and civilians. But one experience I had was the most beautiful of my life. I was nineteen at the time, and a corporal. There was a major with whom I was assigned specific duties. He was between thirty-eight and forty years old and ruggedly handsome. I was assigned to drive him once behind our front lines. It was a bitterly cold winter, and the only place we could find to stay was one room in a small hotel with a double bed.

"The major and myself were the best of friends, and we worked very well together. I believe I fell in love with him the first time we met, but neither of us ever betrayed our feelings for each other. On this night we were in bed together, joking about how officers and enlisted men aren't supposed to fraternize or spend nights together. We laughed and joked in bed when suddenly his hand was on my crotch. We both became very serious—looking into each other's eyes. I was excited by his hand on my crotch, but at the same time afraid because of the army's strict laws against homosexuality. But because of the depth of my feelings for this man, I became very reckless—I wanted so much to hold him and kiss him. I turned my body toward him quickly, took him in my arms, and kissed him on the mouth. I fully expected him to hit me in anger, and that would be the end of my military career. But instead, he opened his mouth and we had the most passionate soul kissing and rubbing together of our horny bodies. I don't think I have ever experienced such loving passion before or since.

"We sucked each other off three times that night and finally fell asleep exhausted. The next morning, I feared when he awakened he might have guilt feelings and really make trouble. However, when he awoke, he smiled beautifully at me, took me in his arms, and we kissed and rubbed our bodies together again. We told each other how much we loved each other and swore we would never betray the other to our superiors. We became dedicated soldiers to our fighting jobs and no one ever suspected our sexual relations or our love for each other. We were an excellent fighting team.

"When the war was over, we went our separate ways. We wrote each other for years, and met each other for vacations together and making love. Then one day, I learned he had been killed in an auto accident, and it really tore me up. I truly loved this man."

"The three GIs I remember making it with were all Puerto Rican former hustlers who had an uncanny ability to spot a fag at 500 yards. I segregated my army job from my personal life as much as possible. I had an immense variety of lovers and sex partners (thirteen years!), but what I most enjoyed was to 'adopt' some starving kid from the street and give him more happiness than he'd ever dreamed of by showing him another human being cared about him."

"As a graduate from high school at the beginning of the war I became interested in flying and to avoid being a foot soldier I joined the RCAF and was soon ferrying Anson trainers across the Atlantic to England. Long cold flights they were in those days but the English lads were warm-hearted and hot-assed, so it was all very worthwhile."

"I was in the army, and though I had several emotional attractions, I did not have any gay experiences except with one beauty of a guy who liked to embrace. I didn't know what the score was at that time."

"In the navy, it was wild—like going to the baths. Especially the marines. They are built like little gods and are very uninhibited."

"I was stationed on an island, population 4,000—all men. I was there for eighteen months and loved it. I got paid for services rendered. But to tell the entire story would take much too much time."

"Pete and I met in the army, in Korea, in 1964. We arrived at the same time, both of us were in the same office, and the first sergeant assigned us to the same room—we were in the same rank and job specialty. We had a lot in common and we hit it off great from the start. It was a 'buddy' bit at first but in a week, we knew each other and took it from there. When we left Korea, we were assigned to the same bases here in the U.S., and with one exception we went together for thirteen years until he died. Yea—we had friends in assignment control in Washington."

"I was in the army for three years during WW II and I had more gay experiences than I can count. When the Ameri-

cans set foot on New Caledonia Island, the French put all
their women under forty into convents. You never saw them.
And there was no whorehouse until almost the end of the
war, when the navy decided to import Australian prostitutes
in hopes of cutting down on the homosexuality. We had Blow
Job Beach, where you could go at night to suck and/or be
sucked; we had Bare Ass Beach, where you could go at night
to fuck and/or be fucked—and these beaches were crowded.
There were also many one-to-one homosexual friendships going on. I had several myself, and you will have to take my
word that each one was really love. One is still going on, although not sexually since we both left New Caledonia in
1945. The man is now my lawyer and tax consultant; I am
the godfather of his first child, herself now married, and the
last child, a beautiful boy now ten, is named after me, and is
the apple of his father's eye. I've had this sort of thing happen a number of times, when the love was stronger than the
sexuality and therefore endured.

"I was sorry to see the draft end. The draft took thousands
and thousands of young men into a new lifestyle where they
had experiences in homosexuality they would never have had
otherwise, and I think that a lot of them became better men
because of it—gentler, wiser, more mature. Again, homosexuality is a part of life, not a way of life, and the more people
who accept this, the better our world will be."

"Throughout the time in the service I found and associated
with a number of other gay people that were in the same situation I was. I feel those relationships (both sexual and
friend) were what made those years in a pseudo-peacetime
army bearable. Sexually, it was not a time of great activity
but no one was celibate unless they chose that way. Most of
my immediate superiors knew I was gay and as long as I did
my job and didn't compromise their situation, along with my
own, they did all they could to make my different assign-
ments livable. Other friends who fought the system and refused to use the system to their own advantage suffered
greatly, and many were given dishonorable discharges due to
being caught."

"I had a lot of gay experiences in the military and the military provided the anonymity I needed to come out without
parental knowledge or involvement. Some of the best friends
I have today were guys I met in the army."

"I got into hot water once and it happened because I had
gone to see *East of Eden* at the base movie and it affected me

so strongly that I came on to my roommate, which was a mistake. He promptly reported this horror to the hospital CO and when that gentleman told my boss, the head of the dental clinic, his reply was: 'I wouldn't press it. It's Pat's word against Dick's. No witnesses. Aside from that, I don't give a damn what he does after five in the evening, but from eight-thirty to five, I need him.' Subsequent to that he said to me, 'Have you been behaving yourself?' I confessed. 'Well, watch it,' he told me. And that was the end of that. I had a good boss."

"After high school, I fell in with a crowd in Los Angeles, most of whom, as I see it now, must have been transsexuals. In that crowd, you either had to like dressing as a girl and 'servicing' straight men, or be a macho gay, who likes boys dressed to look like Ava Gardner and restricts his sex practices to French passive and Greek active. I could not fit into either mold and was told—authoritatively, I thought—that those are the only two ways of leading a gay life. This resulted in a crisis of identity for me. Being drafted into the army seemed desirable to me, since I had hoped that the army would make a 'real man' out of me. Within a few months after induction, I was at a training camp in Texas. I met a gay army clerk-typist there who took me to a gay off-base party. There they were, the most masculine lieutenants and sergeants, looking like Steve Canyon and Tarzan combined, dancing and necking with each other and not a drag queen in sight. After that party, I never again worried whether I was effeminate or a macho gay. Hard as it is to believe in the post-Vietnam age, my almost three years of military service were a liberating experience. I had gay experiences in every army base and later in Europe. During my time of service (1944–46) I knew gay men and women at every level of the military hierarchy, including an air force general who was the lover of a German boy I knew."

For other men, military service was a negative experience sexually:

"I was in the USAF. I had no experiences. I either had to come out or go insane while in the service. I went to a psychologist for help. I was immediately snatched from duty, made to feel less than human, investigated, lie-detected, accused of all sorts of 'despicable' acts against nature, pushed to inform on 'others' and made to keep latrines while waiting for discharge. The worst period of my life and possibly contributed to the great fear I have of really opening up again."

"While I was in the service I had some gay sex, but not very much because I saw what could happen to you if you got caught. This one guy was caught doing something or other and was put up before the review board. He was able to win his case and was not discharged from the service, but the end result was worse than if he had been discharged. No one would be seen with him, and I guess maybe it was mutual as it is possible he didn't trust anyone, figuring it would be a frame-up or what have you. He became a loner and that is rather hard to do—I never saw him with anyone else. Then they found him hanging in the barracks and they said that he had done it himself. But to this day I wonder if that was true or not. There was any number of guys who could have done it to him in fear that he would tell on them."

"I was in the navy, and found it to be a sexual wasteland. Everyone was very uptight about sex in general. Those who were straight, were always frustrated and deep into role-playing. Those who might have been gay didn't talk about it—at least, not to me. Very dreary, really."

"Yes, I was in the military, and that may be part of the reason I've had such a time adjusting to my gayness, since I repressed myself completely. When I think of the gay sex I turned down because I wanted to be as clean as the driven snow before the President of the United States I am mortified. I was part of a team that held high security clearance. We were tested for our sexual reliability and exhorted to be on our guard against homosexual experiences which could jeopardize national security through blackmail. Well, I made it—clean, cold, antiseptic, and feeling nothing for anybody. It has had its cost well beyond the years of service."

"I was especially impressed by the fact that, before or since, I have never heard such loud denunciations of gays— nor, by many of the denouncers, such heated and furtive seeking of gay sex later."

PART SIX:
ON BEING GAY

Do you think there are any reasons that you're gay?

Certainly one of the most controversial and puzzling questions in human relations is the cause (if any) of homosexuality. Ever since the nineteenth century, when psychological theorizing first gained popularity, a wide spectrum of ideas has been offered on the subject. Most of these were negative in nature, because homosexuality was almost universally viewed as a sickness which had to be explained. Nineteenth-century scientists, for instance, viewed it as a degenerative disease of the nervous system. Recently, positive theories have been advanced—positive in the sense that they treat homosexuality in a nonjudgmental way and attempt to discover its origins in much the same way one would attempt to uncover the cause of heterosexual stimulation. Many modern scientists have abandoned attempts to find causes for homosexuality, viewing it as merely a different mode of sexual expression.

The theories advanced until now, however, are still being debated and, as we will see later, many gay men believe that one or more of these do indeed apply to them. Freud was the first to take issue with the "degenerative disease" theory, believing that homosexual behavior in adults was an arrest of what he saw as the normal development from bisexuality through a homosexual phase to heterosexuality. Those who never progressed emotionally beyond the homoerotic phase, in Freud's view, became adult homosexuals. His conviction was that all heterosexuals are latent homosexuals.*

Perhaps the most widely known and repeated theory is one advanced by Dr. Irving Bieber and his co-researchers in 1962. This holds that homosexual development in males is a result of "severe pathologic parent-child relationships," specifically one in which there exists a close-binding, overprotective, often sexually stifling mother and an indifferent, hostile, or absent father. Bieber sees these factors as diverting the homosexual male from his natural inclinations toward hetero-

---

* Sigmund Freud, "The Sexual Aberrations," in *The Basic Writings of Sigmund Freud*, ed. A.A. Brill (New York: Modern Library, 1938), pp. 553–79.

sexuality. Contrary to Freud, Bieber feels that "most men are not latent homosexuals; rather, all homosexuals are latent heterosexuals."*

Research into the origins of homosexuality has also considered genetic and hormonal factors. A frequent retort to Bieber's theory, "My brother grew up in the same family and *he* isn't gay," led F. J. Kallman to study eighty-five homosexuals who had twin siblings. He found that among the forty-five twins in the survey who were fraternal, rates of corresponding inclination toward overt homosexual behavior were about the same as between most brothers and sisters (using a scale determined by Kinsey). Among the forty identical twins (those with the same genetic makeup), there was a 100% incidence of higher-than-normal inclination toward homosexual activity in both.** This was a strong indication that homosexuality may be genetically determined. Although Kallman's findings have been contradicted by later studies and his methods criticized, the findings indicate further study into the possibility of genetic roots of homosexuality.

Hormonal studies have been even less satisfactory. It was at one time believed that homosexuality was the result of an abnormally low level of the male hormone testosterone. Injection of this hormone into homosexual subjects, however, did nothing but increase their sexual drive—toward other men. Other tests have been inconclusive at best.***

The men responding to this survey have no clearer an idea about why they are homosexual than do the clinicians. The range of responses was extremely wide.

Most of the respondents stated either that there was "no reason" that they were gay or that they were born that way:

"I think the reason that I am gay (and that most everyone else who is gay is gay) is that I was born that way. At the

* Irving Bieber, "Clinical Aspects of Male Homosexuality," in *Sexual Inversion*, ed. Judd Marmor (New York: Basic Books, 1965), p. 253.
** F.J. Kallman, "A Comparative Twin Study on the Genetic Aspects of Male Homosexuality," in *Journal of Nervous and Mental Disease*, 115:283 (1948).
*** Judd Marmor, "Homosexuality and Sexual Orientation Disturbances," in *The Sexual Experience*, eds. Sadack, Kaplan, and Freedman (Baltimore: Williams and Wilkins Company, 1976), pp. 378–79.

age of three (yes, three) I was aware of my penis as a sexual stimulus. I began masturbating then and also putting crayons up my ass at the same time. I had no exposure to anything or anyone which would have taught me this. I used as my fantasy object during these three-year-old masturbations pictures of Charles Atlas on the backs of comic books. I also fantasized about my father and my playmates. My parents had nothing to do with my sexuality except that I believe there is a genetic disposition in approximately 10% or more of the population which makes them prefer the same sex. I believe homosexuality is natural and should be treated as such by parents when they discover any tendencies in their children. I think if most gays thought about it, they would realize that their homosexuality is a given that they have no control over, but many of them probably repressed their natural awareness because of the contempt with which homosexuality is treated by churches, peer groups, and the society at large. Heterosexuals would fare no better if 'straight' were a dirty word."

"God made me gay, bless Her!"

"I am the *kind* of gay person I am because of my parents and my upbringing. But I am gay for no other reason that I know of. It is my belief that science will uncover a genetic component for gayness in the unraveling of the DNA ladder at which point the question before mankind will be whether or not to tamper with the natural destiny that mutation mandates. The question will be how to regard exceptions to the norm."

"I feel it is a part of my karmic education, and that when I reincarnated into this lifetime I purposely chose to live the life of the homosexual, because of the previous lifetimes when I might not have been so tolerant of difference. (I was regressed last year to a former lifetime as a Nazi soldier who died freezing to death in Russia.)"

"I believe homosexuality is genetic, or largely genetic. I watched my two-year-old son working a puzzle one day. Just as my ex-wife's father has always done when tinkering, my son bit his tongue gently as he worked. And I thought, that trait—that tiny trait—is *inherited*, not learned behavior. If such a small thing comes from genes, then surely . . ."

"A study out of East Germany has now come out which has been supportive of my views. The study maintains that sexuality is determined at some point in the fetus. I feel that there are few extremes (i.e. 100% homosexual, 100% heterosexual) but that we all fall somewhere in between. Society, the environment, and the psychological makeup of the individual determine the extent to which his sexuality is expressed."

"I think every male is born gay and, naturally, your environment will affect the outcome. In my opinion, there is more conditioning involved in becoming heterosexual than homosexual."

Many of the men do subscribe to the theory that it was their environment—parents, upbringing, etc.—which caused them to be gay:

"My father was so good to me—so loving and warm—that I guess I wanted that to stay with me all my life. After I became an adult I missed the closeness I had with my father. Now I get that closeness from my lover."

"My father contributed a lot by making me feel very inhibited, at times to the point where I actually hated him. He used to call me 'chicken,' or constantly tell me that I was afraid of girls. That sort of talk, especially from one's own father, can make a guy grow up shy and afraid. At least it did me."

"I come from the standard, textbook background: brutal father, a mother more intelligent and understanding than her husband, and an older sister as a role model. But I don't accept that as a total explanation. Otherwise my two younger brothers would be as gay as I am. I certainly wasn't much of a masculine role model for them. A contributing factor—if we accept the idea that homosexuals are made and not born—was my father's constant determination that I *not fail* at anything. He was a 'man's man' in his own eyes, and scared to death that his oldest son would disgrace him. I remember that attitude as far back as I can remember anything at all. Whenever I attempted anything, in order that I not fail at it, he'd 'help' by taking it over and doing it himself. I grew up believing that I couldn't do anything that a man was supposed to be able to. I chose the arts—possibly because of an aptitude—certainly because it was something my father had no skill in at all, and so couldn't take away from me and finish himself."

"I think I'm gay because my mother was constantly harping on me about how evil it was to have sex with girls and she instilled in me a terror of ever getting a girl pregnant. Nothing was ever said about sex with men, so I naturally took to that."

"Neither parent has ever said 'I love you' to me at any time in my life that I can remember. They gave me no reason to copy them because of the constant fighting, swearing, and even physical fighting at times. I have never been complimented by either parent in my entire life but they were always complimentary about me when speaking to others."

"My mother may have unconsciously influenced me. Not by any praising of homosexuality, far from it. But rather, I think I may have picked up a little of her taste—she was always very high on masculinity. Maybe I heard her praise it so much that I decided I liked it, too?"

"Being an only child (or any first-born) seems to help. Having a close mother, distant father. Not caring for boys' play or sports from the start. Being protected. I hate to give these stereotyped reasons but they must have some relationship with being gay. I was shy, not physically confident, afraid of the naughtiness of sex and girls. I was asexual except for fantasies, and even then I would not admit my fascination for boys was sexual. It started very early."

"I was seduced by a male friend at age twelve, just when I recall being curious about girls. My mother was overprotective and wouldn't let me date until high school. Also, Satan wanted to make my salvation as difficult as possible. Some of these reasons may sound ridiculous, but, being gay, as I am, one can assume I've given these matters a lot of rational thought. If none of these reasons had happened, I don't know if I'd be gay today."

"My reasons for being bi—not gay: A. My wife does not satisfy my needs. B. I was seduced by a male in 1964, after six years of marriage, and I enjoyed it. I have been seeing men often since 1968. C. I have a slight preference for women, but men are easier for me to get intimate with in our twentieth-century American culture."

"Physiological: Spongy erectile tissue which makes intercourse difficult. This would make a relationship with a woman unfeasible. Financial: There is no way I could support a family. There is a slight chance that this could change, if I could get a career started. If this happened, and as I get older and less attractive to men, there is a slight chance that I could become heterosexual. Heredity: I have a problem with premature hair loss. There is nothing that can be done about this, and it is a trait which can be passed on to future generations. There is a moral question of whether it would be fair for me to have children."

"My theory for the cause of homosexuality: it is both genetic and developed. That is, given a certain person with a certain genetic makeup and put him in a particular environment and he/she will be gay. No generalizations can be made about either the genetic makeup or the environment."

Unpleasant experiences with women were cited by a few men:

"Maybe it was because girls played games with me even into college, and the guys didn't. The guys knew what they wanted; the girls seemed to be wasting my time . . . not so much 'Wanna do it?' as 'Wanna spend some time with me?' I preferred direct answers, and the girls spent so much time being Cute, Alluring, Unobtainable, Indecisive."

"I would never have chosen to be gay if there weren't many reasons. I have always disliked women because they connive, manipulate, and patronize men to get whatever they want. Almost every married couple I know, the wife and in some cases the children prevented the husband from realizing his full capabilities, desires, dreams, education, or job advancements. Even when I dated in high school I was never really comfortable with a girl. I always kept wondering what she wants out of me. I like men because they are for the most part forward and honest."

"Playing doctor with my male friends was more fun than playing with females as their bodies lacked any unique characteristics—just flat all over."

Some men felt that the glorifications of the male image had a profound effect upon them:

"Even in first grade I can remember being drawn toward my own sex since it seemed men were dominant, powerful, etc. That was what the world showed me and I wanted to be a part of it."

"All the time I was growing up, the man was everything. His opinion counted, he brought in the money, he was the one you leaned on and went to for advice. In my frame of reference women were just around for cooking and cleaning. This was the macho ideal, and I fell for it—by wanting a relationship with a man, not a woman."

"I sometimes think the reason I am gay is penis envy—I always wanted a big one and was attracted to everyone else to see how much they had."

Some men see their homosexuality as a form of rebellion:

"Possibly my innate spirit of rebellion caused me to be gay when assumed straight and straight (functional with females) when assumed gay. I fit no molds except my own. I am my own person, and not an echo of someone else."

"As a teenager, and in my twenties, I had a definite romantic interest in women, but I also took as naturally to loving men as to sleeping or eating. It was a series of unpleasant experiences with homophobic contacts and peers that led me to make a conscious choice of finding out about gay life and subsequently following it."

"My gayness is nothing less than a rebellion against any vestiges of heterosexual traditions, institutions, and mores so as to be in greater communion with the androgynous whole at the core of me. I feel that core growing each time I feel heterosexual civilization dying."

Others see gayness as just one facet of being "different":

"My present working theory is that gayness is the result of one's perceiving that he/she is in some way 'different' from others, either as a result of praise or disparagement of achievements or defects (which may be social, psychological, physical). When one perceives oneself as being different, the difference manifests itself as gayness."

"I've always been 'different' inside. For as long as I can remember, I didn't fit in with boring, mundane things that boys had on their minds. I somehow knew that my thoughts were right for me, however unacceptable they were to others around me. Growing up, I sometimes felt the sting of being different, but I was thankful I *was* different, instead of being a gray, two-dimensional thing that did blindly what others told him to do."

"All I know is I feel different, in a positive way, from heterosexuals. It's like having a sixth sense to their five."

A distinction was drawn by several men between "gay" and "homosexual":

"Gay and homosexual are thought to be the same thing. I don't think they are. Homosexual is a term used to indicate sexual preference. Gay means a commitment to a homosexual lifestyle. Being a homosexual is not a conscious choice

but one dictated by various circumstances beyond the control
of the individual and civilization. I feel that being gay is a
conscious alternative lifestyle and one that is chosen. Before I
determined to come out and take up the gay lifestyle, I
thought up all sorts of reasons as to why I was homosexual.
The reasons varied but mostly centered around the dominant
mother/distant father theory. I felt guilty. I felt God had
abandoned me. Now my feeling is there are so many theories
I do not care about any of them anymore. Why am I gay? I
became aware that there were other people like myself who
did not fit the stereotype of what a homosexual was thought
to be. I felt I would go insane sooner or later if I did not find
other men I could have sex with and find out for sure
whether I liked it or not. I did not consider myself a confirmed homosexual, I was just going through a phase. Once
I got out of the service, I was sure I was homosexual but
didn't want to be classed as gay, as the term gay, meaning
happy, was a contradiction when used for poor homosexuals
trying to get off on one another. Why, homosexuals were the
lowest of the low, down there with criminals of all sorts. Since
I have been with Fred, I have changed a lot and feel I must be
more actively gay so that other people will see what an average gay is like and know that what they had heard or read or
seen is not the *only* picture of what a gay person is. I am gay
because I could not be true to my own feelings if I lived a
fake straight life."

"I am gay because I refuse to live a regimented, dull, 'safe'
life, but enjoy flamboyant, carefree attitudes. I'm homosexual
because I am turned on by men, their bodies and the
power/freedom associated with them, either sharing or being
dominated by that power. I was gay for many years before I
realized I was homosexual."

**Many men admitted that they just don't know the reason
why, and others stated emphatically that they couldn't care
less:**

"I have no idea why I am gay. I came from a happy home;
strong father who is very successful but always found time
for his children; a caring but not weak mother who never
tried to dominate her children; both monogamous and loving;
seldom fought and made up quickly when they did. I was
never considered a sissy. I played football and ran track in
high school. I was considered popular in school and was an

officer in the 'best' fraternity in college. I had my first gay experience after I graduated from college and I sought it out. I am not aware of any gay relatives or ancestors."

"I don't know why I'm gay. I have been since I was little. As a child, I identified strongly with my mother, but was it that which 'made' me gay, or was that *because* I am gay, or what?"

"Having read continually in an effort to determine just what caused me to be gay, I still don't have that answer in full. I am suspect of anyone who feels they are gay for some particular reason."

"I used to try to figure this one out and say that my relations with my parents caused me to be gay. But I have two younger brothers both indubitably straight, so the reasons break down, and I have come to feel that looking for reasons is one form of feeling that gay is sick. I am enormously happy that I'm gay."

"I've had erotic feelings toward men as long as I can remember. I was very close to my father, and we used to sleep together, cuddle, and I was aware that he had a hardon—this might have encouraged my sexual feelings to be directed toward men—though I also used to cuddle with and 'fool around' sexually with my sisters and the little girl next door, so the whole thing really is a mystery to me."

"To spend an inordinate amount of time in analyzing why I'm gay or why I like strawberries shows that I am very defensive, unhealthy, and self-absorbed or on my way to being so. It would never be a mark of health or growth, always the opposite."

"I am at least the fourth generation of not being concerned about the gender of sexual partners and I think my sons will be the fifth."

"Who cares why I'm gay? I'm just grateful that I am!"

One respondent was unhappy that the question was being asked at all:

"This question is one gays are unfairly saddled with. Straights are never asked why they are straight. By asking gays the implication is: being straight requires no explanation, that's natural, normal development, but being gay must be explained—how did you get off the track? I believe that people are born with a bisexual potential. No one is born gay or straight. Most of us become one or the other as we grow up, though a few remain bisexual. There is no *one* cause of being either gay or straight, and any attempts to find such a universal common denominator will fail. There is no reason to consider developing as a straight superior to developing as a gay. The difference is that all the factors that society can readily control are set up to crank out straights. It's no more mysterious or significant that people are mostly straight in our society than that most people raised in a Catholic or Buddhist or Protestant setting turn out *that* way. A few will always go another way.

"I'll be happy to recount why I'm gay, when straights are put to the same test. When they trace their childhood influences to find out how they turned into breeders. Maybe Geraldo Rivera can do a special on the 'struggle for sexual identity' by straights. He can have Warren Beatty on to tell why he flaunts being a heterosexual."

Do you ever feel guilty about being gay? When? Why?

The majority of respondents do not feel guilty about their sexuality. Of the 80% who answered no to this question, many stressed that their current guilt-free attitude was arrived at after much difficult soul-searching. These men view the societal attitudes which made them feel guilty as wrong—not their sexual behavior.

Thirteen percent report that they feel guilt about their homosexuality only at certain times and in certain situations. Some of the men (5%) have not yet been able to overcome the guilt instilled in them over their homosexuality:

"How could anyone live in this Great American Society and not feel guilty about being gay or for that matter any number of things—being different in any way; losing the big game; not scoring the highest grades. And let's not forget all those varied sins our God-fearing religious groups—Protestant, Catholic, Jewish, or whatever—dream up to keep us all in line and their coffers full to overflowing."

"Yes, but I feel just as guilty about sex in general. I used to feel guilty about masturbating."

"I can't seem to get it into my head that it's all right to be gay."

"I feel guilty many times, like when I look intensely at a good-looking guy on the street and people gawk and hoot-call at me. Also, after every 'one-night stand.' Because I've been 'conditioned' to feel it is immoral to be gay, as well as sick."

"It's been so ingrained in my growing up, that being gay is wrong. Is sick. Is illegal. Is perverted. Is all bad things. So naturally, whenever I think of doing something gay, the 'little birdy' says—'You're not supposed to do that.' After a while, you feel guilty even when you know you're with someone who agrees with what you want to do."

"God, yes! I was born feeling guilty about being a cocksucker—who hasn't or isn't or doesn't in this rotten U.S.A. society we have to try and live in and with? Always! 365 days a year, forty-five years running, twenty-four hours a day!! Why? Because *most* everyone tells me I'm an 'abomination, pervert, sick, insane, vile, repulsive, obnoxious, disgusting, revolting, going to hell and burn forever'—etc. etc. etc., ad infinitum."

Some respondents say they feel guilty some of the time:

"I feel guilty when I have to lie to beautiful people who are straight friends or family."

"When straights wonder out loud why you're not married, when you see the happiness of having a child grow up, knowing that you'll never be able to have a child. When holidays roll around and we have each other, but no children to enjoy, and no close association with family."

"I feel guilty when I think about God, because He says He hates it, and I believe Him."

"Usually, when my friends talk about homosexuals (they don't approve), I'll go along with the conversation in order to cover up my gayness. Perhaps I feel guilty because I'm hiding my homosexuality when in fact I should be defending it."

"Yes, I feel guilty—when my lover's children stay with us. Because here's their daddy getting fucked like their mommy and I worry they'll find out and get their heads all fucked up over it."

"Only in tiny brief moments—when it hits home that my parents couldn't know my roommate was my lover, and that we went our separate ways on holidays—Christmas, Thanksgiving, Easter. I don't know if this is feeling guilty—but I have a hard time dealing with my lover being a bunch of miles away on Christmas Eve."

"About the only time I ever feel guilty about being gay is when a gay is used as an example of something that is horrible. I can recall when a demented gay murdered a little girl and the play was, 'look what a gay did to this mere shadow of a child.' I felt guilty as a class, not as an individual. I felt guilty as an American when I visited Hiroshima and Nagasaki in Japan. I felt guilty as a military man when the National Guard killed the Kent State students. I tend to feel guilty as a class."

"I sometimes feel guilty about not bedding down a woman and raising kids. But then I look and see how screwed up my friends' marriages are and how messed up they're making their kids and I feel better."

"I sometimes feel guilty when I listen to fundamental Christians and Roman Catholics talk about homosexuality being a sin. But my lingering love for Jesus Christ lets me know that being gay isn't bad in his eyes. So I try not to listen to fundamentalists."

"There are still times during periods of frustration and depression that I sometimes feel guilty about being gay because I tell myself that some things would be so much easier if I were only straight. However, I quickly realize the fallacy in that type of thought."

"My guilt is in relation to my wife and children, who are hurting because of my gayness. I wish that the social support for being gay which is currently available was present when I was in my twenties. I would probably have been able to recognize my gayness and have changed my lifestyle rather than marrying and hurting others."

"I feel guilty sometimes because I don't feel that I am a forceful part of the gay movement. I may be gay but I feel useless sitting at home while others are working for my rights. But I am not used to working for my rights because as a WASP I had it made and did not have to do anything at all."

80% of the men report either that they have never felt guilt, or that they used to and no longer do:

"As a youngster I felt confused and wondered if I was the only one. But I don't think I ever felt guilt because my feelings were as basic and as natural to me as my brown hair and eyes. I've never had a straight thought in my life!"

"I have never felt guilty about being gay. As a matter of fact I have always felt proud of the fact. I have long contended that a homosexual is a superior person in that he has more or less to prove to the world that he can work as well if not better."

"I used to feel very guilty about being gay, once I realized and accepted the fact to myself that I was. This was when I was in my late teens and early twenties-thirties. I worried about the fact that to lay with another man was sinful and unaccepted by church and society, and I wanted desperately to be accepted by both. Finally, in my middle thirties, unable to withhold my own needs and desires any longer, I broke out of the closet, said 'To hell with it,' and went out and found myself a man!"

"There was a time in my life when I did feel guilty, when I accepted traditional church norms as absolutes and so felt guilty. My reading and conversations have liberated me from most of that feeling. I feel that God loves me and made me as I am. I cannot believe that He will punish me for something as basic to what I am as my gay inclinations. I feel no guilt as far as society is concerned, for I think my sex life is none of society's business as long as I don't impinge on others' freedoms to be what *they* are. I would feel guilty if I tried to coerce or entice someone into homosexual acts, but I never have and don't expect to. Guilt is a function of not being able to accept oneself, of not having it together. I hope by fifty-two I do have it pretty well together. If I don't now, I'm never going to."

"At one time I did. Therapy attempted to use the guilt to push me into heterosexuality. I even underwent the beginning of aversion therapy (the Playboy Therapy at Brigham Young University). Of course it was not 'successful' and no follow-up was ever conducted on its 'success,' which has increasingly irritated me."

"Good heavens, if I felt guilty, I sure as hell wouldn't be doing it, not to mention that I've been doing it for well over twenty-five years. If I did, I think I'd bail out and try living the life of a monk or join a nunnery, or something. No sir, I'm gay and proud!"

"I have *never* felt guilty or ashamed for being gay, but often *fearful* of being fired, physically abused, evicted from my apartment, etc. Recently, during the Anita Bryant furor, I was attacked by some high school students while walking down the street to my apartment. They were yelling 'faggot' and actually threw *rocks* at me! I always carry an icepick, which is not considered a 'concealed weapon' according to California law, just in case I should be attacked again."

"I do not feel guilty about being gay as I don't feel responsible for being gay. How can one feel guilty about something which one has not chosen and about which one acts with consideration for the rights of others?"

"I've never felt guilty about being blue-eyed. In fact, they're a nice shade of blue. Besides, they're a part of me so they must be OK. I hear and read occasionally of guilt feelings, especially in queers and fairies who grew up back in the dark ages. I started sucking dick in the mid-'50s. Thinking back to Ken, Tony, Jim, I can remember how it was, how much I liked it. Two beautiful guys doing something beautiful together. No guilt—none at all."

"Because of my paranoia about my homosexuality, I became extremely mentally ill. In 1970 I was in an encounter with another man in which I panicked because of my latent homosexuality. In the panic, I killed him and in turn I spent four and a half years of unbearable mental stress in mental institutions throughout the state of California. That is why I find it a necessity to fill out this questionnaire: in hopes that it can educate those who have doubts about their own sexuality and in hopes that they realize how vitally important it is to be honest with themselves about their own sexuality. I learned the hard and painful way."

"I don't feel guilty, but I am sometimes embarrassed by gay acquaintances who reinforce the negative stereotypes. I know we don't like to admit it, but there are more than a few PE coaches who use their positions to cruise chicken. I know that straights do likewise, but when you have a bad rep to overcome, whether deserved or not, you have to be as pure as the driven snow."

"Until this past summer when I finally came out, I thought I was a sinner awaiting God's wrath. My training in seminary helped me reevaluate Biblical passages relating to homosexuality and I was able to begin reshaping a much more positive self-image. Now the only time I feel guilty is when I have to lie and pass for straight."

Do you think it is easy or difficult to be gay today?

How do gay men view their position in this country today? The reaction to this question was largely optimistic, but tempered with a realism even those with the most positive outlook were unable to avoid. 28.6% of the men replied that it is

"easy" to be gay today, but many of these offered some miti-
gation of that view in their verbal response. 28.5% were of
the opinion that it is much "easier" to be gay today than in
the past, but still fraught with difficulties. 13.1% think it "depends" on various factors: where you live, how open or
closeted you are, how tolerant your family happens to be,
etc. And 27.4% feel it is quite "difficult" under any circumstances.

**Most of the men (57.1%) feel that it is either "easy" or
"easier" to be gay:**

"I think it is easier and it seems to be getting better all the
time. Maybe Anita Bryant helped our movement by exposing
it. At least people are aware of it now."

"I think it is easier to be gay today and I predict that it
will become more so. Actually people like Anita Bryant and
Company are giving us a lot of free advertising. Millions of
young kids growing up in my day never heard of our way of
life. Don't believe there won't be a lot of experimenting and
general curiosity now. That old sex urge is as strong as ever
and now there are more outlets to relieve all those right-
handed jerk-offs."

"It seems to be easier today than how it was in the recent
past. At least today we aren't burned at a stake."

"It's easy. You're accepted as long as you don't act like a
screaming faggot."

"For me, it is easy. I've been through a lot with myself and
I've simply decided to love myself—what I do, how I do it—
and no one can make me think any differently."

"It is easier because homosexuals take pride in themselves,
they no longer look down at themselves as being sick. Those
who do should seek help, it's unhealthy."

"Having come out to all my aunts and uncles and close
friends, it is a helluva lot easier today. I might have come out
ten years ago if there had been this openness and availability
of reading material, but at that time the *Advocate* was still a
mimeographed publication and my only knowledge was that
stupid portion of *Three Men*, what a lot of crap. In those
days all you could read about were homosexuals who happened to be neurotics, so basically you only read about neurotics who happened to be homosexuals."

"It's much easier than it was a few years ago. Were it not
for my kids, and I suppose my wife, I would come out in a

second. Nobody cares anymore, not even my faggot-hating boss."

"I think it's easy these days to be gay. Because even the straights are trying to be gay these days."

"It is much easier to be gay today than ten years ago. I remember a *Time* essay in 1967 or so which called gayness 'a pernicious sickness.' I was still in the closet then and wouldn't have ever thought about letting anyone know my true feelings. *Time* wouldn't be caught dead taking that attitude today—evidence of the vast change by society in general. In fact the reason we are seeing Anita Bryant and her right-wing friends react so strongly is because they do see that gayness is gaining acceptance, and being the frightened, ignorant children that they are, they cannot understand it and cope with it. I still feel that there are many things which need to improve, however, so that gays can live open, free, honest lives."

"It is easy for me because I'm not Christian. I don't like or believe in their religion, but would never shove it down their throats and I expect the same from them. Christianity is the basis for all the prejudice I have seen and experienced. If it turns out that they're right and their God would damn me for being gay, I would want no part of him anyway. That's my feelings. I allow them to live in peace and can't understand why they can't do the same."

"I was recently in the Castro area of San Francisco and thought it was hot—buddies walking with their arms around each other, or hand in hand, and the cruisin' free and easy. Someday, it won't be just in that one area that this will happen, but it will be all over. It won't be as easy as in Castro but it will be relaxed. I think it's easy to be gay today. Now that the style and costume is butch, the straights are having a hard time spotting us. But we recognize each other."

"The more gay rights are discussed and presented as a viable lifestyle, the easier it will become for a fifteen- or twelve-year-old to recognize what's inside him, to utilize those feelings in planning a productive life without feeling he (or she) has betrayed his (or her) parents and friends."

"It's much easier today. Sure, Anita Bryant is spewing her nonsense, but she's just regurgitating all the old bigotry we used to be subjected to all the time. Now, we have U.S. Senators, public officials, magazines, and newspapers like the L.A. *Times* coming to our defense and telling the truth *in addition* to the hatred and lies. That is definitely a step forward.

Young people coming out now know right off the bat that there are others like them, and they also know that there is a large segment of the population who think they're OK. What I wouldn't have given to have that security."

Others feel either that the situation is "mixed" or that whether it is easy or difficult "depends" on various factors:

"It's both. Within the gay community, among gay friends and acquaintances, it is easy, exciting, rewarding. Many worlds are opened simply on the basis of the common denominator of being gay. But many things are difficult. Relationships with parents and other relatives can be very hard, and there is still the pressure of prejudice and discrimination in jobs—although perhaps less so in college teaching than in other occupations. One of the most difficult things for me about being gay is having to identify myself so often with this single aspect of my personality, having to think of myself in terms of my sexuality—which is, after all, a very private matter, however significant."

"This answer depends on the person's personality. For someone who is outgoing, this is the best time. So many changes for the rights of homosexuals are coming of age. But for someone who is quiet, shy, and a homebody, all the changes in laws and attitudes won't help a bit. I myself am a generally quiet type. I don't go in for barhopping and only have a small handful of friends. This makes meeting *Mr. Right* almost impossible."

"Hmmmm. 'It was the best of times, it was the worst of times.' Like blacks, gays are so close to achieving equality (compared with former times, at least) that injustices are thereby magnified."

"It's easier and harder. It's easier because: it's more open and accepted now. Behavior, dress codes, and self-expression are more relaxed and allow anyone to be more individual now. Being 'gay' is not something to be ashamed of today—our 'consciousnesses' have been raised. It's harder because: With this new freedom and with drugs and back-room bars, few people seem interested in relationships, no matter how brief. Conversation, because it isn't necessary, is almost non-existent, or limited to 'Live around here?' or 'Waddya like?' "

"If you lived in Waynesboro, Mississippi, Selma, Alabama, or Chipley, Florida, it would be suicide. The people of these rural areas (and so many others in the Southeast, and no doubt in other areas of the country) are so ultra-conservative and 'morally right' that it would be justified by *legal authority* if someone opened fire on a gay person in these areas. I love rural America; however, I would not consider living in some places because the residents cannot accept such 'newfangled' ideas as gay sexuality. I think it is easy to live a gay life in places like New York, Atlanta, New Orleans, and San Francisco. The people of these large metropolitan areas are well educated and, as a result, are more liberal and on most occasions would not think twice about whether someone is gay. Overall, one can enjoy his or her life, gay or nongay, no matter where they live. It is just a matter of being *discreet* about it. I am not saying that gays should hide in fear in the closet, rather, they should just be careful when dealing with certain homophobic types!"

"Like anything in this life, being gay is as easy or difficult as you make it for yourself. I really get angry at the flaming-faggot types who demand their rights. If they weren't so damn busy making a spectacle of themselves, they might find the discrimination a lot less. These and their compatriots the screaming queens and leather freaks bring on the discrimination and set back the gay-rights cause thousands of years. Worst of all, they are the fodder for the sick machinations of the Anita Bryants and John Briggses."

"In some ways, being gay in Los Angeles in 1977 is incredibly easy and in others it's nearly impossible. There are plenty of people to be with and most people—or at least enough people—are open about their sexuality so they aren't uptight about getting down to hot sex and it's easy to find people very quickly to satisfy an urge. But there is a cost to all of the above and that is that it's hard to find a lover whose head won't be turned in five minutes by someone else and hard to find someone who will make a commitment because it's so easy to get what you want without making any commitments. Also, the homosexual community as a whole doesn't have much respect for one another. There needs to be some consciousness raising amongst the gays, especially in bars. I mean *we* treat each other like shit, using, taking, rejecting each other without much thought about the other person. I'm guilty, too, your honor."

"It's probably becoming easier, but I think it depends on where one lives. My community is small and extremely church-dominated. Just a few weeks ago, I wrote a letter to the editor of our local paper criticizing Anita Bryant's hyster-

ical campaign of bigotry. On the day the letter appeared, the
paper ran an editorial condemning me and my views, phone
calls from anonymous callers threatened me with God's wrath
and Hell's fires—but my college administrators said nothing
to me about it. Many other calls and letters were in complete
agreement with my views. It's not easy being gay in *this* community."

"It's easy if you're not living at home. But if you're under-
age and gay, it's hell."

**The remainder of the respondents feel that it is extremely dif-
ficult to be gay today:**

"I think it is bone-crushingly hard. Nobody but gay people
can completely understand what a gloriously courageous
thing it is sometimes just to get up and face another day of
confrontations with hostility, bigotry, and loneliness. It is to
be constantly reminded that you are almost completely all
alone against all those people out there who would just as
soon murder you as look at you."

"It is horrific to be gay today in America! Anywhere in
this country, even the so-called liberal places. There *is* more
tolerance than say twenty, thirty, fifty years ago but it is still
a terrible and miserable life most homosexuals have to live in
this country. Unless one is financially able to 'escape' the
U.S.A. we are forced to live in one of the sickest, most
repressed, ignorant societies on earth. I live in fear of not
being able to get a job (or losing the one I have). I live in
fear of physical or mental abuse and harassment from not
only most people but also the police and the judicial system. I
live in fear of ostracism and bigoted hatred from most other
fellow human beings—most of whom I'm not in the slightest
interested in going to bed with and certainly not their children. I live in dread and fear most of the time and last but
certainly not least I live in terror of dying because, as of
now, I'm completely unable to undo or forget that 'God hates
homosexuals, considers them abominations and will burn
them forever in hellfire and damnation!' "

"I think it is *more* difficult to be gay now than before gay
lib opened the doors, because before gay lib, it was a *crime*
to be gay, so if anyone called you names, you could threaten
them with a suit for slander. Then too, the subject itself was
taboo, so people tended to overlook the obvious in order to
preserve 'appearances' and social conventions. Now, if people

think you're gay, they can and do say the most insulting things and openly persecute and ridicule you."

"It's difficult because we are no longer sick, frivolous fairies. Therefore, we must accept the responsibilities and strive to gain our rights. This awareness of being a gay man is both exciting and frightening."

"Very difficult—at least the type of life I lead. To be an admitted homosexual might not be as difficult, although I cannot really speak for them. For me, I will have to lead two lives—one straight and one gay. I can't afford to leave the military (job security, pay, benefits), at least not right now. Even if I did get out of the military soon, I don't think I could admit to the majority of people that I have contact with that I am gay."

"It's difficult because people don't know that gay people are just like everyone else. I had the idea in my closet that it was perverted and sex all the time. Gay people didn't know how to talk to each other—only fuck and suck. I couldn't openly be gay because of my family—they are the most important things in my life. The straight friends that I have that know me have told me that I have changed their whole idea of homosexuality because I am the kind of person I am."

"Difficult. Because most gay-oriented businesses and media oftentimes treat gay folks as less than human and only interested in things sexual."

"It is always difficult to be gay. Always. Society is not set up for gays. It is set up for straights. Society is a jungle and, as D. H. Lawrence states, 'an insane beast.' One simply must be wary of it. Gays are extremely strong. They can live under pressure that would crush a straight in a week's time."

"I think it is very difficult to be gay today because we are in a state of transition. In the larger cities, a lot of freedom of lifestyle has come our way, but I don't think we know quite what to do with it. The macho trip is a kind of homosexual backlash that is self-defeating because it doesn't deal with the reality of what it means to be a man. It's glorified role-playing drawing from straight stereotypes that mask rather than give vent to true feelings. I think the time will come when each gay man will stand on his own and decide for himself who he is and how he will shape his own life, based on what he wants and feels, and not on what the 'scene' dictates. That day is not today."

"Straight oppression and misunderstanding is a problem for all of us. For someone like myself who is bisexual and who does not care to be enveloped into a gay ghetto, the oppression can also come from gays. So many gay men have built up their defenses and have tried so hard to protect themselves from the straight world that they can only deal with other men in the meat-market world of the baths, bars, and discos."

"It is always difficult to be different."

"There are a great many heterosexual maniacs running around loose who make sport of inflicting violence on us. Those of us who do not exercise great care and cunning assume a considerable risk of being beaten or killed by these freaks. The very worst that can happen to a straight dude is to be slapped in the face for making a pass at a girl, while we may very well be knifed on the spot or hunted down and killed weeks later—for every dude I make a pass at I must pass by a hundred others out of a desire to avoid violence."

What do you like most about being gay? What do you dislike most?

"I guess I like the idea of being different from the norm. I dislike all this conformity. I think people should be who they are, no matter how it fits into society's plans. I like loving men, touching them, kissing them, and just feeling I'm a part of them. What I dislike about being gay is the fact that I see so many guys I'd really like to get to know—but this is on the street, in stores, etc. I'm so afraid to talk to them, for fear that I will end up with a busted lip. I dislike people thinking I'm a limp-wristed, purse-carrying, child-molesting man just because I'm gay."

"I like most the comradeship of the gays. It takes very little to make a very good friend in the gay world. I guess we all feel we all need each other. I dislike the way so many guys develop such deep feelings for someone they just met. They really become upset when the guy they met two weeks ago decides he doesn't want to see them again. I'm simply not that insecure."

"I think one of the best things I like about being gay is that being part of a minority serves to enhance my outlook on other minorities. It makes me conscious of sexist attitudes which I assimilated through society, so I could eliminate them. I am more aware of my sexual being and respond to it accordingly. I don't feel that I have any sexual hang-ups."

"I'm sort of glad I didn't turn out like those straights I went to school with, who still live in that small town and think the same things day in and day out and have potbellies and snot-nosed ungrateful kids. I would have been a pompous middle-class bore but for being gay. It cut me off whether I liked it or not and made me fight my own fight."

"I think being gay has made me a better teacher because I have strong empathy for anyone who is the least bit out of the 'normal' flow. I like to make them feel someone cares, and I think the caring is real, because they mirror me. (This sentence has nothing to do with 'gay' or 'sex,' OK?)"

"I like the fact that being gay makes me feel more like a man because I'm in love with men, and they're in love with me because *I'm* a man."

"I think the thing I like most about being gay is that I'm being myself and not trying to be something I'm not, like pretending to be straight, get married and have children. The other thing I like about being gay is that I feel I'm helping in some way to control overpopulation, which I feel is one of the biggest threats to the world today."

"I hate losing some acquaintances because they learn I'm gay. It makes me sad that they're so unsure of themselves they can't communicate with me."

"I dislike being separated from the rest of the human race because of my orientation."

"The things I like about being gay: I'm free of all the Judeo-Christian bullshit that was drummed into my head as a kid. I can relate to men and not feel ashamed. I can cry because I feel I can without embarrassment. And I can be me. What I don't like: the unfortunate games that are played in order to meet or talk to someone if you're in a bar. If you're not macho, you're a queen. If you're not 'womanly' enough you're probably some type of S&M freak and so on. Games are a definite drag. At times I could just scream when I'm at the bars."

"I hate being put down by people because I'm gay. If I'm ineffectual or stupid or irrational or ignorant, that's one thing. But simply because I'm gay? That tells me more about the person attacking me than he/she probably knows about him/herself."

"I'm still in the process of realizing it, exploring it. It has seemed to me, at various times, terribly sad—being left out, somehow, of the crowd, the isolation of being different; and terribly exciting, magical. There is so much to say about it: the zest of the forbidden, the playful mischief, the language and gestures, secret, nearly invisible to outsiders, the sense of having an outsider's view of many of the masks and roles that society offers as the only reality. And the mystery of it: having hit bottom in absolute despair, and some guy walking down the street can trigger a feeling of interest, until one is pulled back into the game."

"The only part that hurts about being gay is straights. I will never understand why they are so afraid. Where do they get off thinking we are all out to put the make on them? Gay guys are better-looking, take better care of themselves, and have much more interesting, open minds."

"I get annoyed by the way gay people belittle themselves and their chances for happiness. Gay love is as real and lasting as straight love, but gay people have convinced themselves that that isn't true."

"I dislike most the image that society puts on us. I'm just as moral as the straight stone-throwers. I wouldn't harm anyone. I wish society felt the same about me. I want to live my life without any social stigmas attached. I want to live without shackles of society's judgment. Is that asking too much?"

"I do not like the fact that so many gay people try to mask themselves as straight or bisexual. I do not like the closet for anyone. Nor do I like roles that some people still try to play—butch/nelly, wife/husband, etc."

"Being gay in certain ways makes me feel special and elite. Like being a hippie did in the '60s. It also outrages people that I feel need to be outraged to loosen them up a little. Although I'm not at all flamboyant about my gayness, I'm honest about it usually and don't mind at all when people get freaked out. And they do, as the saying goes, get used to it."

"I never think of myself as 'gay,' in any exclusive sense, which may sound strange coming from an activist. It's just that I've always had a great deal of self-possession and a sense of personal worth. Sometimes I've abused it (in the sense of forgetting it and getting myself into bum situations) but it has always been there. I've never felt isolated or ostracized. Not even in military school, when I was getting put down with all the usual names during the day and the traffic kept right on coming to my bed at night. I knew it for the hypocritical crock of shit it was even at that age. I don't think there's anything particularly wonderful about being gay.

Or anything disgraceful. Or anything in particular, period. Putting in a nutshell what I could well spend another 2,000 words on: I try to relate to others from my person, not my pelvis."

"I am a gay chauvinist. I think that because of our free time, our discretionary income, and the value system within gay society, we tend to be more aware, informed, and innovative than any other segment of society. I just wish that we could be as kind to each other as we are to straights. Maybe my view of gay life is colored by the fact that my experience is limited to large, metropolitan centers, but I really think that we have it all together in every regard except emotionally. Perhaps it is time to opt for less protection and self-preservation and more vulnerability and warmth."

"The things I like most about being gay are the freedom from responsibility and the male companionship—you never really have to be lonely if you're gay. There is nothing I dislike about being gay."

"Being gay in one's maturity has produced a revitalization of many of life's energies. My lover has been painting with energy. I have been more creative in my work and more loving in my social manner than I have ever been. We go to the theater, the opera, galleries and museums, the movies, and on trips, and our social life is a shared, relatively open activity."

"I dislike the fact that some people naturally assume that that is *all* that I am. Well, I'm me. That means I'm male and so tall and this and that, and I drive a BMW and I swim and I'm a marvelous cook and I'm a good writer and musician and I love to travel and I'm homosexual and I love cats and . . . Being gay is one facet of my makeup. I dislike the people who cannot see beyond that and immediately label me as only a homosexual. And I dislike the gays with whom I have absolutely nothing in common, people I just have no interest in, would not choose to be friends with, people I sometimes would even dislike, assuming just because I too sleep with men that I'm some kind of blood brother. Only in a very limited sense I am—as I am a Democrat and an author—part of their group. I feel a great sense of devotion to the cause of all people becoming free, and I would put gay rights before any other cause I have come in contact with, but I loathe the attitude that I *must* march in the streets with all the others just because I happen to be homosexual. I will do what I can in my own way, on my own time. In fact, I think I have done as much or even more than several of the publicized 'gay leaders'—in my own way, on my own time."

"I dislike bigots and rednecks and some gay conservatives who would cut their own throats and those of all their brothers to keep anyone else from finding out about them. It seems to me that L.A. has quite a few of these. Paranoid pissy queens, who won't attend a gay parade or carnival, because they feel too good to mingle with radicals and street people. It seems like the more successful these people become, the less they care about their brothers or the public image of gays. I respect their choice, but detest their selfishness."

"I very much like the instant sexuality and the opportunity to explore another sexually and then take it from there to whatever plane is mutually acceptable. This 'getting into' a person is the super turn-on to me of being gay."

"I like the honest acceptance of promiscuity, which I think is natural to males. I dislike that most straights assume that somewhere, somehow I must really be effeminate."

"I really like the culture that's taking place in San Francisco. Brotherhood and sisterhood is happening. People are concerned about others' lives. Gay life is a small-town feeling. Our community is getting its shit together. It may be wild and strange to many, but it's ours. In so many ways things are happening that have never taken place before. New thresholds are exciting."

Would you rather be straight?

Only 541 men answered this question, since it was not asked on every questionnaire. Of these, 85% answered that they would not rather be straight, and 15% said they would.

Almost all the men who said they would rather be straight cited the difficulties of being gay in a straight society:

"There are too many negative aspects to being gay. When I graduate and am teaching or coaching, there will be insurmountable pressures from the peer group. Also, I'd like to father kids. I do not want to see myself at sixty sitting in a gay bar. It gets lonely and sad being gay at *my* age. I'd rather be straight or die than see myself thirty-five or forty years from now all alone in this world, and gay!"

"I'd rather be straight so I wouldn't have guilt feelings."

"I'd rather be straight so I could show my girl off."

"I would give a lot to be straight, because it's a straight world."

"Because I love children, I would prefer to be straight. Also, there would be less conflict with my religious beliefs, which I cherish."

The vast majority of the men report that they would not rather be straight, despite the apparent advantages of being straight in a straight society:

"No, I would not rather be straight, because if I were, I'd be somebody else. I certainly couldn't be any happier if I were straight. I enjoy it. Why? Well, I'm a realist and I accepted the fact early on and made the best of it. To ask me if I'd rather be straight is like asking a straight man if he'd rather be gay. How can you answer that?"

"I would rather be who I am and what I am. There's a saying I saw burned into a tree: Who you are at essence is God's gift to you. What you make of it is your gift to God."

"I would not want to be straight. I think gay couples in general get along better than straight couples and have a much fuller life together."

"Had I remained convinced that herd psychology was valid I would probably rather be straight, but with the help of reality therapy, I realize that each person must step to their own music. I am gay and I like it."

"I would *not* rather be straight. A few years ago the answer would have probably been yes, please! please! But the struggle of acceptance is over for me. I'm happy now, and now I can answer with an unqualified no!"

"I tried being straight. It didn't work."

"Sometimes I want a child I can never have. Sometimes I would like to live in an old-fashioned small town—that's almost impossible. I could just never be straight no matter how disillusioned I may get sometimes."

"I would *not* rather be straight. I was involved in a straight marriage, and found it very unfulfilling, especially when I compare it to the lover-relationship I am in now."

"I most definitely would not rather be straight because that would undoubtedly produce other changes in my personality which I'm not interested in altering; even if it did not, I'm perfectly content with matters as they are."

"I wouldn't change my life. I'd die first and my family

would rather see me dead than tortured and living under a
lie. I never knew people were in closets until recently. I do
not understand why."

What do you think are the most important changes that have to be made, by gays or straight society or both, to improve gay life?

Many men in this survey took a great deal of time with
this question and gave it much thought. Most listed several
areas where change would be advantageous. The percentages
which follow indicate the number of respondents who mentioned a particular area, either singly or as part of a list.

**64% felt that educating others about the truths of homo-
sexuality was of primary importance:**

"Education concerning the diversity of gays (as with
straights) would probably do the most to eliminate the stereotypes which create fear and loathing among straights and
gays for homosexuality. A misunderstanding of homosexual
references in the Bible probably accounts for much of the ignorance. For those diehards who will always insist on a literal
translation of those texts, it will be necessary for gays to insist on a strict separation of church and state when interpret-
ing the Constitution."

"The best thing that could happen is for people to learn
enough about human sexuality, so as to accept any act, short
of violence, as natural and beautiful. My upbringing tells me
that what I enjoy and want out of life is wrong, yet my experiences tell me that it's beautiful and right. Understanding
and acceptance of homosexuality *and* sexuality are the
changes that would be of most benefit to *everyone*."

"Young men and women in high school who are perplexed,
deeply troubled, anxious over their emerging sexuality should
be told, at the very least, how and where information can be
obtained to help answer their questions in private. I'm sug-
gesting that this information be found well away from the
charged atmosphere of the public school where peer pressure
is the strongest. We must be realists too, that it is unlikely
that the subject would ever be broached in the classroom. But
the education of our youths who should have accurate in-

formation to help them wind their way out of a Chinese puzzle of social conflicts with sex, especially gay sex, is essential and should not be ignored any longer."

"I think that the straight public must be made aware that gays are not a bunch of sex-maniac deviates who go about trying to seduce everything with a cock between its legs from the age of one to a hundred. I also think many gays should stop attempting to seduce straights who frequently will spend the rest of their lives persecuting them because they thought they might like it or were genuinely disgusted. Rather, we should use the soft-sell approach of education and revelation."

"Almost an underground approach by a gay who is in the accepted professions and trades is necessary. The gay who is thought to be straight could do much to improve homosexual life and the life of the homosexual by infiltrating the straight society through meetings and other encounters and diligently teaching and promoting the gay style rather than peddling his ass. Our society is not yet ready for an aggressive approach to converting people to the understanding and tolerance of gays."

"It would be fine if society would accept the fact that homosexuals cannot help being gay. I think it may even be part of a design of nature, and/or God, that some people are homosexuals. Not every plant or animal has offspring—perhaps some human beings were not meant to marry and have children. Homosexuality may be one way that nature has of preventing too many people from having families. If society could come to see this a bit, they might even realize that the homosexual is doing society a *favor* in that he does not generally produce babies in a world that is being quickly overpopulated."

"An understanding, on both sides, of what it means to be gay or straight. A breakdown of stereotypes, on both sides. Not all straight men are potbellied beer-guzzlers, nor are all gay men limp-wristed faggots. They're all people, whether you approve of their lifestyle or not."

"Educate the public, especially the straight public, since they are the future parents of the future gay children. Make these future parents understand that it's all right if their children are gay so that they can impart to their gay children that it's all right to be gay. Then and only then will we have a generation of happy gays."

"Gays must be more understanding of nongays. Most nongays are so closed up within themselves, they can't do anything open. We have to show nongays what love can be. Couples and singles (and even triples, etc.), both gay and nongay, who really have their heads together, know that it doesn't take law, marriage, or even the sex act to keep them together. They are what they are, doing what they are doing because they want to. And when someone like that loves you, you've got something that all society should know about, straight and gay."

"I think the biggest thing that could happen is for the world to find out why we are gay. Then, not only will we understand ourselves better, but so will society. It's only at that point that society could fully deal with gays. It's difficult to accept something one does not understand."

"Everyone must accept, and try to understand, the facts about homosexuals. We did not choose to be gay, nor can we be expected to willingly want to change our way of life. We (hopefully) enjoy loving other men equally as much as straights love women. If they could view homosexuals by putting themselves in our shoes, then they might find it easier to understand and accept."

"I think society has to realize that sexuality doesn't necessarily have to affect your social life. I believe acceptance will come, in time."

32% feel the solution lies in a lessening of the emphasis on sex and/or more adherence to traditional standards of morality:

"Both gays and straights must stop thinking of homosexuals as primarily sexual beings. Everyone, gay *or* straight, is several things before he or she is gay or straight. I'm a human first, then a man, then a teacher, then a Christian, then an American, a political liberal, and a lover before I'm gay. Heterosexuals are guilty of pointless bigotry, of course, but we homosexuals should take our minds off our genitals long enough to achieve the wholeness and harmony characteristic of well-integrated personalities."

"I think one way to end this situation is for gays to stop calling themselves gays and homosexuals and begin referring to themselves as homosocials, stressing those aspects of our lives other than our alleged gaiety and sexuality."

"Gays must develop the same respect for human interrelationships that apply to hetero relationships, must learn that pure promiscuity violates and injures other people, and that respect and giving are necessary to an ongoing relationship. Straight society then could come to learn over a long, long time that gay love can be respectable and just as meaningful."

"On the part of gay society, I feel that a degree of desexualization would be in order to help us feel more free to love and support each other. I can hug many of my straight friends, male and female, and know that they are only accepting it as an honest show of affection. With gay men it is often seen as a sexual invitation or turned into a heavily flirtatious act, which to me invalidates it. If, at the bars or clubs, we could approach people to converse and only converse, I am sure we would make better friendships and find more love in the long run. But a 'hello' is a come-on, so you don't say it unless you want to come on. It really is unbalanced and therefore unhealthy."

"First the gays need to clean up their act. Every one of the gay publications appeals to the lowest common denominator. I find little dignity in seeing huge cocks semi-erect and ads for jac-pacs, etc. I'm no prude and readily admit I love looking at all of that but I put myself in the shoes of the average straight, sampling at large gay publications. All he will find is a massive obsession with sex and little else. I can see why they are hesitant to accept the gay lifestyle. All they think is we spend our entire private lives sucking, fucking, and jac-packing."

20% feel that gay people should behave publicly in a more circumspect manner:

"Gays should not flaunt their gayness in any public demonstrations if they are extremely feminine, appear in 'drag,' run around screeching, being femininely dramatic, etc. Gays will make much better headway with the general public of straights if all their appearances remain 'straight'-looking in dress, actions and comments."

"Lead a normal calm life without shoving gay life down people's throats. You will be accepted by most straights as long as you act yourself and don't act like a fairy princess."

"I am ashamed not of being gay myself but of being gay as it appears in the ads and editorial line of gay-oriented publications, in the pictures of semi-nude, overmuscled bikers that have become popularly synonymous with gay desire, in the pleading 'just folks' tone of so many gay-rights liberals, in the horrifying misogynist fury of gay-male attacks on Anita Bryant—in all these and similar evidences (seemingly) that gay men are servile, self-seeking, male supremacist, overconsuming parasites. Whenever I meet with someone whose images of gay men are determined by those things, I will not admit to being gay. Then I'll fall back on being queer, i.e., unusual, different, nonconforming to what those things say gay men are. In fact, as a gay man, I almost feel queer, never more so than when I'm with the most vocal of my gay-activist brothers."

"I enjoy sex with men. To me this is and should be the only difference between gay and straight. I believe the 'gay' image was created by a certain type of people who are gay—the other gay people (straight types) are not the types who join clubs, go to exclusively gay public places, join activities of any kind. If those people were straight they would still be the same: gay activists, if straight, would be activists for something else. I don't believe there is a 'gay lifestyle.' It is a lifestyle of a small percentage of gay people who push themselves into the public eye. Therefore, everyone calls that the gay image. When I ask a straight person what he objects to most about gay people, he never mentions sex—only the image he sees in the silly 'fag' types. If more people like David Kopay would speak out, the image could change."

"Gay people have to realize that public sex is more detrimental to us than anything else. It reinforces stereotypes that we profess to want to break down. It isn't fair to have sex anyplace where a nongay person might happen upon you—that's infringing on the rights of others. If all gay people had sex only where others couldn't possibly see them a lot of our public relations problems would be over."

A breakdown of religious taboos was cited as a necessity by 11.5%:

"The liberal religions must somehow convince the diehard conservative ones, especially in the Midwest, that homosexuality is not a sin, that it is a reasonable alternative, helpful in limiting population growth, etc."

"Straights must kick the Bible-thumping, misdirected and misinterpreted Judeo-Christian morality stances. Individual and collective male love, however sloppy and decadent, isn't going to erode or destroy sociopolitical systems!"

"I think religion, and religious-based, doctored-up English laws are gay people's worst enemy in society. I don't think that Western society truly understands human nature. I know several people who are gay who are so guilt-ridden because of religious upbringing, and it is all so unnecessary. Homosexuality is a common occurrence in all forms of nature; why people don't realize (or accept) this is beyond me. Perhaps people are afraid of themselves, pass laws to protect their insecurities, and interpret religious scripture to feed those insecurities."

"Besides acquiring scientific education, straights need to be exposed to the works of theologians who dispute the fundamentalist position that the Bible condemns gay lifestyles. Straights need a new morality, not an old morality."

"Gay people must insist that the church be forced to stay out of political issues, which it is not supposed to get involved in. We're supposed to have separation of church and state in this country. The only time the churches adhere to this is when April 15 rolls around. They pay no taxes, but they have been in the forefront (often initiating and totally supporting) many political battles including those against the ERA, gay rights, and abortion. Whatever people's stands on these issues, they must realize that the church has no business imposing religious morality on civil issues. Why no one has called them on this point I'll never know. It's outrageous, and people have to do something to try and stop it."

45% mentioned political action as a way toward improving the lot of gays:

"Gays must develop a greater gay consciousness and become politically active. They must confront politicians and other decision-makers. They must learn to openly take leadership roles and to serve as role models for other gays (especially for adolescent and pre-adolescent gays). It is up to us to demand our rights."

"We must find a way to join hands around the world. There are millions of us! Enough to turn the tide of history. We must find a way to join in a cohesive unit—free from petty dissension—and work for a common goal. And what other common goal do we have but to be allowed to live our lives with the same freedoms and justices that are meted out to our heterosexual fellow human beings? Let us learn to *vote as a united bloc!* Support those candidates for political office that uphold the rights (constitutional and human) of the gay community. We will prevail through our voting clout!"

"First, we must get rid of 'sodomy' laws. This is the major stumbling block to getting the civil rights legislation passed. Over and over again, I have heard the argument of 'Why give them rights when what they do is illegal?' "

"The entire governmental structure in this country, which has a stranglehold on the economic welfare of gay Americans, is biased against gay people. Gay people do not necessarily need much, if any, special treatment. All they need is legal equality. It is far more important to get changes in the laws and in public administration than it is to try to educate every bigot and every nongay ignoramus about the basic humanity of gay persons. And anyway, who should live so long as to wait for the dullards to catch up?"

"My lover and I try to give our business to gay-owned stores and offices. We have a gay doctor, dentist, lawyer, and CPA. This lets us speak frankly to these professionals about our situation."

"When laws are passed for the homosexuals, they should not be put up to a public referendum, as happened in Miami. It is unconstitutional to *vote away* an individual's civil rights. This should be protected. I'm surprised they let Bryant get away with it, and let her take it as far as she did."

"I feel that gays have supported the so-called straights— their children's schools, for instance—with our tax dollars. If we decline to pay for that it would be hard for them to pay for their own. They can take our money, but they can't accept what we do in our own bedrooms. Bigots!"

"I think that gays must be *peacefully* and *soberly* aware of our responsibility to fight for rights. You've heard of the 'guerrilla warfare' and 'scare tactics' used by some gays against Miss Wholesomeness Anita B, haven't you? Those actions are not helpful to us. Media coverage of peaceful demonstrations and special events that are gay-oriented are good points for our struggle."

"The most effective means at the disposal of gays is the clout of the economic boycott. A person may tolerate or ignore the rallies or parades or letters, but he can't ignore it when his business falls off sharply."

51% felt that a change needs to be made in the social climate, among both gays and straights:

"When the words gay and straight, black and white, male and female are no longer used, we will be at the point of survival for everyone. We are all human beings."

"We must all learn to accept our sexuality and gratify our sexual instincts. We must learn to masturbate without guilt, to have sex without guilt regardless of age. Children and teenagers in particular must be allowed to have sex when and how they want it. Do away with all laws proscribing sexual behavior between children or between children and adults. Raise a generation that knows good, satisfying orgasm as a matter-of-fact, everyday occurrence. Those are necessary first steps, from which the repeal of laws against adult sexual behavior will follow because for a generation raised in sexual health they will be unnecessary and foolish and barbarous plainly before all men's eyes. I am not saying give rapists and molesters license, but rather that free sexual development must not be legalistically constrained. Let us learn to discriminate exactly and in each separate case decide whether rape or love, or indeed mere innocent lust, is involved."

"I'd say straights should be bombarded with TV, newspaper, and magazine propoganda to wean them away from the ingrained hate of gays they are all raised with."

"I think homosexuality has to be regarded as a part of life, not a way of life."

"We have to stop pushing Gay Bars, Gay Bookstores, Gay this and Gay that and become a total society. With all of the Gay this and thats, we are setting ourselves apart from society and trying to be accepted as a separate kind of people. As long as this is continued, we are going to gain very little."

"It is all insanity that we who are different by choice and chance should try following the norm. Let us break away from the one thing that has kept us in chains for so long and establish a better society, a more tolerant society, a better cultural level. Push forward to the next plateau, not looking back and not reacting to the straight society, but showing our mettle and worth."

"Every piece of work I have encountered concerning gays has been negative excluding *The Front Runner* and *The David Kopay Story*. I haven't been able to purchase any more recent studies, although I will soon. The stuff on television has been too tame and too weird at the same time. I think *Soap* is handling it the best even though I don't agree with the extreme. I won't be satisfied until I see a good drama with two decent actors on the tube evolving a positive desirable character situation and ending."

"I hope your work will point out that the gay rights movement is a civil rights movement and that equal rights for gays are being fought by the same conservative right-wing people who fought and are fighting equal rights for blacks, women, and other minorities. Consider Dade County and Anita Bryant. This is no coincidence that the forces of bigotry and hatred are rallying in the South and in the White Southern Baptist Church. This is the South defining its new 'nigger.' (I hope black comedians, in using the term in comedy, have made its use acceptable.) The poor Southern Christians can't use the blacks anymore as their nigger. There's too much pressure on them to lay off. They're anxiously searching for a new nigger. Even Jimmy Carter, who says 'human rights are absolute,' has been strangely silent on the issue of gay rights. So, the South thinks it has found its new nigger—the 'homo,' the 'queer,' the 'pervert,' the 'child molester,' the fictionalized and misrepresented gay. Bumper stickers have appeared reading 'Kill a Queer for Christ.' It is up to gays to make this twisting of the doctrines of Christ apparent to straights. We must not allow gays to become American's new nigger."

"Gay money directed where it will do the most good—for example, the Muscular Dystrophy donations from gay sources were praised by Jerry Lewis on national television. I was so proud to be gay that day! Groups of gay students volunteered their time to speak on panels for college classes on the subject of gay living—a positive image created by emphasis on constructive endeavors of gay men and women. Deemphasize the sexuality and understand the gay humanity. Keep gay pride and dignity alive by good example and an occasional pie in Anita's face. It shows we have a sense of 'earnest' humor."

"There should be more gay PR. The National Gay Task Force, etc. should carry out a PR campaign aimed at Middle America to make people aware of the gay lifestyle and, especially, its similarities to the straight lifestyle."

"Gays should protest when a crime is referred to as 'the homosexual murder case.' The fact that the man is a murderer has nothing to do with the fact that he's a homosexual. Richard Speck was never referred to as 'the heterosexual murderer of eight student nurses.' But if he were gay and they were male pre-med students, it would have been 'those hideous gay murders,' and people would have thought 'those

gays are so sick.' But when a straight man murders a girl, it's
never 'we straights are so sick.' We can't let them get away
with this anymore."

"I hope to see the day when the 'gay community' has self-
help clinics established in all areas of the world. These clinics
would offer classes in homophile history, sexual education, art
and culture, psychology (interpersonal communications and
guided psychodrama), would offer housing and job referral,
have a VD clinic, in-house counselors, activities, and do
research into the community needs as well as be an information center and interagency advocate for all citizens in the
area serviced by the clinic. The staff would cater to the needs
of the homophile but also work with and for the integration
of the whole population served by and for the better understanding, health, and recreational needs of the community."

**20% felt that the most important changes must be made on
a purely personal level:**

"We need a stronger bond, a more tender and accepting
stance toward each other. We need, as someone has said,
enough of a group consciousness that some actions would
rightly be deemed 'treasonable'—so strongly developed would
be our loyalty to one another."

"The greatest flaw in the gay subculture is the infectious,
self-perpetuating, hypocritical, phony, and arrogant attitude
which many gays assume. The homosexual's worst enemy is
the gay lifestyle itself because its degradations and inhuman-
ity are insidious. Anita Bryant, as a visible, vocal, definable
target, is far less dangerous. An injection of honesty, sincer-
ity, and self-control into homosexual relations would produce
important and valuable improvements in the lifestyle."

"I think it would help homosexuals to learn what it is like
to love a woman. No, I'm serious. Nine-tenths of the gay
people I've met have told me they've never had sex with a
woman. Aren't they missing something? I also think it would
help if we could tone down our sexual hang-ups."

"Straights need to know that gay sex feels good, too. Some
gays that have never experienced straight sex should try it
and find out it may be more fun than they realized. Both
straights and gays need to learn to love more."

"*Get rid of guilt.* It is the single most destructive element
in any sexual problem. Just accept yourself, your feelings,
your desires, the whole goddamn bag, and don't feel guilty

about it. If that could be done, the possibilities for man are unlimited."

"Gays should really start getting into people as people other than getting into how nice one's body is or how hot they are, because that causes more head problems than I can imagine. If we get to know the people's minds as well as we do their bodies, in the long run it would save a lot of heartache that gays experience too many times."

"I think one vital change for both gays and straights is to get away from using sex as a weapon. The fact that this happens says something about the moral/ethical climate of the day. This is, of course, related to exploitation and manipulation through role- and game-playing. Subcultures tend to exaggerate the worst features of the parent culture and gays become their own worst enemies when they fall into 'sex as games' traps. What's needed for most Americans is a good lesson in basic ethics and a keener awareness of morality."

"Gay people need to broaden themselves, diversify their interests, educate themselves, train themselves to be able to participate in many facets of life. This is advice that could be given to anyone, but gays in particular, I think, need it. Too many gays are totally unaware of the world around them except what the latest disco hit is and what's new in *Gentleman's Quarterly*. They're fluff-headed pretty boys who think of nothing but their appearance and sex. What happens to them when they get older and less beautiful? What will they have to offer a partner then? And when they're old and lonely, they'll blame being gay rather than the real culprit—themselves, for being so vacuous. Many of them even blame being gay for a lack of a lasting relationship right now. But what do they have to offer another human being except a nice piece of ass? As I once heard, 'Man does not live by bed alone.' You have to be able to talk to someone else, you have to be able to interest someone else. You can't be interesting to another unless you are interested in other things."

"I strongly feel that gays in important positions should come out of the closet, whenever possible, because they can do a lot for our self-esteem and egos and they can also give society in general a truer picture of our intellect, might, perseverance, history, lifestyles, and our diversity. Those gays that cannot afford to leave the closet can also help, and should, by offering money contributions or support to gay activists. Any gay who prefers to remain inactive or who continues to pass for straight is my oppressor."

Do you consider yourself happy? Why or why not? If not, would changes in your sex life make you happier?

For years, homosexuals have been painted as unhappy, pitiable men and women. Psychoanalytic studies abound with case histories of patients made wretched by their inability to handle their sexual orientation; literature and film until very recently pictured homosexuals as lonely, miserable, sometimes suicidal (*The City and the Pillar, The Boys in the Band, The Sergeant,* to name just three). Happy and well-adjusted homosexuals were almost never depicted—and when they were, they were most often represented as flamboyant and effeminate.

The picture of the unhappy homosexual thus presented was certainly not without basis in fact. We have seen throughout the responses in this book the tremendous difficulty homosexuals have in adjusting to a society with which they feel at odds. But the responses to this question by the men in this survey indicate a radical change in gay men's attitudes about their lifestyles. It is partly, if these responses are any indication, due to a greater acceptance by society than ever before. It is also due to a diligent private effort on the part of these men to come to grips with their sexuality and accept it in a positive way.

Seventy-two percent of the respondents describe themselves as "happy." An additional 6% term themselves "fairly happy" and another 2.6% consider themselves "content." Thus, over 80% of the men in this survey feel good about their lives. Of the rest, 4.9% said that their feelings on the subject were "mixed" and 12.6% describe themselves as unhappy.

Of those who consider themselves unhappy, most indicated that their unhappiness was caused by factors other than their homosexuality:

"I do not consider myself to be happy, but that is not because I'm gay. It's due mainly to the lack of someone special. If you mean becoming heterosexual by stating 'changes in your sex life,' that wouldn't make me happier. I know what I want—and it's not a woman."

"I am not happy at this point in my life, but my problems

of insecurity, fears, etc. ad infinitum would not be solved, nor would they be any different if I were straight."

"My unhappiness springs from dissatisfaction with the powerlessness of my fellow men and women to affect their lives where alien forces—arrogant bureaucracy, callous businesses, wilfully stupid institutions and their political supporters—frustrate and hamper and seriously wound them. Changes in my sex life might make me happier individually, but they wouldn't alleviate the unhappiness I feel every time I consider the general foolishness and lack of compassion of the powerful of our society."

"I think that there are times when unhappiness is appropriate and healthy. Generally I am optimistic. Certainly (based on the 'tastes' I have had of married life—and I always refer to marriage in terms of another homophile male) I would have much more reason to be happy were I married. I would float!"

Some men do feel that their unhappiness relates to their homosexuality. Most of these, however, are reacting to society's view of them, not to their homosexuality itself:

"I'm not very happy. I feel very distressed over recent attempts by certain individuals to perform genocide on gay people. I feel that if I wished to walk down the street or through a park holding hands with my boyfriend, I should not be harassed or humiliated."

"No, definitely not. With the attitudes and repressions forced upon me by most of society, in this country today, I would have to say no, changes in my sex life would not, in themselves, make me any happier. I do not believe that I can or ever will be completely free of the 'Bible' and so-called 'Christian' attitudes toward homosexuals. I sincerely try not to 'judge' others from these points of view but I find it impossible not to judge myself. In this case I find only a hopeless situation. Life is intolerable lived alone and without love and its natural expression, sex. But death is equally untenable and frightening as I cannot completely forget the awful 'punishments' awaiting me. One might consider here why so many alcoholics are homosexual; are they seeking 'oblivion?'—the in-between life and death—the limbo of nonexistence but also nondeath?"

"I am uncomfortable with the dual life I have to lead. One life with my family, my straight life. The other life with my men friends, my gay life, when I go into San Francisco for an evening. In my gay life I am open, candid, go with my feelings, and give full rein to my emotional and physical needs. I would be happiest if I could live one type of life and not have to act so conservative and straight. I think I could handle acting straight during the day at work if I could then be myself away from work."

Some of the men are unhappy with their sexuality itself:

"I think finding out if I'm gay, bisexual, or straight might make me happier because I would know what kind of person to look for to spend the rest of my life with. If I found out that I was really straight, that would be a plus because I feel that women are a lot more dependable and supportive than men in an ongoing relationship."

"I do not consider myself as happy, primarily because of loneliness and having no special person to share my life with. Also because there's something holding me back from making a total commitment to someone because of the insecurity of gay relationships. The only changes in my sex life would be if I could stop looking at every sexual encounter as a potential lover and enjoy it for what it is at the moment."

"Probably changes would help—I used to be bisexual but now women turn me off sexually unless I'm drunk. I wish I could have sex with women as well as men as I once did."

"I am angry that I cannot be with men (gay or straight) without wanting to do a number with them. If sex weren't so important to me, I could interact with men without trying to put the make on them."

Some men feel "mixed" about the state of their happiness:

"I find happiness in work; when it's going well, I'm happy—and I'm apt to have fun with sex. If work isn't going well, I feel guilty about sex and try to avoid it."

"I'm happy, then I'm not happy. I have a theory about existence. I believe that everyone has to have one thing, animal, vegetable, or mineral, that is absolutely hassle-free. For instance, if a person owns a house, but doesn't have a partner or a social life, then the house becomes an absolute that provides a moment of respite from complete mental suicide. If a person has another person, but no job or home, then the person is the absolute. At present, I have two or three absolutes

(I'm working on the definition) so I'm happy. But as a person ages, absolutes grow in scope or narrow in scope. So I'm unhappy because my desire for a partner to breathe life into the other absolutes is intensifying. Understand?"

"I'm relatively happy because I have a fair circle of gay friends with whom I can relate; but I am bitter about straight 'friends' who exclude me from their social functions because I'm not married or don't go with a girl."

"Changes in my sex life would make me happier. At the present time I feel that I am defining myself as a positive worthwhile person through gay sexual experiences. When I am with men, I feel complete, whole, and worthwhile as a person. I need to increase the level of my sexual activity to assist in defining myself as a person. It would also reduce the level of intensity which I put in the sexual relationships that I now have. Part of this is being newly gay and experiencing gay sex and its meaning."

"I am generally happy. I would not want to be not gay any more than a Jew would not want to be a Jew. Being gay is not easy; but it is good to be gay nevertheless. My sex life would be much better if society would get off my back and just let me live/love and let live/love. What causes me the greatest unhappiness is the fear and resentment I feel concerning the threat of loss of property, economic opportunity, and unequal treatment by judges and juries and other governmental agencies. There are times when I am very unhappy about the entire social situation in this country. I am not, after all, living in a fool's paradise. I am conscious of the social realities; and I am very angry about the very real discrimination that gay persons face in this country and elsewhere in the world."

Nearly three-quarters of the men report that they consider themselves happy. Many of these profess a general happiness not necessarily associated with being gay:

"Yes, I am happy. I'm happy to be here, happy to be breathing, happy to be healthy, happy for all the good things life has to offer. I struggle with the bad things, but they do not necessarily make me unhappy. They distract me at times, but don't change my outlook much."

"Rather than changes in my sex life making me happy, I believe that if you are happy, your sex life will be more satisfying. Too many gays think that sex is going to make them happy. It should be a result of their being happy first."

"Yes, I am happy. I am beyond being hurt."

"I consider myself as happy as any straight person. In the sex arena, I have what I want and too, I also have had partly, I suppose, something of the benefits of the straight life, too. I've been father to a boy. Taken him for his first haircut, ballgames, etc. That sort of thing. Listened to his woes, spanked him, etc. He's illegitimate but his mother has been a close friend of mine since before he came along. I don't think changes in my sex life would make me happier. I am content with what I am."

"I work at being happy. If something bothers me, I change the cause of it and create my own happiness. I no longer wait for happiness to come to me, because it never will unless I work at it."

Other men attribute their happiness to being gay:

"I consider myself very happy. There are so many joys I've gotten out of my life and being gay, that they far outweigh the bad."

"I am happy. I feel more sexually liberated, and thus less sexually motivated in my lifestyle, than I did a year ago."

"I generally feel I have the best of both worlds, being well situated professionally, and pretty well adjusted in the straight world (playing the straights' 'confirmed bachelor' act); and then to be able to swing into free-spirited gay life whenever, and for whatever, I wish. A special way of living and experiences I regret straights won't allow themselves to know—or me to reveal."

"Becoming aware of my being gay has caused the most profound changes in my appearance, attitudes toward living, and future outlook—all positive."

"I consider myself very happy. After getting out of an eight-and-a-half year straight marriage and 'finding myself,' I couldn't be much happier or more fulfilled."

"I consider myself happier now than at any previous time in my life. Basically because I'm in love with a wonderful man and we're going to build a life together."

"I consider myself happy because I know myself and I'm not afraid of my feelings like so many people are."

"I am extremely happy with myself and with being gay. I feel one reason I'm happy is because of my attitude toward gay life—I feel my sex life is my business, and no one else's, as long as I'm not hurting anyone."

"I feel pretty good about myself because I've said to myself, Yes, I'm gay and there's no excuse to use for the things I do. I've accepted it and most of my straight friends have also and their feelings toward me haven't changed."

"The conflict with my wife is very difficult, but I feel really good about my gay life, friends and sex. Thus, I am happy."

"I'm very happy with my lifestyle, my friends, my lover, my interests, and myself. I attribute all those things to being gay."

"It's been a long transition from my first bar through the too-many-tricks days in between, to today—when I seem to be one of the few people with a smile on my lips as I wander through the too often grim bars in D.C. and elsewhere. From long-haired kid to short-haired man, from saying I know who I am to knowing who I am, it has been an experience I wouldn't trade for all the accepted cultural security you could offer me. Anytime now that I get scared, I think of my friend Leonard Matlovich, and I calm down. Life can be a bitch, but I can get through it."

AFTERWORD

Preparing this book has been a tremendously moving and educational experience for me. I have been educated both by many of the replies and by my own research done in connection with analyzing the replies. I was faced with a decision at one point: whether to include much of what I had gathered through research, or simply to allow the respondents to speak their minds with a minimum of intrusion of my own comments. I chose the latter course, injecting external material only when most necessary, usually to point out myths being debunked. In doing so, I have reprinted some scientific opinions opposed to homosexuality or treating it negatively. There have, however, been highly positive approaches to the subject, certainly within the last few years. These, I feel, reinforce many of the opinions expressed by the respondents, and I recommend them for further reading of a scientific or academic nature.

The "Kinsey Report," *Sexual Behavior in the Human Male*, published in 1948 by W.B. Saunders, is often quoted (inaccurately, for the most part) for its statistics on the prevalence of homosexuals and homosexual behavior among all men. But it is far more valuable because of Kinsey's highly enlightened view of the general public's attitude toward sexual variance. I would like to quote several passages from a long section of this report:

> It is unwarranted to believe that particular types of sexual behavior are always expressions of psychoses or neuroses. In actuality, they are more often expressions of what is biologically basic in mammalian and anthropoid behavior, and of a deliberate disregard for social convention . . .
>
> . . . Most of the complications which are observable in sexual histories are the result of society's reactions when it obtains knowledge of an individual's behavior, or the individual's fear of how society would react if he were discovered. . . .
>
> . . . The reactions of our social organization to these various types of behavior are the things that need study and classification. The mores, whether they concern

food, clothing, sex, or religious rituals, originate neither in accumulated experience nor in scientific examinations of objectively gathered data. The sociologist and anthropologist find the origins of such customs in ignorance and superstition, and in the attempt of each group to set itself apart from its neighbors. Psychologists have been too much concerned with the individuals who depart from the group custom. It would be more important to know why so many individuals conform as they do to such ancient custom. . . . Too often the study of behavior has been little more than a rationalization of the mores masquerading under the guise of objective science."*

It is unfortunate that such cogent Kinsey ideas have been lost amid statistics. The book is now out of print, but should be available in local and college libraries.

One of the strongest ancient customs in America is our religious training. It is vital to an understanding of the opposition to homosexuality to understand the history of religion. In *The Church and the Homosexual* (Pocket Books, paper), Father John J. McNeill explains and takes issue with many of the religious bases for homophobia. It is required reading for anyone attempting to converse rationally with those whose hatred of homosexuality is "based on scripture."

Several books generally discussing homosexuality in a favorable light are valuable to an overall understanding of the issue. *The Homosexual Matrix* is a recent work by C.A. Tripp (NAL, paperback) in which he sheds light on the origins of homosexuality by discussing the origins of heterosexuality as well. *The Same Sex* is a collection of essays by such renowned researchers as Wardell Pomeroy, Evelyn Hooker, and Lewis I. Maddocks, published in 1969 by the Pilgrim Press. The best book on the subject to date was published in 1967: *Homosexual Behavior Among Males* by Wainwright Churchill, M.D. (Hawthorne Books). It is dedicated to Kinsey. *Sexuality and Homosexuality* is an exhaustive study by Arno Karlen (W.W. Norton), and *The Sexual Experience*, published in 1976 by the Williams and Wilkins Company, is an excellent textbook for those interested in all aspects of sexuality from a largely clinical perspective.

---

* A. C. Kinsey, W. B. Pomeroy, and C. E. Martin, *Sexual Behavior in the Human Male* (Philadelphia: W. B. Saunders, 1948).

Lastly, the subject of coming out, especially to your family, has been handled beautifully by two very different books. *A Family Matter* by Dr. Charles Silverstein (McGraw-Hill) discusses how parents can best cope with the news and gives advice and personal stories. It is very positive and a good book for a gay person to give his or her parents when the moment comes. *Consenting Adult* is an extraordinary novel by Laura Z. Hobson told from the viewpoint of a mother whose son has just informed her he is gay. Her initial reaction and her eventual acceptance make for highly emotional reading.

These books, along with this one, offer any individual heavy artillery in the war against ignorance.

J.S.
Los Angeles, California
October, 1978

STATISTICAL
BREAKDOWN OF
REPLIES

"When did you first realize you were sexually attracted to members of your own sex?"

"Always":	69	(06.7%)
"Very young":	10	(01.0%)
Ages 3 to 5:	71	(06.8%)
6 to 9:	211	(20.3%)
10 to 14:	425	(40.9%)
15 to 18:	158	(15.2%)
19 to 24:	58	(05.6%)
Over 24:	22	(02.1%)
No answer:	14	(01.4%)
	1038	(100%)

"At what age did you have your first homosexual experience?"

Ages 2 to 5:	54	(05.2%)
6 to 9:	167	(16.1%)
10 to 14:	429	(41.3%)
15 to 18:	193	(18.6%)
19 to 24:	145	(14.0%)
Over 24:	38	(03.6%)
No answer:	12	(01.2%)
	1038	(100%)

"Have you told your family that you're gay?"

Yes:	526	(50.7%)
No:	492	(47.4%)
No answer:	20	(01.9%)

"What was your family's reaction?"

Good reaction:	213	(40.5%)
Bad reaction:	132	(25.1%)
Mixed:	54	(10.3%)

First bad, getting better:	42 (08.0%)
First bad, then acceptance:	19 (03.6%)
No answer:	66 (12.5%)
	526 (100%)

"Do you ever pretend to be straight?"

Sometimes:	320 (30.8%)
Usually:	282 (27.1%)
No:	423 (40.8%)
No answer:	13 (01.3%)
	1038 (100%)

"Used to":	108 (25% of "No" replies)

PART TWO: GAY MALE SEXUALITY

"How often do you have sex?"

Once or twice a week:	223 (21.5%)
Three or four times a week:	182 (17.5%)
At least once a day:	170 (16.4%)
As often as possible:	77 (07.4%)
It varies:	69 (06.7%)
Almost every day:	65 (06.3%)
Two or three times a week:	47 (04.5%)
Once or twice a month:	45 (04.3%)
Very little:	33 (03.2%)
Not enough:	25 (02.4%)
Two or three times a year:	22 (02.1%)
No answer:	19 (01.8%)
Once every two weeks:	18 (01.7%)
"When I feel like it":	16 (01.5%)
About three times a month:	10 (01.0%)
Never:	6 (00.6%)
"Frequently":	6 (00.6%)
Others:	5 (00.5%)
	1038 (100%)

"Do you enjoy one-night stands?"

Yes:	545 (52.5%)
No:	313 (30.2%)
"Sometimes" or "depends":	128 (12.3%)
No answer:	52 (05.0%)
	1038 (100%)

"Do you enjoy affection during sex?"

Yes:	931 (89.7%)
No:	47 (04.5%)
"Sometimes" or "depends":	42 (04.0%)
No answer:	18 (01.8%)
	1038 (100%)

"How do you most often reach orgasm?"

Masturbation:	551 (53.1%)
"It varies":	250 (24.1%)
Anal intercourse:	118 (11.3%)
Fellatio:	106 (10.2%)
Rubbing bodies:	5 (00.5%)
Heterosexual intercourse:	3 (00.3%)
No answer:	5 (00.5%)
	1038 (100%)

"Do you enjoy giving fellatio?"

Yes:	914 (88.0%)
No:	79 (07.6%)
Sometimes:	34 (03.3%)
No answer:	11 (01.1%)
	1038 (100%)

"Do you enjoy having your partner ejaculate in your mouth?"

Yes:	806 (77.7%)
No:	155 (14.9%)

Sometimes:	66 (06.4%)
No answer:	11 (01.0%)

	1038 (100%)

"Do you enjoy receiving fellatio?"

Yes:	936 (90.2%)
No:	43 (04.1%)
Sometimes:	44 (04.2%)
No answer:	15 (01.5%)

	1038 (100%)

"Do you enjoy 69 (mutual fellatio)?"

Yes:	520 (50.1%)
No:	453 (43.6%)
Sometimes:	50 (04.8%)
No answer:	15 (01.5%)

	1038 (100%)

"Do you enjoy anal intercourse?"

Yes:	796 (76.7%)
No:	123 (11.9%)
Sometimes:	46 (04.4%)
Depends on partner:	19 (01.8%)
Depends on position:	17 (01.6%)
No answer:	37 (03.6%)

	1038 (100%)

"During anal intercourse, are you usually top or bottom man?"

Both:	534 (51.5%)
Bottom:	236 (22.7%)
Top:	198 (19.1%)
No answer:	70 (06.7%)

	1038 (100%)

"Do your emotions differ when you're on top from when you're on the bottom?"

793 men answered this question.

Yes:	512 (64.6%)
No:	159 (20.0%)
Sometimes:	122 (15.4%)

	793 (100%)

"Do you ever go to the baths?"

No:	567 (54.6%)
(of these, 115 "used to")	
Regularly:	364 (35.1%)
Infrequently:	97 (09.3%)
No answer:	10 (01.0%)

	1038 (100%)

"Do you ever have sex in restrooms or other public places?"

No:	763 (73.5%)
(of these, 72 "used to")	
Regularly:	132 (12.7%)
Infrequently:	133 (12.8%)
No answer:	10 (01.0%)

	1038 (100%)

"Do you engage in any unusual sexual activities?"

None:	729 (70.2%)
No answer:	12 (01.2%)
Yes:	297 (28.6%)

	1038 (100%)

Activities	*Percent of total response*
Watersports:	192 (18.5%)
S&M:	163 (15.7%)
Active fist-fucking:	150 (14.5%)

Bondage and discipline:	129	(12.4%)
Humiliation:	87	(08.3%)
Passive fist-fucking:	85	(08.2%)
Scat:	32	(03.0%)
Spanking:	12	(01.2%)
Others:	6	(00.6%)

856 (82.4%)*

"Do you use drugs, sex toys, or pornography during sex?"

None:	421	(40.6%)
Pornography:	525	(50.6%)
Drugs:	445	(42.8%)
Toys:	347	(33.4%)
No answer:	34	(03.3%)

1772 (170%)**

"Are you ever aroused by uniforms, leather, garments, odors, and the like?"

No:	615	(59.2%)
Uniforms:	261	(25.7%)
Leather:	196	(18.8%)
Other garments:	184	(17.7%)
Odors:	192	(18.5%)
Parts of body:	80	(07.7%)
No answer:	19	(01.8%)

1547 (149%)**

"Have you ever paid or been paid for sex?"

Neither:	668	(64.4%)
Paid:	131	(12.6%)
Been paid:	128	(12.3%)
Both:	103	(10.0%)
No answer:	8	(00.7%)

1038 (100%)

*Percentages total more than the 28.6% who answered "Yes" due to multiple answers.
**Percentages total more than 100% due to multiple answers.

"Is the size of a man's penis (including your own) important to you?"

> **Others':**
>
> Not important: 432 (41.6%)
> Very important: 381 (36.7%)
> Somewhat important: 213 (20.5%)
> No answer: 12 (01.2%)
>
> _____
>
> 1038 (100%)
>
> **Their own:**
>
> Somewhat important: 373 (35.9%)
> Very important: 321 (30.9%)
> Not important   229 (22.1%)
> No answer: 115 (11.1%)*
>
> _____
>
> 1038 (100%)

"Do you consider yourself masculine?"

> Yes: 786 (75.7%)
> "Somewhat":   78 (07.5%)
> No: 62 (06.0%)
> "I'm a man":   51 (04.9%)
> "Androgynous":   31 (03.0%)
> No answer: 30 (02.9%)
>
> _____
>
> 1038 (100%)

PART THREE: RELATIONSHIPS

"How would you characterize your emotional involvements with men?"

> Buddies: 565 (54.4%)
> "It depends":   151 (14.5%)
> Equals: 62 (06.0%)
> Father/son: 60 (05.8%)
> Brothers: 46 (04.4%)
> Lovers: 31 (03.0%)

*The unusually large number of "No answers" to this question resulted because many men answered the first part of this question, and either forgot or preferred not to comment on their own size.

"Just sexual":   20 (01.9%)
"Varies with
same person":   10 (01.0%)
Husband/wife: 7 (00.7%)
Master/slave: 6 (00.6%)
Other: 37 (03.6%)
No answer: 43 (04.1%)
                            ————————————
                            1038 (100%)

"Do you have a lover?"

No: 543 (52.3%)
Yes: 430 (41.4%)
No answer: 65 (06.3%)
                            ————————————
                            1038(100%)

"Do you and/or your lover have sex with others?"

Yes, both of us: 281 (65.3%)
Happy with this: 183 (65.1%)
Not happy: 69 (24.6%)
Ambivalent   25 (08.9%)
No answer: 4 (01.4%)

No, both of us: 105 (24.5%)
Happy with this: 77 (73.3%)
Not happy: 22 (21.0%)
Ambivalent: 4 (03.8%)
No answer: 2 (01.9%)

Just me   26 (06.0%)
Happy with this: 21 (80.8%)
Not happy: 3 (11.5%)
No answer: 2 (07.7%)

Just him: 13 (03.0%)
Happy with this: 4 (30.8%)
Not happy: 8 (61.5%)
No answer: 1 (07.7%)

No answer: 5 (01.2%)
                  ————————————
                  430 (100%)

"Do you and your lover live together?"

Yes:	255	(59.3%)
No:	158	(36.7%)
No answer:	17	(04.0%)
	430	(100%)

"Would you like a lover?"

Yes:	476	(87.7%)
No:	62	(11.4%)
Ambivalent:	4	(00.7%)
No answer:	1	(00.2%)
	543	(100%)

"Would you want to live with your lover?"

Yes:	285	(59.9%)
No:	150	(31.5%)
Ambivalent:	25	(05.3%)
No answer:	16	(03.3%)
	476	(100%)

"Do you prefer men younger, older, or the same age as yourself?"

16-24 age group: 236

Older:	145	(61.4%)
Same age:	71	(30.1%)
Younger:	15	(06.4%)
No answer:	5	(02.1%)
	236	(100%)

25-30 age group: 313

Same age:	163	(52.1%)
Older:	99	(31.6%)
Younger:	44	(14.1%)
No answer:	7	(02.2%)
	313	(100%)

31-40 age group: 215

Same age:	96	(44.7%)
Younger:	80	(37.2%)
Older:	33	(15.3%)
No answer:	6	(02.8%)

215 (100%)

41-49 age group: 151

Younger:	75	(49.7%)
Same age:	61	(40.4%)
Older:	10	(06.6%)
No answer:	5	(03.3%)

151 (100%)

50-77 age group: 107

Younger:	71	(66.4%)
Same age:	21	(19.6%)
Older:	7	(06.5%)
No answer:	8	(07.5%)

107 (100%)

PART FOUR: WOMEN

"Do you have sex with women?"

No:	839	(80.8%) (218 of these "used to")
Yes:	179	(17.3%)
No answer:	20	(01.9%)

1038 (100%)

"Are you now (or have you ever been) married to a woman?"

Never been:	835	(80.4%)
Used to be:	126	(12.2%)
Am currently:	54	(05.2%)
No answer:	23	(02.2%)

1038 (100%)

"Was (or is) your wife aware of your gay activities?"

Yes:	97	(53.9%)
No:	60	(33.3%)
No answer:	23	(12.8%)
	180	(100%)

"What are your feelings about lesbianism?"

Positive:	697	(67.1%)
Negative:	211	(20.4%)
Ambivalent:	107	(10.3%)
No answer:	23	(02.2%)
	1038	(100%)

"Do you ever dress in women's clothing?"

No:	944	(91.0%)
(48 of these used to, 29 as children)		
Sometimes (Halloween, etc.):	51	(04.9%)
Yes:	27	(02.6%)
No answer:	16	(01.5%)
	1038	(100%)

"Would you rather be a woman?"

No:	1007	(97.0%)
Sometimes:	12	(01.15%)
Yes:	07	(00.7%)
No answer:	12	(01.15%)
	1038	(100%)

PART FIVE: PROBLEMS

"Have you ever been arrested for a sexual activity?"

No:	939	(90.5%)
Yes:	83	(08.0%)
No answer:	16	(01.5%)
	1038	(100%)

"Have you ever had any of your rights denied you because you are gay?"

No:	748	(72.1%)
Yes:	186	(17.9%)
No answer, don't know:	104	(10.0%)
	1038	(100%)

"Have you ever had any form of sexually transmitted disease?"

Had crabs:	548	(52.8%)
Never had any:	322	(31.0%)
Had gonorrhea:	251	(24.2%)
Had "V.D.":	128	(12.3%)
Had scabies:	124	(11.9%)
Had syphilis:	78	(07.5%)
Had hepatitis:	23	(02.2%)
Had herpes:	19	(01.8%)
Had venereal warts:	18	(01.7%)
Had non-specific urethritis:	17	(01.6%)
"Others":	5	(00.5%)
No answer:	10	(00.9%)
	1543	(148%)*

"Have you ever been in the military?"

No:	670	(64.5%)
Yes:	360	(34.7%)
No answer:	8	(00.8%)
	1038	(100%)

"Did you have gay sex while in the service?"

Yes:	230	(63.9%)
No:	120	(33.3%)
No answer:	10	(02.8%)
	360	(100%)

*Percentages total more than 100% due to multiple answers.

PART SIX: ON BEING GAY

"Do you ever feel guilty about being gay?"

No:	837 (80.6%)
Sometimes:	138 (13.3%)
Usually:	57 (05.5%)
No answer:	6 (00.6%)

1038 (100%)

"Do you think it is easy or difficult to be gay today?"

Easy:	297 (28.6%)
Easier than	
it was:	296 (28.5%)
Difficult:	284 (27.4%)
"It depends":	136 (13.1%)
More difficult:	10 (01.0%)
No answer:	15 (01.4%)

1038 (100%)

"Would you rather be straight?"

(Note: This question did not appear in all the publications which reproduced the survey. Therefore, only 541 people answered this question.)

No:	460 (85.0%)
Yes:	81 (15.0%)

541 (100%)

"What do you think are the most important changes that have to be made, by gays or straight society or both, to improve gay life?"

Educate people about the true nature of homosexuality:	659 (63.5%)
Basic changes would have to take place in the social climate:	534 (51.4%)
Political action should be taken:	469 (45.2%)
Place less emphasis on sex/adhere to traditional mores:	336 (32.3%)

Gays should endeavor to improve themselves:	296	(28.5%)
Gays should behave better in public:	212	(20.4%)
Break down religious taboos:	119	(11.5%)
Others:	91	(08.8%)
No answer:	7	(00.6%)
	2723	(262%)*

"Do you consider yourself happy?"

Yes:	749	(72.1%)
No:	131	(12.6%)
"Fairly happy":	61	(05.9%)
"Mixed":	51	(04.9%)
"Content":	27	(02.6%)
No answer:	19	(01.9%)
	1038	(100%)

*Percentages total more than 100% due to multiple answers.

About the Author

James Spada is a freelance journalist whose work has appeared in such publications as *Us* magazine, the London *Daily Mirror*, *Coronet*, *Los Angeles* magazine and *In Sports*. He has written on the subject of homosexuality for the Los Angeles *Times*, *The Advocate*, *Christopher Street*, *In Touch*, *Gold* and *The Alternate*, among others. He is the author of career biographies of Barbra Streisand and Robert Redford, and has been Editor of *In the Know* magazine. He served as a campaign press aide to Senator Edward M. Kennedy in 1970 and is currently working toward a Master's Degree in Professional Writing at the University of Southern California.